Again he thought of that day.

He could still remember that jolt of awareness when he'd spotted her, the gut-twisting connection. He could still see the wild banner of lush red-gold silk that was her hair, hear that throaty voice. He swore he could almost smell the clean scent of soap and sunlight on her neck. He could taste the surprising sweetness of her lips. She had been so alive that day. So compelling. So earthy and sensual, the exact opposite of the ethereal beauty of his own wife.

He'd known better. And yet, he had found himself kissing that girl as if he'd been a thirsty man drinking at a deep well. And he carried that single memory through the ensuing years of pain and drama.

What if the ensuing years had been different? Would he have kept better track of her? Would he have wondered what had happened to the sharp, bright girl he'd met?

He would never know. He would never know if he could have changed Fiona's life. Or his own...

Praise for the Drake's Rakes Series

Once a Rake

"Dreyer dazzles readers with her incomparable gift for creating heartbreakingly real characters and her inimitable flair for fusing sexy passion and dangerous intrigue in a richly emotional, wickedly witty, and altogether enthralling historical romance."
—*Booklist* (starred review)

"4 ½ stars! Dreyer is a master storyteller who merges intrigue and passion perfectly…*Once a Rake* is hard to put down and difficult to forget."
—*RT Book Reviews*

"This series is so thoroughly engaging, so emotionally taut, that it's difficult to wait patiently for each new adventure. Her fans will be ravenous for this one."
—*Library Journal*

"Entertaining, well-written, and emotionally satisfying."
—LikesBooks.com

Always a Temptress

"4 ½ stars! [Dreyer's] novels have every hallmark of a memorable historical romance: passion, unforgettable characters, an engrossing plot. May she continue to deliver her fantastic historicals!"

—*RT Book Reviews*

"Fueled by a surfeit of sizzling sensuality, chilling suspense, and delectably dry wit...Dreyer again deftly combines deadly intrigue and sexy romance in a swoon-worthy read."

—*Booklist* (starred review)

"A perfect ten! The characterizations make *Always a Temptress* an awesome read...a tantalizing tapestry of romance."

—Romance Reviews Today

"One of the jewels within the story is the wonderful band of supporting characters we encounter...I enjoyed this book for the suspense, the romance, and the humor that was beautifully mixed together in a wonderful story."

—Fresh Fiction.com

"A super Regency undercover romance starring a tough combat veteran and a courageous heroine. Their pairing make for a fun thriller, but it is the support cast at Rose Workhouse and an orphanage that brings a strong emotional element to an exciting, complicated historical."

—Genre Go Round Reviews.blogspot.com

Never a Gentleman

"Exquisite characterization; flashes of dry, lively wit; marvelous villains; and a dark, compelling plot that unfolds in tantalizing ways."

—*Library Journal*

"A pure joy to read! Dreyer displays her phenomenal sense of atmosphere in an emotionally powerful and beautifully rendered love story...the consummate storyteller makes the conventional unconventional. Combining beautifully crafted, engaging characters with an intriguing mystery adds depth."

—*RT Book Reviews*

"As always, Ms. Dreyer has written an engrossing story which will entice the reader into the world of the Regency."

—Fresh Fiction

"Superb...an intoxicating read."

—The Romance Readers Connection.com

Barely a Lady

One of *Publishers Weekly*'s Best Books of 2010
A Top Ten *Booklist* Romance of the Year
One of *Library Journal*'s Best Five Romances of the Year

"Dreyer flawlessly blends danger, deception, and desire into an impeccably crafted historical that neatly balances adventurous intrigue with an exquisitely romantic love story."

—*Chicago Tribune*

"Vivid descriptions, inventive plotting, beautifully delineated characters, and stunning emotional depth."

—*Library Journal* (starred review)

"Romantic suspense author Dreyer makes a highly successful venture into the past with this sizzling, dramatic Regency romance. Readers will love the well-rounded characters and suspenseful plot."

"*Barely a Lady* is addictively readable thanks to exquisitely nuanced characters, a brilliantly realized historical setting, and a captivating plot encompassing both the triumph and tragedy of war. Love, loss, revenge, and redemption all play key roles in this richly emotional, superbly satisfying love story."

"Top Pick! 4 ½ stars! An emotionally powerful story... unique plotline...intriguing characters."

Also by Eileen Dreyer

Twice Tempted

Eileen Dreyer

FOREVER

NEW YORK   BOSTON

Forever
Hachette Book Group
1290 Avenue of the Americas
New York, NY 10104
www.HachetteBookGroup.com

Printed in the United States of America

First Edition: November 2014
10 9 8 7 6 5 4 3 2 1

OPM

Forever is an imprint of Grand Central Publishing.
The Forever name and logo are trademarks of Hachette Book Group, Inc.

The Hachette Speakers Bureau provides a wide range of authors for speaking events. To find out more, go to www.hachettespeakersbureau.com or call (866) 376-6591.

The publisher is not responsible for websites (or their content) that are not owned by the publisher.

To the women of science who worked without
acknowledgment
for so long, especially the women of
astronomy, who
were usually relegated to doing the math.
They really were called computers.

Acknowledgments

My thanks to everyone who has helped bring Alex and Fiona to life. To my agents, Andrea Cirillo and Christina Hogrebe. To all of Grand Central, especially Amy Pierpont and Leah Hultenschmidt, who shared the gestation of this book, and Claire Brown for another fabulous cover. To Maggie Mae Gallagher, assistant extraordinaire, who has saved more than my sanity.

To my writing community, who also helps keep me sane. The Divas, of course. MoRWA, the Pubs. To the Aspen contingent—I know we gave ourselves a name, and if it hadn't been a very long night I'd remember it—who taught me to successfully brainstorm and went to watch meteors with me and let me test out my new astronomy knowledge.

To my readers, who have been faithful and supportive, even when I've taken longer than I should to finish a story.

And finally, to those who have helped me research astronomy, which I have fallen madly in love with and would totally immerse myself in if I had any skill at math whatsoever.

To John Beury of the St. Louis Astronomical Society and the late lamented Wired Coffeeshop, my guide to the night sky, for his patience, graciousness, and generosity in introducing me to the wonders of the night sky (without John, I doubt Fiona and Mairead would have been astronomers, no matter how much they wanted to). I swear the books are coming home. I have added the works that John gave me that helped me research this fascinating field to my research page. (Okay, I'm also giving a shout-out to my pretend scientist boyfriend Neil deGrasse Tyson. You're such an inspiration, I'll even forgive you Pluto.)

The Regency period was a golden age of amateur scientific research, from astronomy to physics to geometry, chemistry, paleontology, geology, engineering, and more. It has been a pleasure meeting the amazing minds of the age. But especially the women, who languished in obscurity for far too long. All of the scientists mentioned in this series were real. All made substantial discoveries and contributions to their fields. I hope I've inspired somebody to learn more about them.

Twice Tempted

Prologue

Hawesworth Castle, Yorkshire

Lady Fiona Maeve Ferguson Hawes received her sentence in a white room. White marble, white brocade, white porcelain, white-painted oak. The cold, spare temple to her grandfather's pretensions.

Walking so silently she failed to strike an echo from the gleaming floor, Fiona came to a stop at the edge of the Aubusson carpet. She wanted to worry at the ivory muslin of her dress. She wanted to run upstairs and throw herself on her bed, where she could sob herself dry. Instead, briefly, she pressed her hand to her chest, absurdly afraid that the chaos that battered her would spill out all over her grandfather's stark marble floor.

She couldn't seem to draw a good breath. She hadn't since Ian's friend Alex Knight had told them the news. Since he had ridden away again, taking with him the last of her childhood dreams.

Oh, Ian.

Gone. Her brother was truly gone. He had left before. He had fought in the king's wars since she had been a child. But he had always come home. He had always done his best to keep track of his twin siblings, and do his best by them, especially after mama had died.

No more. This time, Fiona and Mairead would be truly alone, especially when her grandfather delivered the verdict he was so anxious to make.

"You took long enough to get here, girl," he barked, rising from behind his massive desk and stepping forward.

"I was seeing off Alex Knight," she answered with a dip of a curtsy. "Considering he was kind enough to deliver the news of Ian's death in person, I assumed that you would not wish me to stint on Hawesworth hospitality. Was I mistaken?"

She was rewarded with the cold glare that had once made her tremble.

"I hope you didn't waste your time setting your sights on him," the old man said, his voice thick with disdain. "The likes of him will have nothing to do with the likes of you."

She refused to flinch. "He left unmolested."

If he had been the kind of person to react, her grandfather would have gone red. As it was, he froze into a tower of disapproval. Hands clasped behind his back, he stood straight as a subaltern on parade, the sun limning his pure silver hair and magnifying the immense dignity of his person.

To be truthful, Fiona's grandfather could have stood in a barn naked and disheveled, and it would still be obvious that he was the current holder of one of the nation's most illustrious titles. He carried the marquessate of Leyburn in his bones, in tendon and viscera and brain. And he never ever let anyone forget it. Especially the misbegotten twin granddaughters he'd been forced to take in four years earlier when they'd had nowhere else to go.

"I give you enough credit to know why I called for you," he said, his voice crisp.

She had known before Alex Knight had finished giving his news. "I imagine you intend to find a way to blame Mairead and me for Ian's alleged crime."

"Nothing alleged about it," the marquess snapped. "You heard his friend. Pulled a gun in front of a shipful of witnesses and tried to shoot the Duke of Wellington." He snorted, shaking his head. "I should have known he was a traitor."

You should know even now that he wasn't.

"As for you..." The marquess pulled out his watch and flipped it open. "You have about twenty-five pounds of accumulated pin money between you both, which is yours to keep, along with what you can carry." He snapped the watch closed. "I have an appointment in Leyburn in an hour. I don't expect to see you when I return."

"What about Mairead?" Fiona asked, hands clenched to hide their trembling. "Do you think she can simply wander the roads?"

He shrugged. "By your own account, she's done it before. Wouldn't have even known there was a life like this if I hadn't interfered. Besides, it saves the embarrassment of trying to foist her off on society."

Of foisting either of them off. Something he never would have done anyway, which they both knew.

"I have done my duty," he insisted as if he'd heard a protest. "That is all that can be asked. This family goes back to the Conqueror. I will *not* have it fall to scandal."

And the scandal of two granddaughters who had survived on the streets could be erased if the girls disappeared as if they'd never come.

Fiona fought a flood of panic. Where would they go? It

had been so long since she had kept them safe out on the streets. Eight long years. Had any of her skills survived? Her instincts? Where could twenty-five pounds take them?

Well, standing here soaking in the marquess's contempt would offer no ideas. Without another word, Fiona turned for the door.

"Where will you go?" he barked.

Fighting for calm, she turned back and lifted an eyebrow, unaware how identically she copied him. "I don't believe that can be of any interest to you, sir."

Home, her heart cried. *Get ye back to Edinburgh, where you know the streets and the people and the price of a meal.*

"Of course it is of interest to me," he snapped. "I demand to know that you won't do anything more to sully my name."

Glad to at least get a bit of petty revenge for all the slights she had suffered under this roof, she smiled. "In that case, Grandfather, I fear you are doomed to suffer disappointment."

And without another look at the grandfather she had once thought would be her salvation, Fiona Ferguson walked out, shutting the door behind her.

Chapter 1

Four weeks later

It took a lot to surprise Alex Knight. But there he stood in the White Salon of Hawesworth Castle staring like a simpleton at the hall door that had just slammed in his face.

"Bloody hell."

Three days of hard riding to bring the Marquess of Leyburn the best news possible, and the old bastard had blindsided him.

Standing alongside him, Chuffy Wilde gaped like a landed trout. "Bit dense, I know," Chuffy said, scratching his nose with a pudgy finger, "but did the marquess just say he threw his granddaughters out into the snow?"

"Yes," Alex answered, still staring after the old man. "I believe he did."

Throwing open the doors, Alex strode into the hallway to find the marquess climbing the sweeping white marble staircase, his hand on the polished rail, his back as rigid as his morality. If the old tartar hadn't been moving, Alex could have easily mistaken him for one of the statues that lined the steps.

"A word with you, sir."

The marquess didn't stop. "I have said all I wish to."

"Perhaps you did not understand me," Alex said, his voice terse. "Your grandson is alive and exonerated of the charges of treason. Ian has even been commended by the Duke of Wellington himself for his courage. Surely that is excellent news."

Not from the old man's expression. "Do you perhaps believe me to be hard of hearing?"

"I believe you must have misunderstood me, or you would never have walked away without securing the safety of your granddaughters, as any gentleman would."

His expression frozen in disbelief, the marquess stalked all the way back down the stairs. "You question my honor, sir?" the old man demanded in glacial tones. *"Mine?"*

"A man of *honor*," Alex retorted, "would not have abandoned the women under his care, no matter the provocation. Where are they?"

The marquess lifted a vague hand. "They left after your last visit. It is no longer my affair."

That took Alex's breath. He'd heard the term "seeing red." He understood it now. Delivering the news of Ian's death was one of the hardest tasks Alex had ever taken on. Fiona had been devastated by it. And Alex had left her. To this man.

"Do you mean that you threw your granddaughters out of your house the same day they learned that their brother was dead?"

The marquess's expression grew, if possible, colder. "You are new to your title, Lord Whitmore," he said. "Perhaps when you have worn it a bit longer, you'll begin to comprehend just what is owed to it. My line has been unblemished for eight hundred years. It will remain so."

The silence was shattered by an explosive laugh. Alex

turned to see Chuffy bright-eyed and chortling. "Beg pardon," he apologized with a wave of his hand. "Hilarious. Saintly family and all. Leyburn title is as straight-laced as Prinny's parlor. Chock-full of pirates and brigands. Pater told me so."

"Fribble," the marquess spat. "Your father must despair of you."

Chuffy's smile only grew. "Does. Have a question, though. He'll want to know. Ferguson's exonerated. Why ignore the girls now? Bad form and all."

"He is still a spy," the marquess snapped. "No *gentleman*," he said, glaring at Alex, "lowers himself to such behavior. As for his sisters…" He shrugged. "They are probably already back on the streets from which they came. I have found another heir. You may tell them. What those Fergusons do now is not my concern."

Alex blocked his way. "Four years ago, at *your* behest, I brought your granddaughters to you. How can you just throw them out like this?"

"They survived just fine before, and they should have no trouble surviving now. The skills that kept them clothed and fed before I found them are never forgotten by women like that."

Alex went cold. He had met Fiona only twice, but each time he had come away respecting her more. What kind of monster could look into those glorious blue eyes and not see the bone-deep honor there?

"Exactly what do you mean, sir?" he asked, his voice dangerously quiet.

The marquess's smile was sour. "Come now, Whitmore. How do you think those two ate when they were living on the streets of Edinburgh? Kind Scottish fairies did not drop apples in their laps."

Alex struggled to breathe. "They were no older than fourteen when Ian found them and got them into Miss Chase's Academy."

The marquess sneered. "Plenty old enough for that business, sir. And don't think I am being dramatic. That she-wolf pulled a knife on me once, did you know that? She carries it in her garter. My secretary once forgot himself enough to challenge her to a shooting contest. He lost. He was lucky I didn't dismiss him on the spot. *She* was lucky I didn't toss her out onto the moors. And I haven't even had the nerve to find out what other 'talents' she possesses. Well, no more. I will not feel threatened in my own home."

Chuffy was shaking his head. "Won't keep Ferguson away. He'll find out. Wouldn't be here when he comes, I were you. Bit protective and all."

The marquess glared. "I don't care if your father was my friend. Get out."

Chuffy blinked. "Not without the ladies."

"I told you. They're not here."

"Got to be somewhere."

Somewhere. *Christ*, Alex thought. How would he possibly find them? It had been four weeks.

"If we don't find those women," he promised the old man, "Chuffy and I, along with every one of our associates, will spend every day and every farthing we possess between us ensuring that the *ton* knows exactly what happened here. You will be more vilified than Princess Caroline, and twice as unwelcome. I also wouldn't count on supplanting Ian in the succession. He has friends, too."

Alex saw the threat reach the marquess. The old man paled; his eyes narrowed. Fortunately for him, the old man refrained from delivering another opinion. With no more than a jerky wave of his hand, he stalked up the stairs.

"Don't know about you," Chuffy said, pushing his glasses

up his nose, "but I think it's time to talk to people who really know what goes on."

*   *   *

They spent the next four hours interviewing the staff and came away with no more than outrage, grief, and carefully couched fury at their employer. Fiona's abigail sobbed, chef all but shattered his chopping block as he slammed down his butcher knife on unsuspecting mutton, and the butler, a stiff-rumped old tartar with a profile like a penguin, methodically tore apart the linen handkerchief he had been folding. Alex had a feeling that if a vote were held, every person on that estate would have walked over a burning marquess to hand Lady Fiona a glass of water.

It didn't help him find her.

"Tha'll bring them safe home," the housekeeper begged, fierce brown eyes awash in tears. "Won't 'ee?"

Alex lied, unable to admit to either of them how slim his chances were. "I will. Do you have any idea where they went after they left here?"

"Coachie took girls to Black Swan in Leyburn."

"And from there?"

She could only shrug, looking even more lost. "Stage goes all over, think on."

No one else could offer more. So Alex and Chuffy began at the Black Swan, a gray coursed rubble stone building that anchored the market square of Leyburn. The proprietor, a thin, rather somnolent man of a height too great to fit beneath his own doors, remembered helping the women onto the London coach. Beyond that, he could say nothing certain, except that Lady Mairead had been sore distressed and Miss Fiona quiet, as usual.

With night coming on, the men had no choice but to secure rooms and repair to the taproom, where they were served full mugs of ale and a serviceable game pie. They spent dinner at a scarred oak table by a desultory fire trying to decide how to proceed.

"No friends to go to?" Chuffy asked, his attention on his food. "Your sister heard from her? School chums and all."

"No. Pip would have alerted me. Especially if she learned that they'd been evicted from their home. Pip has a finely honed sense of justice."

The first time he'd met Fiona had been in response to his sister's sense of justice.

Chuffy grinned. "Little spitfire, Pip," he said, pushing at his sliding glasses. "Popped me in the nose once for insulting the Ripton chit." He rubbed at that appendage. "Not intentional, o' course. Had no idea she was so shy. Never forget now."

Alex was nodding, but he really wasn't paying attention. He was remembering the first time he'd seen Fiona Ferguson four years ago. She had been sixteen and running away from the school her brother had put her in. Alex, hung over and surly from too much brandy the night before, had gone after her at Pip's insistence.

And then, chasing down the coach he thought might be carrying her, he had seen Fiona lean out the window. Tall, stately, with a square face, high cheekbones, and startling blue eyes. A mature beauty on a deceptively fragile girl. And the most glorious red-gold hair he'd ever seen, gleaming even in the rain like precious metal. She had been as bold as brass, fearless, focused on finding her sister, whom she thought was in some kind of trouble. She had fit that glorious hair to a farthing.

But when he'd seen her four weeks ago, she had changed.

Quieter, tidier, as if she were a foot squeezed into a too-small shoe. That barely tamed light he had unconsciously sought in her stunning blue eyes had been gone, replaced by a disturbing placidity. She had been expensively clad and shod in Indian muslin and kidskin, groomed to a fare-thee-well. And oddly pallid.

What had happened in the last four years to douse that ineffable spirit? A spirit that had survived a childhood of hardship, upheaval, and death, all by her sixteenth birthday.

Why had Alex not realized that Fiona's promising future had gone wrong? Had she even had a season? Suddenly he couldn't remember. Certainly not when his sister Pip came out. The year after? He had been on the continent through much of that season, interceding between Wellington's paymaster and the Rothschilds.

He was furious, suddenly. At the marquess, at the vagaries of life. Mostly, at himself. At his assumption that the only thing Ian's sisters had needed four years ago had been warmth and a full belly. That when he had brought Fiona to that great house in the Yorkshire dales to meet her grandfather, he had delivered her to paradise.

After all, she and her sister had spent their lives scraping by, alone except for a brother who was never there. Wouldn't it be wonderful to have a family again?

But he had judged her family against his own, and he knew perfectly well how unfair that was. He had the love not only of his mother and sisters, but a stepfather who had taught Alex most of what he knew about being a gentleman. To Alex, the greatest gift a person could be given was a family. He'd forgotten that not all families were worth coming home to.

It was Chuffy's portentous throat-clearing that yanked Alex back from his thoughts. He looked up to discover a middle-aged man standing at their table, his curly brimmed beaver clutched in his hands.

"Lord Whitmore?" the man asked. At Alex's nod, he smiled. "Oh, thank heavens. I was afraid I'd missed you."

Alex and Chuffy both stood to receive the unprepossessing gentleman, Chuffy's napkin still tucked into his neckcloth.

"Can we help you?" Alex asked.

The man put out his hand. "Gilbert Bryce-Jones. The marquess's secretary. I just returned to find the marquess ready to lop off heads and the staff all in a fuss. Seems a pair of gentlemen called his lordship to task for failing his responsibilities."

Hands were shaken, names exchanged, and outerwear removed. Reclaiming his seat, Alex took a draught of his ale and evaluated the newcomer, who seemed interchangeable with most other secretaries he'd met. Trim and tidy, with unremarkable features and neatly cut, mouse-brown hair, as if seeking anonymity.

"Bryce-Jones?" Chuffy asked, fork and knife back in hand. "Know your family. Good *ton*, no luck with money."

Bryce-Jones chuckled, but Alex caught a glint of discomfort in his gray eyes. "You're absolutely correct, my lord," the secretary said, his right hand brushing against his marcello waistcoat, as if expecting to find something there. "I am fortunate that my cousin the marquess was kind enough to give me a position."

Chuffy shook his head. "Not kind at all. Cheese-paring old misery guts. Must be sharp in the brain box."

Obviously uncertain how to react to Chuffy, Bryce-Jones turned to Alex. "I'm sorry I wasn't there when you came. Although I doubt I could have been more help."

Alex waited for the innkeeper to bend like a slow crane to

deposit Bryce-Jones's ale on the table and leave before answering. "You truly have no idea where the women went?"

"No." Bryce-Jones picked up his mug, but didn't drink. "I can't begin to tell you how worried I am about them. If it were in my power, I would have sent Bow Street after them. If only I'd been here..."

"You weren't?" Alex asked.

Another sorrowful shake. Another quick swipe at his vest. "In London for the marquess. I came home to find Ladies Fiona and Mairead gone and the staff inconsolable." He leaned in as if sharing a secret. "They were greatly loved."

"Even Lady Mairead?" Alex asked. "I've heard she can be...difficult."

"You don't know her?"

"We've never met. I was looking forward to it."

Bryce-Jones smiled, his expression almost paternal. "Lady Mairead is...special. I worry about her, though. She doesn't do well when she is forbidden her routine."

As if in response, Chuffy began scratching the side of his nose. Alex paid attention. Usually when Chuffy started worrying at his face, something bothered him.

"Mrs. Weller said the marquess's grandson is alive and vindicated," Bryce-Jones said. "That is wonderful. When should we expect to see the viscount?"

It took Alex a moment to realize that the man was speaking of Ian Ferguson. When Alex had been introduced to him, the Scot had been no more than a lucky street gypsy from Edinburgh who had chivvied and lied his way into a commission in the Black Watch. Even when Ferguson had learned that, far from being a bastard he was the heir to a marquessate, he had never thrown his position around.

"I don't know when he'll be released to return home," Alex said.

Bryce-Jones nodded. "Of course. I hope then the marquess can make his peace."

"Can't 'til we find the girls," Chuffy said, pulling off his glasses and wiping them with his handkerchief.

"I don't know if this will help," Bryce-Jones said, reaching into his jacket, "but they had quite a correspondence."

Alex's head snapped up. "Who?" he asked. "The twins?"

Bryce-Jones pulled out a packet of letters and handed them over. "Some odd characters, from all over. No one we ever met, of course. Could they have sought refuge with one of their correspondents?"

Alex picked up the packet and began to riffle through it. There were about eight envelopes in all, a few from foreign countries. Alex recognized a few names and frowned.

"Have you read these?" he asked, looking up.

The secretary smiled. "The ones in English. They're fascinating, aren't they?"

Alex nodded, his focus on a return address in Slough that belonged to a familiar name. Caroline Herschel. The letter was in German. More important, it seemed filled with complex mathematical equations.

"Well," he said, checking a few more addresses. "It's a place to start."

"Please keep me apprised." Bryce-Jones frowned. "I realize the marquess seems intractable, but he'll want to know."

"If you'd like," Alex said, his attention now on a letter from Pierre LaPlace, who was saying something about black holes. "I'll give you my card...oh, no, wait. They're up in my room." Scraping his chair back, he stood. "Chuff?"

Chuffy's head snapped up and he blinked. "Keep you company, Bryce-Jones."

Alex took all the time he could. It was an old tactic. If Chuffy gave the signal, it usually meant he needed some time alone with the person they were interviewing. He rarely failed to learn something interesting. It was amazing what people told Chuffy.

By the time Alex got back, Bryce-Jones was sitting back in his seat, his ale mug in his hand, smiling. Chuffy was checking his pocket watch, which he'd pulled from a plum-and-silver-striped waistcoat.

"No, no," he was saying. "Appreciate the offer. Late. Need to be up early."

"Here's my card," Alex said without sitting.

Bryce-Jones was forced to stand to accept it, and Chuffy followed suit. After that it took only five more minutes to get the secretary out the door, after which Alex and Chuffy secured a bottle of brandy and glasses to take upstairs.

"What did you find out?" Alex asked as he followed Chuffy into his room and shut the door.

Chuffy stretched out on Alex's bed as if it were his own. "Closemouthed as that minx fella."

Alex couldn't help but smile. "Sphinx, Chuff."

His eyes opened. "Egyptian cove? Furry hands?"

"The same."

He nodded. "That. Didn't even admit that he hates the old man. Does. Thinks he's smarter. Probably is."

"And?" Alex knew there was more. There always was with Chuffy. Getting it was like bringing in a recalcitrant trout, though.

Chuffy was scrubbing at the side of his nose again. "Not sure. Marquess stiff-rumped as a deposed king. But something in the way Bryce-Jones described him made me think there's more. Lion?"

Brandy bottle in hand, Alex paused. That would certainly alter the picture, now, wouldn't it? The Lions were the group of highly placed aristocrats Alex and Chuffy had been investigating over charges of possible treason when they'd been pulled to deliver Ian's good news to Fiona.

Fiona. Dear God, where *was* she?

"I haven't heard anything that might implicate the marquess," Alex said, his gut sour with dread. "But you're right about his attitude."

Alex handed Chuffy a glass of brandy and some of the letters Bryce-Jones had given him. "What do you make of these?"

One look had Chuffy sitting up. "Zounds." Opening the letter more fully, he shoved his glasses atop his head and held the paper close, as if the German would be easier to translate. It took a minute of reading before he looked up. "Do you know what this is? And from whom?"

"Equations of some sort," Alex said, pouring them both out a tot of brandy and handing Chuffy his. "From someone named Gauss."

"Someone?" Chuffy set his glass down untasted. "Only one of the greatest mathematicians of the age. He seems to be debating a theory using Euler's formula in something…I'm not sure what, though. I don't recognize it."

This time Alex admitted surprise. "You? Impossible."

Chuffy was nibbling on his thumb, his lips moving as he scanned the letter. "Astronomy ain't my field. Need to ask the pater."

Alex nodded, not understanding any of it but the fact that it took complex mathematics to get Chuffy to speak in complete sentences.

"Didn't you say they lived in the streets?" Chuffy demanded. "How could they have learned this? It's advanced, even for me. Have to be wrong."

Alex downed his drink and poured another. "Not wrong. Their mother spirited them to Scotland when they were young to save them from their father. You remember Viscount Hawes."

Chuffy shuddered. "Didn't die soon enough."

"Ferguson supported them all with army pay from the time he was fifteen. He came home some time later to find his mother dead and the girls living under a bridge. But as I said, they were already twelve or fourteen or so. The marquess didn't step in until Hawes died and left him without heirs."

"Might have known."

"Tell me these letters will help us find them."

Chuffy was shaking his head, his focus obviously on the squiggles and letters and numbers. "Depends on whether they feel comfortable battening down on any of these folk. Not sure I would, but I've never had the nerve to correspond, either."

Alex separated out a few letters. "Fiona bought coach fare to London. A few of these addresses are in the vicinity. We might as well look there first."

Chuffy began to carefully fold his letter. "Read the others later. Right now, need to do some more work on those blasted ciphers."

Alex looked up. "No luck?"

"Dead annoying. Have half a dozen messages. Have a whole bloody poem full of keywords. Nothing seems to fit. Awful poem. Hurts my eyes."

Alex cuffed him on the shoulder. "Well, if anybody can crack the thing, it's you."

It was the Rakes' greatest secret. No one who met Chuffy would think him a code-breaker without equal.

Chuffy frowned. "Feel like Octopus, solvin' riddles all the time."

Alex tried not to smile. "You mean Oedipus? Well, it

could be worse, Chuff. He did solve the Sphinx's riddle and get the fair princess."

"Don't want a princess. Want to sleep." Handing over the letters, Chuffy gave a mournful sigh. "Might have known it'd be back to the minx fellow."

Alex grinned. "The Sphinx is actually female."

"Figures." Chuffy shook his head and slid his glasses back into place. "At least I don't have to tell Drake we're deserting the princess's house party. I'll let you do that."

Alex felt a new weight drop on his chest. An old weight, really. A weight Chuffy didn't know about. "I'm not sure Drake will understand."

Chuffy gave him a look that reduced him to a first-former. "Gentlemen first, old lad. Spies second."

Gentlemen first. But was he? Alex wondered.

The truth twisted in his gut like bad meat. Gentlemen didn't betray their friends. Gentlemen didn't sell their souls to retrieve incriminating letters. Alex had done both not a week earlier, at the house party he and Chuffy had been monitoring. But at the time he had convinced himself that he could save Ian once he'd saved his own family.

It hadn't worked out that way.

Alex couldn't shut his eyes without seeing Ian Ferguson torn and bloody and bowed from his encounter with Minette Ferrar, only still alive because others had found him. He couldn't think of what he'd done without wanting to vomit.

Every day he promised to make it up to his friend somehow. And now, already, he had failed him again.

He had to find Fiona for Ian.

He had to find Fiona for himself.

"Indeed, Chuff," he said, downing his drink as if the matter were that easy. "I wouldn't be able to face my father if I deserted two innocents just to save the nation."

Chuffy gave that little huff of his as he bundled the letters. "Others can save the nation. No one around for the ladies. Not worried, though. White Knight and all."

Alex's stomach lurched again at the hated appellation. "I'm no White Knight, Chuff."

Chuffy blinked. "You are. Always do the right thing."

Alex clenched his brandy glass so tightly he almost snapped the stem. "Don't you dare burden me with that kind of nonsense. No one can always do the right thing."

But Chuffy's smile was complacent. "First time I met you, down at Eton. Being beat to flinders. Got your lights darkened for me. Never forget. Haven't changed."

Have, Alex thought, his gut on fire. Only Chuffy still saw the world in absolutes. Mortals like Alex had had their ideals eroded by time trudging along battlefields, lurking in alleys, betraying friends, being betrayed by friends. By lovers and wives. A man didn't come out of that unscathed. He learned too quickly that he couldn't save everybody.

God knew he hadn't saved his wife. He hadn't even saved Ian Ferguson.

But Chuffy wouldn't understand. So Alex grabbed the letter in Chuffy's hand. "I'll notify Drake that we've been detained. He can get Beau Drummond to take over. He was in the princess's train anyway."

Climbing off the bed, Chuffy suddenly grinned. "Your sister's there. Be happy to help, I'm sure."

Alex groaned. "Pippin? Don't even think of it. I am not letting Pip loose anywhere near a government investigation. She'd muck it up more royally than Prinny's marriage."

Chuffy gave his head a ruminative shake. "Not so sure. Sharp as scissors, Pip."

"And too inquisitive by half. Don't encourage her,

Chuffy." Finishing his own brandy, he put the decanter away.
"Now, go be Oedipus."

Long after Chuffy left, Alex stood at the window thinking. He knew he should get back to Sussex and follow up on
that blackmail attempt. He should ride hard for London and
confer with the Rakes, the untidy group of gentlemen spies
Drake led.

But he couldn't face Ian Ferguson. Not until he'd made
some kind of amends. Not until he'd brought home Ian's sisters. Until he made sure they were safe.

Until Fiona was safe. Until she knew she wasn't alone
again with no help and no friends and no hope.

He thought again of that day four years earlier when he'd
met her. He could still remember that jolt of awareness when
he'd spotted her, the gut-twisting connection from just the
sight of a girl leaning out a coach window. He could still see
the wild banner of lush red-gold silk that was her hair, hear
that throaty voice.

He smiled at the memory of her standing before him, head
back, back straight, determination a living thing in her. He
remembered being surprised. He'd set off after a petulant
schoolgirl and stumbled over an Amazon. A young, painfully
earnest warrior who only wanted to see her sister safe.

He still didn't know why he'd kissed her. Maybe it was
because she had looked so frustrated, so lost when
she'd gotten so tangled up in the briars. Maybe it was the
fact that she'd been the most honest thing he'd seen in
four months spent trolling London's underbelly. He just remembered the scent of clean soap and sunlight on her neck
as he bent to free her from her prison. He remembered being humbled by her bravery.

He remembered that he'd been surprised by her innocence and backed right off. And he remembered that he'd

carried the memory of that moment with him through the ensuing years of pain and drama, when futility had eaten away at the marriage he'd once seen as a miracle, and around him the world had shown itself to be a place of deceit and violence.

What if he hadn't been married the first time he'd met Fiona? Would the ensuing years have been different? Would he have kept better track of her? Would he have missed seeing her the year she should have debuted and wondered what had happened to the sharp, bright girl he'd met?

He would never know. He would never know just how different his life could have been if he hadn't fallen so hopelessly in love with Amabelle Taverner. He would never know if he could have changed Fiona's life. Or his own.

Fiona was a strong woman. If Alex hadn't already known that from her life story, he certainly would have realized it the day he'd delivered the bad news about Ian. She had stood up to her grief and her grandfather's animosity with amazing courage. But she was more alone than ever, penniless and friendless, with Mairead to care for.

It was up to Alex to find her. Not just for her own sake, or her brother's. For his own.

* * *

In a paneled library two hundred miles away in Mayfair, a tall, lean, middle-aged gentleman sat at his desk going through the mail. The room was silent, even birdsong failing to breach the heavy windows, the man's only company an elderly hound bitch who lay curled up before the fire. The man was so absorbed in the letter he held in hands that betrayed a faint tremor that it took him a moment to hear the knock on his door.

The white of his thick hair gleamed in the candlelight as he set down the letter and looked up. "Enter."

Another unmemorable young man cast in shades of medium brown stepped into the room, a missive in his hands. "I beg your pardon, sir, but we've just had word. Madame Ferrar has been safely recovered from the authorities."

The older gentleman went still. "Good. How?"

The younger man shrugged. "The communiqué doesn't say. Just that she left behind a jarvey with his throat slit. The militia has mounted a full search for her, but she is already out of the area."

The man behind the desk rubbed at his forehead, his eyes closed. "Good. I admit I was a bit worried. She is the best assassin in Europe, but one doesn't wish to chance our odds with her in custody. Tell them to get her safely back here as soon as possible. I'd rather she didn't do any more solo jobs. Her habit of leaving behind calling cards like that is beginning to be commented upon."

Privens, poised at the edge of the carpet, scribbled on his notes. "Yes, sir."

"What about the other matter, Privens?" the man asked, reaching under his reading glasses to rub his eyes. "The missing message from Hawesworth."

Privens shifted on his feet. "No luck, sir. We don't know if they did it on purpose, but the ladies must have carried it away with them."

"I doubt they did it on purpose. It was in code, wasn't it?"

"Yes, sir."

The silver hair gleamed as the man nodded. "Have we found them yet?"

"We're having Whitmore followed. Our bet is that he won't rest until he finds them. Especially after what happened with their brother."

"Whitmore, eh?" The older man smiled and picked his mail back up. "A tidy solution all round. If he balks at helping us, make sure he knows what he owes us."

The older man's smile was satisfied. "It was a lucky day we stumbled across those letters, Privens. Strap me if it wasn't."

Privens seemed to be having trouble swallowing. "Yes, sir."

"Well, make sure we don't botch this. We need to find those women. And then we need to find that message. Christmas is coming up fast, and everything has to be ready for the attack." Tidying his desk, he rose to his feet, so that he looked down on the secretary. "In fact, let Madame Ferrar go along to search. It will keep her busy. And as a woman, she should know where they would hide the thing."

"Yes, sir."

For a moment there was silence. The older man looked up. "Well? What else?"

"If we find out that the Ferguson women are actually involved, do you wish us to ask for further instructions?" he asked, the missive crackling a bit in his hands.

The old man's eyebrow rose. "Can't you take care of them yourself?"

"Of course, sir." The younger man bowed. "They won't bother you again."

The older man nodded and returned to his work. "See to it."

Chapter 2

For the fifth time that day, Fiona Ferguson thanked the education she had received at Last Chance Academy. It had been an awful school, but the staff had definitely beaten the maidenly arts into its students. Because of it, Fiona could draw a figure, sing a tune, play a reasonably melodic piano, sew a sampler, and set a dinner table. All of which she taught to the Blackheath neighborhood girls, along with Latin, Mathematics, Globes, and Natural Philosophy.

As she accompanied the last of her students to the door, she thanked her friend Margaret Bryan most of all for the chance to do both, at least for now. If not for Margaret, Fiona and Mairead would have been back on the streets. Instead, at least until the lease ran out in two months, they had a roof, some furniture, and a bit of egg money.

Fiona also had a blistering headache, but that was because of the sleep she was forfeiting trying to keep their heads above water. And that was such a familiar state that she barely noticed it.

"We'll come tomorrow, then, Miss Fee?" eight-year-old Nancy Peters asked as Fiona knelt to button her coat.

"No, my dear. Tomorrow is Saturday. Your mother will need you about the shop. But I expect you to practice your addition and your curtsies."

Giving a gap-toothed grin, the tiny girl with her white-blond braids dropped almost to the ground. Chuckling, Fiona helped right her. "You will be curtsying to the likes of Mrs. Walsh, Nancy. Not the queen."

The little girl's grin was still cheeky. "But Mrs. Walsh thinks she is the queen. Will Miss Mary be here when we come back?"

"Oh, I expect so. She is just busy working today."

Nancy gave a solemn nod. "Counting stars."

"Exactly. Now, off with you before your mother worries."

She taught children of shopkeepers and chemists, pupils Margaret had groomed and then been forced to leave because of frail health. Fiona hoped her friend's health would benefit from her move to Margate. They had a debate to finish over Fermat's Last Theorem.

In the meantime, though, at least for two months, the very lucky Ferguson sisters would keep up the town house where Margaret had run her school for children of enlightened parents. Within that time, Fiona prayed she would be able to find another place they could afford to stay and teach. If not...well, she had faced uncertainty before. And if there was one thing Fiona Ferguson excelled in, it was dealing with uncertainty.

After watching the little girl hop down the steps of the tidy brick row house, Fiona closed the door and returned to the south parlor to clean up the slates and books Margaret had loaned her.

Anyone from Hawesworth Castle would have been appalled at her living conditions. Rather than the hundred servants Hawesworth enjoyed, she and Mairead had one female helper and one man-of-all-work they shared with two other families. More often than not she was paid in foodstuffs and services. In fact, Fiona's next chore for the day was to help Mrs. Quick figure out how to stretch the ham hock Nancy Peter's butcher father had exchanged for the week's lessons.

Since most of the furniture had gone with Margaret, the guest salon was graced with no more than a tinny pianoforte, an unpretty brown settee, two stiff-backed chairs, and a few odd tables Fiona had negotiated for French lessons, which was plenty. If Fiona and Mairead were working, they sat at the dining table Fiona had acquired from the rag-and-bone man. If they weren't, they shared the warm kitchen with Mrs. Quick. The only rug resided in the schoolroom, and the only artwork had been done by her students. She and Mairead shared a bed, rationed coal, and turned cuffs and hems. Other than that and the roof over their heads, they had nothing.

They had everything. They were off the streets. They had food and heavy cloaks and a bit of coal for the fires. They had their correspondence from their friends around Europe, which was their only frivolous expense, and the Royal Observatory up the hill. And they had each other. For that Fiona was most grateful. Now that Ian was gone, Mairead was all she had left in the world.

That thought brought Fiona up sharp, leaving her standing alone in the echoing room, slates in one hand, the other hand pressed against the shard of grief that had lodged in her chest. Considering how little she had seen her brother Ian while growing up, she was surprised how sharp her grief still sat on her shoulders. It was as if a foundation stone had gone missing from her house, threatening its stability.

No, she thought, eyes briefly squeezed shut. It was as if she had been left to balance a heavy, unwieldy load on only one leg. She had done it before, of course. This time, though, there was no hope of regaining that balance. Mama was gone, Ian was gone, and the only person left who loved her was Mairead. And Mairead couldn't help her. It was Fiona's task to help Mairead.

Deliberately opening her eyes, Fiona put the slates away and set off for the kitchen, in the hopes she would find Mrs. Quick preparing dinner.

"There you are," Mrs. Quick snapped from where she was chopping carrots at the counter. "Last of the brats gone?"

Fighting a grin, Fiona lifted her apron from a hook by the door and slipped it over her head. "Indeed, they are, Mrs. Quick," she said as she reached around to tie it. "You are once again safe from shrill voices, sticky fingers, and the tramp of small feet."

In response, Mrs. Quick went after her carrots as if they were tender young necks.

Mrs. Quick was another new experience, left behind with Margaret's blessings. A large, rigidly groomed woman with a taste for bright colors and sherry, the housekeeper was dour and acerbic, the majority of her interactions consisting of her opinions on the twins, the school, and the world. Nothing pleased Mrs. Quick except a perfect pie crust, and she thought women knowing Latin or mathematics went against all that was holy.

On the other hand, she enjoyed nothing more than a challenge, and trying to help Fiona stretch their budget to make ends meet was a definite challenge. Besides, this was the only house that put up with her temperament. Even Mrs. Quick's sister had declined the opportunity to take her in.

She seemed to understand Mairead better than most, though, and had some excellent ideas for keeping her occupied. If she was the price Fiona had to pay for warmth, food, and safety, she was glad to pay it.

"Well, then, Mrs. Quick," she said, smiling. "How may I assist you?"

Mrs. Quick gave her a quick scowl. "You can get out of my kitchen. Sit down somewheres. You look like death on a stick."

Fiona managed a smile. "How could I? We're rich today, Mrs. Quick. An entire ham hock, and we didn't even have to step out into the fog to get it."

But Mrs. Quick was correct. She was beginning to feel like death on a stick.

Mrs. Quick gave an impatient *hmmph*. "You tell me. What good is Latin to a butcher's daughter?"

Fiona sat at the scrubbed table and picked up an onion and a knife. "Maybe none. But maybe Nancy will become a governess herself. Think of the opportunities a good understanding of the romance languages provides."

Mrs. Quick didn't bother to answer. She just reached over, snatched the knife from Fiona's hand, and pointed it at her. "Your sister will be here soon. You'll get no rest then. So get it now." Fiona balked, but Mrs. Quick smacked her wrist with the flat of the blade. "Go on. Nuthin' you were gonna do I can't."

When the older woman also grabbed the onion, Fiona knew it was time to surrender. Getting slowly to her feet, she smiled. "I would kiss you," she said, "but I fear it would only make you more severe."

"I'd wallop you like a redheaded stepchild," the older woman said, then pointed toward the back stairs and resumed her glare.

Fiona smiled and waved, but she obeyed. Sleep did sound seductive, come to think of it. Just a bit, like a refreshing sip of water. She could lay her head on a soft pillow and dream of sines and cosines. Of ham hock-and-vegetable soup.

It was inevitable, of course. Halfway up the stairs, she was brought up short by the sound of the front door knocker. She knew she should go down and answer it. She spent a moment making sure her lace collar was flat against her ubiquitous black kerseymere dress, perfectly aware she was hesitating as long as she could in the hopes Mrs. Quick would intervene.

Just when she'd decided to turn around, she heard the slam of a knife against a butcher block. "Don't you worry yourself," came the strident notes of sarcasm. "I was just dyin' to talk to strangers."

Then came the footsteps, sharp, precise, impatient. Fiona smiled.

She was turning to follow, when she heard a man's voice. "Excuse me. Is Mrs. Margaret Bryan at home?"

Fiona stumbled to a halt, her heart seizing. It couldn't be. Could it?

Just the possibility took the stuffings out of her knees, landing her on the steps like an eavesdropping child. She couldn't breathe, of a sudden; it felt as if bubbles had been caught up beneath her sternum, like champagne drunk too quickly.

"Mrs. Bryan don't live here anymore," Mrs. Quick snapped.

Fiona held her breath, as if it could improve her hearing.

"Could you provide us with her new address?" the voice came again. "It is very important."

It was he. Oh, dear God, it was. She squeezed her eyes shut. She swore her stomach did a complete flip inside her chest. The last time she'd felt like this was four years earlier, in a cow pasture on a rainy spring day, as a man sliced off her hair with a knife. As he bent to kiss her. She swore she could almost smell the fresh-mown hay in that damp field, could feel the sure clasp of a man's hand and the skittering of unrecognized arousal. She had been sixteen, and he had come to take her back to school. He had been kind. She had fallen head over heels in love, a girl too new to anticipation to understand its peril.

The only other time she had seen him, he had come to deliver the news that her brother was dead. He had still been so kind. But it was only now that she noticed.

She didn't even remember getting up from the stair, but suddenly she was running down the hallway toward the foyer to see Mrs. Quick poised before the open front door, hand on hip, face pursed in displeasure at the sight of the two men on the stoop.

"I don't know where she is, and if I did I wouldn't tell you," she said and gave the door a good push.

"Wait!" Fiona called, slowing down, as if it would make her look less frantic. "Let them in, Mrs. Quick."

"Don't think I should," the woman retorted with a squint at the two town bucks. "Don't need their kind nosin' around the school."

Fiona almost laughed out loud. "I sincerely doubt the gentlemen are here to ravage our children," she said, hoping they couldn't hear how overwhelmed she felt.

Taking in a surreptitious breath, she stepped past her housekeeper. "Lord Whitmore," she said with a smile. "It is so nice to see you."

It was beyond nice. It was beyond anything. He was truly standing there before her, wind-chapped and tousled, sleek as a big cat. He had such broad shoulders, such angular, chiseled features, with only an odd cant to his nose to make him seem human. Fiona was afraid her heart would simply seize up, battered by joy and grief.

"By God," he said suddenly, staring at her. "It really is you."

She saw a strong emotion cross his features. Shock? Relief? Before she could decide, he strode up and grabbed her hands. "You have no idea how glad I am to see you."

Fiona caught her breath. It was the same, when he touched her, that arc of lightning, the surge of warmth that flooded her as if she had just rediscovered the sun.

She smiled up at him, praying she didn't look as upended as she felt.

"I, uh...," she said, and had to clear her throat. "Won't you both come in? You were looking for Mrs. Bryant?"

"Actually," Alex Knight said, grinning, his hands still chilly and hot at once around hers. "We were looking for you."

Fiona blinked, somehow disengaging her hands. "Me? For heaven's sake, why?"

"You know them?" Mrs. Quick demanded with an accusing squint as the two men stepped past her and removed their beavers.

Fiona swallowed. "The Viscount Whitmore was a friend of my brother," she said. "This is our housekeeper, my lord. Mrs. Quick."

Alex bowed to the rigid woman. "Mrs. Quick." Then he motioned to his shorter, rounder, bespectacled companion. "Lady Fiona Hawes, may I present Charles, Lord Wilde."

"Chuffy," the shorter man insisted with a bow and a smile that seemed to exude from every inch of him. "The rest is too much."

Fiona dipped her knee. "How do you do... er, Chuffy?"

"Hawes?" she heard from behind her. "And who's that when she's at home?"

Fiona flinched. "I prefer to be known as Miss Fiona Ferguson, if you don't mind, Mrs. Quick. It is so much easier."

"Lady?" Mrs. Quick sneered. "Why not say so? People'd be tripping over themselves to get their brats into your school."

"I have my reasons." Fiona removed her apron and handed it to the woman. "Thank you for your help, Mrs. Quick. Miss Mairead will be home soon. We have to get dinner finished."

The housekeeper crossed her arms and stayed put. "Already is. I assume *she's* a lady, too."

Fiona gave up. "Why don't you join me in the parlor, gentlemen. I have a fire there. Would you like some tea? Mrs. Quick would be happy to get it for us."

Mrs. Quick snorted. Fiona turned for the parlor. Laying their hats on the boulé table by the door, the men followed.

Fiona felt as if she were suddenly walking across an uncertain floor. She had the shivery feeling one gets upon waking from a vivid dream to wonder where she was. What was real. The air seemed to close in on her, and she felt off balance. Why were they here? What did they want? What more could they take from her?

The only thing that kept Fiona from panicking completely was the small satisfaction of shutting the parlor door in Mrs. Quick's face. She waited for the inevitable *hmmph* and receding footsteps before turning to the men.

"I apologize for not having anything stronger than tea," she said, walking over to settle onto one of the chairs so the men could enjoy the marginally more comfortable settee. "This is a girls' school."

Flipping their tails, the men gingerly perched on the couch. Fiona had the most ridiculous urge to giggle.

"You have your own school?" Chuffy asked, looking around. "Mighty successful in six weeks."

She smiled. "No. I have been watching over it for Mrs. Bryan. She had to relocate to Margate for her health and didn't want to leave the children without teachers. Fortunately, Mairead and I were able to help. You truly want to see me?"

She felt so overwhelmed. Beset by memories and the dry remnants of old dreams.

"Searching everywhere," Chuffy said, pushing his glasses up his nose.

Alex's smile was rueful. "We intended to question your correspondents as to your whereabouts. Mrs. Bryan was the first."

She blinked. "My..."

"You really know Gauss?" Chuffy demanded, head up, eyes alert. "Carl Gauss?"

Fiona struggled to keep up. "Well, yes. But how did you know?"

"Your grandfather's secretary. Mr. Bryce-Jones. Worried about you."

She felt her heart shrivel. "Ah, so you've been to see my grandfather. I am sorry for that. He is not the easiest person. Especially now. You see, he has a rather violent aversion to the idea that the family tree might contain a..."

Pain sliced through her chest. Poor Ian.

"Traitor," Chuffy supplied for her with a big nod. "Not."

She blinked. "Pardon?"

Alex leaned forward. "We have news."

For a moment Fiona thought Alex might take her hands again. He didn't. She felt the loss of those fingers deep in her chest where the remnants of old dreams still smoldered. Useless dreams. Dreams she had no right to. Her grandfather had made sure to acquaint her with that sad truth.

"News," she repeated stupidly. "Something to do with my grandfather's edict, I assume. I cannot imagine he failed to tell you of our banishment."

"He did. But what if I told you that you could go home?"

She blinked. The feeling of disorientation grew. "I would say no thank you."

Alex smiled back, and Fiona was the one leaning forward now, as if she could warm herself on him.

"Even if it meant having your brother back?" he asked.

She stared at him, her mind frozen. For the longest moment, she couldn't seem to comprehend what he was saying. Something about Ian.

"But I can't have my brother back," she whispered, thinking that his smile was suddenly cruel. "You told me so yourself."

"I was wrong. We all were. Ian is alive."

She sprang to her feet. "What?"

He rose as well. He stepped closer, but she backed away. Her heart was suddenly pounding in her chest, and there seemed to be a roaring in her ears.

"We were just at Hawesworth Castle, Fiona," Alex said, his expression so gentle as he reached out to finally reclaim her hand. "We went there to give you the good news. Ian is alive. More than that, he has been cleared of all charges. In fact, he's helped us bring in several traitors and given us information that might lead to more."

She kept blinking, as if that would bring the world back into focus, Alex's strong hand her only anchor.

Alive. Ian alive. Safe. Innocent. All of them innocent of scandal.

Still the numbness didn't dissipate. She rubbed at her forehead, as if that could help clear the confusion. "I don't understand."

With gentle hands, he eased her back into her chair and knelt before her, his hands on the arms of her chair. "I can't tell you everything. I can't even tell you where he is. There is still some danger to him, and it is considered better for him to remain in hiding. In fact, you can't tell anyone about this yet. For his protection."

She searched his eyes for deceit, for cruelty. She found none, only compassion, only joy. "But he is safe? He's well?"

Alex nodded. "I'm sure he will get in touch soon. He'll want to introduce you to your new sister-in-law."

Fiona gaped like a simpleton. "My, he *has* been busy, hasn't he?"

Alex reclaimed his seat. "In fact…"

She raised a hand. She didn't want to know more. She was having enough trouble breathing as it was. "We won't go back," she said baldly. "I refuse to expose Mairead to that nasty old man again."

Chuffy snorted. "Good sense. Come with us."

She knew her eyebrows were halfway up her forehead. "Come with you? Where?"

If she had expected an answer, she was disappointed. Alex looked at Chuffy. Chuffy gaped at Alex and shook his head. "Forgot that."

"You forgot where you want me to go?"

"We'll figure something out," Alex insisted. "The point is, you don't need to stay here any longer. You should return to your rightful place in society—" His smile blossomed. "If for no other reason than to rub your grandfather's face in your success."

He was still smiling. Fiona's heart felt as if it were splitting. How did she tell him? How could she ever admit the truth? No matter what he wanted, it was far too late to go back. It always had been.

She opened her mouth to answer, when she heard the front door slam. A reprieve. She needed to think. She needed to plan. Mairead would give her the chance.

"It is my sister," she said, lurching back to her feet. "I would appreciate it if you didn't say anything to her yet about Ian. She... doesn't tolerate shock well."

"You're certain?" Alex asked, rising as well.

She was nodding when the library door slammed open. But it wasn't Mairead. It was a scruffy boy of twelve, bent over, a hand on his thigh, panting as if he'd climbed St. Paul's. Fiona's relief evaporated.

"Well, Tim?"

"You... gotta come..." He threw an arm wide. "Up the hill. She's... she's... gonna do herself harm." This time he shook his head. "You gotta come."

Fiona gave a brisk nod and waved him back. "Get my cloak, Tim."

The boy ran out without another word. Fiona turned to the men. "We will have to postpone the rest of this discussion, gentlemen. I must see to my sister."

"We'll help," Chuffy offered, moving toward the door.

Fiona grabbed his arm. "You will not. It will only upset her more. If you wish, come back tomorrow afternoon. By then I will have broken the news to her. But for now, I must leave."

"But surely you would do better with some help," Alex protested.

For the first time since the two men had knocked on her door, Fiona was able to laugh with real humor. "Oh, Alex. I have been handling Mairead since I was in leading strings. Now go on with you. I will see you tomorrow."

"She won't hurt you?"

They didn't need to know the truth. "Of course not."

And before they could question her further, she walked over to Tim, collected her cape, and swung it around her shoulders as she strode out the door.

Chapter 3

Four hours later, Alex still felt confounded. She was safe. It was all he could think. After the panic that had driven him all the way down from Yorkshire, the all-too-vivid images of what might have happened to Fiona and her sister, the sleepless nights and frantic driving, she'd been safe all along. Safe and fed and busy.

He had seen her and wanted to yell at her. He'd wanted to grab her in his arms and whirl her around until she couldn't stand. She was thinner, and strain tightened her features. She was still the quiet, contained woman he'd met again in Yorkshire, which made him angry. She needed the chance to recover that bright spirit that had so set her apart. She needed to remember what it was to feel safe.

Well, he was damn well going to give her that chance.

But for now he had other issues to deal with. He had finally caught up with Marcus Belden, Lord Drake.

"I appreciate your seeing me," he said, following Drake into the man's library.

Drake didn't look up from where he was pouring both of

them a tot of brandy. "I'm the one who was looking for you, old lad."

Yes. Alex knew. He accepted his glass without a word and claimed one of the green wing chairs that braced the Adams fireplace.

Drake claimed the other, pouring himself into his chair as if boneless. His eyes half-lidded, he reclined with his snifter on a crossed knee.

A dark horse was Alex's friend Drake. Blond and blue-eyed in the finest British tradition and an earl in his own right, he was suave, handsome, and deceptively easygoing. As opposed to most of their other friends, though, Alex knew Drake's history. And a man with that history carried more sins and secrets than Alex ever could. A man who had gathered fifteen highly placed aristocratic sons to do clandestine work for the government under the guise of a club of rakes had brains, determination, and a quiet zeal. As a rule, though, it was an almost impossible feat to catch any of it.

"So the old man simply tossed Ferguson's sisters out?" Drake finally asked, his mellow voice barely sounding interested. "Seems a bit excessive. They didn't point any guns at national heroes."

Alex scowled. "They threatened the revered name of Hawes by being intimately related to a traitor."

"But you just cleared up that misconception."

Alex shrugged. "Evidently no one is allowed to accuse the marquess of being wrong."

"And you wish to...?"

Alex looked up to see the telltale flicker in Drake's eyes that betrayed him. He was interested, all right. "I wish to see that they are established in the *ton*. I wish to rub that old bastard's nose in their success."

"A tall order."

Alex's smile was rueful. "Even as we speak, Chuffy is over at Lady Bea's dumping the butter boat in the hopes she'll take the girls on, at least until Lady Kate gets back from her honeymoon."

Drake cocked an eyebrow. "Lady Bea is all that is admirable, of course," he agreed. "But are you certain Lady Kate is interested in squiring a couple of untested chicks about the marriage mart? That is not quite Lady Kate's reputation."

Lady Kate's reputation was for high living and outrageous behavior.

Alex grinned. "Who in their right mind would snub Lady Kate? Especially now that she is married to an eminently respectable war hero like Harry Lidge?" Shrugging, he sat back and sipped at his brandy. "Besides, if we're lucky the girls will be leg-shackled before Kate gets back from her honeymoon. Where did she go again?"

"Venice." Drake had a smile like a well-fed cat, which meant that there was more to the story. "I look forward to meeting the girls. I only wish I could be there when they meet Lady Bea."

"I don't suppose you'd rather…"

An eyebrow went north. "Be there instead of you? No thank you. I will happily sustain myself on your stories."

Alex looked away into the gentle shadows of the richly paneled room. "Actually, I should get back down to that house party, now that the princess is arriving."

Drake's eyelids all but closed. "No, actually. You shouldn't."

Alex froze, his snifter halfway to his lips, his heart stumbling badly. "Because I can no longer be trusted?"

Drake tilted his head just so. "Can you not?"

Alex slammed his glass on the table. "Don't be an ass.

Of course I can. I reported that the Lions contacted me, didn't I?"

"You also left your post and let them get to Ferguson."

Alex couldn't remember ever seeing such a flat, opaque expression in his friend's eyes before. It made him feel sick. "Don't think you can flog me more than I already have. It was inexcusable, and I take the blame."

"And we never found out what it was they wanted to tell you."

"No. We didn't. But you must know I'll come to you the minute I hear from them again. Nothing is more important. Not my honor. Not my life."

Silence stretched, sticky and impermeable, as Alex met Drake's unrelenting gaze.

Without ever betraying a reaction, Drake took another sip of his brandy. "Actually, you'll probably be here for a completely different reason. Your father's home."

Alex swore he stopped breathing. "What?"

"Sir Joseph has returned from St. Petersburg. Your mother and sister remained."

This time Alex couldn't manage a word. He simply couldn't imagine any situation that would separate his mother from his stepfather.

"Is he in trouble?"

"Not the kind you think." Alex took a breath. "It's his heart. He has suffered two attacks and has come home to evaluate his health."

Alex was on his feet before he knew it and heading for the door.

"Not yet," Drake said calmly. "You need information before haring off."

Alex stopped, his hand still on the door, his heart racing. "Then get on with it."

"He has not put out the word that he is here or contacted your sisters, so don't act the town crier. But the Foreign Office felt that you should be notified."

"Thank them for me."

Drake nodded. "His excuse for returning, if anyone should find out, is that he is bringing dispatches and briefing the prime minister on the Holy Alliance nonsense the tzar is attempting to force down our throats." Drake shook his head. "Mysticism and politics rarely make a good marriage. But the tzar is insistent."

Alex blinked, still distracted. He knew he would need this information for some reason. "Will we join the alliance?"

"No. But they're going to have to be watched. So far Prussia and Austria have signed on for the betterment of kings and posterity. Sound familiar?"

Alex returned to his chair. "You think the Lions are involved?"

"Wouldn't you?"

Alex rubbed at the bridge of his nose. "It would appeal to them, certainly. A return to absolute rule." He huffed in dry amusement. "I can imagine what father had to say about it."

Finally Drake smiled. "Loudly. Which is why I have someone else keeping a close eye on him. Not you," he amended, obviously seeing Alex's intent. "You would only draw more attention to him. Which would do nothing to ease the stress on his heart."

Alex found himself staring at the brandy left in his snifter. "I am allowed to see him, however."

"Of course. Any change would be suspect. While you're there, I would count it a favor if you'd evaluate the possibility that our clever Lions have a hand in this business with the tzar."

Alex nodded and pulled out his watch to check the time.

Yes, his father should be home. "I'll let you know," he said, standing. "Does my father know about the Lions?"

"Not yet. Being so far away, he's been well out of things since before the plot was discovered. Now, with his heart…" He shrugged.

"Let me assess the threat from the tzar before they decide," Alex suggested. "And my father's health. I won't have him endangered."

"There isn't a soul in government who'd argue with you." Drake rose to his feet. "Why don't you consider this a bit of a hiatus, then? Visit with your father and see to the Ferguson sisters as a favor to me. Are you going to eventually return them to Yorkshire?"

Alex pocketed his watch and shared a grim smile. "Lady Fiona insists on going by Miss Fiona Ferguson. What does that tell you?"

"What do you truly think of their chances on the market?" Drake asked.

Alex considered the remaining brandy in his glass. "Well, I've only met Fiona, but she is a stunner. Tall, same red hair as her brother, excellent figure. Every inch a lady."

"Even though she spent her formative years living beneath a bridge?"

Alex glared, not certain why he should feel so defensive. "She was only reduced to that for a few years." He couldn't help it. He shared his own sly smile. "Leyburn does say she carries a knife, though. And is quite proficient on pistols."

The eyebrow rose again. "Something to remember."

"Her grandfather certainly thought so." Alex flashed a grin. "I can't say he was wrong. I truly cannot see her being easily importuned."

"And the sister?"

Alex shrugged. "I'll find out tomorrow. The way people

talk of her, though, I doubt she'll be an easy sell. And I don't see Fiona deserting her."

"Another challenge, then." Drake finished his own glass. "Which would be much more difficult if one were to lose objectivity."

"There's no need for unsubtle warnings. I have not succumbed." Finishing the dregs of his drink, he got to his feet. "Now, if you don't mind, I'm off to be surprised that my father is home."

Chapter 4

He saw his father. His stepfather, to be precise. But as Sir Joseph Knight had acted as his parent for twenty of his thirty years, Alex disdained the difference. A distinguished fifty, Sir Joseph was lean, soft-spoken, and blessed with a thick head of pure silver hair marred only by a slice of red over his right eye. Before taking himself off the marriage market, he had been known as the Silver Fox.

Alex walked into the library of the house on Bruton Street to find Sir Joseph sitting at the sleek Chippendale desk working on some files. Alex's stomach dropped. The changes in his father weren't great; he was a bit thinner, his color less robust, his hair somehow dulled. But Alex felt the dimming of the steady life force that set his father apart. He had been worried before. Now he was afraid.

"So, left your wife to all those elegant Russian princes, have you?" he said, hoping his voice sounded hearty. He didn't care if the throne was at risk. He wasn't going to add to his father's burdens.

Sir Joseph looked up and smiled. "I told them not to bother you. I'm sorry."

Alex strolled over to the drinks cabinet and poured himself another brandy. He wasn't much of a brandy man. Today, he thought, he would excuse the lapse.

"Indeed you should be," he said, pouring a glass for his father and carrying them back with him. "I was called away from babysitting a friend's sisters. Before that I was at a crushingly boring house party with Princess Charlotte."

"The same one your sister Pip is undoubtedly terrorizing?"

He grinned. "The very one. Considering the guest list, I sincerely doubt she can get into too much trouble. Besides, Beau's there."

His father smiled. "Poor man. I wonder if he's realized yet that our Pip is unstoppable."

"He should. He's suffered her hero worship since she was three."

Standing, Sir Joseph waited only long enough for Alex to set the glasses on the desk before pulling him into a hug. "It's good to see you."

"You, too, sir." Alex returned the hug, briefly closing his eyes at the familiar scent of vetiver cologne, which immediately resurrected every feeling of safety and comfort he'd known as a boy. The slight rasp in his father's breathing ruthlessly dispersed it. "I'm surprised you got away without at least mother."

He is too thin, Alex thought, his own heart stumbling. He could feel what good tailoring was camouflaging. Thank God Drake had given him time off. He could focus on making sure his father regained his strength.

"Your mother is furious with me for haring off so quickly," Sir Joseph said, stepping back to retrieve his brandy.

"She and Cissy are well, I hope?"

His father chuckled. "She and Cissy are setting the Russian court on its ear. It is one thing for an Englishwoman to converse in French. But when she also discusses recipes with the cook in Russian and comparative religion with an orthodox priest in Greek, she upsets everyone's expectations. They aren't certain whether they should distrust her or adore her."

Alex nodded. "They chose adore, of course. She is impossible to resist."

His father's eyes softened. "That she is."

Alex stood back and faced his father. "Does she know?"

For the first time, Sir Joseph looked less than sanguine. "You do, then."

"The government worries when its most vital diplomat feels under the weather."

Sir Joseph's smile was tired. Alex thought his shoulders slumped, just a fraction, as if he'd been holding himself up.

Taking his drink, Sir Joseph settled into one of the armchairs before the fireplace and waited for Alex to join him before speaking. "It was undoubtedly stupid of me to make that voyage home, just because of a bit of discomfort."

"Is that what they call heart seizures now? Discomfort?"

Alex won a faint smile. "I didn't want your mother to know. She would worry."

"She will find out, you know. It's inevitable. And I wouldn't want to be in your shoes when she does. What do the doctors say?"

"What they've said since I was twenty-five. I injured my heart with that bout of rheumatic fever, and I must be careful." A sudden winsome smile lightened the thin face. "But careful is such a dead bore."

Alex knew he should argue with his father. Make him see

some sense. But when Sir Joseph Knight smiled like that, kings and emperors tripped over themselves to please him. It was Sir Joseph's secret, one Alex wasn't even certain his father understood. Sir Joseph was such a gentle soul that people around him lived in fear of disappointing him. God knew Alex did. Had from the time Sir Joseph had first introduced himself to a nine-year-old boy to ask his permission as head of the family to marry his mother.

Alex had often wished he had his father's knack for controlling people with kindness, but he didn't. He wasn't patient enough, or nice enough, or capable of seeing good in even the worst person. His father lived to negotiate. The only thing Alex hated more was always being disappointed with the inevitable results.

If Chuffy wanted to see a White Knight, Alex thought, considering the comfortable creases of his father's face, this was where he'd find him.

"Why come home?" he asked instead. "The travel had to have been grueling."

His father shrugged. "Not as much as you think. We came mostly by sea, and I like sailing. It's so peaceful, so free of brangling."

It was Alex's turn to smile. "At least diplomatic brangling. I understand the Tzar has a new bee in his bonnet."

Sir Joseph scowled. "Oh lord, yes. Somehow he's gotten himself involved with some harebrained female claiming to be a mystic, who has talked him into forming a Holy Alliance that would codify divine right."

Alex let an eyebrow slide north. Drake had been right. This was right up the Lions' alley. "Where did the mystic come from?"

"God only knows. She's nothing but a poseur, but the tzar can't see that. He is in a fever of religious purpose. He's already talked Prussia and Austria into joining him. And he's nipping at my heels like a terrier." He considered the remaining brandy in his glass. "Another good reason to come home. And one your mother understands. I'll go back in a few weeks. As soon as I get my brief from Liverpool. And Alexander's fervor wanes a bit."

"Are you sure?"

The older man looked up. "I am careful with my health, Alex. I always have been. But I will not be put out in the sunshine in a Bath chair. Your mother understands that."

Alex wasn't so sure she did, but now wasn't the time to have that argument. "Do you have any appointments this evening? What about sharing a beefsteak at Whites?"

His father nodded. "I would enjoy that. You can tell me more about this friend's sister you're babysitting."

"Sisters. They're named Ferguson," Alex said. "Sisters of my friend Ian."

His father's eyebrows soared. "The one who died shooting at Wellington?"

Ian knew he was breaching a trust, but if his father wasn't a secure repository for the truth, no one was.

"No one knows yet. I only know because I was allowed to tell the girls. Not only did Ian not die trying to kill the duke, he saved him and helped bring in the people who were the actual perpetrators. For some reason the government doesn't want that information out yet. More conspirators, probably. So they asked Chuffy and me to notify the marquess and Ian's sisters."

"They."

"Some government drone named Thirsk."

His father nodded pensively. "I see. How did you become involved?"

Sir Joseph didn't know of Alex's clandestine activities.

Sir Joseph didn't understand the need to lie or steal or murder, even for a good cause.

So Alex shrugged. "Ian has been a good friend. When we heard the reports that he'd died, his friends drew lots to see who would inform his family." Sipping at his second brandy of the day, he let his gaze wander to the fire. "I lost."

"And?"

"And I rode up to Yorkshire to tell Lady Fiona. I had evidently no more than cleared the property before her grandfather the bloody marquess tossed her and her sister out onto the street." He had to pause for a moment, the jagged remnants of fury catching his breath. He shook his head. "Who would do such a thing?"

"The Marquess of Leyburn, obviously. I wish it were a surprise. The surprise, actually, is that he took in those girls in the first place, considering his aversion to scandal."

"Well, it was a surprise to me!"

Alex sought the wisdom of his father's eyes. Soft brown, wise, just a little saddened by too much knowledge.

"I was the one who delivered the girls to that man," Alex said. "I never even thought to ask if they would be welcome. I just assumed..."

"Because you have a mother who could never turn anyone away."

Alex thought of the friends who had camped out at their house during holidays. "And a father who abetted her shamelessly."

Sir Joseph's smile was sweet. "How could I possibly turn her down?"

Suddenly Alex's chest felt as if it would tear in two. He'd forgotten how much his parents loved each other...no, not forgotten. Put away somewhere safe. Able to avoid it when they were gone where he didn't have to see the proprietary touching and telltale smiles and shared amusement in life. It was what he'd wanted from his own marriage. It was what he'd thought he had.

For about a year.

"What are you going to do?" his father asked.

Alex's head snapped up. "Pardon?"

"What are you going to do? About the girls? Have you found them yet?"

"I've only met the one. Fiona."

Splendid, sensuous Fiona. As buttoned down as a vicar's wife now, but the fire was there; he knew it. He just had to give her a place where it was safe to remember.

"And?"

Alex looked up, surprised by his lapse. "She and her sister managed to land on their feet, teaching school for a friend."

"Well, that's good."

"No, it's not." Restless and impatient suddenly, he got to his feet and stalked over to the window. He wasn't sure why. There was nothing really to see. The yellow fog of the last few days lingered, dirtying everything and smelling of sulfur. "Fiona and her sister are daughters of a viscount. Granddaughters of a marquess. They have no business living a threadbare existence working like drudges."

As quickly as possible, he filled his father in on the tentative plans for the girls. When he finished, there was a long silence, punctuated by the snap of the fire and the steady metronomic ticking of the old clock in the hallway.

For a long moment, the silence held. Alex almost smiled. It was an old tactic and an effective one. Sir Joseph knew Alex would become impatient and return for his father's reaction. With one last look out at the muted street, he did just that.

"And then when I get them settled with Lady Bea," he said, reclaiming his seat and his glass, "I think I'll finally do a bit of travel. I just found out that Lady Kate and Harry Lidge have gone off to Venice. It sounds warm, doesn't it? And bright."

His father had the gentlest smile. "You could come to St. Petersburg if you'd like. Your mother would love to see you."

For a moment Alex was afraid he would give himself away. Of course he couldn't go to St. Petersburg. He couldn't go anywhere. Not until he was certain Fiona was finally assured of her birthright. Not until, God help him, he found out just what a blackmailer might have of Amabelle's that could ruin him. That could ruin his family, which would be so much worse.

So he grinned and finished his brandy. "I said warm, sir. If I want to be cold, I can just stay here and speak my own language."

"What about the estate your uncle left you with that fancy title? Have you been able to visit yet?"

"Maybe for Christmas. I'm sure the staff would far rather have a bit of a break. I understand Uncle Pharly was a bit of a task master."

That got a full grin from his father. "Which is exactly how I'd describe you."

Alex grinned back and got to his feet. "Oh, I think for once I shall be a man of leisure. Hunts and harvest festivals and whacking away at the front lawn with a scythe. The bucolic life for me."

"You won't last a month."

Alex met his father's gaze and allowed a bit of truth to seep through. He had long suspected that his father was wrong. He was so tired. He thought he'd been tired since long before Amabelle died. But since then, he knew he'd expended far too much energy supporting his cover as one of Drake's hedonistic rakes. And when he wasn't showing the world how carefree he was, he was exposing the crawly, nasty things that lurked beneath the rocks. Could a stint in the country really be worse?

His father rose. "And in the meantime…"

Alex followed. "In the meantime, I was hoping you wouldn't mind my battening down on you for a bit. That mausoleum I inherited on Jermyn is fit for neither man nor beast."

His father frowned at him. "You aren't moving just to keep an eye on the invalid?"

Of course he was. "Of course I'm not. I began to pack the minute my bedroom ceiling landed in my bathtub not five minutes after I'd gotten out."

His father knew he was lying; he could tell. But a gentleman simply did not call his son a liar. Especially when that son believed he was being helpful.

"I probably won't even be here all that much," Alex said. "Tomorrow I hope to bring Lady Bea to meet Fiona and her sister Mairead. I won't be able to plot my campaign until then."

His father didn't smile, as he'd hoped. "I see."

"In the meantime, I will see you tonight for dinner, sir. Right now I'm due at Tatt's."

He had hugged his father and turned to go, when a single word drew him up short.

"Alex." Alex heard a wealth of history in his voice.

He turned, suddenly sure he didn't want to hear what his father had to say. "Sir?"

His father's gentle brown eyes looked almost liquid. "Don't waste more years paying penance."

Alex's head snapped up. "Pardon?"

His father smiled. "The first time I met you, you were gathering your lead soldiers to melt down so you could sell them to buy... what was it?"

Alex's gut crawled with discomfort. "A Christmas goose for the staff. They were working without pay. It was the least I could do."

"You were eight. It was not your fault that your father was a... disappointment...."

"Don't try to wrap it in clean linen. He was a wastrel."

Sir Joseph's smile never changed. "Nor was it your fault that Amabelle was imperfect. But what you can learn is that you weren't put on this earth merely to heal and atone for everyone you meet. Be careful that you don't find yourself trying to save Ferguson's sisters all by yourself."

Alex felt as if a band were tightening across his chest. His laugh was harsh. "Good heavens, sir. Why would I want to do that? The last time I tried to save anyone, it was my wife. And she was so grateful, she committed suicide."

* * *

He had been the one to find her; Amabelle had made sure of it, timing her act to the second, so he would return from a hard trip to find her lying in the bloodred bath, her hair floating about her like obscene seaweed, her eyes open and opaque, somehow looking despairing and accusing at once. He had yanked her from the tub, screaming curses, and tried to stem the flow of blood from her gaping wrists, even knowing he was too late, that he had been too late before he'd walked in the door. He had exhorted her, begged her, bullied her to live. He had kept on until his staff finally pulled him off and covered her up.

Her suicide note had contained one line. *I cannot do*

it anymore. And only Alex had known exactly what she'd meant. Only he had come to suspect the depth of her need, the impossibility of filling that gaping hole, the lengths to which she would have gone to try.

He hadn't truly understood, though, until three weeks ago, when he had received the letter from the Lions.

We believe you would want to know. We have found your wife's letters.

It would be enough to ruin them all. A member of the family who had committed treason, even if she hadn't fully comprehended it. After all, she had just repeated overheard conversations to her lovers. How could she know what they would do with them?

How, indeed?

Alex was so caught up in memories as he walked that he turned the wrong way on Piccadilly without realizing it and strode through progressively deteriorating real estate. His first hint of the extent of his wandering was a piping voice at his elbow.

"Cur, gov, you don't 'ear nuffink, does ya?"

Stopping in the midst of teeming foot traffic, Alex looked down to see a scrawny boy of maybe ten glaring up at him from beneath the most disreputable top hat he'd ever seen. "What am I supposed to hear?" he asked.

The boy huffed, as if Alex were the greatest idiot walking. "Me, 'course. Tryin' to get y'r ear since bloody 'aymarket. Got a message f'r ya."

Alex wanted to smile, but he knew better. Ragamuffins like this were all business and fragile dignity. Alex bent to hear the boy over the din of passing traffic, street vendors, and broadsheet sellers. "Indeed. And what would that be?"

"You be Lord Whitmore, right?"

For the first time, Alex felt a frisson crawl down his back. "I am."

The boy nodded and pulled a crumpled letter from his pocket. "'Bout time you showed up. I bin waitin' at that 'ouse nigh on a week. Was told you'd give me a yellowboy for the delivery."

Alex raised an eyebrow. "An entire yellowboy? It must be important, then. Who gave it to you?"

The boy shrugged, sending layers of grimy wool shifting about his skeletal frame. "Dunno, do I? Some toff. Seen 'im a coupla times at the Blue Goose. Said you was to read it and answer one question with a nod or a head shake."

"What question?"

"Do you understand what the letter means?"

Instinctively Alex looked around, as if he could divine any unusual interest in their conversation. There was no one obvious, of course, in the teeming streets. Vendors, servants, flower girls, carters, tinkers, and a goosegirl, her flock wad-dling toward Smithfield on their tar-covered feet.

"Ya gonna read it, then?"

Alex jerked back to attention to see the boy's hand out. Digging into his pocket, Alex handed over a quid. In ex-change the boy dropped the now grimy, crumpled letter into his hand.

"Good day to ya, gov."

"Wait," Alex said. "What's your name?"

The boy glared. "Why you wanna know?"

Alex shrugged. "Just like to know who I'm doin' business with."

"Y'r doin' business with the cove at the Goose. But I'll give you me name anyways. Wednesday. Lennie Wednes-day. See ya round, gov."

And off he ran.

Alex was still shaking his head at the sight of all those clothes flapping around the running boy when he opened the seal on the letter. He stopped cold.

A letter wrapped in another letter. Alex recognized the handwriting on the interior one and froze. Amabelle. Instinctively he looked around him, even though he knew the sender wouldn't be anywhere in the crowds that poured through the narrow streets toward the market. Not if they had set Lennie to wait for a week.

He bent back to the letter.

We're glad you've been to see Sir Joseph. His health has worried us all. Which is why we know you wouldn't want to burden him with more problems. You might not know it, but about three years ago, your father hit a bad patch with investments. Then, suddenly, he found money somewhere. If you read this letter, you might know why. As you can see from it, your wife indicts herself. But she also indicts someone else. Someone in a delicate situation. Believe us when we say there are more letters like this. The next time you hear from us, you will undoubtedly wish to follow the instructions that will release to you another.

Three years ago. His father had mentioned something about investments. But a ship had come in they'd thought lost. Hadn't it?

With trembling hands, Alex opened the interior letter; the one in Amabelle's ornate hand addressed to Geoffrey Smythe-Smithe, a scoundrel if there ever was one. One name jumped out at him, though. An impossible name. An unthinkable betrayal. Sir Joseph.

Five minutes later, Alex was still standing in the middle of the walk, the crowds passing around him like a rock in a fast-moving stream. He should return to Drake's and show him this. He should bring it to the Home Office. He closed his eyes. He couldn't. The threat was valid. This letter could kill his father. It would definitely ruin him.

It couldn't be true. If Alex believed it was, he would have to jettison every belief he had. And yet, the letter was damning. And allegedly there were others. Alex couldn't breathe. What would they want? Would it end up costing his father anyway? Would Alex have to betray not only his country but his father?

He thought of the promise he had only recently made to Drake, that he would not fail to contact him the minute the Lions approached. Nothing was more important than his duty to his country, he'd vowed. Not honor. Not life.

But what about his father? Just what would a charge of treason do to that magnificent heart?

Alex stood for a long time. Before he moved on, he gave one nod of his head. He never went back to Drake's.

* * *

Fiona had expected to see Alex and his friend Chuffy again. After all, they had promised to return, and she had prepared for it, slipping into her best black twill gown with its Irish lace collar, and tucking her hair up into braids that wrapped around her head. She hadn't expected to welcome the elegant older woman who followed them in. She certainly hadn't expected that woman to step up without an introduction, lay a papery hand against Fiona's cheek, and say, "Sanctuary."

They all sat now in the library, where Fiona and Mrs.

Quick had pulled the extra chairs and set out tea and seed cakes. Fiona felt as if she were back in school sitting before the charity board. She sat ramrod straight, terrified her teacup would begin to rattle.

She knew they meant well. But they didn't understand. And she couldn't tell them.

"We were hoping your sister would be here," Alex was saying, looking no more comfortable than Fiona felt.

Fiona took a look at the mantel clock, which seemed to be ticking unnaturally loudly. "She should be in a few moments. She has been up the hill this morning."

"Sure that's wise?" Chuffy asked, frowning. "Upset and all."

Fiona managed a weak smile. "She would be more upset if I kept her home."

Lady Bea nodded briskly. "Ritual. Soothing."

She had been speaking in that kind of incomprehensible way since she'd arrived. Fiona was used to cryptic conversations. There were days when that was the only way Mairead spoke. But Fiona was used to interpreting Mairead. She didn't know this lady.

"Is there really a reason to wait for her?" Chuffy asked Alex.

Alex, looking even more uncomfortable than Fiona felt, shook his head. "I imagine not. Have you told your sister about Ian yet?"

Fiona wasted a quick look at the smiling Lady Bea.

Alex smiled. "We have no secrets from Lady Bea."

"Wouldn't do us any good," Chuffy agreed with a nod of the head that sent his glasses sliding down his nose. "Find out anyway."

Lady Bea patted Chuffy's knee.

"Have you told your sister?" Alex repeated.

Fiona caught his gaze, unsure why he was making her feel so off-kilter today. It wasn't as if he were angry or stiff. His rich brown eyes were soft and smiling, his posture easy as he sat with his own cup balanced on his fawn-stockinette-clad knee. Even so, she felt odd shivers chase down her spine, and she wanted to fidget.

"Change comes slowly to Mairead," she finally said, briefly looking down at her teacup. "She doesn't like surprises. I told her, but it will take a while longer for her to admit it."

"But we don't have time," Chuffy said. "Little Season coming."

Inexplicably, Lady Bea was nodding and smiling again.

"But surely your sister would want to know that your brother is alive," Alex said. "You need to make her understand."

Fiona bristled. "Lord Whitmore, I appreciate your help in this matter. But you do not know my sister, and I resent your speaking as if I don't, either."

"No offense meant," Alex said, flushing a bit. "But before your sister arrives, we need to know what to expect from her."

"In what way?"

"Well..." He looked over to the old woman, who nodded again.

"Would she shy at attending a few routs, a ball maybe," Chuffy said. "Not Almack's—"

Lady Bea suddenly waved a hand. "Paralyzing."

Chuffy nodded and shoved his glasses up his nose. "Rather play two-handed whist with the mater. But your sister..."

Fiona was feeling more confused by the minute. "I don't understand."

"How do you think she would do in a social setting?"

Fiona's heart clenched. She instinctively straightened, too familiar with this line of conversation. "She is not one for social functions. She is...shy."

Fiona saw the looks on all three faces that betrayed their skepticism over her term. She well knew Mairead's reputation and limitations as well as she knew her own, and she refused to apologize.

"But if your sister said yes?" Alex asked.

Before Fiona could answer, the library door swung open to slam against the wall, and a whirlwind descended. Both men jumped to their feet as if to confront an enemy. Fiona followed more slowly. She knew exactly what they would see, and she wanted to know their reactions. It should not have been important to her, but it was. More than anything, she needed to know how the men would behave in the next few minutes. Particularly Alex.

"Can you believe it?" the whirlwind demanded, unwinding a hunter-green muffler from around her neck and pulling off her bonnet to reveal a mass of fire-red hair just a bit lighter than Fiona's and the sharpest blue eyes in Britain. "He refuses. Simply refuses to allow me to apply to be an assistant. Me, who helped him calculate the fluctuations in Eta Aquilae, and the Astronomer Royal doesn't believe I have the *intelligence* to handle his telescope. Well, I am more than his computer, and so I told him. Fee, you have to do something." Abruptly, she froze, finally catching sight of the visitors. "What have you done?"

The men were on their feet, jaws dropped.

"*This*," Alex demanded, "is 'poor Mairead'?"

Chapter 5

Alex knew he was gaping. He couldn't help it. Fiona should have warned them.

The newcomer was staring at him, her hands fluttering oddly in the air, as if pushing the visitors away. "I don't know them," she protested, brow pursed. "Why are they in my house?"

"We have visitors, sweetings," Fiona said, hurrying up to capture her sister's hands and quietly murmur to her as her sister stared at the interlopers as if they had dirtied her floors.

He wasn't certain what he had been expecting of Fiona's sister. But the way everybody talked, he'd thought...well, he'd thought he would meet a short, misshapen girl of limited intelligence, who had to be protected from a harsh, mistrustful world. He supposed he had expected an overgrown child.

He hadn't expected a goddess.

Fiona had said she had a twin, of course. But somehow Alex hadn't expected an identical twin. *No*, he thought, almost shaking his head. *Not identical, exactly.* Fiona was compelling, with high, broad cheekbones, startling blue eyes, and hair the color of fire. She stood at almost five feet ten inches and moved with the grace of a natural horsewoman. Ever since he'd met her four years earlier, he had known she would mature into a rare beauty, and she had. Her sister had the same features, from square face to tumbling red-gold hair. She stood as tall and walked with the same fluid power. But she wasn't the same. She was *more*.

Fiona was beautiful. Her sister was luminous. Otherworldly. Breathtaking. Her hair wasn't just thick and curly. It was alive, dancing around her shoulders like one of the seven veils. Her eyes had enough of a violet tinge that they compelled comparison to flowers and evening skies. Her skin had the hue and texture of unearthly fine porcelain, and her hands, now in flight, were as graceful as soaring birds. Even her figure, only hinted at beneath a hideous mustard dress and rumpled apron with overfull pockets, was the stuff of fantasies.

There was no one thing Alex could put it down to, this stunning otherworldliness that set her so far apart. But it existed, and it made him question every assumption he'd made about the intelligence of anyone who'd met her.

And yet, amazingly, he had no reaction to her. No accelerated heart. No tightening in his groin or urge to possess. Those, he realized, he reserved for Fiona.

"Mairead," Fiona said, standing so she filled her sister's view. "You remember my talking about Ian's friend Alex."

The sister blinked as if being woken suddenly from sleep. "No."

Capturing her sister's hands midflight, Fiona turned toward Alex, continuing as if the answer had been affirmative. "Well, this is Alex Knight, Viscount Whitmore. You have never met him, but he is the gentleman who brought me home from school to Hawesworth Castle four years ago. The one who brought us the news about Ian." Swinging around, she motioned just beyond Alex. "And this is, uh, Lord Wilde."

"Chuffy," Chuffy said, sounding curiously complacent. "Everybody says so."

Lady Edna Mairead Ferguson Hawes blinked a couple more times at Chuffy. "You're not sure?"

He shrugged. "Enough for the engraver."

"And here, Mairead, is Lady Beatrice Gilbey," Fiona finished, turning to include Lady Bea, who simply waggled her fingers at Lady Mairead, as if catching sight of her across a crowded ballroom.

"They have come about our good news, Mairead. You know, that Ian is alive."

It was a small movement, but Alex caught it. Every muscle in the sister went taut. She was ready to bolt, but Fiona, smiling, kept tight hold on her. The sister took on a faint resemblance to a panicked horse. Her nostrils even flared, as if she smelled danger.

"Will you join us, Mairead?" her sister asked, her voice brisk.

Fiona's twin spared one more panicked look at the intruders—funny, how Alex suddenly felt like an intruder—and then turned back to her sister, as if no one else inhabited the room. "Where is it, Fee?" Her voice sounded thinner, fretful. "Please. I think that woman has it."

Fiona never looked away from her sister. "She is resting against it, dear. Don't you want her to be comfortable?"

Obviously a harder question than it seemed. Mairead Ferguson began to rock, her hands clutching Fiona's as if she were in danger of falling. "Please. These people, I can't...I..." She was drawing in air now like a landed fish.

Alex almost got to his feet, as if that could help. Fiona held her sister's gaze.

"You will have it soon, sweetings. It is safe."

"This?" Lady Bea asked, pulling a pillow from behind her back and holding it up. The size of a large book, the square was tattered and covered in needleworked thistles.

Before she could say more, or Fiona react, Mairead broke free and grabbed the pillow to her chest, closing her eyes. "Sorry," she said, still gasping a bit. "Sorry. It isn't your fault, ma'am. I should never have let it out of my sight."

Lady Bea was still smiling as if she understood. *"Ego te absolvo."*

Mairead's eyes sprang open and she laughed. "You look nothing like a priest." Without a pause, she turned on her sister, the pillow still clutched close. "I *must* get time on the great refractor," she insisted. "If my calculations are correct, the light from my Cepheid variable should be fluctuating again in the next few days, which would prove the orbit of the companion star. I need to catch the exact time so I can make precise calculations. Fiona, you must do something. You must talk to Mr. Pond. You must get me time. You told me that since we couldn't live near Caroline and William, we would live here so I could have the chance at the observatory's instruments. You even agreed to do his computing so he would give me time. But he isn't. He won't. *Make* him, Fiona."

"It is too late this afternoon, Mairead," Fiona said, and Alex was impressed by her steady calm. "Of course I will speak to Mr. Pond in the morning. But for now, sit down for a few minutes and greet our guests."

And before Alex knew it, Fiona had drawn her sister all the way to the settee, where she sat her next to Lady Bea, who patted the girl's hand as if she were a child deserving sweets.

Lady Mairead blinked like a baby rabbit and rocked a bit in place, arms around the small pillow. "No, Fiona. No, now. Please. I won't sleep. You know I won't."

"Of course you won't, sweetings," Fiona said, seating herself in a chair next to her sister without letting go of her hand. "You will be up with me watching the night sky. But now I'd like you to give your greetings to our guests."

"I don't want guests. I don't want news. I want to see my *star*."

"Pond, eh? Astronomer Royal?" Chuffy asked with a nod. "Good chap. Bit old-fashioned. Friend of the pater's. Help, if you want."

Lady Mairead scowled, giving Chuffy a once-over that reminded Alex of his aunt Euphrania dressing down a deb. The only thing the girl was missing was a lorgnette.

"Who are you?" she asked again.

Chuffy grinned. "Chuffy. Just Chuffy. Can go next week, if you want. Busy now."

"You are interested in astronomy?" Fiona asked him.

"Don't know a star from a seagull. Might like to learn."

"Do you know mathematics?" Mairead demanded. "There is no point in pursuing an interest in astronomy unless you understand mathematics."

Chuffy shrugged. "Some."

Alex coughed, but kept his thoughts to himself.

"You really know Gauss?" Chuffy asked, giving his glasses another shove.

"Of course we know Gauss," Lady Mairead snapped. "He has a fine mind. We're discussing a new vision of geometry, aren't we, Fee?"

That was when Alex noticed that Fiona had released her sister's hand and sat back a bit. Mairead was stroking her pillow like a cat.

"Indeed we have, Mairead," Fiona said. "We can talk about Mr. Gauss over tea."

Lady Mairead's head came up. "Tea?"

"I'm sure Mrs. Quick has it ready."

She received another blink, a nod, and her sister calmly returned to her feet.

"Help," Chuffy offered, popping up.

Fiona's sister jumped back from him as if he'd pushed her, but she didn't seem distressed. "We're having ginger-bread," she said and, depositing the pillow in Fiona's lap, walked out the door, Chuffy right on her heels.

Alex wished he could just close his eyes. He had had a surfeit of eccentrics lately. He had a feeling it was about to get much, much worse. And he wasn't at all sure he had enough patience left for them. He needed to get back to his father. He needed to ferret out who had sent that blackmail letter. He needed a few minutes alone with Fiona to assure himself she was all right. That she was happy to see him.

"He really doesn't notice how beautiful she is, does he?" Fiona asked.

Alex opened his eyes to see her staring out the door. "Chuffy? Oh, in a 'what a pretty sunset' kind of way."

Fiona nodded and sank back into her chair, still looking bemused. Alex had a feeling she was even more over-whelmed than he. He caught himself just shy of going over to sit next to her. Taking her hand. Offering support.

"Mairead never just goes off with other people," she mused.

Lady Bea chuckled. "Chuffy," she said, as if that were an-swer enough.

For anyone who knew Chuffy, it was. "Chuffy is the most nonthreatening soul in the kingdom," Alex assured Fiona. "Your sister truly enjoys astronomy?"

Fiona smiled. "I am not sure 'enjoys' is the proper term. 'Obsesses over' might be closer. Lives for. Breathes and sleeps. I still cannot believe how lucky we were to end up in a school at the south end of Greenwich Park. She walks to the observatory every day. I know she is impatient with Mr. Pond, but he has been very kind to her. Of course, we have been doing some of his calculations. He should be gracious."

Again Alex had to rearrange his assumptions. "You both have?"

She shrugged. "Mr. Pond actually has several people helping him. And he would be foolish to pass up a mind like Mairead's."

A mind like *Mairead's*. No mention of how singular her own brain must be to be doing mathematical calculations for the Astronomer Royal. Alex felt more and more disconcerted. Somehow he'd thought he knew everything about Fiona. Everything that mattered, anyway. Hadn't he saved her once? Hadn't he kissed her out in a pasture? But he was just beginning to realize how little he did know. And how much he wanted to change that.

Now Lady Bea patted Fiona's hand, which made Alex smile. "Bryan," the old woman said. "Of course."

Only a few days ago, Alex wouldn't have understood the reference. But he'd studied up on Fiona's odd collection of correspondents, and found that the Margaret Bryan she had inherited the school from wasn't merely a school principal. She was a brilliant mathematician and natural philosopher in her own right, having published several seminal works. The Ferguson twins were looking more interesting by the minute.

On the other hand, how well would a pair of mathematician/astronomers fare in the shallow pool of the *ton*? It was a question he had never thought to ask.

"Does this mean we have to find you a telescope for when you move?" he asked with a smile.

Fiona's head snapped up. "Move? What move?"

"Chuffy and I didn't come merely to tell you about Ian," he said. "We've come to bring you back."

She stiffened. "Back? I told you. We are not going back. And I cannot believe the marquess would be any happier than I if we did."

"I agree. He's not worth wasting time over. But you are both granddaughters of a marquess. The daughters and sisters of viscounts. You should have had a season two years ago. We're here to see you returned to your rightful place in society."

Fiona Ferguson had the strangest smile on her face, as if Alex were the sweetest, most ingenuous boy she'd ever met. "No, Lord Whitmore. You won't."

He felt like growling. "First of all, I already told you. It's Alex. Second, why the deuce—er, why not?"

She was back on her feet and striding over to the window, the pillow clutched to her chest. "It isn't that I don't appreciate your concern," she said. "And I do thank you for telling me about Ian." She turned and frowned. "He really is alive."

Alex could understand the need for reassurance. "He really is."

She nodded, looked out onto the yellow fog that blanketed Southvale Road. "It will be good to see him. Please give him our direction when he is free to travel."

Alex was on his feet, too, suddenly impatient. "Lady Fiona, you know I cannot do that. If I left you here alone, your brother would have every right to take my head. And I wouldn't blame him." Standing, he approached. "When we came yesterday," he said, "we failed to give you a viable path for returning to your lives. But Lady Bea has offered that path. She would be pleased to invite you to live with her and be sponsored by her and her sister-by-marriage, Lady Kate Lidge. Lady Bea wanted to come herself to make certain you knew how delighted she is to welcome you both."

Lady Bea nodded with a beatific smile. "Diamonds."

"You have no responsibility toward us, ma'am," Fiona said to Lady Bea, who was still smiling. "I would not wish to put you out."

Alex heard an abrupt bark from the doorway and looked up to see Chuffy, who pointed behind him as he walked in. "Women shoved me out of the kitchen. Lady Bea. You inconvenienced?"

"Golden cage," the old woman said, now frowning. "Need out. Need...quest."

Chuffy grinned. "Lady Bea has been companion to Lady Kate, who's a real pip. Up to every rig and row and never happier than when she's setting the *ton* on its ear. Lady Kate's on her honeymoon, though. Imagine Lady Bea's bored out of her stays."

Lady Bea giggled and smacked him on the arm. He grinned back at her.

"Excuse me, ma'am," Fiona said. "But how can you know you would enjoy having us? You have only just met us. I know you cannot have mistaken my sister's personality as a sweet and biddable one. She cannot tolerate crowds, bores, or bad music, and she will say so out loud. And we will no longer be parted. For any reason."

"Anathema!" Lady Bea proclaimed.

Alex grinned. "She means your being separated."

"I got that," Fiona answered. "But what of our work?"

Alex could wait no longer. He took her hand, cradling it in his own as if a woman with hands this strong and elegant needed protection. "You wouldn't have to work ever again," he said. "I promise."

For a long moment she just looked at him, and Alex felt the creeping decay of his certainty. He couldn't remember a time when any woman had told him no for any reason. He couldn't imagine this woman he had kissed four years ago disdaining his help. Suddenly he was fighting the urge to pull her close to him, to insist. To collect her like an heirloom to protect.

She pulled her hand away as if it burned and backed up a step, never looking away from him, the picture of dignity and strength. "Ah, but you see, Lord Whitmore, you've made the wrong promise. We have no wish to be relieved of our work. We have students, and Mairead has her chance on the refractor, and we both have our computations to keep us busy and well fed. I think this is the place for us now."

And then, as if the conversation were finished, she turned back to the window. Alex felt that rejection lodge in his chest like a peach pit, which confused him. He was here to help her; that was all. Her answer wasn't personal.

But suddenly, it felt personal. He had known more beautiful women. Hell, Fiona's *sister* was more beautiful. Amabelle had been more beautiful, all soft, plump curves and vulnerability. There was nothing vulnerable about this woman.

And yet, he had to help her. He had to have her with him, where he could watch her. Even though he knew damn well she probably wouldn't tolerate watching.

"Lady Fiona," he said. "Begging your pardon, but you know that isn't an option. Not for you. Your birth precludes it."

"My birth precluded my stealing apples from carts to eat, my lord," she said quietly. "It precluded picking pockets for handkerchiefs and hiding in tavern corners waiting for drunks to drop a coin or two. But I have done that, too."

"When you needed to. You no longer have to work. You have the right to enjoy the benefits of your station."

That, finally, was what got her to turn, and he almost stepped back. Her eyes gleamed with a cold fire that froze him. "I have spent the last four years doing just that, my lord. *Enjoying my station.* Which meant that my sister and I were secluded in the country like a pair of madwomen, not allowed to travel, or interact with anyone else of our class, and certainly not of any other class, while our grandfather attempted to restore the family reputation."

"Marquess," Chuffy huffed. "Bad form."

Alex saw something more in Fiona's eyes. Something hard and unforgiving, something forged in fires he would never face. Fiona Ferguson was trying to share a truth no one in this room could understand, and it snaked down his back like a portent.

"I would be no credit to you, ma'am," she told to Lady Bea. "My sister and I would always be freaks, useful for nothing better than gossip. 'Those Ferguson girls. Came from the slums, don't you know. The older one is known to carry a knife about her person, and stole food at school. Not good *ton*, my dear. Not good *ton* at all,' " she mimicked with brutal effect.

Just as Alex knew she would, Lady Bea shook her head. "Noisy birds."

Alex saw Fiona's expression soften. He saw the briefest gleam of unspeakable pain darken those celestial eyes as she walked over to seat herself beside the old woman and take her hand. "You are all that is kind, ma'am," she said, her voice as soft as regret. "But it is those noisy birds who make up your world. Who welcome or exclude you at their whim.

The last thing I would want to do is to destroy your standing in your own world. I have been outside it my whole life and do not miss it in the least. You, I think, would suffer. My grandfather would see to it."

Alex saw tears in Bea's eyes, where he'd never seen them before. The old woman lifted a papery white hand to cup Fiona's cheek. "No Joan," she said.

Frowning in confusion, Alex looked over to Chuffy.

"Warrior?" Chuffy asked, his forehead pursed.

Fiona never looked away from the old woman. "Martyr," she said softly. "Nor am I, ma'am. It so happens that I truly love the life I have chosen to live."

Alex couldn't accept her conclusion. He couldn't leave her here in these bare rooms and menial conditions. It wasn't right. He refused to admit that he couldn't tolerate the idea that Fiona Ferguson would choose to take herself out of his life.

"You won't be able to continue once Ian is back," he challenged. "Your brother won't allow it."

Fiona smiled up at him, but again the smile was edged in steel. "We'll see. Besides, I cannot imagine his new wife would welcome a pair of awkward spinsters into her home, nor wish our interference in her life."

"Not so sure about that," Chuffy said.

Alex finally found a reason to smile. "Indeed. I never got a chance to tell you who your brother married, did I?"

She frowned, still holding Lady Bea's hand. "Does it matter?"

"Oh, I think so. He married your friend Sarah Clarke. Sarah Tregallan Clarke."

Finally he had surprised her. She lost all color for a moment, her mouth a bit agape, her posture rigid. "Sarah? No. No, how could he?"

Alex shrugged. "Providence, I'd say. He washed up on her land, and she saved his life."

"Friend?" Lady Bea asked.

"We... uh, we went to school together."

Alex challenged her. "At Miss Chase's Academy along with my sister Pip and Lady Elizabeth Ripton."

Lady Bea's head came up. "Dorchester?"

"Yes," Alex said. "The Duke of Dorchester's sister."

Predictably, Lady Bea made a disdainful noise deep in her throat. "Awkward. Balderdash!"

"With all modesty," Alex said, hand to his heart, "Lady Bea is saying that if these are your friends, you are already in the heart of the *ton*."

He might have carried the argument if at that moment Fiona's sister had not slammed open the door yelling, "Tea! Tea, tea, tea, tea, tea!"

And then, coming to an abrupt stop, almost causing the housekeeper to slam into her back, demanding, "Are you still here?"

"You're right, of course," Fiona said quietly. "Who could ever consider us awkward?"

Getting to her feet, she strode over to intercept her sister before Mairead could escape.

Chuffy anticipated her. "Promised tea," he said evenly, stepping in front of Mairead before Fiona could reach her.

Mairead froze in place, glaring down at the chubby baron who only came up to her shoulders. "We did?" she asked.

He gave her a grave nod that sent his glasses skidding down his nose. "You did."

And, amazingly, the Amazonian Mairead giggled like a girl and gently pushed his glasses back up into place. "Then tea it is."

Alex looked over, expecting to see Fiona smile. She was

staring, certainly, her hands wrapped around that pillow as if gaining purchase. But she wasn't smiling. She frowned, her jaw working, as if she were chewing over the words she wanted to say.

"Mairead?" she said, holding out the pillow.

Her sister didn't seem to notice her. "You like seed cakes?" she was asking Chuffy.

Chuffy patted his straining green-and-yellow-striped waistcoat. "Does it look like there is anything I don't like?"

Without even looking over to her sister, Mairead took Chuffy's hand and led him over to the chairs. Behind her, Mrs. Quick was shaking her head as she finally entered the room with the loaded tea tray. Alex sat back and prepared to repeat his invitation. He would not let Fiona Ferguson win this argument.

* * *

By the time Fiona finally convinced her Good Samaritans to go home, she had a raging headache. Alex had been determined that Fiona and Mairead follow him home. At least to Lady Bea's home. He had gone so far as to call Fiona a fool. And all she had been able to do was sit silently and wait him out. She couldn't say yes. And she refused to tell him why. Alex had always been her white knight, the only person besides Ian to look out for her. The last thing she wanted to do was disillusion him.

By the time she closed the door on her guests, she was reduced to lying on the brown couch with a lavender-scented cloth over her eyes.

"He said he'd help," she heard, and knew that Mairead had returned to reassure herself of the momentous change in their lives.

"He did," Fiona assured her, not moving.

That was another thing contributing to her headache. Mairead's behavior with Chuffy Wilde. Mairead didn't take to strangers, especially men. But she had spent quite twenty minutes explaining Cepheid variables to the guileless young man while he nodded, wide-eyed and adorably cute. Fiona had the feeling he hadn't understood one word out of four, but he'd positively egged Mairead on, smiling all the while. And every so often, without interrupting her lecture, Mairead had reached out to shove his glasses back up his nose. She had willingly touched a stranger.

Fiona couldn't remember the last time that had happened.

"Did he mean it, do you think?" Mairead asked, her voice unbearably hesitant, her arms once again around the pillow.

"Oh, I think he did. He said he would be back on Tuesday."

She heard Mairead march closer. Mairead always marched, as if on a mission. But then, she probably was. Everything Mairead took an interest in was all-consuming. Mathematics, astronomy, music.

"Do you want me to play?" Mairead asked, her voice curiously soft.

Fiona did like to hear Mairead play. Her sister wasn't a restful musician, but she was talented. She played with the same precision that she mapped stars and the kind of energy that spoke of Mairead's use of music as release.

Fiona lifted the rag to see a curiously uncertain expression on her sister's face. "What's wrong, Mae Mae?"

Mairead's eyes dipped. "You don't look right."

Fiona smiled. "I'm fine. Just a little tired from arguing with Lord Whitmore."

From fruitlessly wishing she could allow him closer.

Mairead sat in one of the chairs with a *plump*. "The tall one."

"Yes. The tall one. The male tall one."

She actually got a grin out of her sister. "I think he likes you. He kept smiling."

Fiona almost hid behind her cloth again. Oh God, that was the last idea she needed to get stuck in her sister's head. Mairead wasn't merely brilliant and quirky. She was relentless. If that idea took root, she would worry it until it lay in shreds at her feet. She certainly didn't need to know that Fiona's fingers still tingled from their contact with Alex's hand. She didn't need to sense the grinding disappointment that followed his exit.

Fiona sat all the way up, trying her best to hide the pain that pounded through her skull. She was nauseated with it, and that always upset Mairead. Mairead needed to know that there was a solution to every difficulty. So far neither of them had come up with one for Fiona's headaches.

"Lord Whitmore feels proprietary toward me," Fiona explained, deliberately laying her hands in her lap. Rubbing at her forehead would distress Mairead all over again. "Remember, he was the one who first brought me to Hawesworth."

Mairead thought about that a moment. "I miss my telescope."

"I know, dear."

"And the library." Abruptly, Mairead sat next to Fee, jostling the couch and Fiona's head. "Oh, Fee, do you think we'll ever find another library like it? Who knew that the inclination toward the stars could run in a family? I actually held a copy of Bayer's *Uranometria*." She shook her head in wonder. "Imagine. Me, holding a star chart from 1603 in my very hands. All the stars given the names we now call them."

Fiona's heart melted at the longing in her sister's eyes. "I know, sweetheart. It was such a discovery. And you were the one who unearthed it."

Mairead scowled. "Who would ever think to pile dozens of agriculture magazines on top of it? Treatises on dirt, when the heavens lay beneath."

Fiona's heart seized. She so wanted Mairead to have everything she wanted. She wished with all her heart she could return her to her telescope and library. But Fiona suspected she had poisoned that dream. When her grandfather had informed her of the eviction, she had finally informed him of her opinion of him.

"You could go back, Mae Mae," she ventured. "You got along just fine before I got there."

Her sister was already shaking her head with a violent force that made Fiona wince. "Absurd notion, Fee. *Absurd.* After the things that nasty old man said about you? I would sooner spit in his soup."

Fiona had to smile. *Oh, Mairead. You valiant girl.*

Was she wrong? Fiona wondered. Was she needlessly keeping Mairead from comfort and companionship? Did they always have to rely only on themselves?

She closed her eyes against the scrape and weight of old pain. Yes. They did. She had tried so often to rely on others, making the mistake of hoping that this time things would change. And every time she had been cut loose and left drifting. Better to never be disappointed again. No one knew what was better for Mairead than she did. No one loved her acerbic, brilliant, frustrating sister as much as she.

"We don't have to go with strangers again, do we, Fee?" Mairead asked, her voice unbearably small.

Fiona wrapped her arms around her sister. "We do not, sweetheart. We will live here, teach children, and save up our computing fees so we can buy a real telescope. We can set it up in the back garden and watch for comets, like Caroline and William."

Fiona regretted mentioning the names the minute she did it. Mairead's head came up with a snap and her eyes flashed. "You promised," she accused. "You promised that we would live near them. That we could visit and talk and maybe, if we were very lucky, use their twenty-inch telescope. We could even help them grind lenses. We got very good, didn't we? It is my dream, Fee. You know that. To sit at the feet of William and Caroline Herschel. To help. To add my name to theirs in the rolls of history."

Fiona finally gave up and rubbed at her temple. "We've spoken of this, sweetheart. The Hershels live twenty-five miles away. We have to live here, where we can support ourselves. We were very lucky to have a friend as generous as Margaret."

Alex Knight could get you to the Herschels' home in Slough, temptation whispered.

Mairead was scowling and picking at a loose thread in the pillow. "We could find a school to teach at near Caroline."

"We could. In time. But for right now, we should be happy to exchange correspondence with Caroline as we take advantage of our location. Don't you think?"

But Mairead wasn't pacified. "We could if Mr. Pond let me on the great refractor."

"Chuffy said he would be happy to come back and speak to Mr. Pond with you." Fiona paused, trying to decide how to bring up the next important topic. She finally gave up and just asked. "You seemed to like him very much, Mae Mae. Chuffy, I mean. Do you want to go with him to the observatory?"

Fiona wasn't sure what reaction she expected from

Mairead. What she got was a considered frown, which was
unusual. Mairead made up her mind in a blink and then refused to change it. The fact that she was debating something
made Fiona uneasy.

"He is a very nice man," Mairead finally said, looking up,
her eyes wide and troubled. "He says he knows some mathematics. Do you think he was lying?"

Fiona smiled. Mairead was otherworldly. She wasn't
blind. Since their eleventh birthday men had been telling her
lies to get close to her. Mairead had somehow managed to
see through most of them.

"Is it important to you?" Fiona asked her.

Again Mairead cogitated, her head tilted just a bit. "I
don't know. I suppose it must be if I'm asking, don't you
think? But he truly seemed interested, and not that many
men are." Suddenly she flashed a bright, impish smile. "Not
many men understand so much as a parallax."

"And he did?"

"He did. He said it is used in gunnery. He couldn't have
been in the artillery, could he? He didn't say. He didn't say
much about himself." She looked startled. "And he listened.
He didn't look. Do you know?"

Fiona nodded. It took an exceptional man to be more
interested in what Mairead said than how she looked saying it. "Then I don't think he was lying. Maybe we could
invite him to dinner one night, and you can discuss your
work."

Mairead actually flinched. "Oh, no. No thank you. I don't
have time for that. It will be enough that he gets me on the
refractor and goes away. Don't you think?"

And before Fiona could answer, Mairead leapt back to
her feet. "I have a puzzle I'm working on. Do you want to
help?"

"A puzzle?" It was always a challenge keeping up with Mairead's quicksilver mind.

She was bouncing on her feet. "Yes. I found it in the castle. But I can't make it out."

"What kind of puzzle, Mae?"

Mairead shrugged, her attention already lost. "Words. I like word puzzles."

Fiona nodded. "I know. Maybe later, sweetings, all right? For now, I believe I'm going to simply lie here and rest."

Again Mairead paused, poised on the balls of her feet like a bird coiling to take flight. "Would you like the pillow, Fee?"

Fee smiled up at her, knowing what a sacrifice her offer was. "Oh, sweetheart, thank you. But I don't think so. I think I'm happy when you have it."

Mairead nodded anxiously. And then, suddenly, she rushed up to Fiona and bent to kiss her. "Be better, Fee."

And without another word, she sailed out of the room, leaving her sister to contemplate the upheaval in their lives. The noise that would, in the end, signify nothing. Alex Knight had come here to be kind. To redress the harm the marquess had done. Alex had done it because he was a gentleman. Fiona understood that. Even so, she had once again watched him walk out the door and seen her own dreams depart with him.

How had he become so wrapped up in them, those faint longings for a normal life? A home, a family, a loving husband. She had known better since she had walked into Miss Chase's Academy and compared her life to those of the girls around her. They would all fulfill the promise of their looks, breeding, and wealth. She would grow old protecting her sister from the harsh world outside and nurturing the genius that gleamed behind those amazing eyes. The two of them would live and die together, sharing a history, a love of natural philosophy, and the special bond that came from sharing the same womb. She had known that all along.

Suddenly, though, since Alex Knight had come back into her life, it hurt. It hurt in ways she couldn't describe. He had cracked the door on a future she had only allowed herself to imagine once, in the courtyard of a country inn, only to have it quickly and ruthlessly snuffed out. This time she would have to be the one to slam that door shut again. No matter how much it hurt.

Chapter 6

Alex knew he shouldn't be so angry. He had tried his best, after all. He'd used logic, guilt, coercion, and blackmail, but Fiona Ferguson had chosen to stay where she was: in a middle-class neighborhood teaching tradesmen's daughters.

He should damn well be relieved. After all, he'd succeeded in locating her. And she was safe. He had ridden his horses into the ground for two hundred miles, dreading what he'd find. If he found her at all. Terrified that he had failed Ian again. That he had failed *her* again.

But there she was, with a fairly comfortable roof over her head, food to eat, and a pastime to keep her occupied until her brother could get free to oversee her care. It should be enough. It certainly should have dispensed his obligation to her.

It didn't, and it made him want to hit something.

Trying to work off his frustration, he paced his father's library, bow window to roaring fireplace to overfull floor-to-ceiling bookshelves that had been his childhood playroom.

Usually the room soothed him, bathing him in the scents of woodsmoke, tongue oil, and leather binding, the light pouring like warm milk across old Turkey carpets.

Even as little time as he'd spent here over the years, it held some of his best memories. It was in this room Sir Joseph had declared him an adult, passing over a snifter of brandy and asking about his days at Christ Church. It was here he had curled up on the floor on cold winter days as a boy, reading Mallory and Homer and Dante while Sir Joseph had worked on government reports, the two sharing a masculine retreat from all the women in the house.

If he'd thought the room would provide a haven from thoughts of the women today, though, he was sadly mistaken. Fiona Ferguson followed along every step of the way. Stubborn, willful, obdurate Fiona Ferguson.

Stopping at the front-facing window, he looked out to where the light was finally breaking through the sick yellow fog. That wasn't what he saw, though. Suddenly he saw a country road on a soft spring day, the rain-swollen clouds scudding over the trees. He could smell the rain-dampened earth, the pungent scent of livestock, and the thick sweetness of the gorse. He could see her, a splash of color among the gray green.

She had been cursing. He smiled, remembering it. The poor girl had slipped going over a stile in an attempt to escape him and gotten her hair completely tangled in the briars.

"I'm afraid you're going to have to be shorn like a sheep," he'd told her, his knife in hand, his own gut clenching at the idea of sacrificing that magnificent treasure.

Any other woman would have wailed, pleaded, threatened. Fiona Ferguson had only closed her eyes and said, "It doesn't matter."

It had. He knew. But she was obviously not going to be the one to let on.

Back then he had seen her as a schoolgirl, a bird too unfledged to understand what she was trying to do in escaping school. Now he knew better. She had been fledged long since, growing up too fast and learning too much. Strong in ways no woman he knew was, but vulnerable in more.

She deserved so much more. A real home. Friends, family, the chance for a brighter future than living out her days in spinsterish isolation with her odd sister. And in Alex's head, he knew her brother would provide that. But from the very moment she had stood toe-to-toe with him four years earlier, refusing every lure that might keep her from seeking out her sister, something connected her to him. Something more than an obligation to her brother.

His father was right, of course. He did have a habit of picking up strays. It had been true at Eton, where he'd saved both Chuffy and Nate Adams from upperclassmen, and true after, when he'd gained a valet in a poker game rather than see the poor man further abused by the cheating sot he worked for.

But Fiona was different. She was, in an odd way, his, and had been from the moment he'd kissed her. And no matter where she went in life, what she did, he would still feel compelled to watch over her.

He even admitted, standing here alone, that his compulsion wasn't purely altruistic. There was an indefinable something about Fiona, a humming energy that seemed to radiate off her like sunlight. A smooth, certain strength that dared a man to challenge her. A tightly leashed sensuality that taunted any man who came too near.

He'd come too near, and his cock stood to attention just thinking about it. Heat curled in his gut, and a chill snaked all the way down to his balls, a sensation of prescience. Of inevitability. Of carnality recognizing like to like. The schoolgirl had grown up, and his body knew it.

If he had any sense in his head, he would leave her be. Let her struggle to make ends meet far away from civilization with only her sister and an acerbic housekeeper for company. Let her squander her life on imaginary numbers and pinpoints of light in the sky. He had better things to do. He had a father to protect and a blackmailer to catch. He had a nation to protect. And she had the right to a more honorable friend.

It didn't matter. He didn't seem to have a choice. He would protect Fiona Ferguson whether she wanted it or not.

"'Lo, gov," a cracking tenor voice broke into his reverie. "Lady Bea says as 'ow you might want to see me."

Startled, Alex looked up to see a lanky, towheaded lad leaning against the library doorway. Perfect timing, he thought, considering one of the tools he'd decided to use in keeping watch over the Ferguson girls.

"Thrasher," Alex greeted the boy, turning away from the window. "I'd ask how you got into my father's house, but I assume it would be pointless. Are you off duty, or is this your new livery?"

Grinning like an imp and clad in a set of tattered woolens, a grimy kerchief tied about his neck, the boy tipped a jauntily-perched bowler. What was it with scrubby slum brats and unique headware? Alex wondered.

"Off duty, aren't I?" The boy sauntered in, scanning the library as he came. "Caught me in a...private interaction with the stable lads, Lady Bea did."

As typical of her rather eccentric house staff, Lady Kate had hired the young urchin to be her tiger when he'd tried to pick her pocket. Thrasher had answered by being the house's best source of information, shady connections, and shadier pastimes.

Alex nodded wisely. "How much did you take off the lads?"

The boy's grin was as brash as a gypsy with a bad horse. "Three crowns an' a month's ridin' lessons. Paltry lot. Can I do f'r ya, gov?"

"A couple of things. Sit down."

Thrasher looked as if Alex had offered him the house silver. Flipping off his hat, he plopped into one of the leather armchairs and crossed his legs.

"I need someone to do some babysitting," Alex said. "Probably only a few days until I can make better arrangements. In Blackheath."

Thrasher focused on tossing his bowler onto a bust of some long-dead Knight in the corner. "Not my lay, gov."

The bowler spun through the air with deadly precision and landed on the bewigged relative at a stylish cant.

Alex smiled. "No, I wouldn't think so. Besides, no offense, but I'm thinking of someone bigger. Someone who might defend the ladies if necessary. Do you think Finney might be able to help?"

Finney, being an ex-boxer and Lady Kate's butler, was certainly a better option than using anybody in Sir Joseph's house. If Alex asked Soames the butler to intercede, that worthy would swoon right along with Alex's valet, the everpristine Mr. Marsh.

"Finney?" Thrasher said. "'e just might. Knows a lotta big coves, does Mr. Finney. She in trouble, this gentry mort?"

"No, not at all. She is just a woman on her own, and I'd rather not have to worry. She is being a bit stubborn about moving someplace safer."

A rush of longing slammed through Alex, distracting

him from the lengthening silence. He could watch her, he thought, close up.

And then her brother would have another reason to shoot him. If she didn't first.

"Ya want I should scare 'em out?" Thrasher finally asked. "I could do that."

Alex's head came up. "What? Good God, no. I don't want you to do anything. I especially don't want her to know anybody is there."

Thrasher gave him a look that spoke of a street child's impatience with toffs and shrugged. "Just a thought."

"I'll need a daily report, Thrasher," he said. "Does Finney read and write?"

Thrasher let loose a disdainful snort. "In Lady Kate's house? Even the potboy writes. Daftest thing you ever seen."

Alex nodded. "Have Finney come by. We need to begin soon."

Thrasher was getting to his feet when Alex straightened. "One more thing."

The boy stopped.

Alex considered the thinning fog outside for a second. "Have you ever met a lad named Lennie Wednesday? Resides somewhere in your old neighborhood."

Thrasher scowled. "Ya think I know every kid was born in the Dials?"

"You'd have a better chance than I would. He's about your age. Probably a product of the flash houses." When he still got blank disinterest, he changed tactics. "He said he hangs about the Blue Goose. Do you know of it?"

"Sure. It's a 'ell in St. Giles where the young swells go to lose their money. You got some money you wanna throw away?"

Alex didn't answer right away. If he could find Lennie

Wednesday again, maybe the lad could point out who had given him the note. Maybe Alex could find a way to defang his enemies before they had a chance to strike.

"I'd like to go there tonight," he finally said.

The boy cocked his head. "If ya want to blend in, dress down an' don't say nuffink. Ya wanna go as a swell..." He shot Alex a blinding grin. "Dress up an' look stupid."

Alex grinned back. "That should be easy enough."

Walking over, he plucked Thrasher's hat from where it sat. "Ask Mr. Finney to stop around when he's able."

Accepting his hat, Thrasher hopped over the arm of the chair and held out his hand. "Well, if that's all I can do..."

The boy was staring at his hand, as if it had managed to hold itself out, palm up, all on its own. Alex wanted to laugh. Instead, he flipped a coin that Thrasher caught like a bird snapping at bugs.

Alex nodded. "Tell Finney they'll need to begin tomorrow. I'd rather not leave the ladies unprotected."

Thrasher tipped a finger to his bowler. "Anything you say, y'r worshipfulness."

*   *   *

An hour later, Alex was still sitting at the desk staring at a distressingly empty sheet of paper. Acting stupid was going to be easy, he realized. He already felt stupid. He still had no notion of how he was going to convince Fiona Ferguson to see sense and desert her students. He had finally written down his first suggestion when Sir Joseph strolled in.

"I leave the country for six months and you take over my house," he greeted Alex casually.

Alex looked up to see that his father looked even more worn than the day before. Alex had meant to confront him with the letter. He kept thinking there had to be some rational explanation, but what if there wasn't? How could he bring it up now, though, when his father's color was even worse?

So he smiled, as if the world had not been upended. "Soames has been tattling again, I take it."

Sir Joseph smiled. "Something about a tatterdemalion pickpocket making free with my office behind my back."

"Soames forgot infant mastermind and incipient scoundrel," Alex said. "One of Lady Kate's projects."

Stepping up to the desk, Sir Joseph noticed Alex's aborted list.

"'Buy telescope'? Does this signify success or failure in your attempt to recover Leyburn's granddaughters?"

Glad he hadn't written down the other suggestions he'd been considering, Alex came out from behind the desk. "Failure. I have just sent a letter informing the marquess's secretary that while the marquess's granddaughters are safe, they have no interest in society, which should make him happy. They are content being computers for the Astronomer Royal and teaching scrubby brats to count."

His eyebrows soaring, his father eased into one of the green leather armchairs by the fire. "Mathematics? Good lord. Bluestockings."

Alex joined him and shared a grin. "Worse. Astronomers, although I wouldn't call Fiona a bluestocking. She is quite formidable, however... actually, I think they both are. You should see their correspondence."

"It doesn't sound like your typical debutante to me. Are you sure you shouldn't simply leave her alone?"

Alex successfully fought the urge to snap at his father. Sir Joseph didn't know how special Fiona was turning out to be. Or Alex's debt to her brother. How could he?

"Do you really think we should abandon her, simply because her grandfather did?" Alex asked instead.

His father had pulled out his watch and was wiping the face with his handkerchief. "Do you wonder why she doesn't want to be rescued?"

That stopped Alex for a moment. "Well, obviously her grandfather impressed on her how undeserving she was to enter society. He kept her locked away for the last four years. She hasn't even made her bow."

The wiping stopped, and Sir. Charles looked up. "Why do you think that is?"

Alex scowled. "Because she grew up in a slum."

His father, the most patient man in Christendom, merely nodded. "Is that all?"

"What?"

"Before you do rescue her—because I have no doubt you will do so—you might want to find out if there is anything you don't know."

Alex felt something unpleasant crawl around his gut. "I imagine there's a lot I don't know, like how it would feel to live under a bridge."

His father's gaze was piercing. "And what else?"

"What else? What do you mean, 'what else'?"

"Don't be dense, Alex. How did she and her sister survive? Just how long were they living under the bridge before their brother found them?"

Alex thought of the vague allegations her grandfather had made and felt sick. "Are you telling me to ask her?"

"No. But I'd go check that her grandfather had them thoroughly investigated."

Alex stared, unnerved by the temptation in his father's words. A frisson slithered down his back, and his heart sped up a bit. Did he really want to know about Fiona's life before her rescue? Did he want to know why the marquess had hidden her away? Did it matter?

"Don't you think that's a bit underhanded?" he asked.

His father smiled sadly and snapped his watch shut. "It's very underhanded. But would you rather do a bit of clandestine work or humiliate that girl by having her secrets exposed in public? Do you think she deserves that?"

Alex's heart rate kept increasing. He felt suddenly unbalanced, as if the sure earth had dipped. The whisper of temptation grew louder, and he looked away from his father, as if the idea needed grave consideration.

"I would rather not give the marquess the satisfaction of asking," he finally said.

Sir Joseph waved off the consideration. "You don't have to. I know who he uses to make his inquiries, an excellent Bow Street Runner named Barkley. I used him to investigate that young man who wanted to marry Cissy last year."

Alex was surprised into smiling. "Is that why the lad made that sudden trip to Antigua?"

"No daughter of mine is going to be tied to a man who will gamble her into poverty. I'll contact the runner and tell him to see you. Do you need me to wield my formidable diplomatic skills?"

Alex lost the urge to smile. "I think I can manage. Thank you."

They had both risen, and Alex returned to the desk and his paper, when his father stopped in the doorway. "You haven't asked her to marry you yet, have you?"

Alex looked up, the almost-empty paper in his hand. "No, sir."

Sir Charles nodded. "If you're tempted, just remember Amabelle."

If anyone else had said that, Alex would have leveled

him. But the gentle concern in Sir Joseph's voice sapped some of the sting from the words.

Nothing could sap the sting out of the memories. Sir Joseph was right. Alex had married Amabelle to save her, a bird with a broken wing. He'd thought that his love could heal a girl too fragile for the world, a woman who only saw her worth reflected in men's eyes. The marriage had been doomed long before it began.

No one would compare Fiona Ferguson to Amabelle, of course. Amabelle had been delicate, small-boned, and big-eyed, like a china doll too easily injured. It had been her very neediness that had drawn him. Drawn him and every other man within hailing distance, all wanting to soothe Amabelle's life, ease her way, since she couldn't seem to do it herself.

Alex actually smiled at the idea that anyone might describe Fiona that way. Fiona waited for no one to help her. She relied on no one and asked for nothing. Alex thought he knew why. Who, after all, had not disappointed her, especially the men in her life? When could she ever have had the chance to lean on someone other than herself?

It was reason enough to help her. It wasn't reason enough to marry her.

Nor, he thought, finally smiling, would she allow it. She'd as likely beat any man off with a broom who was foolish enough to make such an offer.

Still. Was it a sin to want to see her cared for? To offer sanctuary from the responsibility she carried on her shoulders like a yoke? To wrap his arms around her and gather her in, where he could teach her to cherish life?

Alex suspected she would say yes. It was a sin. And she would probably be right.

It didn't banish the fantasy that plagued him of Fiona

in his bed, that glorious hair her only cover, her eyes languorous and her body flushed from a long, slow bout of lovemaking. It didn't ease the heat in his groin or the temptation to wonder whether he could kiss her again and make their lives turn out differently.

* * *

"What do you mean there's more?" the older man demanded.

"We got the note today. There is a watch...."

The older man rubbed the bridge of his nose. "I know all about the watch, Privens. It carries the key."

Privens nodded miserably. "Hasn't been seen since the women left. My contact believes one of them might have inadvertently carried it away with them."

"Or stolen it." The old man thought for a moment. "Have you found them yet?"

"We're not certain. We saw Whitmore and Wilde going into a school belonging to one Margaret Bryan down in Blackheath. I thought we could check it out. Possibly talk to Mrs. Bryan."

"Forget talking to Mrs. Bryan. Talk to Whitmore. Remind him what's at stake if he doesn't cooperate. Find those girls. Find that watch. And make sure you find out what they know. I don't care how you do it. Just do it."

The younger man wanted to protest. He believed in the old man's mission. The government did need change. The Princess Royal would make a much more appropriate monarch, especially with select aristocrats guiding her hand.

But he couldn't get past the idea that innocent people had to die to assure her succession.

"Privens?" the older man barked. "Did you hear me?"

Privens swallowed and nodded. "Yes, sir." And, unable to think of an alternative, backed out the door.

* * *

The night was cold and clear. Fiona lay on her back on the hard, sloping lawn before the Royal Observatory and considered the stars. Thousands of them, millions of them, all participating in a slow, precise dance that glittered across the deep night sky.

Just as she always did, Fiona first sought Orion. There, newly stretched across the southwest sky to announce the onset of winter and anchored by two of the brightest stars in the sky, blue Rigel and red Betelgeuse. Orion was her anchor, the first constellation she had ever identified all those years ago in Edinburgh. A warrior, her Orion. An even better guide, she always thought. Her cornerstone in the heavens.

"Do you want to look through my telescope, Fee?" Mairead asked next to her, where she bent over a small Galilean refractor telescope Margaret had lent them.

"No thank you, sweetheart. I'm happy visiting with old friends."

Mairead grinned down at her, her teeth gleaming in the dim light. "You flirting with Orion again?"

"He is the truest man I know."

Mairead chuckled. Fiona didn't. If it weren't for the night sky, she never would have believed that there was something dependable or constant in life. She would have had nothing to counter the vagaries that had beset her from her earliest childhood.

It hadn't been anyone's fault. Certainly not her mother's. Her mother had worked herself to death in order to feed and clothe her girls. Not Ian, who had sent every spare shilling home from his army pay. Not Mairead, who had stood right by her during the worst and never complained.

Well, Fiona thought with a small smile, *Mairead had never complained about anything but her stars*. Nothing else mattered, after all. No one. Fiona had a small piece of her heart, but the heavens held the rest.

"I think I'd like to discover a comet," Mairead mused, eye to the telescope, notebook on her knee.

"Everyone wants to see a comet," Fiona retorted. "They're so pedestrian. Look for something rare. Something unique."

Mairead frowned down at her. "Comets are rare. If they weren't, Caroline wouldn't be getting the royal stipend for finding them. If comets weren't rare and wonderful, Napoleon would never have convinced himself that the comet of 1811 was a sign for his victory in Russia."

"Much good it did him."

Fiona knew Mairead was grinning. "His loss was not the fault of the comet. But think if I could name another comet that lit up the night sky the way that one did. All those people across the world looking up at Comet Ferguson. Fee?"

"Yes, Mae Mae."

"Don't you think that if I found a comet the king would give me a stipend, too? Then I could help with expenses."

Tears crowded Fiona's throat at her sister's offer. "Caroline has found eight comets, dear." Reaching over, Fiona took her sister's hand, her own heart aching. "Besides, you help quite a lot with your computations. And you help teach some classes."

Mairead never took her eye away from her stars. "Oh, teaching children to count. Fee, anyone could do that. Even Lord Whitmore's friend."

Fiona looked over. "Chuffy?"

Mairead didn't face her. "Yes. Him. He'd better come Tuesday."

Fiona closed her eyes, unsettled by something in Mairead's tone. "Oh, I think he will." And if he inadvertently hurt Mairead with his attentions, Fiona would destroy him. She didn't know how. But she would.

If only Alex Knight hadn't found them. It was an awful thing to say; she knew it. She had seen the look on his face, after all, when he'd recognized her. He had been so visibly relieved, as if she had been a child he'd lost at a fair. He and his friends sincerely wanted to help. They wanted to make life better for her and Mairead.

How would she ever convince them that they couldn't? That the best thing they could do was leave the two of them alone to live in virtual anonymity, their lives devoted to the stars? How could she explain that she simply couldn't bear another disappointment? That the only thing worse than loss was loss on the heels of hope? She had survived that swing too many times, every time picking up the pieces again, carving out a little corner where she and Mae could survive, and worse, weathering Mairead's desperate distress every time their lives changed. They had barely reached equilibrium again, with only a few outbursts to mar the days, when Alex and his friend descended.

And what about her? How was she supposed to withstand the storm of sensation his touch set off in her, the quick lightning that she swore lived in his hands, the showers of warmth in his kisses. How was she to barricade herself against the memories he carried in with him like an incense-scented breeze?

She had held them off for so long, folded them away in the dark where they couldn't torment her. And yet, one touch of his hand, one smile from those earth-brown eyes, and she could smell clover and soft rain. She could feel the touch of his fingers sending chills down her neck. She could hear the rumble of his chuckle and the lowing of cattle in the next pasture. She had been kissed before. She had been kissed since, some welcome, some not. She had never been kissed like that. She had never ever reacted to a kiss like that.

She had been sixteen and so new to her new life that she'd still been hoarding bread under her bed at school, just in case the food ran out. She had roomed with three other girls who, if they hadn't met her there, would have passed her by on the street without a thought. For the first time in her life, she had been living without Mairead because Mairead had gone home. She had been kissed by the most handsome man she'd ever seen and then sent back to school, as if it had changed nothing.

It had not been the first time nor the last she had faced disappointment. But it had hurt the worst. Even worse than the day he had walked away after destroying her world with news of Ian.

And now Alex was back. What was she to do? How was she to keep him at arm's length? How was she to survive the hope that had already begun to bloom in her chest? Pointless hope. False hope.

But false hope tasted no different than real hope, which meant it was going to hurt even worse when the disappointment inevitably came.

So she lay on her back out in the cold night and watched the immutable stars, calculated their paths, and reminded herself that if nothing else, she would always have them. She would always have the stars, and she would always have Mairead. And since she would, she could deal with anything else.

She wasn't quite so sanguine two hours later when she found herself in the throes of one of Mairead's episodes.

Episode. A kind name for a tantrum.

"They're my things!" Mairead screamed, red-faced and weeping, her arms windmilling as if she might fall. "You can't touch my things! Nobody can touch my *things*!"

They were in the dining room where Mairead had laid out her work in precise bundles, one for her own calculations, one for Mr. Pond, and one for Mr. Gauss. Only the stack meant for Mr. Gauss was out of order. And the compass and ruler Mairead had left at precise right angles to the papers were off by about ten degrees. Someone had touched Mairead's things, just as she said.

"I've been with you all evening, sweetheart," Fiona said, catching Mairead's hands in their mad arc and holding tight.

Mairead was trembling as if she had a fever. She kept tapping her toe on the groove she'd worn in the old rug. "Mrs. Quick, then. Mrs. Quick touched this. She *knows*, Fiona. She knows I cannot work in disarray. Did she do this to torment me? I need to speak with her, Fee. I need to speak to her *now*."

Fiona sighed. "Mae, it is four in the morning. Even if Mrs. Quick set your papers on fire, I would not wake her. If we do, there will be no breakfast in the morning. No fresh bread and jam."

Just as she knew it would, that brought Mairead to an abrupt halt. "Oh."

"Can I let you go now?" Fiona asked.

Mairead closed her eyes and nodded. Fiona let go of her sister's hand and quickly restored the table to order. "There, now. Let's go up to bed. We have children coming in a few hours, and it would not aid our reputations at all if we slept through Globes."

Without opening her eyes, Mairead grinned. "Maybe not our reputations," she said, turning for the door. "But it would certainly make the children happier."

With the ease of long practice, Fiona slipped an arm through Mairead's and guided her up the stairs. It was probably a good thing to happen, she thought. At least it put a quick halt to the dangerous memories that had plagued her up on that hill.

Even so, as she climbed the stairs, she laid her fingers across her lips, where four years ago Alex Knight had kissed her, and with tears in her eyes, she smiled.

Chapter 7

Tuesday came, and so did Lord Wilde. Chuffy, he kept insisting every time Fiona tried to be polite. She was on her way to the dining room with a pile of newly washed curtains in her arms when she came across him in the front foyer.

"Nobody answered," he said, spinning his hat in his hands. What hair he had stood up in little peaks all over his head, which he attempted to pat down. "Wilson's despair, don't you know."

Fiona smiled. "Your valet?"

"Since I was breeched. Excellent man."

Poor man, she thought, noticing that the little baron's waistcoat had a loose button and his pantaloons bore evidence of the street. She imagined he was one of those people whose pristinely ironed attire rumpled the minute he stepped through his front door.

"With your permission," Chuffy said, "come to get your sister."

Fiona smiled. "You truly know the Astronomer Royal?"

"Mr. Pond?" Chuffy gave an enthusiastic nod. "Was at

Trinity with the Pater. Gave him his first telescope." He shrugged. "Never rubbed off."

Fiona tilted her head. "Then why should you go out of your way for Mairead?"

If she hadn't seen it, she wouldn't have believed it. Chuffy didn't simply smile. He seemed to glow, as if his happiness radiated outward. "Deserves it, doesn't she? Brilliant. I can tell. Shouldn't have to worry about day-to-day things." He shrugged. "Day-to-day my forte, ya see? Nobody notices, but it is."

"And do you know mathematics?" she asked. "Mairead won't let you help her do anything if you can't even discuss her work."

"Your housekeeper know math?"

"My housekeeper is a housekeeper, Lord Wilde. You are not. Mairead sees absolutes."

Chuffy nodded. "No worries. I can keep up. Does she like phaetons?"

Finally Fiona smiled. "She adores phaetons. She'll demand you let her drive. Don't, please. We don't need to terrify the population of Greenwich."

Chuffy pressed a hand to his heart. "Word of a gentleman."

For a second Fiona was afraid she would make a rude noise. She had never had good luck with the word of a gentleman. But then, she thought, none of those gentlemen had been Chuffy. One look at this small, innocuous, bespectacled man told her he was as innocent in his way as Mairead was in hers. He meant what he said.

"If you insist on being Mairead's white knight," she said, turning, "come into the dining room. I believe she is working there."

"No white knight. That's Alex."

She halted. "Pardon?"

"His nickname. White Knight. Too perfect for his own good." Chuffy beamed again. "Or ours. Hard to live up to."

"I imagine." She could also easily imagine how Alex had earned his moniker.

She let Chuffy open the door for her and entered the dining room, her footsteps echoing briskly across the parquet floors. There, bent over a collection of papers on the scarred oak table, sat Mairead, chewing the end of a pencil. Not a hair was out of place from her tight bun, and her bishop's blue roundgown looked as if Mrs. Quick had just taken a hot iron to it. She was mumbling and tapping her fingers on the table.

"Look who has come to call, Mairead," Fiona said, depositing the pile of maroon drapes on the empty end of the table. "Chuffy is here for your excursion."

Mairead startled to attention, blinking as if she'd just faced a bright light. "Is it Tuesday?"

"It is," Fiona said. "Why don't you get your pelisse, sweetings? It seems nippy outside."

Beside her, Chuffy stepped up to the table, his attention focused on Mairead's work. "What do you have there?"

Mairead pulled the paper closer to her. "Word puzzles. The last one from the castle."

His expression was odd. "Word puzzles?"

"Grandfather used to share these with Mairead," Fiona said. "Just games."

"They look like codes."

Mairead stood, her hand still on the paper. "I enjoy frequency analysis. It clears my head for more difficult mathematics." Quickly she looked down at her work. "Although I can't seem to figure this one out."

"Do you accept help?" Chuffy asked diffidently.

Mairead glared. "No." And then, gathering the papers to her chest, she stalked off.

"She'll be getting her outerwear," Fiona assured him.

She looked up from where she was gathering the curtains to find Chuffy jotting notes in a little notebook, letters collected into groupings of four, very much like Mairead's puzzle. He was moving his lips.

"You remember the puzzle?" Fiona asked, surprised.

Not looking up, he nodded. "Like to take it with me. Finish it. Rather a hobby with me as well."

Fiona went back to her curtains. "Please don't tell Mairead if you are. Especially don't tell her if you figure it out before she does."

"Doesn't like the competition?"

Fiona smiled. "Oh, no. She really doesn't notice competition. She simply can't abide missing out on the thrill of discovery."

Bobbing his head, Chuffy shoved his glasses up his nose. "Quiet as the grave."

Fiona nodded and pulled the stepladder up before the window.

"Wouldn't you like to come along?" Chuffy asked. "Nice day out."

Fiona collected the drapes and climbed. "Oh, no thank you. I have an appointment this afternoon. The parent of a new student, I hope."

A widow with a bit of extra money, which would help add a bit of a cushion.

Still peering down at the puzzle, Chuffy nodded absently. Conversation died until Mairead returned, straw bonnet in hand, buttoning her pelisse one-handed. Seeing her, Chuffy grinned in delight and held out an elbow, which she took.

"Don't forget to thank Mr. Pond," Fiona told her sister. "Do you have the orbital equations I finished for him last night?"

Spinning around on Chuffy's arm, Mairead nodded. Fiona knew that was as good as she was going to get and turned back to the drapes.

*   *   *

Alex Knight had not had a good few days. He kept waiting for another missive and spent the rest of the time searching for Lennie Wednesday, who seemed to have gone to ground. Which meant that Alex spent his days culling gossip from his clubs, evenings at paralyzingly boring *ton* events, and nights giving every appearance of being cup-shot and seeking low play at the Blue Goose. Which left him tired, lighter in the purse, and fighting a chronic headache.

He didn't even have an excuse to visit Fiona Ferguson. Finney sent Thrasher with regular reports from the men who watched Fiona's house, ex-fighters like Finney, who were finding the job pretty boring. School for the nippers in the morning, working at the table or cleaning the house in the afternoon, and lying out in the cold on the ground in Greenwich at night. The women didn't see any men but the butcher's boy at the back door, didn't go out except to market and church, and didn't seem to have acquaintances except for the tykes and their parents coming in and out. Queer as Dick's hatband, the men said, but light enough work for the pay.

Alex couldn't imagine how Fiona could prefer such a restricted life to the one her standing could afford her. He couldn't bear to think of her living in a self-imposed exile like this, with only tradesmen's families for company and a distracted astronomer for mental challenge. She needed more. She *deserved* more.

Why did she refuse it?

He wouldn't know until he saw the Bow Street Runner, but that gentleman was out of town.

Alex knew he should wait for concrete information before approaching Fiona again. It could be disastrous to promise what he couldn't deliver. And yet here he stood on her doorstep, his tiger behind him walking his bays in the damp chill of another overcast day. He knocked on Fiona's door and waited. He knocked again. Unsettled by the silence that met him, he looked around. He didn't see Finney's man, but he didn't expect to. The street was busy with everyday traffic, the walkways a river of pedestrians taking advantage of a fog-free day.

He should knock again. He took one more look around, realized no one was taking any notice of him, and opened the door.

The house smelled of baking and beeswax. The entry was empty, the sunlight slashing across the oak floor. And then Alex heard the sound of singing. Closing the door behind him, he removed his hat and caped greatcoat.

He stopped a second just to listen to Fiona's scratchy soprano and smiled. Finally, proof that she was human. The girl had no clue how to stay on pitch. She did know Gaelic, he realized. Even off-key, she made it sound soft and hushed. Setting down his outerwear, he followed her voice down the hallway to a door that opened into a dining room of some kind with a sadly battered oaken table covered in open books, papers, inkpots, compasses, and an azimuth. Three hardback chairs surrounded the table, one adorned with a cast-off gray woolen shawl, and a beautifully painted star chart covered one wall. And there, perched on a stepladder at one of the windows, was Fiona, dressed in a spring-green gown, her hair beginning to slip from an untidy bun. Stretched on tiptoe, she was reaching up to hang a panel of heavy velvet curtains.

He almost groaned out loud. Stretching up like that, she elongated her sleek silhouette and placed the sweet sweep of her bottom right at face level. Raw lust clawed at him. He briefly closed his eyes, fighting the urge to grab hold of her. Knowing damn well that no good could come from staying. He should just run for the door.

And yet, he didn't.

She went on to the next verse of her song, completely unaware he stood in the doorway.

> *Noble, proud young horseman*
> *Warrior unsaddened, of most pleasant countenance*
> *A swift-moving hand, quick in a fight,*
> *Slaying the enemy and smiting the strong.*

Alex opened his eyes and stepped into the room. "Singing about me?"

It was a stupid thing to do. Fiona shrieked in surprise and spun around, overbalancing herself. She shrieked again and dropped the drapes. Alex leaped across the room just in time to catch her as the ladder tipped her off.

"Oommph," he grunted, catching her before she landed on the floor.

Suddenly his arms were full of delicious woman. He could smell cinnamon and vanilla and warm female. He could feel the silken slide of her hair against his mouth, and he found himself starving.

"You great lummox," she snapped, wiggling free. "You scared the life out of me."

Before she could feel just how strongly she affected him, he set her on her feet. "My apologies. It just seemed as if you were calling me."

Her hand to her chest, as if calming her heart by force, she straightened, making it a point to brush down her dress. "I was not," she retorted, her voice shaking just a bit. "If I was calling anyone, it was Bonnie Prince Charlie."

Alex arched an eyebrow. "A little late for that, isn't it?"

She didn't smile. "If you must know, it was a lullaby my mother used to sing to us."

He arched an eyebrow. "About Bonnie Prince Charlie?"

"Why not?"

He chuckled. "Usually mothers in England prefer to sing to their babes about angels and moons and stars and such. Not doomed rebel leaders. I wouldn't think the latter would be particularly restful."

Fiona bent to gather up the drapes. "Nevertheless, it was what mother sang, and her mother before her. Another Scottish trollop, my grandfather would say."

Alex was startled by the dispassionate tone of her voice. "Did that insufferable old reprobate call you that?"

She briefly met his gaze and went back to work.

Alex could think of nothing to say that didn't involve threats of violence. Suddenly he wanted to march back to his phaeton and drive straight up to that white mausoleum on the moors and rearrange that haughty face.

"No wonder you don't trust society," he finally managed, crouching to help gather the weight of the drapes.

Her smile was quick and dry. "Oh, I don't concern myself enough to care for their opinions. I am certain being Scottish is bad enough. But being Scottish and a woman *and* interested in astronomy?" She rolled her eyes. "'Oh, my dear, it simply isn't done.'"

Alex straightened, arms full of material. "You're right. I can't imagine how any self-respecting mother would let you near her chick. You might taint them with...*knowledge*."

Fiona smiled. "A most frightening prospect."

"Well, what about those of us who actually enjoy a bit of knowledge? Will you deprive us?"

She began to sort out the curtains. "Of course not. Why do you think I teach school? I plan to help create a social class of shopkeepers' children who will intimidate their betters into realizing that they are not so much better after all."

Alex helped her, an odd effervescence ballooning in his chest. "Ah, I see. A radical. You, madam, are a threat to social stability."

That incited the brightest grin yet. "Oh, I do hope so."

Alex gave her an exaggerated frown. "Definitely puts paid to a visit with Prinny, then. We don't need the man to have a stroke."

"I wouldn't mind meeting Mr. Wilberforce," she said, climbing up her ladder.

Alex came within a hair of grabbing her arm and pulling her off before realizing that if there was any action that would put paid to his chances to help Fiona, that would be it. Instead, he gathered much of the weight of the curtains to ease her job and stood just behind her.

Exactly where he had the best chance to inhale that curiously erotic scent of cinnamon and enjoy the unmarred slope of her derrière. Just close enough for his body to go instantly on alert, as it always seemed to do around her.

"Let. Go," he finally heard and looked up.

She was glaring down at him and tugging on the material. He grinned. Her eyes went unnaturally dark, the pupils dilated, her breathing shallow. Ah, so he wasn't the only one who felt the surprising attraction. With tortuously slow movements, he eased out the material, running his hand up so that it accidentally brushed against hers.

He heard a sharp intake of breath and almost broadened his smile. He knew it was cruel, but he couldn't help it. Suddenly he wanted to know that the attraction he felt was truly shared. That she was as unsettled as he. As aroused.

He wanted to savor these moments because he knew damn well that after this she would be a fool to let him this close again.

"Isn't maroon a bit dark for in here?" he asked, brushing her hand again and coming away with a shower of chills that tightened his balls. "With all the dark wallpaper, it's not exactly sun-soaked."

She yanked hard on the material, as if that would really make him give it up. "True. But maroon is an excellent camouflage for stains from everything from candle smoke to water damage. The curtains maintain the image of a prosperous school. It is not necessary, however, that they are closed so tightly we cannot see the sun."

He eased out a bit more, this time accidentally brushing against her hip. It truly was an accident. It didn't stop his body from clenching even tighter or her from jumping back. He caught her again just as she was about to fall off the ladder.

"You might want me to hang these," he offered, an arm around her hips. "Might be less dangerous."

"Oh, I doubt it," she managed in a breathy voice, not moving from his grip. "After all, if I get you in a position to be precariously balanced with your hands full, I might just be tempted to shove you all the way through the window."

He grinned. "You never would. Windows are expensive."

She tilted her head a bit, and her hair gleamed copper. "Hmmm."

"Trying to think of a way to give in gracefully?"

"Trying to figure how long it would take to afford a new window."

He laughed out loud. "Minx. Come, it would be easier for me to reach. I am taller than you." Putting his foot on the first rung, he lifted himself closer. "And to be fair, not that many people are."

"I only stand five foot ten," she protested.

He grinned. "And the average English male stands about five foot nine. In his boots. With a hat on."

She scowled, but he saw the humor glint again in her magnificent blue eyes. "Believe me, Lord Whitmore. I am well aware of the fact."

He arched an eyebrow. "Lord Whitmore again? Please, Fiona. Don't do that to me. When I hear 'Lord Whitmore,' I think of my uncle, who had six fingers and thought bathing was a trick of the devil."

She giggled. "I can understand your wanting to maintain the distinction."

"Every time you call me Lord Whitmore, I will call you Eloise."

She glared at him, the curtains clutched to her chest like bedclothes, as if she were a maiden in threat of seduction. "You wouldn't."

He shrugged. "It is your name. Lady Eloise Fiona Ferguson Hawes."

"No one knows," she hissed.

He leaned in very close. "I do."

She reared back and almost tipped the ladder again. "That is patently unfair."

He shrugged and reached up for the curtains. "All is fair in love and safety."

She refused to budge. "I do not believe that is precisely the quote."

Grinning, he put his foot on the second rung, just beneath her. "Close enough."

And then he made the mistake of looking into her eyes. Her blue, blue eyes, which were suddenly black with arousal. He heard the sharp intake of her breath and saw the erratic pulse beating at the base of her long white throat.

His own body reacted just as it had every time he'd gotten close to her. He focused in on her, his grip on her tightening. Still she didn't move, caught in the circle of his free arm, her hip pressed against his chest, her mouth just above his. All he had to do was climb another rung, and he could satisfy a four-year-old craving.

His heart was galloping suddenly, and he could feel a bead of sweat roll down his back. He could see a glow on her forehead, her upper lip. Her eyes widened, as if she could read his thoughts, and he could scent something new. Arousal. Need. Hunger. His own body was shaking with it. He swore his cock had taken on a life of its own, and his brain simply shut down.

He leaned a bit closer, his foot still on the step beneath her and paused, giving her a chance to escape, to clout him in the head if necessary. She didn't. She watched him the way prey might a raptor, unsure and wary. He didn't blame her. He wasn't certain how much control he had over himself. It had been so long since he'd had a woman. So much longer since he'd really liked the one he had.

Slowly, so he didn't startle her into tipping the ladder, he rose up and set his other foot on the rung. She was frozen in place, one hand fisted around the blood-deep velvet, the other clenched against the ladder, as if she were still uncertain whether to use it.

She didn't. She inhaled, her mouth opening just a bit, as

if there wasn't enough air. As if she were struggling to stay afloat.

Sink, Alex wanted to say as he lifted himself face-to-face with her, mouth-to-mouth. *Sink into me*.

"I knew it!" a voice screeched behind him, shattering the moment. "What did I tell you about lettin' them jackanapes in here?"

Fiona reared back as if he'd attacked her, again throwing the ladder off balance. Alex instinctively pulled back to stabilize them. He pulled back too far and the ladder tipped.

There was a lot of yelling and a couple of muffled thuds as Alex landed on his back, cushioning Fiona's fall. He wasn't so lucky.

"Are you all right?" Fiona asked immediately, leaning over him.

"Serves him right," the housekeeper snapped from the doorway.

He had hit his head so hard he was seeing stars. But he was smelling cinnamon and Fiona, so he really couldn't complain.

"That is enough, Mrs. Quick," he heard. "Alex? Your eyes are open. Can you hear me?"

Rather than admit that he was too distracted by the plump pressure of her breast against his chest to answer, he simply closed his eyes and groaned. The act would have been unworthy of him if his head weren't pounding and his arse aching from hard contact with the floor.

"Mrs. Quick," she was saying, her hand on his cheek. "See if Mr. Clemson is outside. Send him for the doctor."

He knew his injuries didn't merit such concern. "No doctor." He blinked a couple of times until the multiple Fionas resolved into one. "I'll live. My head is a bit bruised is all."

In retaliation, she took away both her hand and breast, which almost set Alex to groaning again. She actually smacked him on the arm. "Then don't frighten me like that...*again*."

"Don't know why you let him in here at all," came the grumble from the doorway.

Untangling them both from the curtains, Fiona sat up. "Thank you, Mrs. Quick. I think we're all right now."

"Ya think that, do ya?"

Fiona gave her the kind of glare that betrayed her aristocratic heritage. The housekeeper, still grumbling, clasped her hands in a parody of good servile behavior and stalked off down the hall.

Fiona looked back down to where Alex lay, and he could see the cost of the last tumble on her face. He should have been outraged. He was lying in a nest of curtains with a fresh headache and the humiliation of his fall, and she was...laughing.

She tried so hard not to. She held her hand to her mouth. She shook her head. He could see her shoulders heave. He would have chastised her, except the minute he opened his mouth, he burst out laughing, too.

"You are not very beneficial to my *amour propre*," he wheezed up at her.

She couldn't stop laughing, full-throated, full-bellied, as if too much suppressed laughter had simply spilled over. "I...I...didn't..."

"Mean it," he managed, making it up as far as sitting beside her. "Yes, I know."

She frantically shook her head. "Think anything could be so...funny!" She was gasping, bent over her hands at her waist. "The look on your face!"

He had meant to get up, to reassert his mastery of the situation. He refused to sacrifice this perfect moment with her on the floor. Wrapping an arm around her shoulder, he wiped at the tears that coursed down her cheeks.

"It's not that funny," he groused.

She started laughing again. "Oh, yes, it is. You can have no idea of how long it's been since I had the chance to laugh. Since I last saw your sister, I think."

He had to grin. "Well, yes. Pip would set anybody to laughing. She's a ridiculous little thing."

For that he got a resounding smack on his chest. "Do not dare speak ill of my best friend." She hiccupped, her eyes widening a bit. "My only friend, actually. Except for Sarah and Lizzie. And now that Sarah is married to my brother, I have no idea at all how we will meet again."

There was the faintest plaintive note in her voice that made Alex want to curl her completely into his arms and shield her from hurt. Dear God, how lonely she must have been. "I promise," he said instead, "I fully respect my sister's loyalty. It's her good sense I frequently question."

Her breathing was evening out. She nodded. "Pip does have a knack for acting before thinking."

"She's like a whirlwind."

"She needs to finally capture her Beau," Fiona said with a definite nod. "That would settle her."

Alex snorted. "Poor Beau. He'd never have another moment's peace."

And for a long moment, they just sat there in a pool of sunlight and velvet, his arm around her and her head on his shoulder. It felt so good. So whole.

It couldn't last. If he didn't move, he'd damn well take her here on the floor. He opened his mouth to tell her, and then made the mistake of meeting her gaze again.

Her lips were still parted, but she wasn't laughing anymore. He could see the pulse jumping at her throat, and her hands were clenched again, as if she was trying hard to keep them to herself.

He didn't know why. Lifting his own hand, he cupped her cheek. Again he gave her the chance to pull away. Again she didn't. His own heart started to skip around. He was rock hard. There was no longer a question. He had to kiss her.

She didn't just smell of cinnamon, she tasted of it. Cinnamon and coffee and hunger, except he thought the hunger might have been his. Her mouth was so warm, so small, so delicious. He had wrapped her to him, now, both hands holding her still, his thumbs stroking her jaw. He heard a groan and thought it might be she.

And then he had his arms around her, and he was running his hand over her back, his mouth still fused with hers, his body thrumming like a harp. He pulled on her, bringing her back down to that nest of curtains. And she came, her arms wound around his neck, her mouth open and welcoming, her breasts cushioning and lush.

Four years ago he'd known. He'd known that it would feel like this to hold her, to bear her to the ground, where he could touch her, taste her, devour her. He'd known and he'd put that knowledge away, burying it too deep to hurt him.

But how could it hurt him now? He was no longer married. He could disappoint no one. And Jesus, he thought nothing had ever tasted so erotic in his life. He could have her. He could show her just how magnificent her body was, how much she deserved. He could make her sing, by God. He could...

He wasn't certain what alerted him. Suddenly it was clear to him that he was seducing a young woman on the floor of her dining room, and if he was caught there would be no way out of ruin. Or marriage.

This time when he reared back, he was the only one to lose his balance.

Chapter 8

She couldn't breathe. She couldn't think. She was tumbled like a rag doll on a pile of velvet and hard wood, her body on fire. Her skin felt as if were galvanized, her breasts were heavy and shivery, and she thought her bones might be melting. And he was...just...standing there, his back to her. Fiona couldn't believe it. Lurching to her feet, she stumbled back from him. Her dress pulled oddly against her breasts. She looked down and blanched. How had it become so mussed? She knew, though. She could still feel his hand on her breast. His mouth on hers. His body...

Spinning around, she tugged her bodice back into place. She heard him move behind her and squeezed her eyes shut, as if it would block out the last few minutes.

And then he spoke. "I'm..."

She spun around and glared at his back. "If you say sorry," she snapped, feeling wild, "I swear, I will gut you like a carp."

He looked over his shoulder at her. "That's not the way I meant it."

She recognized the look in his eyes. She'd seen it four years ago, the last time he'd kissed her. Shame, regret, shock. It made her want to strike out.

"I don't regret the kiss," he finally said. "I regret the locale."

He was clenching his hands, as if grabbing on to control. For some reason, that made Fiona feel better. She didn't know how to answer him, though. He was correct. The last thing she needed was for anyone to see her cavorting on the floor of her dining room, even though it had been the most wonderful moment of . . . well, the last four years.

She almost groaned. And she had a new parent due to arrive soon. Wouldn't that have just put a period on her school?

Trembling like an ague victim, she bent to once more pick up her curtains. "You could at least turn around and face me," she accused.

His laugh was sore. "No," he said. "I really can't. But I do think I should hang those curtains anyway."

Fiona took a considered look at the heavy material bunched in her hands. "Fine," she finally said. "If it will help me get done more quickly."

Nodding briskly, he shoved the ladder back under the window and climbed. With Fiona feeding him the material, they were making quick work of it when they were interrupted yet again, this time by the slam of the front door.

"Wait until I tell the lads down at White's," came a voice from the dining room doorway.

"You will do no such thing, Chuffy," Alex said, not even looking toward the door, "or I will tell your father exactly what you were doing last week instead of attending your mother's soiree."

There was a stricken silence. "You wouldn't."

Fiona looked over to see Chuffy standing there in curly brimmed beaver and caped coat, mouth agape, glasses half-way down his nose. Fiona desperately hoped he couldn't see how hotly she was blushing.

"I would," Alex promised, his focus on the curtains. "Hello, Lady Mairead. Did you see the Astronomer Royal?"

Fiona deserted her post to go help her sister out of the coat she seemed to be having trouble with.

"It's not right," Mairead was muttering. "It just isn't. That's all."

Oh, no, Fiona thought, seeing the agitation in her sister's movements. "Weren't you able to see him?" she asked.

Chuffy doffed his hat and unbuttoned his coat. "Did. Nice chap. Gave us tea."

Mairead snorted and batted Fiona's hand away. "He gave *you* tea," she huffed.

"Did you get time on the great refractor?" Fiona asked, stepping back.

Mairead kept fumbling with her buttons. "Of course we did." She looked up, jabbed a finger toward Chuffy. "*He* did. Not me. *Him*."

"Can't be angry about that," Chuffy argued with a faint smile.

Mairead stopped her actions, her head snapping up and her eyes blazing. "Yes, I can. I can. I *can*."

"But why?" Fiona asked.

And then she saw the tears in her sister's eyes and ached for her. "Because *I* should have gotten it. *I* am the one measuring the orbits of the Cephei variables. *I* am the one calculating the parallax correction."

"Actually, I am doing that," Fiona said.

It was as if her sister hadn't heard her. "I am the one who corrected his first assistant on his calculations. I am the one who knows the names of every one of the Messier objects and where to find them. Not *him*."

Again she jabbed that accusatory finger at Chuffy, who just grinned. "I'm the one who knows the pater."

Fiona would have been upset for the kind little man if he hadn't been smiling at Fiona as if she were a Christmas gift.

"Think she's upset cause it took a man to convince Pond," he offered. "Especially that it took a man who don't know a planet from a petunia."

Mairead actually shrieked at him. Stomping into the salon, she came back with the pillow, held against her breast like a baby. Then she did the oddest thing. Her movements strangely gentle, she reached over and shoved his glasses up. And Chuffy beamed at her.

"Use whatever means you need," he told her with a shrug. "I'm means."

Fiona clenched her own hands, suddenly unsure of her sister. "Sound logic, Mae," she offered gently.

Mairead swung on her, shrieked again, and stalked off, her coat still half-buttoned, her face all but buried in the old pillow.

Fiona managed a grin. "Not the answer she was looking for, evidently. Thank you anyway, Chuffy. I truly appreciate the effort you went to for her."

Chuffy bowed. "Pleasure. Help you hang, Alex?"

Alex kept shaking his head, as if it would help clear the confusion. "As a matter of fact, Chuffy, yes. Get over here."

They had just gotten the last of the curtains hung when the front door knocker sounded. Fiona hurried the men along.

"Thank you for your help," she said. "I know you have other places to be."

"Sale at Tatt's," Chuffy said to his friend as they returned to the front hall and collected coats. "Come along? Carter has a luminato for sale."

"Lusitano," Alex corrected, looking at Fiona. She must have betrayed her distress because he smiled. "Perfect timing, Chuff. We can leave Lady Fiona to her work."

Passing right past them, Mrs. Quick opened the front door. Fiona heard a soft woman's voice answer, the accent strong.

"Good time for us to leave?" Chuffy asked, watching as a sylphlike woman in black stepped inside.

She wore widow's weeds, even to a heavy veil obscuring her features. Fiona couldn't take her eyes off the woman. She would give anything to be as delicate and graceful as her visitor.

"Welcome, madame," she said, stepping forward. "If you would like to follow Mrs. Quick into the parlor, she will provide tea while I will see these gentlemen out."

"Tea," the widow answered, her voice musical and sweet. "'ow lovely." She turned and dipped a curtsy toward Alex and Chuffy. "A pleasure, *messieurs*."

She wasn't exactly petite. Willowy, though, with the kind of lush breasts men seemed to favor. Standing next to her, Fiona felt like a plow horse. As the lady passed into the parlor, Fiona looked back at the men to see them staring at the retreating figure, their mouths just a bit slack.

Alex waited until the door to the parlor closed. "French?"

Fiona almost sighed. "Belgian, I believe. Or Swiss. A war widow. She is relocating here with her daughter."

"Good for her."

"Thank you for your help," Fiona said, her hands still clenched at her waist. It was a safe place for them, she thought, especially when they seemed determined to brush Alex's hair off his forehead. "Both of you."

"Our pleasure," Alex assured her with a placid smile as he slipped on his greatcoat.

Alongside him, Chuffy was standing at an odd attention, his head tilted, staring at nothing.

"Chuffy?"

Chuffy's head jerked around. "Smell anything?" he asked.

Fiona immediately inhaled, afraid she would smell smoke. All she could smell was the faint spice of cologne.

"Oranges," she said, eyebrow raised. "How lovely. It must be Madame's. I certainly have no oranges."

Chuffy kept frowning. Alex was staring at him, as if expecting some revelation. Fiona didn't know what to do. She needed to get into that parlor, but she couldn't go until the men left.

Suddenly Chuffy came to life and grinned. "Drives you mad, don't it? Catch a whiff of something familiar, can't place it."

Alex chuckled. "If it's oranges you smell," he said, popping his curly brim atop his head, "odds are you're thinking of Covent Garden. They sell oranges at intermission," he told Fiona, as if she were a rube, which she supposed she was. "We'll have to take you both to the opera some night so you can see for yourself."

Fiona didn't bother to answer. After all, what good would it do to tell Alex that neither she nor Mairead had the wardrobe for the opera? As precipitously as they had left Hawesworth Manor, they were lucky they had the wardrobe for teaching.

Fortunately, the thought seemed to be passing, and she was able to get them out the door without too much more fuss. Stopping before the small pier glass in the hallway, she quickly tidied her hair and made certain her dress was restored. Then, drawing a breath, she opened the door to the parlor.

Inside was one of the most beautiful women she had ever seen, well rounded, with flawless porcelain skin, great blue eyes, and honey-blond hair. Clad in unrelieved black, with her heavy veil lifted over the back of her mourning bonnet, she rose from Fiona's one good chair with the grace of a dancer.

"Mademoiselle Ferguson," she greeted Fiona with a gracious smile, her accent thick. "I 'ave 'ear so many good things about you."

Smiling, Fiona approached. "Madame Fermont, how do you do?"

The two women exchanged curtsies and reclaimed seats.

"You 'ave the gentlemen here, I think?" Madame asked. "I am not sure, me, that this would be a good...mmm, 'ow you say, scenery for my Nanette."

"Of course, madame. But please do not worry. They were friends of my brother, whom I recently lost, come to assure themselves of the welfare of myself and my sister."

"Ah *non*, dear child. I am of the most sadness for you."

Fiona dipped her head. "Thank you."

Madame wagged a finger at her. "But most 'andsome men, *oui*?"

Fiona blinked, a bit startled by the woman's playful tone. "Em, well..." Looking toward the door, as if she could better envision them, she shrugged. "I suppose. But they were being my brother's good friends. Nothing more."

Madame smiled. "''andsome men are rarely 'nothing more,' *mademoiselle*."

Suddenly Fiona wanted to go out and come back in again, as if that could help this conversation make more sense. "You said in your letters, madame, that your daughter is now eleven years."

For the longest moment, Fiona wasn't at all certain madame meant to answer. But then, with a knock Mrs. Quick shoved her way into the room with a full tea tray and set it down before Fiona. With a quick scowl at the Frenchwoman, she stalked back out.

"Tea, madame?" Fiona asked.

Madame watched the door close and then began to pull off her gloves. "*Oui. Merci.* A bit of sugar if you will. My Nanette is not yet eleven. Next month."

Fiona poured tea and spent the next hour coaxing Madame Fermont into making a down payment on her daughter's education. Fiona would have loved to say that Alex Knight was summarily forgotten. She had a feeling, though, that even Madame Fermont knew that he wasn't.

* * *

Two nights later, everything changed. Fiona would never know what woke her. She had finally fallen into bed well after midnight, the complex calculations she had been doing for Mr. Pond still spread out over the dining table alongside Mairead's precisely aligned stack and the night candle snuffed in the hallway. Fiona always slept hard, exhausted from the day's toil and the burden of Mairead's obsessions. She laid herself down on her third of the bed and did her best to avoid Mairead's outflung arms.

Closing her eyes, she tried to stay awake long enough to plan the next day in her head, arranging her schedule like a chessboard with room for surprises. She got no further than the arrangements she needed to make for their science walk in the park.

It was odd, what woke her. It wouldn't have on a normal night. Mairead was mumbling in her sleep, rolling in place with the pillow in the crook of her arm, as if trying to soothe herself over some unsolvable puzzle, like why the students weren't held rapt by her stars. She nudged Fiona, but not hard enough to leave a bruise. But suddenly, with that little bump, Fiona was wide awake and staring into the darkness. Had she heard something? The clock downstairs? The charlies outside calling the hours?

A scrape. The tinkle of glass. An odd whooshing sound downstairs.

She sat straight up in bed. Downstairs? Someone was in the house. Mrs. Quick wouldn't leave her little quarters behind the kitchen for a French invasion. Besides, Mrs. Quick wasn't that heavy.

Fiona's heart lurched. Her mouth went dry. What should she do? Wake Mairead? She looked over to see the frown on her sister's face, the frilly nightcap half-off, and her braid draped over her shoulder.

Go downstairs? No. There was nothing down there worth stealing, but maybe the thieves would satisfy themselves with the ground floor. But if they didn't, she would need a weapon. Sliding silently out of the bed, she looked wildly around the room. A poker. A warming pan full of cold coal.

Oh, well, beggars couldn't be choosers. She hefted them both in one hand and crept toward the door. Then stopped. Exactly what good would that do? Wouldn't it be better to lock the door?

Excellent. She set the weapons on the bed and turned the key, which squealed in the darkness. She caught her breath. She swore her heart was just going to tumble out of her chest. She hadn't heard the intruder in the last few minutes. Could he be gone? Had he moved back toward Mrs. Quick's lair? Oh, and if he had, could Fiona leave her unprotected?

The woman might not even get as far as the kitchen and the skillets before she was set upon.

Fiona unlocked the door with sweaty hands and picked the poker back up. Tiptoeing out of the room, she turned to close and lock the door, to keep Mairead safe, when she smelled it.

Oh, no. She whipped around and stared over the banister. It couldn't be. Not in her poor little school.

It was. Smoke.

Poker in hand, she spun around and fumbled with the lock.

"Fire!" she yelled, shoving the door open and pushing Mairead almost out of the bed.

Mairead popped up like a jack-in-the-box, blinking.

"Hurry, Mae!" Fiona urged, bending to pick up shoes and hurl Mairead's at her head. "We must get out."

"Mrs. Quick," Mae answered, catching the slippers and shoving her feet into them.

"Her, too. Come. And take this." Shoving the warming pan into Mairead's hand, Fiona turned back to the hallway. There should be no lights in the house except the faint wash of moonlight. No sound but the fretful pop and moan of old wood. No smell beside beeswax and mutton from dinner. But smoke lent the air a sharp edge. A shuddering fall of orange washed the walls, and Fiona heard a crackling that didn't bode well. And even in the faint moonlight Fiona could see the fingers of smoke wrapping around the spindles of the banister.

She grabbed Mairead's free hand and headed for the stair. Then she stopped, planted Mairead, and ran back for the pillow. If they lost that, there would be no consoling her sister.

"Why am I wielding a copper pan?" Mairead asked sleepily.

Fiona dragged Mairead down the stairs. "Because I heard someone downstairs right before I smelled the smoke."

"And if we see him, we'll bash him?"

"We'll bash him two feet shorter," Fiona assured her, hoping she sounded positive.

She was terrified. The flames were licking up the schoolroom door and along the wall. Fiona reached the bottom floor and turned for the back of the house.

"Mrs. Quick!" she yelled. "Fire! Get out!"

There was no one else in the house. The intruder must have escaped. On the way by the schoolroom, Fiona saw her precious slates piled on a floor littered in paper.

"My computations!" Mairead screamed, pulling for the dining room.

For a moment Fiona hesitated. Could she trust Mae alone while she rousted Mrs. Quick? Mairead did not handle surprise well.

Fiona followed Mairead into the dining room where the air was still fairly clear. Grabbing up the satchel they used to carry their work back and forth, she began to randomly stuff papers and books inside, along with the astrolabe and compasses.

"No, Fee!" Mairead cried, her hand fluttering uselessly. "I'll never get them straight."

"You won't get them charred, either," Fiona said, grabbing Mairead's hand again. "Come along, sweetings. It is time to go."

The tan-and-pink wallpaper was curling off the walls, and the smoke obscured the top half of the hall. Fiona bent low and pulled Mairead down with her as they ran back for the kitchen.

"Mrs. Quick!"

A thick shadow detached itself from the dark. "What in

blazes are you two up to now?" Mrs. Quick demanded as she hopped on one foot, shoving the other into a shoe.

Since the handyman slept out in the mews, this was their complete contingent. Fiona began to relax. At least they would get out.

"Here," Mairead said, holding the warming pan out to the woman. "I'm no good with these."

Mrs. Quick didn't even think to refuse. The three hurried through the darkened kitchen, the increasingly loud flames throwing shadows against the back wall. Fiona saw the door and all she could think was that she needed to get these women out. All else could be taken care of. She had started again before. She would certainly do it again, even though this time she didn't even have the money her grandfather had given her.

Mairead was the one to reach the door first. With her free hand, she turned the knob and pulled. Fiona had a moment's thought to what—or who—waited for them outside. After all, that fire had not set itself. Before she could open her mouth to urge caution, though, Mairead was running through the door.

And then, suddenly, Mairead tripped and went sprawling, and Fiona almost went down with her.

They had reached the back garden, which seemed oddly empty and quiet. But there was some obstruction on the ground. Something large and lumpy and soft.

"Mae?" Fiona asked, seeing that her sister was rising to her knees.

There was something on her robe. Something dark and splotchy. Fiona was about to step over whatever was on the ground and see to her sister, when Mairead lifted her hands. And stared. And stared.

"It's a man," she said in an oddly dispassionate voice.

Fiona froze. Memories flashed before her; hard, desperate memories, cold, darkness, and little Mae, crouched on the ground. Sobbing. "It's a man."

Fiona sucked in a shuddering breath and blinked. Just as she'd shoved her paperwork into that bag, the memories were shoved away where they wouldn't hurt her. Where they wouldn't hurt Mae. She bent to see what it was Mairead was staring at.

"Dear sweet Jesus on a cross," Mrs. Quick breathed, bent over the other side of the big, lumpy, soft obstruction that laid sprawled almost directly across Fiona's back doorway. "Sweet, sweet Jesus."

And then she began vomiting in the grass.

Fiona bent closer. The moon spilled gray light, washing away color. It didn't need it. She knew too well that in the moonlight blood looked black. That dead flesh looked fish white, and that staring dead eyes had no glisten to them. There was no question. The man lying in her back lawn was dead. He was violently, viciously dead, the blood pooled around him like a brutal halo. He was dead because his face had been cut to ribbons, only his staring eyes left intact.

"Fee? *Fee?* Not again!"

In the end, it wasn't the smoke or flames that brought the neighbors. It was the sound of Mairead's desperate screaming.

Chapter 9

Alex downed a bumper of brandy, slammed it on the stained, gouged sticky table, and shoved his money to the center. "All," he growled, making sure to slur.

Four other men sat at the table with him, all members of the aristocracy out for a bit of slumming, all regular visitors to the Blue Goose. Slouched in their seats, drinks in hand and cravats pulled, they stood out in the tavern like daisies in a garbage heap. Even completely cast away, they couldn't loosen their posture or dirty their linen enough to make them look native to the dive. Hell, even their faces were too clean.

Their eyes were mean enough, Alex thought, staring down Cyril Weams, a bony, balding, badly dipped second son who frequented taverns like the Goose and won a disproportionate number of times, even from Alex. Especially from Alex lately. It seemed every time Alex arrived at the Goose, Cyril was already there with Bart Smithers and a bumpkin of a baronet named Purefoy they had been sponging from.

Alex knew Weams cheated. He suspected Smithers did

as well. This wasn't the time to call him on it, though. Not when the front door had just opened and a familiar top hat bobbed through.

"Gov," Alex heard at his elbow.

"Go get him," Alex said quietly.

Thrasher slipped through the crowd that had gathered around the card game and followed the top hat toward the tap. Alex went about finishing the kill.

"Well, Cyril?" he asked.

Cyril was sweating. Alex didn't like Cyril. Besides cheating and keeping company with the likes of Bart Smithers, he liked to take advantage of young girls. Alex was happy to take Cyril's money.

It was winner-take-all on high card. Alex had drawn a knave. Cyril's fingers hesitated over the deck. Cyril was shoving the rest of his money into the center of the table when Alex saw it.

Oh, hell. Not now. But he couldn't ignore so blatant a move. As quick as an adder, Alex slammed a hand down on Cyril's wrist. The room around him went dead silent.

"Only the cards in the deck, old man," he drawled, his voice perfectly calm.

Cyril went red. "How dare you...?"

Alex reached his free hand under Cyril's wrist and drew a king from his sleeve. Cyril howled in protest. Alex ignored him. He was gathering the money and shoving it into a drawstring bag. "Now I know why you prefer the atmosphere at the Goose, Cyril," he said very gently. "Undoubtedly wise."

Pandemonium broke out. Cyril jumped up, almost oversetting the table. Glasses splintered. Liquor spilled, adding to the puddles on the floor. Alex refused to react. He simply stood and walked away from the table. Men pounded him on the back. At least three barmaids offered him everything from dinner to having his baby. He ignored them all. He needed to get back to the private room where Thrasher waited with their prey.

He wasn't a moment too soon. Thrasher had Lennie Wednesday by the collar of his tattered tweed coat, and Lennie wasn't happy. The only reason Thrasher wasn't sporting a broken nose was because he could weave faster than Lennie could swing.

"Sit down," Alex barked.

Both boys stopped. Lennie's sharp blue eyes got big. "Gor," he breathed. "You."

"Yes." Alex pulled out a chair and sat. "Me."

Lennie still gaped. Big blue eyes. Smooth cheeks. Layers of oversized clothing topped by a surfeit of worn tweed and that execrable battered top hat shoved low over his ears.

"Thank you, Thrasher," Alex said, not looking away from the younger boy. "I have this now."

It was Thrasher's turn to gape. Alex didn't blame him. No person of sense should do business without a backup in this neck of the woods. But it wouldn't do him any good for Thrasher to know this particular business.

"I'll be out in a minute," Alex said. "See if you can find a hackney."

Huffing in outrage, Thrasher slammed out the door. Alex turned back to consider Lennie, who stood balanced on the balls of his feet as if coiling to bolt.

"A big secret, is it, gov?" Lennie asked with a knowing smile.

"Is there any other kind, Lennie?"

Leaning against the wall as if he'd spent a long life propping up buildings, Lennie shrugged. "Don't let it get around. Might cost ya more."

"From you?"

"Nuh. I'm an 'onest bloke, I am. Me mam woulda 'ad me lights and liver, other."

Without waiting for the boy, Alex sat down at the scarred, stained table. "How old are you?" he asked, his attention on the bag of money he was tossing in his palm so that it made a tempting clinking noise.

Lennie's eyes were riveted on the bag. "Twelve."

He was ten or Alex was blind. Even so, Alex nodded absently. "Have a seat. I have a proposition for you." He lifted the bag. "And a bit of memory stimulant."

Lennie plopped onto a chair as if his knees had given out. "Won't kill nobody. I got me principles. And I ain't no nancy boy."

Alex fought a grin. "I'm glad of that. No. I do not want you to kill anyone. I want you to point someone out for me."

"The cove what asked me to deliver the message?"

"Yes."

The boy laughed. "Well, that's easy 'nuff. You was jus' playin' cards with 'im."

Alex caught his breath. "Which one?"

"Yeller 'air. Bad teeth. Looks like a starvin' 'ound."

Alex felt as if he'd been kicked in the gut. "Good God. Cyril Weams?"

The boy shrugged. "If that's 'is name. Smells like sewage."

That was him. "Has Weams asked you to deliver messages before?"

His attention on the bulging bag, the boy shrugged. "Coupla times. Coupla punters wiff bad luck. Poncy toff named Evenham. I 'member him special. 'e cried."

Evenham had also killed himself. Alex still wasn't sure whether he'd done it because he'd loved another man or because the Lions had used that secret to force him to help liberate Napoleon from Elba.

"Do you remember anyone else?"

The boy's eyes shifted uneasily. "Naw."

"Because you have a bad memory, or because it could be injurious to your health to remember?"

For that he got a quick, blinding smile. "You ain't 'alf-stupid, gov."

Standing, Alex picked up the bag. "Seems you have a choice, Lennie. You can stay here and take a chance that the people who hired Weams to hire you won't wish to minimize their risk. Or..." He held up the bag. "You could throw your lot in with me. Regular food, improved working conditions, a chance for advancement."

His attention still on the bag, Lennie grinned even more broadly. "An' just f'r the cost of a few names."

Alex didn't move. "Ask Thrasher if you want. I don't lie."

Alex wasn't certain why he didn't want to let this child back onto the streets. The neighborhood was full of them, tough little beasts hardened in flash houses and back alleys. For some reason, this one tugged at something perilous.

"Do you have any family?" he asked.

The boy scowled and looked away. "No."

There was a story, but Alex didn't think he'd be the one to get it. Reaching over, he picked up the bag. "Tell you what. I have a friend in Blackheath named Miss Ferguson who needs some help, but doesn't want to admit it. If you can't bear life with her, I'll bring you back myself."

Lennie's gaze stayed locked on the money. "What about Weams?"

"I'll take care of Weams. What do you say?"

Lennie refused to meet his gaze. Even so, the boy gave a quick, jerky nod. Alex tossed over the bag, which was snatched out of the air like a magic trick.

"If you're smart," Alex said, "you'll let Miss Ferguson

store this for you. There's enough there to keep you off the streets."

The boy sat for a long time, just staring at the plump bag in his long-fingered hands.

Alex nodded and stood. "All right, then. I'd appreciate it if you'd keep this Weams business between us. If you think of any other names, tell no one but me. All right?"

Lennie nodded without looking up.

"What say I take you to my housekeeper tonight, and we'll visit Miss Ferguson in the morning?"

The boy got to his feet. He really was a little dab of a thing, Alex thought as he walked around to open the door. He hoped to hell the lad could find a way to be comfortable in Fiona's world.

"Mister?" Lennie whispered as he came level with him. "I think I'm gonna be thankin' ya."

Alex couldn't help but smile. "I wouldn't worry about it 'til you know you have reason. Besides, first thing Mrs. Soames is going to do is scrub you until your skin's raw."

Lennie flashed amazingly white teeth. "Might wanna tell 'er I bite."

Alex shoved him through the door. "You tell her. I'm going to be looking for Weams."

"Try 'alf Moon Street," Lennie suggested, stuffing his hat back down over his jutting ears. "'as rooms there."

Alex grinned. "I knew you'd be a good investment."

"'ey, Lennie Wednesday!" somebody yelled as they walked through the late-night crowd. "Weams was lookin' f'r ya!"

Lennie nodded. "On my way there now, Sully. Thanks."

Weams, Alex thought as he followed Lennie out the door and into the damp chill of the autumn night. He couldn't say he was surprised at anything Weams might be involved in. The man was a parasite.

Well, he thought, turning to where he could make out Thrasher standing alongside an old hackney, *at least I have a name. I wonder if Weams has the letters, or he's just another intermediary.*

It would be something to discover after a few hours of sleep. Right now Alex could barely put one foot in front of the other.

"Thrasher," he said, reaching the carriage. "Lennie's comin' with us."

Alex thought for sure that his night was over. He gave brief thought to asking Mrs. Soames for some hot water of his own until he pulled out his pocket watch to see the time. Two a.m. Ah well, he'd slept in his dirt before.

He had just reached for the door to pull himself up when a shadow separated itself from the darkness and ran their way. He and Thrasher and Lennie all reacted identically, crouching into readiness for attack. Alex pulled out his pepper pot. Thrasher and Lennie both had blades in their hands.

"Thrasher," a low voice called, sounding urgent. "It's me. Frank! That you, m'lord, what hired us?"

The hulking shadow stepped into the faint glow cast by the gaslight on the walk to reveal the doughy, misshapen features of one of Finney's ex-boxer friends who had been helping to watch Fiona.

"What is it?" Alex demanded, stepping up.

"You gotta come," the man said. "You gotta come now. It's the ladies."

*   *   *

Alex heard it before the hackney even stopped, an otherworldly keening that lifted the hair straight up off his neck.

"What the blinkin' 'ell," Thrasher breathed next to him.

Alex felt that awful sound in his gut. He could smell stale smoke now, wet ash, and destruction. He saw the remnants of a neighborhood crowd clumped on the lawn next door. And there, in Fiona's house, a window that blazed in candle-light. So the school hadn't been a total loss.

If only that was the worst of it.

"I ain' goin' in there," Lennie protested, hand caught in the strap. "It's 'aunted."

"Don't be daft," Thrasher retorted. "That's just Miss Ma-reed. She's upset."

"Wait here," Alex told the jarvey as he jumped out, the two children behind him.

A couple of people turned to see him run up the stairs. He ignored them. The smell of smoke was growing thick and heavy, and the sound of Mairead's ululating wail unnerved him. It rose and fell in regular waves, unstopping, as if she didn't even draw breath. Alex didn't bother to knock before pushing open the door and running in across a fire-blackened floor.

"Fiona?"

"In here." Her voice was quiet, calm, as if he had caught her reading *La Belle Assemblee*.

He hadn't. She sat on her ugly brown sofa in a drab brown cotton wrapper and slippers, her arms around her sister, rocking, rocking, that ubiquitous little pillow caught between them. Humming and stroking her sister's hair as Mairead, eyes closed, mouth open, hands clenched in the air, kept up that unnerving noise.

"Are you all right?" Alex asked, pulling over a chair of his own and sitting.

Fiona looked up at him, and he could see that her eyes were red-rimmed and her hair straggled down the side of her neck. There was soot streaking her stark white features, and the faint freckles that sprinkled across her nose stood out in sharp relief. Her eyes, those large blue pools of calm water, seemed flat as mirrors, shock robbing them of emotion.

"Fiona?"

She looked over as Thrasher and Lennie slammed into the room behind him.

"Y'r not leavin' us out there with that bunch," Lennie said in a raspy voice.

"This is Thrasher," Alex said. "And...uh, Lennie. He's helping me as well."

Fiona nodded, as if strange urchins tumbled into her salon every day. "Thank you for coming," she said, leaning her cheek against her sister's head. "Who told you?"

Alex couldn't think past that noise. He couldn't imagine it happening enough that Fiona was used to it. "Isn't there something we should do for her?" he asked. "Um, a bit of laudanum, perhaps?"

She shook her head. "No. This will work itself out in a bit. She had a shock."

Alex looked around. "Well, of course she did. Your house caught fire. Do you know how?"

The salon seemed untouched, but Alex had seen the scorched walls in the entryway and passage.

"It isn't the fire that has distressed her," Fiona said, her voice still soft, calm. "The neighbors and Sun Fire actually put it out quite quickly. It's...the other."

Alex looked around again. "Other? What other? I was only told about the fire."

"Out back. He's out back."

Alex looked more closely to see that Fiona wasn't quite making eye contact. Her fingers, stroking her sister's hair, were trembling.

"Should I go out and help him?"

She sucked in an unsteady breath. "You might want to." Alex was halfway across the floor before she said more. "Someone doused my schoolroom in lamp oil."

He froze, his heart lurching. "Lamp oil? Has someone threatened you?"

Say yes, he silently pleaded. *Let this be someone angry at the idea of girls being educated.* He looked back, but she wasn't facing him. Her eyes were closed. She kept rocking, and suddenly he wondered if Mairead was the only one who needed the rhythmic comfort.

Alex unerringly found his way down to the kitchen, where the housekeeper was sweeping up shattered glass and ash, her graying hair sticking out of a sleeping cap. The fire had damaged the front hall, classroom, and kitchen, it seemed. Enough to cancel classes for a bit. Enough to silence the sharp tongue on the housekeeper, who just watched him in mute misery as he walked past.

There was another clump of people in the back garden. Torches flickered, casting writhing shadows and muting the faces of the men who bent over the ground. Voices were hushed, as if they stood in a cemetery.

Then he saw what they all bent over.

"Good Christ," he breathed, his stomach revolting. "What is that?"

One of the crowd, a short, squat man with a thick head of dark hair stepped forward. "'oo are you?" he asked, standing in front of the scene as if protecting it.

For once Alex threw around his title. "The Earl of Whitmore," he said in his best Lords voice. "I am a friend of the ladies' family. Now, what's going on?"

The little man nodded. "Constable Byrnes, my lord, and I have to ask...do you know this man?"

He stepped aside. Again, Alex's stomach heaved. "How could I possibly tell?"

The body was large and curled up on its side, arms tucked in, as if protecting its belly. The head, though, was thrown back, frozen in the final throes, and Alex could see...disaster. It looked as if the man had lost a fight with an animal, the face slashed to ribbons, the neck gaping, the blood black in the shadows, the teeth bared in an awful rictus, the flesh that surrounded them gone. Alex's mouth went dry and his heart began to gallop. This was more than the work of a neighborhood bully.

"It's Crusher," Alex heard behind him, and he turned to see Thrasher standing like a stone in the doorway, his face stark white, his focus on the grisly body.

"You know 'im?" the constable asked, notebook suddenly in hand.

Thrasher looked up at Alex, his expression suddenly unbearably young. "'e's one o' Mr. Finney's friends. One o' the watchers."

"Watchers?" the constables echoed, his attention caught.

Alex truly thought he would be sick now. He looked back down at the body and then at the constable. "For the Ferguson ladies," he said. "They were here alone, and I was their brother's friend and wanted to protect them. I thought to hire some help."

"Their brother..." The man looked down at his notebook. "Colonel Lord Ian Ferguson? The one what tried ta kill the Duke o' Wellington? *That* brother?"

"He..." But Alex couldn't say it. He needed permission. "Lady Fiona said that the fire was set," he said instead.

"It was. Do you know of anybody might want to harm the ladies?"

"No."

Yes. Could he have been protecting the wrong person? Had he led the people who did this right to Fiona? Fisting a hand, he rubbed at his temple.

He had to speak with Weams. He had to speak with Drake. He had to know that he hadn't just compounded his sins.

The constable was shaking his head. "No civilized person would do this. Even after what their brother did. Besides, the brother's dead. Can't make no difference."

Alex caught himself once again just shy of disagreeing. "I need to get those women out of here."

"You just wait a minute, my lord," the man protested, stepping up.

Alex whipped around. "My home is in St. James Square," he said. "I will be at your disposal. But I am not leaving these women in a burned-out house without protection. Do you want their deaths on your hands, Constable?"

And until he spoke with Drake, he couldn't tell the constable why.

"The ladies will speak with you tomorrow," he said, leading the way back into the house. "But I don't think you would want to be the one to put them in further peril."

"Peril? What do you mean?"

Alex stopped so fast the man almost slammed into him. "What do I *mean*? Someone set a fire here tonight and then proceeded to filet the man I set to watch the women. What more peril do you need?"

The little man just stood there. "They musta known the attacker," he insisted. "Nobody does this to strangers. You got any ideas?"

"We can speak tomorrow as well. Now, Constable, unless you have something purposeful to say, I would suggest you let me get these women someplace safe and leave you to your crime."

And without waiting for an answer, he stalked off.

"''oo's gonna tell Mr. Finney?" Thrasher asked behind him, his voice small.

"I will," Alex said, his gut twisting hard. "It's my fault."

It was his fault that he hadn't warned the ex-boxers just how dangerous their task was. But then, he hadn't known. How could he?

How could he? If the Lions had done this, he had plenty of evidence how dangerous they were. How ruthless. Wasn't he one of the examples, after all? Hadn't they boxed him into a corner from which there seemed no escape?

But what purpose could be served by terrorizing innocent women? Why torture a stranger? Unless they had taken to exacting revenge on their enemies, this made no sense. And nothing Alex had ever seen or heard about the Lions would point to that.

Maybe Drake would have some ideas. After the women were settled, Alex would have to contact him.

By the time Alex walked back into the salon, Mairead had stopped keening. Now she was deathly quiet and staring, and Fiona, still rocking, was stroking her cheek. Alex suspected this was no improvement. He wished he could have taken the time to be gentler with them both. At least to wait until Chuffy came to jolly Mairead out of her hysterics.

"You saw what was in the back garden," he said without preamble. "I believe you'll agree with me that you have no choice now but to come with me."

"I need to speak with the constable," Fiona said. "And... clean. And Mrs. Quick..."

"Will be coming with us. You cannot stay here, Fiona. You know that."

Sighing, she closed her eyes. "I know."

That should have made him feel better. She was finally allowing him to help her.

Looking at her now, though, the blue of her eyes oddly hollow and spectral, her skin the color of parchment, her hands betraying a fine tremor as they stroked her sister's hair, he knew she had lost more than just her independence tonight. She looked smaller, more fragile, more dimmed than ever before, as if she were fast running out of strength.

Without thinking, he crouched down in front of her, commanding her attention. "We'll find out who did this, Fiona," he said. "We'll find out and make them pay. And then we'll find a way to bring you back here to your students."

The worst part of that lie should have been that she recognized it for what it was. It wasn't. The worst part was that she simply nodded and helped her sister to her feet, without a word of protest. As Alex watched her carefully guide her sister up the stairs, he made another vow, one he meant to keep. He vowed that no matter what, he would make someone pay for what had happened tonight. And he would do everything he could to keep Fiona from ever looking like this again.

Chapter 10

The hackney that pulled up before the Knight residence in St. James Square was packed like a turnip wagon, carrying not only Fiona, Mairead, and their pitiful luggage, but Mrs. Quick and Lennie, with Alex riding up with the jarvey. If Fiona had felt more in the mood, she would have found it amusing. As it was, she simply felt crowded, sick, and frightened.

Mairead hadn't spoken since she'd stopped keening. She hadn't protested being dragged or dressed or guided, simply held on to that poor, ragged pillow and followed instructions. She had acted the same way once before. But not in a long time. A very long time. Her arms wrapped tightly around her silent sister, Fiona wasn't certain whether to pray that Mairead broke back out of her cold shell or that she didn't. Not yet, anyway. Not until they could be alone to deal with the fallout.

"Cor," she heard at her other elbow. "Swells live good, don' they?"

Fiona looked down at her newest companion. Beneath

that squashed, filthy top hat was a heart-shaped face that had almost been completely masked by dirt. Pointed little chin, big blue eyes, heartbreakingly young voice. Even more heartbreaking, caution that Fiona recognized all too well.

"This swell does," she agreed, still rocking Mairead in her arms so her sister wouldn't notice how the movement of the carriage changed. "He's an earl."

Lennie whistled. "Crikey."

"Don't worry," Fiona reassured them both as she assessed the stark white marble facade that stretched up four stories behind the black grilled fence. "He is a very nice man. He'll make you feel very welcome."

She had no idea whether he would or not. It didn't matter. This was where Alex had brought them, and evidently this was where they would stay. Fiona knew she should resent Alex's high-handedness. She should challenge his right to take over her life, as if she had never faced danger before. As if she hadn't survived worse.

As if she wouldn't again.

Still, she couldn't quite whip up any resentment. Worse, she suspected she was relieved. *Cautiously* relieved, she amended to herself. It seemed like such a luxury to have someone else help bear some of her burdens, even though she knew perfectly well how it usually turned out when she allowed it.

Can't I simply enjoy it for the moment? she thought. Rest a bit, knowing that Alex would at least try to help her? It couldn't make the disappointment any worse when she ended up having to reclaim the weight later, could it?

She rubbed at her smoke-irritated eyes and sighed. Of course it could. She knew from experience.

The carriage ground to a halt, and Fiona caught sight of Alex's long leg as he swung down from the box, then his torso, then the back of his head, his hair near black in the predawn gray. Even in the disreputable attire he had affected, he could never be mistaken for a denizen of the slums. His posture was too instinctively straight, his presence too striking, his calm authority too ingrained. He was a leader. A touchstone. He assumed responsibility the way another might a uniform.

Just the sight of him threatened Fiona's hard-won equanimity. Just the sound of his voice made her want to lay her head in his lap and ask him to hold her, to forestall the trembling weakness that gathered in her like swarming bees. The sight of him made her want, oddly, to weep. And she hadn't done that in years. Not since the last time Mairead had gone quiet.

When Alex pulled open the door this time and reached in a hand, Fiona closed her eyes, just a moment. Long enough to snap that connection that seemed to inexorably grow between them, fed now with the memory of sunlight and drapes.

Then, turning to Mrs. Quick, she smiled. "You first, Mrs. Q. I need to get Mairead settled."

Mrs. Quick grabbed Alex's hand and stepped down, followed by Lennie. Fiona watched the latter's disembarkation and wondered at the disparity of what she saw in the child.

Then, suddenly she knew. *Of course*, she thought with a smile. If she hadn't been so distracted, she would have seen it right away. She was a bit amazed that Alex hadn't.

"Come along, Mae," she murmured to her sister, prying her sister's hand from her own. "Alex Knight is here to help us get to our beds. Take his hand, please."

"Not our beds." Mairead sighed, head bent over the pillow. "Not ours."

"No, sweetings," Fiona agreed, gently pulling Mairead's

hand toward Alex's outstretched one. "Not really. I know. But ours for tonight. Ours until ours are ready again and not reeking of smoke. Your lungs won't tolerate our house right now."

All the while she spoke, she nudged her sister toward the door and then followed when Mairead stepped down.

"We'll stay here today, Lady Mairead," Alex said, his voice as calm as Fiona's.

That got Mairead's eyes open, but not for the reason Alex thought, Fiona knew.

"I am *not* a lady," Mairead seethed, yanking her hand back. "Not any *kind* of a lady. Not as long as that selfish, sanctimonious son of a bitch lives. Do you have my books, Fee?"

One foot on the ground, Fiona managed a grin. "In the boot, Mae. Now come along before we outrage the entire neighborhood. And apologize for your language, please. We might not be ladies, but that does not make us soldiers on leave, either."

Mairead's giggle was high and frantic. Fiona held her breath.

"My apologies, my lord," Mairead managed, still giggling as she dropped a perfect curtsy in the street. "I seem to be all about in my head this morning."

Alex was kind enough to smile back. "Miss Mairead," he said, bowing back, "if I had been through what you have tonight, I would have used language that brought a sailor to blush. You are excused."

His levity seemed to have broken her mood, at least for now. Fiona knew that sleep would be perilous for the next few days, for both of them. Mairead hadn't been the only one to trip over that poor man. But for now, they were managing.

"I see we have guests," she heard as they were ushered in the front door.

Fiona looked up to see a dapper white-haired gentleman in perfect evening attire stepping into the foyer with some papers in his hand. Not as tall as Alex, he was slim and sleekly handsome, with the merriest hazel eyes she had ever seen and a rather unhealthy pallor to his skin.

"I'm sorry, sir," Alex said, looking discomposed. "I thought you were still gone."

The man had a gentle smile. "House parties are a bore. Got back just a bit ago."

Alex ushered Fiona forward. "I hope you don't mind that I've brought company."

Lennie whipped off his top hat and bowed. Mrs. Quick curtsied.

The gentleman waved a hand. "Of course not. Introduce us, please."

"Mairead," Alex continued with a tense smile. "Forgive me, but formalities must be observed. Lady Fiona, Lady Mairead, may I present my father, Sir Joseph Knight. Father, Lady Fiona and Lady Mairead Hawes. They prefer to go by the name Ferguson, though."

"A pleasure," Sir Joseph said with a smile and a bow of the head. Fiona nudged Mairead into curtsying alongside her, the pillow still clutched to her chest.

"Your names are different," Mairead said, head tilted. "And Knight outranks you."

"Only in the College of Arms," Alex said with a grin. "Sir Joseph has been my father since I was ten. I would have no other."

For a long moment Mairead just stared at them both. "Huh," she finally said. "Interesting."

Considering the last they remembered of their own father

had been stepping over his drunk form on the way out the door, Fiona could understand Mae's bemusement.

Alex gestured to the remaining guests. "Their housekeeper, Mrs. Quick, and Lennie, who has assisted us. Chuffy and Thrasher will be along shortly. "

"Already here," Fiona heard from the doorway and turned to see Chuffy hurrying in, followed by Thrasher. "Heard. Bad business. Oranges. Should have known."

Alex frowned. "Oranges? What should you have known?"

But Chuffy ignored him. Instead he walked right up to Mairead, who only flinched a bit when he took her hand. "Miss Mairead?" he asked, peering up at her. "Here to help. All right?"

Fiona could feel the fine tremors swell in her sister and wanted to hurry her along. Mairead's feet were planted, though. "Yes, please," she said, reaching over to give Chuffy's glasses a little push. "I don't have a house."

Chuffy's smile was so sweet that Fiona almost smiled back. "I know. I'm sorry."

"I assume they'll all need a place to stay," Lord Knight said.

Fiona saw that Alex's smile was tentative. "For a day or two, I think."

His father nodded to Lennie. "Young man, pull that cord, please. We'll have the rooms readied immediately."

Fiona saw that Mairead hadn't taken her gaze from Chuffy. Reaching into his pocket, Chuffy brought out a handkerchief and rubbed at the soot from her face. Fiona was torn. She instinctively wanted to push Chuffy away, to be the protective barrier for Mairead she'd always been. And yet, Mairead was calmer than any time tonight.

"Thank you, Sir Joseph," Fiona said, turning back to

Alex's father. "I would like to get my sister to bed, if I may. She has had a bad night."

Fiona thought of the keening, so recently ended, and prayed that nothing started it up again. She thought of the perilous state of her own control and wanted to protect it. What belonged in a burned-out school in Blackheath did not in a house in Mayfair.

"I shall get Mrs. Soames, shall I, sir?" came a starchy voice from the direction of the green baize door. Evidently the butler had been roused.

"Indeed, Soames." Sir Joseph gestured expansively. "Rooms for everyone."

Chuffy looked up, still holding Mairead's hands. "Security here. Finney insisted."

Alex turned to Thrasher. "You told him."

Thrasher shrugged. "He knew. Said it's not your fault. It 'appens."

"What happens?" Alex's father quietly asked.

Fiona shuddered. She could still see that obscenity, could still feel the splashes of blood congealing on her nightdress.

Alex turned to his father. "I'll explain when I get the ladies settled, sir. I'm sorry. I don't suppose you'd like to spend a day or two at the club to avoid all this."

His father gave him a steely look. "I would not. I might suggest securing a chaperone, however. This is essentially a gentleman's house."

Alex nodded. "We can call upon Lady Bea to come."

Sir Joseph frowned. "You would put that gentle lady at risk?"

Both of the younger men grinned. "Tougher than you think," Chuffy said.

"I'll explain," Alex said.

Sir Joseph frowned. "Soon, I hope."

"As soon as the ladies are settled, sir," Alex promised.

All the men were about to disperse when Fiona turned. "Excuse me. Lennie, will you help us upstairs?"

Everybody turned surprised eyes on her, especially Lennie.

"Get my books," Mairead said. "They are quite heavy. I need to lie down, Fee. Please. I'm sorry. I'm tired. You understand. It's been a... a long..."

It seemed that Sir Joseph was a master of adaptability and affability. Within minutes Mrs. Quick was ensconced in a small room in the servants' wing, Thrasher was sent off with a note for Lady Bea, and Lennie was helping Mairead and Fiona up the stairs, Fiona's portmanteau bumping at each stair.

As Fiona was guiding Mae up the steps, she saw Alex take hold of Chuffy's arm. "Oranges?" he demanded. "What did you mean?"

Chuffy blinked. "Oh, right. You weren't there. Minette Ferrar, my lad. Plays with the things. Should have picked up on it. Have a feeling it's her new signature."

Fiona stopped on the spot, her skin crawling. Madame Fermont had smelled of oranges.

"Oh, bloody hell," Alex breathed, actually paling. "We need to tell Drake."

"You need to tell *me*," Fiona said, causing all the men to turn her way. "Is this about my guest for tea the other day?"

For a minute she didn't think anyone was going to answer. Then, with an abrupt shifting of his feet, Alex sighed. "After you get your sister settled, if you'd come back down to the library. You'll be shown the way."

She wanted to ask more, but suddenly knew she shouldn't. Not in front of witnesses. Especially not in front of Mairead, who was already fragile as isinglass. So she

nodded and continued to climb. God, she was so tired.
Pulled like taffy and aching to her very heart. It looked,
though, as if she wouldn't see her bed any time soon.

Fiona accompanied Mairead to a very pretty yellow-and-
white suite that overlooked the back garden and came with
two bedrooms and a young maid named Suzy. Fiona did no
more than pull off Mairead's slippers before covering her up
and dousing the candles, asking Suzy to stay in the dressing room for now in case Mairead woke. Taking time only to
splash her face with lukewarm water, she crept back out.

She'd meant to return right to the library. Instead Lennie
waited for her in the sitting room. Sighing, she stopped to
assess the fine features and large eyes. "I believe you need to
tell Lord Whitmore the truth, little one," she said.

Lennie froze like prey scenting a hunter. "What?"

Fiona was desperate to get downstairs for some answers.
So she faced her new friend with a smile. "Either you tell
him, Lennie," she said gently, "or I will."

* * *

This night was fast becoming a nightmare. The last thing
Alex wanted was to bring yet more danger to his father's
doorstep. If he could have, he would have personally bundled Sir Joseph up and dropped him at White's, at least until
he could get the women out and the letter investigated. It was
unconscionable to put more strain on his father's heart.

This was also not the way Alex had envisioned telling his
father about Drake's Rakes. He wasn't certain he'd thought
to tell his father at all, especially since he'd seen that damning letter. If Sir Joseph actually had shared troop reports
with a known traitor, Alex could be compromising more
than just the Rakes by revealing the truth.

But Alex refused to believe that Sir Joseph Knight, who had taught him the meaning of honor and loyalty, would compromise his own integrity. He could not imagine a world in which the most honorable man in Britain would sell out his country.

He would not have betrayed his friend, as his son had.

"It's a good thing your mother and sisters aren't here," Sir Joseph said, when Alex finished bringing his father up to date. "I would have flayed you alive if you had put them in danger."

"I would rather not put you in danger, either," Alex insisted.

Not surprisingly, Sir Joseph waved him off. "I am no porcelain doll, boy. I worry about your sister Pip, though."

Alex was pacing again, back in his father's study. "I'll make sure Beau keeps her busy at that house party."

"For how long?"

Alex stopped by the front window. "Well, once Chuffy gets back with Lady Bea we'll decide where she and the Ferguson sisters will be safe. We'll be moving in one, two days at most. But the danger won't end until we can stop Minette Ferrar. I can't begin to tell you how sorry I am, sir."

He was stunned when his father came up and hugged him hard. "Don't be absurd. If we didn't take chances we would do ourselves and our country no good."

Alex hugged his father back and thought how frail he felt. "I know. I just wish you weren't involved."

His father smiled. "Actually, I believe I might enjoy this. Diplomacy can be deadly dull. And those are two very fetching young ladies."

Alex let loose a bark of laughter. "Wait 'til I tell mother."

"Pish. Your mother knows that I appreciate a pretty girl. She also knows what a fool I would be to risk her good opinion."

Alex rubbed at smoke-irritated eyes and thought how stretched Fiona must feel. "Chuffy should be back soon. I believe it's time to roust my good friend Marcus Drake from his comfortable bed. It serves him right."

"Don't you have something else to do first?"

It actually took Alex a moment to remember. "Oh, damn. I do." He rubbed his eyes again. "I don't suppose you'd rather tell our guest that she gave tea to the same notorious assassin who slit a man's throat in her back garden."

"Not actually, no."

"It's all right," Alex heard behind him. "Your guest already knows."

Chapter 11

J umping to his feet, Alex whipped around to see a Fiona he had never seen before standing in the doorway. Like with the signs of his father's deteriorating health, not everyone would have realized how strained Fiona was right now. She stood quietly in another soft black gown, her hair as tidy as her person, her expression calm, her hands quiet, her spine straight as steel. She looked taller somehow, stronger, more certain. And yet, he could almost feel the tension radiating off her body. He could sense the fragile edge of control she straddled.

And he had to take what little peace of mind she had left. Hurrying over to her, he held out his hands. She literally flinched, as if his touch would burn her. Instinctively he knew. It wasn't that she was afraid of receiving his comfort, but of revealing her own distress. The minute he touched her fingers, he would know for sure the cost of this night on an already emotionally bruised and exhausted woman.

So he stepped back and motioned her to a chair. As she neared, his father stood and approached. "I hope everyone here has made you welcome, Lady Fiona," he said, his diplomat face on.

She smiled, and most people would have been delighted. "Everyone has been lovely, Sir Joseph. Thank you. I am sorry we had to intrude like this."

Sir Joseph took her hands without her permission. "You are always welcome, my dear."

She startled, her eyes up, her back rigid. "Thank you, sir."

"I believe you two have some talking to do," Sir Joseph said with a final squeeze before letting Fiona go. "And as my son has been reminding me far too often for my own *amour propre*, I need to catch up on my sleep."

Alex waited until he saw Soames meet Sir Joseph at the stairs with a night candle before turning back to Fiona. "My apologies. I just wanted to make sure he had help upstairs."

She looked back the way she'd come. "He is not well."

A statement, not a question. Alex shook his head. "His heart. He simply will not admit his weakness and slow down."

"Then we should not be here."

"Nonsense," Alex said, wishing she would sit. "I'm having a brandy. Can I offer you something?"

She wiped at her eyes with the heels of her hands. "Do you know, I believe you can. Just don't tell the parents of my students."

"Oh, I think they'd understand."

As he poured the two tots, he watched her. She looked completely pulled. Unutterably tired, as if tonight had taken the stuffings right out of her. Lennie had said that he'd seen Fiona scrubbing at her hands like Lady Macbeth trying to get the congealed blood from between her fingers, burning her nightdress rather than even try to clean it. And yet, she exuded such strength. Such implacable purpose. She had been impossibly gentle with her sister, and yet, when she had turned to Alex from the stair, she'd looked like an outraged queen. Iron-willed and diamond-hard. A warrior ready for battle.

Could he be wrong, though? Could her control be no more than pretense? The camouflage donned by a splintered soul?

Whatever the truth, her indomitable will humbled him. After all, what had he suffered in comparison? He had lost a wife he'd no longer loved. He was being threatened by that wife's weaknesses. He had never gone hungry, been cold, been alone in the world except for a sister who was more child than friend. He had never really been responsible for another human being. Not the way Fiona had.

No. The way Fiona *was*.

The walls she had built around her were formidable; he thought it was the only way she'd survived. But suddenly, he couldn't bear the idea that behind their solid height, she stood alone.

He wanted so badly to wrap her in his arms and cushion her against any injury, any slight, any threat. He wanted to soften the edges of life for her and ease the furrows between her eyebrows. He wanted her never to have to worry again, even though he didn't have the right.

The best he could do now was hand off her glass.

"We need to talk, Fee. Won't you sit?"

For a moment she held her glass, peering into the liquid as if it were a mirror. He wished she would settle in the chair. Maybe what he had to say would impact her less. Instead, she lifted the glass and downed half its contents in one convulsive swallow.

"Is this about Madame Fermont?" she asked, not facing him.

He wasted a look to the shuddering fire, as if it held his answers. "Not Madame Fermont. Madame Ferrar."

His gut cramped. They had been so close. They could have caught her. They could have kept her from doing this to Fiona.

There was nothing to do but tell her the truth. As calmly as he could, Alex shared what he could about the Rakes and Minette Ferrar. "We have run across her several times," he said. "She is ruthless, crafty, vicious, and relentless. And, as you can tell by her visit the other day, she's rather like a cat who likes to play with her victims."

Fiona wandered over to the windows, the brandy snifter tucked against her chest as he'd seen her clutch that pillow, her gaze out into the darkness. "But why would she bother with us?"

Alex briefly closed his eyes against the sudden memories of a damp, cold room, Ian's battered face, the smiling Minette. This he wanted to tell her least of all. "She...er, met up with your brother Ian a little while ago. She was unsuccessful."

Fiona's expression was flat, once again too calm. "You mean she wasn't able to murder him? Like that man in our garden?"

Alex knew he didn't have to answer. She already knew. The color had leached from her face. "Ian is fine," he assured her. "I thought we had Minette locked away. It is evident I was wrong. After I leave you, I'm going to find out why."

It was her turn to close her eyes. When she opened them, she sat in a whoosh, as if her legs had given out. Alex stepped up, but she held him off with an upraised hand. "So what were we?" she asked. "Revenge?"

"I don't know."

She raised her eyes to him, and he fought to remain where

he was. She was horrified, but he didn't think she was astonished. He wondered if any evil in the world could surprise her anymore.

"Why didn't she kill us?"

He sat down in the matching chair. "I don't know that, either. Maybe to draw out Ian so she can have another try at him."

"But you won't let her."

Her eyes. So blue, so deep. So defiant. Alex smiled. "Is that a question or a command?"

"Both, I think."

"No," he said. "We won't. We will protect you and Mairead until we know for certain we've captured or killed the woman, and then we'll reunite you with your brother and Sarah."

She shuddered again, briefly closing her eyes. "Who was he? The man who...who died? Does anyone know?"

This might hurt worst of all. "His name was Crusher. He was an ex-boxer I hired to watch over you and Mairead."

She lifted accusing eyes. "So you knew this...Ferrar woman was after us?"

"No!" He shoved a hand through his hair. "I just saw two women alone and wanted to protect you. That's all."

She dragged her free hand down her skirt, as if to scrape something away. "It isn't all. That man is dead. He's dead...horribly."

"Believe me," Alex told her. "I know. Which is why you must promise you will let us protect you. Minette Ferrar is no ordinary criminal. She is relentless. And the only way we're going to catch her is to work together. At all times."

Fiona looked into the darkness outside the window again, as if it were instinctive when making a decision. "We cannot go back to the school."

"You cannot."

"We cannot travel on."

"Not until this is decided."

She was nodding, as if any of this made sense. "I wonder..."

"What?"

Her laugh was abrupt, her crystal blue eyes dark. "Whether I will ever live a normal life. So far, it has been...decidedly un...un..."

Her voice faltered to a halt. She bent her head, rubbed at her eyes with shaking fingers. Alex knew she was fighting for control. His own throat ached with her unshed tears. "It's all right to cry," he said, leaning close enough to hear the quick rasp of her breath.

"No," she grated. "It is not. I don't have...the luxury."

He brushed a strand of hair back from her forehead. "But you just saw a man murdered. You might have died yourself. And you've just lost your house. Your school. You have a right to a moment of weakness."

That got her head up and her eyes open. "Mairead and I have seen dead men before," she said baldly, the steel back in her spine. "We have almost died a dozen times. The only way to keep it from actually happening is for me to always be on my guard."

Her voice suddenly sounded as ancient as death; her eyes, those luminous sky-blue eyes, looked even older. He had walked battlefields, and yet he couldn't imagine his own eyes looking as bleak. As lonely. As relentless.

"There is a difference now, though, Fiona," he said. "This time you're not alone."

Even in the dimness he saw the truth skim across her eyes. She had been told that before, and by him. She had believed it, and it had turned out to be a lie.

No wonder she couldn't bear to be held, he thought. Hate

and disdain were easy to fight against. But how did you survive the awful temptation of friendship?

It wasn't right. She should never again have to stand alone, afraid to accept the comfort of another human. He wouldn't allow it.

In that moment he deliberately ignored the fact that he was asking her to trust him again. To trust the man who had deserted not only her, but her brother.

Cupping her chin in his hand, he lifted her face to him. "You are the strongest woman I know, Fiona Ferguson. But from now on, I vow to you, you will not be alone. Not to deal with Mairead or Ian or schoolchildren or that surly bastard you call a grandfather. I will be there."

He almost said it, almost committed the fatal error of offering to be her lover. Her helpmeet. He almost committed himself to a mystery, when the lesson was still so new from his last foray into that perilous morass. When he more than anyone knew that she would be making a bigger mistake than he if she said yes.

She didn't answer, just gazed up at him, her eyes wide and bright in the dimness, her skin pale as a dream, her lush hair a conflagration, even in the dark. He couldn't bear it a minute longer. Plucking her glass from her suddenly limp fingers, he set both down on the table and returned to her. And then, winding his fingers through her hair, he held her still for his kiss.

He tasted the salt on her lips. He smelled the faint trace of smoke in her hair. He savored the satin of that hair and the velvet of her skin. He saw her eyes close and her lips open, and he feasted.

At first, she stilled, as if surprised. Her breaths came more quickly, and Alex could feel the thrum of her pulse at her throat. He sank into the lush pillow of her mouth and felt himself losing his way. He deepened the kiss, plundering the silken depths of her mouth, sparring with her, his control fraying more with every sleek slide of her tongue against his. He tightened his hold, pulling her to her feet and wrapping his arms around her, pulling her flush against his body, crushing those luscious breasts against his chest, savoring the plush comfort of her body. He was hard as stone, aching so badly he couldn't catch his breath. He swore his body was on fire. It had never happened like this before. Not ever. Not even with her.

He had meant to comfort. He was about to consume. And yet, if there had been no interruption, he wasn't at all certain he would have stopped.

Fortunately for him, the very distinct sounds of arrival echoed from the entry hall. He pulled back, gasping. Desperate to return to her arms, starving for the taste of her on his tongue. Her eyes were closed. She held perfectly still, her head bent, her chest rising and falling quickly. Alex knew he was shaking worse than she.

"I believe…Lady Bea is here," Fiona murmured. "I should…"

She made a vague motion and opened her eyes. Alex thought he could easily drown in their depths, dark as night, deep as secrecy. He fought an irrational urge to grab her hand and run with her. He didn't care where. Somewhere they could be alone.

"If you would greet her," he managed, turning away. "I'll be along in a minute."

She didn't move, not for the longest time. Alex held his breath, his control all but eroded. *Go,* he thought, desperate. *Go before I ruin everything.*

She left, her steps measured, her gown swishing gently around her legs. And for the longest time after Fiona left,

Alex stood where he was, his hands splayed on his father's desk, his head down, his body screaming in protest, his brain offering up fantasies of his body entwined with Fiona Ferguson's.

It was so wrong. It was the breaking of every oath of honor he had ever taken. But if Lady Bea hadn't arrived just then, he wasn't sure he would have let Fiona walk away from him.

Fiona Ferguson Hawes. *Lady* Fiona Ferguson Hawes. A woman who deserved better than a quick tumble. A granddaughter of a marquess, no matter how she'd spent her earlier years.

How *had* she spent them? The longer he went without that runner's report, the less he was certain. *The skills that kept them clothed and fed before I found them are never forgotten by women like that.* Her own grandfather's words. What skills had he meant? Could it be that she was not innocent? That she had never been, even the first time he'd met her four years ago, a gamine queen in a cow pasture?

No. No, that had not been the kiss of an experienced woman. Even the kisses they'd shared the last few days had seemed unpracticed, impulsive. Not the seductive forays of a woman who made her living rousing desire. Surely he would know.

Surely.

"All right?" he heard next to him.

"Fine," he said, straightening. When he saw the concern on Chuffy's face he had to smile. "I have been battling unholy thoughts, Chuff."

Chuffy's frown deepened. He pulled off his glasses and applied his handkerchief. "Don't worry, White Knight."

Alex almost laughed in Chuffy's face. He was planning to hunt down the man who was blackmailing him, and he hadn't so much as informed Drake. He had come within ame's aces of taking Fiona like a two-penny whore, and he couldn't say for sure if he would have felt any guilt. "Oh, Chuff," he said, patting his friend on the back. "What is it exactly you see through those spectacles?"

Chuffy's expression was as guileless as ever. "Same as you. Brought Lady Bea. What now?"

Alex scrubbed at his face. "Well, I for one am about to have a tête-à-tête with our friend Drake. I have the most annoying sense that he won't be as surprised by Madame Ferrar's return as we were."

"Want me along?"

He shook his head. "My father is a bit low on stamina at the moment. I'd appreciate your keeping watch here. When I return we'll figure out where to go."

Chuffy hooked his glasses over his ears. "Have an idea. Grandmother's dower house. Out of the way. Pop over when I need some quiet to work on ciphers."

"That might be the perfect place."

They were walking out of the room when Chuffy stopped. "Reminds me. Ciphers. Think Lady Mae has some."

That brought Alex to an abrupt halt. "Some what? Ciphers? What do you mean?"

Chuffy scratched at his nose. "Had some papers she was working on. Said they were word puzzles she got from her grandfather."

Alex frowned. "Her *grandfather*? I have trouble believing that old curmudgeon shared games with anyone, much less his granddaughters."

Chuffy suddenly looked very serious. "What if he has her decoding messages for him? Bright girl and all."

I don't have time for this right now was all Alex could think. "How do you know it's a cipher?"

Chuffy shrugged. "Don't. But she had a strip of paper with a string of letters in groups of four. Snatched it away before I could copy more than a few groupings, but it looked familiar. Like the communiqués I've been working on. Think it needs a key."

Alex felt a chill of prescience snake down his back. "The poem?"

Chuffy shrugged. "Tried every word in that poem on the messages we've already intercepted. Tried 'em backward. Don't fit."

"Why do you think they'll fit here?"

"Don't. Wouldn't mind another eye on it, though."

Alex took a minute on that one. What he and Chuffy were considering was against all the rules. They had no business bringing civilians into the mix. Especially when it might put them in further danger.

They could also be the break the Rakes needed.

"See if she'd like to help you," he said.

Chuffy looked up. "Big decision," he said.

Alex sighed. "I'll tell Drake. Right after I wring his neck for putting these two women in danger."

Chuffy huffed. "Give him a twist for me. Not right. Not such a sweet girl."

Alex's head snapped up. "Sweet girl?"

Chuffy blinked, as if Alex were the most stupid man on earth. "Lady Mae. Mean to make her Lady Wilde."

Alex found himself staring at his oldest friend wondering how to tell him he'd just run barking mad. Wondering whether to tell him the possible scandal he was courting, the impossibility of a good outcome. "Do you really think that's a good idea, Chuff?"

Chuffy's answering smile was unbearably sweet. "Don't think I have a choice."

Which was when it struck Alex. No matter what he learned from the runner. No matter what his own father said, or Drake or Fiona or Ian. He wasn't sure he did, either.

God, he wished it were that easy.

* * *

"She did *what*?" the old man bellowed.

Privens barely kept from running back to the house. He wished with all his heart he could have waited until the old man had come in from shooting. As it was, he was sharing bad news with a man who was holding a fully loaded Purdy in his arms.

"She...er, used her knives on the watchman. The team had no idea. They were in starting the fire so they could get the women out to search their bedroom. They'd had no success on the main floor."

"And did they find anything in the bedrooms?" The old man could look quite terrifying, actually, when his choler was up. And it was definitely up. Not the Privens blamed him. This was a cock-up of major proportions.

"No, sir." Privens looked away, possibly at his last sight of a late autumn sky. "The women...er, never quite made it outside. The guard had been left in the back doorway."

The old man actually closed his eyes and cursed. "Was there any reason for her actions, or was she just bored?"

"She didn't say, I'm afraid. She just...laughed."

"Where. Is. She?"

"Uh, Madame Ferrar?" Privens was beginning to shake now. "We don't quite...know."

The eyes snapped open and twin blue fires blazed. "Well, find out. This has gone far enough. She is a liability, and I will no longer tolerate it. If you can't get her safely to the continent, where she may slaughter the French and Swiss to her heart's desire, than eliminate her. I don't care. But do something!"

"Yes, sir."

"It doesn't alter the original problem. Where are the Ferguson women?"

Privens could barely get the words past his suddenly dry throat. "Well, sir, we, uh, don't know that, either. We believe Whitmore snuck them away."

Privens didn't need any words to know that if he was forced to deliver one more message like this one, it would be the messenger who was eliminated.

"Then you had better locate Whitmore, hadn't you? We need those women found." The old man lifted the Purdy and sighted along its twin barrels, causing a sweat to break out down Privens's back. "I hate wasting those letters on something this trivial. We could have coerced that prig Knight into compromising Foreign Affairs for us." Sighing, he let the gun drop. "Well, we'll have Weams find something else for us. There is always something else."

"Yes, sir."

Privens had almost made his escape, when the old man had one final thought. "Oh, and Privens. We're running out of time. If anyone else finds out we've lost that message, we'll be in serious trouble. I don't care how the team recovers the items the Fergusons took. Just make sure they get them."

Chapter 12

Alex was not polite about invading Drake's house. He pounded on the door as if the street were on fire, only to have the door opened almost immediately by Drake's new butler.

"He'd better be here, Wilkins."

The older man winked. "I believe he heard a rumor you might be on a tear, sir, and headed this way."

Alex removed his hat and greatcoat and handed them over.

"May I ask how you are tonight, sir?" Wilkins asked, his eyes still twinkling.

Alex scowled. "You may not, you traitor. You deserted me, Wilkins."

"Lord Drake made me a better offer."

"He offered you more heads to crack. You are a barbarian."

Wilkins bowed quite formally. "Only after hours, sir. Come this way."

They found Drake bent over a billiards table potting a shot. "Grab a cue, Knight."

"If I grab a cue, I'll beat you over the head with it. Did you know that Minette Ferrar was on the loose?"

Drake straightened, his face impassive. "I assume you do."

"She presented herself to Ian Ferguson's sister as a possible client for her school. Chuffy and I walked right by her. But since we didn't know she was at large, we never suspected her. Which meant she was then free to set fire to the ladies' house and carve a man into Sunday roast in their garden."

Every time Alex thought of that grisly scene, of that horrible keening and Fiona's ashen features, he battled a fresh explosion of rage. He wanted to kill Minette Ferrar himself. He wanted to know she was as terrified as her victims.

Drake exhaled slowly, resting the cue on the ground. "That *is* unfortunate. Are the ladies unharmed?"

Alex frowned. "If you don't count shaken and frightened and sick. They tripped over the body when they were fleeing the fire."

Drake looked down. "Minette wants to draw out Ian, of course."

"I told Fiona that would never happen. I hope I wasn't lying about that, too."

That brought Drake's head up and Alex was considered by lazy blue eyes. "What else were you lying about?"

Alex met his gaze implacably. "That they weren't in any danger. My credibility is stretched a bit thin right now."

"Where are they?"

"My father's house, which complicates things even more. Chuffy has retrieved Lady Bea. I'm hoping to get them all out by tomorrow."

"Where?"

"Where no one will think to find them," Alex said. "Especially you."

*   *   *

Four hours later, Fiona was back in a carriage rebruising the same patch of hip and bottom she had bruised on the last carriage ride, squashed between the window and Mairead in another job coach. She didn't care where Alex was taking them, as long as they arrived soon. Ever since they had left his father's town house and set off on this rambling trek meant to lose any interested followers, she had been dividing her time between Lady Bea's carriage sickness and Mairead's increasing distress. Even Chuffy had stopped trying to soothe her, evidently having run out of platitudes. The best Fiona could do was offer a flask of spirits—a bit to Mae, a bit to Lady Bea, and a bit more to herself.

"I want to get out," Mairead kept whining, her voice pitched perfectly to pierce eardrums. "I want to go home."

"A little selfish, you ask me," Chuffy finally retorted, arms crossed. "Lady Fiona might want to see my surprise, even if you don't."

"I don't. I want my house. I want my bed and my telescope and my books."

"We have your books, sweetings," Fiona said, her fingers numb from where Mairead was squeezing them. She didn't have the heart yet to tell her sister that the tabletop telescope Margaret had lent them had been lost to the fire, its beautiful little lenses cracked like windows from a hard frost. "We'll be there soon."

Fiona wasn't at all certain how much more she could tolerate. She had had less than three hours' sleep in the last twenty-four, her own stomach roiled with the movement, and the brick at her feet had long since lost its warmth. She had spent two hours being interrogated by a Bow Street Runner, a magistrate, and Chuffy, and spent another two talking Mae into getting back into the coach.

Fiona was aching for rest, twitching with nerves at the thought that they might be followed by Madame Ferrar or any of her henchmen, and still distracted by the kiss she had shared with Alex.

Distracted. What a pale word. Her body still hummed, as if she should shed light. Her lips still felt tender and her breasts heavy. And tears, useless, frustrating, unfamiliar tears, backed up in her throat as if that one kiss had loosened her hold over them.

She didn't want to succumb. She couldn't afford it. Not around Alex, and not now.

Fiona actually thought of grabbing the pillow from Mairead and burying her own face in it. Maybe she could resurrect the last trace of the lavender they'd slipped inside. Maybe she could remember the older scent of heather and gorse. Anything to soothe the growing clamor in her head.

"Well, I think you're ungrateful," Chuffy suddenly said, as if he had run out of patience.

Fiona's eyes popped open to see Mairead staring at him as if he had bitten her. "And you are a selfish beast," Mairead hissed, worrying at the thread on the old pillow in her arms. "How dare you press me? How *dare* you? You don't understand."

"Oh, but I do," Chuffy said, leaning forward a bit. "You want to play with your toys. You haven't even noticed that Lady Bea and your sister don't feel at all well."

"Oh, no, I—" Fiona didn't get any more out before Chuffy glared at her. Chuffy!

Mairead turned on her, eyes wide and glistening. "Fee, no. I'm sorry. I'm so sorry."

"Now see what you've done," Fiona growled across the

coach as Mae threw herself into Fiona's arms, pillow and all. "I am perfectly fine, Mae. I believe Lord Wilde was just quizzing you."

Chuffy tilted his head like a curious bird. "Got her attention, didn't I?"

Mairead straightened like a shot. "Do you mean...do... Don't...*ever*...do that again. Don't, don't, don't, you miserable slug of an invertebrate! You're the one giving Fee the headache."

Fiona couldn't believe it. Chuffy grinned. "Do too have a backbone," he insisted. "Enough to keep you on your toes, my girl."

Mae opened her mouth to argue. Fiona held her breath. Lady Bea, her eyes still closed, smiled as if she were listening to beautiful music. Fortunately for them all, the coach swung around a long curve and pulled to a jangling, rattling stop before a low-roofed, rambling house Fiona could barely see in the first wash of dawn. Elizabethan, she thought, comprised of old brick and gables, with a forest of chimneys on a meandering roofline, a plain oaken door, and a surfeit of mullioned windows.

At any other time, Fiona would have been delighted with the place. It was just the kind of venerable old lady she would have loved to explore from top to bottom, seeking out secrets and ghosts and surprises. At this moment, though, all she could think of was getting to some kind of bed she could sink into.

Chuffy pushed the door open before they had fully stopped and hopped down, lowering the steps. "Well, Lady Bea," he said, hand up to her. "Join the party?"

The old lady stepped down into the early morning chill and assessed the building. "Bastille," she pronounced with pursed lips.

"Wound me, ma'am," Chuffy protested, hand to plump chest. "Not prison at all. Jewel box, ready to hold only the most precious gems."

Lady Bea patted his cheek and stepped aside as her maid followed her out.

And then it was Mae's turn. "Are you going to behave now, Lady Mae?" he asked, hand up to her. "If you don't, can't share my surprise."

"Really, Chuffy," Fiona protested, gathering scarves and reticules. "Could you let it wait until we get in out of the cold? I, for one, am fractured."

"Beast," Mae protested.

Fiona took her sister's free hand. "Go on, sweetings," she begged. "He won't eat you."

Mae's laughter cracked through the early morning air. "He should be more worried that I shall eat him."

Her movements did not echo the force of her words. She climbed out as if she were exiting a cave, stiff-legged, her movements halting, her eyes squinted against the frail light. At least she exited on her own, Fiona thought, perfectly happy to remain behind for a moment longer in the quiet and shadowy coach. After the upheavals of the last few days, Fiona had expected to have to carry Mae out of the coach over someone's shoulder kicking and screaming, using the pillow as a weapon.

Maybe Chuffy had done a good thing after all.

When she looked around to gather the detritus left behind, it was to see that Mae had forgotten the pillow entirely. Grabbing hold of it, she clutched it to her own chest, the comfort far outweighing the size of the poor old thing. She was just thinking that maybe she could avoid leaving the coach altogether when Alex stuck his head inside. He was tousled from riding alongside, his cheeks wind-roughened and his eyes an almost unearthly gleam in the dim morning chill. Fiona's heart did an odd flip at the sight of him, and she knew she blushed.

"Brace up," he greeted her with a commiserating grin, his hand out. "You have to get down sooner or later."

She did her best to smile. "Do I have to? It is so nice and quiet in here all of a sudden."

Even so, she took hold of his hand. His fingers closed around hers, and she fought the heat of them, the sharp sense of comfort.

"I believe your friend Chuffy is more diabolical than he seems," she said, letting Alex help her down the steps, the pillow still in her arms.

The air was heavy with moisture, the movement creating eddies. Lennie had hopped off the coachman's perch and stood hunched in his too-small coat, hands in pockets, the hat crushed over jug ears. Another problem Fiona needed to deal with.

"Your sister did seem uncommonly testy this morning," Alex said, dragging her attention back.

"Just a fair warning," she said. "I do not believe she will be moved again. At least not 'til she gets some sleep."

"I don't believe it will be necessary," Alex promised. "Besides, now that she's out she seems better pleased."

"I promised you a treat if you came along, didn't I?" Chuffy was saying as he walked Mae away from the coach, her hand on his arm. "Close your eyes."

Mairead did just that. Fiona couldn't believe it. Mae followed no one's guide except hers when she was lucky. Especially when she was already in high dudgeon.

Chuffy guided Mairead to the center of the drive. "Now. Go ahead and look."

They all looked. There where a fountain should have sat

was a plain stone one-story building with what looked like a pipe sticking out of the roof. Except that Fiona knew that it was no pipe. She sucked in her breath at the sight.

"Is that what I think it is?" Mairead breathed in wonder.

Fiona knew Alex was watching her, but she couldn't help but smile.

Not as brightly as Chuffy, however. "Promised I'd make up for taking you away from the observatory, didn't I? Well, like to present you to the Wilde stargazer. Only way Grandmama could get the pater to visit. Put a telescope on the lawn."

There were tears tracing down Mairead's cheeks. Fiona made an instinctive move to comfort her. Alex held her back. She glowered at him, but before either could speak, Mairead launched herself into Chuffy's arms and kissed him, almost lifting him off the ground in her enthusiasm.

Lady Bea chortled and clapped her hands. Alex grinned. Fiona gaped.

"Might want to close your mouth, old girl," Alex said. "You look like a landed trout."

She looked over at him, completely unnerved by Mae's behavior. This simply wasn't like her. Not even with Fiona.

"You don't like Chuffy's treat?" Alex asked, his face crinkled with good humor.

She opened her mouth a couple of times before turning back to watch her sister jabber with Chuffy about azimuths and declinations. "If he hurts her…"

Chuffy was beaming like a child as he reached up to right Mairead's tilted bonnet. There was no question how gently Chuffy held Mairead's hand, or how attentively Mairead stood with her head bent over his, smiling.

"You obviously don't see what I see," Alex said.

She did. But she had seen it before when men were smitten with Mae's looks. She had seen men do any number of surprising things to get her sister's attention. But she had never seen Mae respond this way before.

"You don't know Mairead like I do," she insisted. "This is all new territory for her. And the only place she handles new territory well is a dark sky."

Alex grinned. "She seems to be handling this well." Then he leaned close and whispered in her ear. "Although if you haven't had *that* talk with her, now might be the time."

Fiona almost boxed his ears. Mairead was patting Chuffy on the head like a precocious child. Chuffy was chuckling. Lady Bea patted them both on the arm. And suddenly Fiona was worried that Mairead might be more at risk than she'd feared.

"'From sullen earth, sings at heaven's gate?'" Lady Bea suddenly asked.

Chuffy blinked. Mairead let go of him and stepped back as if she'd been chastised. Bea beamed at her. "The river flows."

"Oh!" Chuffy said, laughing. "Exactly. Need to get inside. Come along, then. Let's see who's home." And putting out two elbows, he led the ladies up the low steps.

Alex turned back to the carriage where the grooms were setting down Bea's trunk and the coachman sat quietly in his red-banded top hat. "All right, John," he said up to him. "Make a show of picking up ladies on Bruton Street and then off to the North Road with you. I don't want to see any of you in London for at least a week. And if you're stopped, you don't know anything but that you were told to take the ladies to Selby."

Fiona saw a brief flash of teeth beneath the top hat's shadow before the man lifted a finger to it. "Moi pleasure, m'lord. Lads 'n I'll toast y'r good 'ealth in every tavern along the way. We'll take good care o' Minnie an' Poppy."

Alex nodded. "All right, then. You've dealt with this lot before. Have a care."

Fiona waited for the carriage to pass before Alex noticed her. "I'm sorry," he said, stepping up. "I thought you'd followed the rest of them."

She wrapped her arm around the little pillow. "I just wanted to say thank you for going to all this trouble. I know it wasn't easy, especially in such a short time."

For a moment Alex just looked down at her, his bittersweet brown eyes near black, his forehead pursed. But the mood seemed to quickly pass.

He held out an elbow. "Don't think of it," he said, smiling down at her as she laid her hand on his arm. "Chuffy lives for things like this. It really is too bad he couldn't join up. He would have been a brilliant quartermaster. I should warn you, though. The staff is new to the house. They are all members of our group."

She looked over toward the somnolent house. "Rakes?"

"After a manner. One of our members, Diccan Hilliard, recruited a group of servants and waitstaff who took to calling themselves Diccan's Household Army. They are placed in some very high-level homes and have brought some of the best information we've received."

She nodded, thinking of the servants she'd known and their infallible grapevine. "I can imagine."

"The only person we're missing is their ringleader. Woman named Barbara Schroeder. I understand she's on another assignment."

Fiona was staring. "Schroeder?" she echoed. "But our headmistress at Last Chance was..."

He grinned down at her. "Barbara Schroeder. Amazing

woman, isn't she? I couldn't think of anybody better to take over when we tossed out that martinet who had been in charge."

"Miss Chase," Fiona said, shaking her head. "I don't believe it. I'm amazed Miss Schroeder allows herself to work as a domestic. We always thought she came to us from a German riding academy. She's a whiz on a horse."

Alex chuckled. "It would have been more likely that Diccan met her at a dance hall. Great…er, well…"

It was Fiona's turn to chuckle. "She's a beautiful woman. I'm sorry we couldn't meet again."

"I'm sorry as well," he said. "No one else knows you are here. It means you won't be able to go outside except to the small walled garden in the back. No one can even suspect."

She nodded thoughtfully. "Then please remind Chuffy to impress upon the staff that they are not to mention Slough."

Alex frowned. "But we're not in Slough. We're near Burnham."

Fiona chuckled, even with her pounding head. "Mairead knows the geography of Berkshire like her prayers. We are no more than three miles away."

"It's so important?" Alex asked.

"If you want her to stay here it is. As you might remember, Last Chance Academy is no more than a few miles west of here. The reason they asked Mae to leave there was that she kept running away."

"To Slough? Why?"

"Because that is where William and Caroline Hershel live."

"The astronomers?" They'd come to a halt just outside the door.

She nodded. "With all of their telescopes. Mae considers them minor deities. One of the only ways I could get her away from Hawesworth was to promise we would move closer to where they lived. She yearns to simply sit at Caroline's feet and let brilliance drip onto her head like nurturing rain."

Alex shook his head. "I had no idea. You don't have any more surprises like that in store for us, do you?"

She frowned and looked to the door, but Lennie was gone, probably hiding somewhere. "Actually..."

Alex dropped his head. "I knew it. You're actually frauds. Actresses sent to bedevil us. Spies for Prinny. Spies for our mothers."

She wanted to grin. "We are nothing of the kind. In fact, we aren't the surprise. Lennie is."

He frankly stared. "Lennie?"

"Yes. Lennie will not be sleeping in the stable with the lads."

"Why?"

Finally she found a smile. "Because Lennie's name is really Adeline. She's a girl."

Alex gaped. "A...How did you know?"

That actually made her laugh. "Don't be silly. Mairead and I disguised ourselves as boys for years. It was far safer on the streets. Lennie doesn't know it yet, but she will not return there. I won't allow it."

He nodded, still wide-eyed. "Of course."

They turned back to the house. "How did I miss that?" he muttered.

"Don't feel bad," she said, waiting as he held the door for her. "I would never have guessed if I hadn't used the same tricks. Big hat, bigger clothes, exaggerated swagger."

"Did she tell you how old she actually is?"

"Twelve. That is why I will keep her. Twelve is a danger-ous age. Her disguise won't hold out much longer."

She didn't know how she would afford another mouth to feed, especially after the fire, but that didn't matter. She would not leave another child to the despair of the streets.

Alex still stood in the door staring at her. "Does she need a dress or...something?"

Fiona found herself really grinning. He looked so sud-denly uncomfortable. "No. Until we sort out this business, I would rather she protect her disguise. I just wanted you to know."

He nodded. "You sure there aren't any other surprises I should know about? Pets hidden in bandboxes, jealous beaus following on horseback?"

Fiona's heart lurched. Yes. There were surprises. But not the kind that could be shared in an entry hall full of wit-nesses.

"No beaus," she said, stepping past him. "No pets."

"Excellent. Then I can manage an hour or two of sleep before I must head out again. Shall I show you to your room? You can meet the staff after you've had a rest."

She looked around in surprise to see that they were the last ones in the entry. There were only three night candles on the drop table by the ornate wooden staircase to light the way, even though the dawn had begun to seep through the windows beyond.

"How do you know where I'm going?"

He grinned. "Chuffy assigned your suite first."

Handing off a candle, he laid his hand against her lower back, setting off a fresh shower of chills. Fiona was so tired. She couldn't remember the last time she had actually been nauseated with exhaustion, and the headache she had been brewing in the coach was setting in. She should want nothing but to become horizontal on a bed. A couch. The floor. Whatever she could find.

But she didn't. She wanted more time with Alex. She wanted the warm strength of his hand against her back and the encouragement of his smile before her. She wanted to talk with him and listen to him and just sit with him.

Which meant she should send him off as fast as she could.

"Will you be all right?" he asked, opening the door into the sitting room she and Mae would share.

"I'll be—"

"Fee?" she heard behind her. "Fee, do you have it? I can't sleep."

And there, just as she should have expected, stood Mairead, rocking from one foot to the next, her arms wrapped around her waist. Fiona found she could still smile.

"Here, sweetings," she said, handing over the pillow. "I have it. Now get into bed before your feet get cold. I'll be in to make sure you're settled as soon as I talk to Alex."

But Mae didn't move. She just leaned a bit to see out the salon window.

Fiona fought a rush of impatience. "Night will come no faster by your looking for it, Mae. Get some rest now."

Mae's smile was halfhearted. "I'm not certain I can."

Fiona kissed her cheek. "Work on your word puzzle in your head."

Mae shook her head. "I am stumped. I will work on Mr. Gauss's geometric equations instead."

"In your head. While you're horizontal."

With a shy bob of the head to Alex, Mae spun around, trotted into the bedroom, and closed the door. Fiona turned around to see the bemused frown on Alex's face.

"Do you mind my asking?" he said. "The pillow seems important."

Fiona took one last look back, as if she could see it, and then faced Alex.

He returned her gaze and she hesitated, the easy words lost in the expression in his eyes. Pity? No. Sympathy? Not really. What, then?

"It's quite simple, really," she said. "Our mother stitched it. A thistle to remind us of our heritage. It is the only memory of her we have been able to hold on to." She shrugged. "A bit of a talisman, really."

He looked back toward the door, then to her. "Nothing else?"

"Our red hair." She grinned. "And our height. Drove grandfather mad."

He was nodding absently, as if it all made sense when she knew it couldn't.

As long as he didn't pity them.

"We came away from Edinburgh with a lot more than most," she insisted.

That, finally, ignited a smile. "Yes, you did. Now, the only thing you have to do is rest. There is the telescope and a fully stocked library if you have need of occupation."

"And you?"

He scrubbed at his hair. "I will have to go out," he said. "I have some business to attend to. And I'll be taking Lennie."

Fiona frowned. "You will ensure her safety?"

"As well as I can. Chuffy will stay, and Finney is supplying armed guards. You will be perfectly safe here."

All she could do was nod. She still felt so stiff and uncomfortable, suddenly, knowing he was about to walk away. Her hands were clenched again at her sides to keep them out of trouble, her breathing measured so that she didn't inhale his scent. He was nothing special. Just a man. Taller than she, good-looking, but so were many men. So he had eyes the color of bitter chocolate. So he had a dimple in his left cheek and a scar on his forehead. So he could move like a fencer and kiss like a rogue. It shouldn't be enough to make her dumb and nervous. But she felt dumb and nervous. She felt as if she were watching him deliberately walk away. And after last evening, it seemed a betrayal.

"Are you all right, Fiona? Do you need anything before I go?"

She looked up at him in astonishment. Her body all but seized with sudden longing. Did she *need* anything? She needed to be back in his arms, where it was safe. Where she felt free and alive. She needed the heat of his mouth, the sure balance of his hands. She needed...

"Nothing. I'm fine. Will we see you tomorrow?"

She could see a flush creep up his neck, as if she were disconcerting him. Selfishly, she hoped so. At least a little bit.

"I might be back tonight. I'll be sure to check at the telescope for you."

Again silence fell, thick and elastic. Fiona wanted him gone now, before she humiliated herself again. She went as far as to take hold of the doorknob, when she swore she heard growling. She looked around. She looked back. There was something different about Alex's eyes. Something...fierce. She froze.

"Oh, damn it!" he snapped and grabbed her.

She got out no more than a squeak of surprise before she was in his arms being kissed. Being ravished, his hands roaming, his arms surrounding her. And his mouth. Oh, his mouth, soft, strong, ferocious, easing hers open and invading with his tongue. She couldn't believe it. She couldn't breathe. She couldn't think, only feel, as showers of chills raced through her and sapped the strength from her knees. She lifted her own hands and wove them through his lovely thick hair. She met his tongue with hers in a sinuous dance, relishing the sleek texture, the bold invasion, the tastes that lingered between them. She was gasping, holding on for dear life, struggling to breathe when she was crushed up against his chest, her breasts fairly flattened.

She had just really settled into a rhythm, just felt as if she could easily sink into oblivion on his kiss, her heart slamming against her ribs and her belly on fire, when she heard it. Faint, thin, fretful.

"Fee!"

This time Fiona was the one to pull away. Her body screamed in denial. Her chest felt as if it were bound. She fought to find her feet again and then her knees.

And then she saw his eyes. Shocked again. Regretful, even when they were still nearly black with desire.

"Fiona."

"Do not even think it," she snapped. Then, with a shove at his chest that unbalanced him just enough, she slammed the door.

She went in to see about Mairead. But before she did, she paused a moment, just for herself. And she smiled. And for the first time in a long while, she meant it.

*   *   *

She could smell onions. Onions and cabbage and sewers. It was dark. It was always dark. Dark and damp, the walls constantly dripping. She was so tired, her feet aching and her back worse. She had been bent over a desk all day and up on Calton Hill the night before watching stars. It was a silly thing to do, really, especially considering how hard they worked during the day, but not two weeks earlier Mr. Playfair had revealed the most marvelous surprise. Like a conjurer, using a telescope for a wand, he had pulled away the black velvet of night to show her a mystery. A miracle. What he called a nebula—right there dangling off of Orion's belt, a boiling, light-studded cloud limned in starlight. A remnant, maybe, of blasted stars or the embryo of a new planet. Creation soup, bubbling away out there in the endless dark.

She had fallen hopelessly in love. With the telescope, with the sky, so silent, so sure. So pristine and precise when the world around her was anything but. She carried the images back down the hill with her and along the cobbles of Holyrood Road as she and Mae trudged back to the vaults under South Bridge, where they were living, pausing only to collect the lumps of coal that had fallen from passing carts.

Mr. McMurray, for whom they worked in the oculist shop, would have tried to house them if he'd known. But Mr. McMurray had no room and less money, what with his sick wife and their half-dozen bairns. So Fiona let him believe that she and Mae still lived in their midlevel apartment on Borthwick's Close. And he let Fiona do his books and Mae learn to grind lenses. Even at her age, he said she had a talent for it.

As for Mae, she had found heaven. Now that she knew what filled the dark sky, she could think of nothing else. Her lessons, her work, her dreams all revolved around the day she would grind lenses for her own telescopes. She would be so good William Herschel himself would ask her to help him build telescopes.

But that was no more than a dream. For tonight they had to eke out a dinner from root vegetables and stale bread. Fiona retrieved the candle stub she left in a crack between stones and pulled out her tinderbox. The sound of the scrape was loud in the gloom. She hoped Mae was tucked back in

*their vault with her candle and the mathematics book Mr.
Playfair had lent her. Fiona hated to leave Mae here, where
she only had Mrs. Gordon in the next vault to watch out for
her. But Fiona refused to take Mae to her second job. Mae
would never understand; it would frighten her.*

*Lifting her candle, Fiona began to weave her way
through the darkness. She didn't call out to Mae as she crept
through the rooms. If Mae had her nose in a book, she would
never hear her, hopefully long lost in the galaxies.*

*"No...don't...Fee...Fee, please..." Fiona stopped.
Mairead sounded wrong.*

*Then she heard a sound that chilled her to her soul. "Fee
isn't here now."*

*The voice was low and raspy, a bit breathless. Fiona's
mouth went dry. Her heart started hammering against her
ribs. Where was Mrs. Gordon? How could no one hear this?*

*Blowing out her candle, she bent to drop her pitiful pile of
coal and food on the ground. Then, her eyes acclimating to
the dark, she crept forward, praying she wouldn't alert him.*

*There was the sound of a rip, then a slap. Mae cried
out. The time for stealth was past. Frantic, furious, Fiona let
loose a wild, echoing Highlander's cry and charged into the
dark.*

He turned around.

Fiona lurched upright in her bed, gasping for air. It was
light out, not dark. It was warm and soft and comfortable.
She hadn't slept on cobbles in a long time. Still she couldn't
stop shaking, suddenly cold again, swamped in despair. It
seemed that soft beds and full bellies weren't protection
against old nightmares.

Bending up her knees, she rested her forehead on them,
willing her heart to ease, the panic to recede back down her
throat.

"Fee?"

Fiona jumped, the hesitant sound so like her dream that for just an instant, she wasn't sure.

"Yes, Mae?"

Mairead pushed open the bedroom door and stepped in. She was still in her nightclothes, her braid coming loose, her face soft with sleep. She was so beautiful, even mussed and rumpled and half-awake, the pillow wrapped in her arm. Fiona knew better than anyone how lovely Mae was, and yet every so often, it startled her all over again.

"Are you all right?" Mairead asked, looking afraid.

Fee held out her arms, and Mairead came to sit on the bed for a hug. "Everything's fine. I just had an old dream."

She knew perfectly well why, too. She had taken too large a step, started to believe that with Alex she could be different. She could be more. That she deserved the comfort of his arms, his smile, his strength.

He had tempted her with the possibility of life. Of hope. Of that most seductive of concepts, a normal life. And for a moment, she had believed.

"We're safe now, though, Fee," Mairead insisted, peering at Fiona as if she could see the truth. "Aren't we?"

Fiona didn't think so. Not really. But she couldn't tell Mae that. "We are," she assured her sister. "The nightmares are over, sweetings."

Oh, God, she prayed as she gave her sister another hug. *Let that be true.*

Chapter 13

The address was unimpressive, a town house on Half Moon Street that contained a rising gambling hell on the ground floor and rented rooms above. Alex stood in the street a moment, assessing egress and exit, possible escape routes and dark corners. Half Moon Street passed directly from Curzon to bustling Piccadilly, without any alleys to separate the houses. Weams's building was only three houses from Piccadilly and Green Park beyond, where there would be room to run.

"All right, then," he said and turned to where Lennie stood in that odd, rumpled top hat of hers. "I want you to stay right here."

"Stay here?" the girl echoed in tones of high dudgeon. "What f'r?"

"Because I know Weams, and I told Lady Fiona I would not put you in danger."

The girl snorted in derision. "Then why'd ya bring me at all?"

Alex fought hard not to grin. "I brought you to recognize people you might have seen with Weams. Other compatriots, victims. You see any, you whistle. When I'm finished, we'll go on to the Blue Goose and try again."

Still the girl wasn't appeased. "How ya gonna dub the jigger, then?"

Alex did smile then, understanding the cant. "Get inside? Easy. I brought the locksmith's daughter."

He brought a set of picks he could use in his sleep after his time with the Rakes.

Alex was sure the child wasn't appeased, but she did at least resign herself to pacing the walk as if waiting for horses to hold. Giving her a nod, Alex went inside. He had letters and identities to retrieve. Since Weams didn't have the intellect or cunning to pull off blackmail like this, someone had set him loose. History suggested the Lions.

The first two flights of stairs were fairly elegant, with runners and wall lanterns lighting the way. The third set, though, showed the diminishment of rank and fortune. The walls were dingier, the wood bare and narrow. Old servants' quarters, Alex guessed. Running up on almost-silent feet, he reached Weams's door without any alarms and pulled out the picks.

He did knock first, just in case. When he got no answer, he made quick work of the door and slipped inside.

They were typical bachelor's rooms, heavy on hunting prints and strewn in the detritus of a careless life: wine bottles, racing forms, toppled boots, and a snowfall of yanked-off cravats littering the furniture. Whoever cleaned up after Weams should be sacked immediately.

Something about the place sent the hair up on the back of Alex's neck. A sense of disquiet, as if he had just barely missed something or someone, their movement still unsettling the air. There was no place to hide in the sitting room. Hand poised to retrieve the knife in his sleeve, Alex pushed the bedroom door gently open.

The first thing he saw was that the window was wide open. So he'd been right. The room wasn't cold yet, so it couldn't have been open long. Scanning the empty room for surprises, he strode past the bed to look out, but there was nothing to see. Three stories of brick wall down to an untidy garden that opened onto the next street. A brave escape, if that was how the previous tenant had gone. There was nothing to grab on that wall but corner bricks and window casements.

Pulling his head back into the bedroom, he made a more careful assessment. The space bore a striking resemblance to the sitting room, tossed in apparel and generally rumpled. Stale and sad, with no more than the bed, a night table, and a worn wardrobe occupying the floor.

Then Alex saw the open portmanteau on the bed and felt that chill of prescience grow. The case was only half-filled, shirt and shaving kit untidily shoved in, as if the man was anxious to pack up and get away.

Now, why would someone stop packing when it seemed a matter of urgency? Alex was about to search the room for any clues when he heard a high, shrill whistle. Spinning around, he ran for the hall door.

Lennie was already halfway up the stairs. "Gov, quick. I jus' saw Weams's valley. 'e recognized me and bolted straight through out the back door."

Weams's valet? "You're sure?"

"Yeah. 'e's as big a weasel as 'is nibs."

Lennie ran past Alex into the apartment and straight through to the bedroom window. "There! Running toward Shepherd Market."

Alex saw a portly, balding man weaving through the back garden. "Stay here," he snapped.

"You'll never catch 'im," Lennie protested, bending out the window.

Alex set her aside. "Yes, I will." And before Lennie could protest, he swung out the window.

Oh, hell. Those handholds didn't look any larger, now that it was his turn to use them.

"Lor', lumme," Alex heard above him as he shimmied down the three stories as quickly as he could using those slick window casings and corner bricks. The minute his feet reached the grass of the back garden, he took off after the lumbering valet, who looked just as rumpled and unkempt as those rooms.

Fortunately, the man was in no shape to escape. Alex caught up with him halfway down Shepherd Market, puffing like Tevithick's little steam engine and sweating as if it had been high summer.

"Here." Alex grabbed the man's arm. "You'll have a heart seizure. Slow down."

The man made one attempt to pull away. It was no contest. "I got...nuthin'...to say."

"Of course you do," Alex said easily. "You just have to have enough wind to say it. Now come along. I imagine Weams has a fair supply of spirits up there. We'll share a tot, and you can tell me everything you know."

The man's head whipped up, eyes hard and thick lips twisted even as he gasped for air. "Scarpered, has he? Might a' known. Sodding bastard."

Alex shored him up and turned him back. "I understand you are his valet."

The man shrugged. "Quit a sennight ago. Was coming to try to squeeze last month's wages out of the rum-touch."

"Well, I'll tell you what," Alex suggested as he guided him back up the garden. "You tell me what I need to know, and I'll pay your back wages. I'd give you a reference, but I've seen that apartment."

The man needed only a moment to think about it. "Best offer I'll get."

Alex dragged the valet, one Millard Bixby, up to the apartment, where they found Lennie perched on the gray settee in the sitting room, feet swinging off the ground, nose in the latest racing sheets. Alex again had the urge to look around, make sure Lennie was safe. He simply couldn't shake that sense of unease.

He sat the valet in a chair. "I was going to ask if you were still all right, Lennie, but I see you're gainfully occupied."

Lennie grinned up at him. "Fancy a flutter, gov? Seems they're givin' good odds on Playmaker in the fifth at Doncaster."

"Put that paper down, you repellent brat."

Lennie complied. "How are ya, Mr. Bixby?"

Mr. Bixby did not yet have the air to answer. Alex poured two brandies from the depleted drinks table. "And no, Lennie. You don't get one. Now, go back down and keep watch. If you see anything suspicious, whistle, just like before. That was brilliant."

"How 'bout I wait in the hall?" Lennie asked. "Cold as a whore's heart out there."

Looking at the impish child jump off the settee, Alex found himself freshly disconcerted. Not by the child's preternaturally mature behavior. By his own blithe disregard for the child's safety in dragging her into this. Oh, Thrasher had been this old when Lady Kate had found him. But somehow, this child was different. More innocent, more vulnerable, hidden away within an oversized disguise and a memorable top hat, only her sudden, whimsical smile and good grammar betraying her.

Had Fiona had a top hat to hide beneath? How had she disguised that flame-bright hair and unforgettable face? How had she protected Mairead? Suddenly it was important to know. It was important to protect this child from the streets since he had never had the chance to protect the other one.

Alex waited until Lennie stepped outside before turning to the much pinker Mr. Bixby. "Now, then," he said, handing off the alcohol. "Do you have any idea where Mr. Weams is? His suitcase is open in his room, but there is no evidence of him."

Bixby's head came up, and he was frowning. "That's not like him. If he was running, nothing would have stopped him. Strong sense of self-preservation, that one."

"Would he have climbed out the bedroom window if he heard me coming?"

The valet laughed. "Not if God himself were chasin' him."

That was what Alex was afraid of.

"Well, then maybe we'll get a chance to see him yet." Crossing his legs, Alex settled back and deliberately sipped, as if he had all the time in the world. "In the meantime, I would like you to tell me where he hides things. False drawer bottoms, trunk bottoms, a slit in his mattress."

Bixby had trouble facing Alex. "I don't know anything. Why would I?"

"Because you simply aren't the kind of man to leave anything to chance. Like maybe loose change that might make up for not getting paid in a month?"

He snorted. "There's no money here."

Alex cocked an eyebrow. "Then what would you have

returned for? I don't see any silver or artwork worth the effort."

Silence. Alex noticed that Bixby's hand trembled.

"Let me make an educated guess. You have helped Mr. Weams blackmail people. And like any good blackmailer, Mr. Weams has kept some of the evidence close by in case he needs to run. Can't expect an unpaid body to pass up a chance at it himself."

Now Bixby was sweating. "You can't prove that."

Alex offered a smile that had struck fear into the hearts of lesser men than Bixby. "But I don't have to. This has become a matter of national security. I can make you disappear, and no one will take notice. *No* one."

He took another sip. Bixby's eyes darted around, unintentionally targeting at least one hiding place. Then he made the mistake of meeting Alex's implacable gaze again and folded like a lady's fan.

"You have it right. He's squeezed dukes to moneylenders. But he doesn't always get money. Papers, sometimes. Favors. At least that's what he says. Sometimes I don't know what he gets. He just passes it along somewheres. I do know he's stone-cold feared of whoever *that* is."

Alex got up to search the room as if his heart weren't suddenly pounding. "Have you heard any reference to the Lions?"

Bent over the empty bottom desk drawer, it took him a minute to notice the silence. When he finally looked up it was to see a paralyzed Bixby. The man honestly looked as if the Lions would storm through the door any moment and slaughter him.

Alex straightened. "I assume that is a yes. What do you know?"

But Bixby remained silent. Alex was patient. He went

back to the drawers. "Empty," he pronounced, shoving the last one shut.

Bixby laughed. "Somebody wasted their time emptying that lot. Nothin' but bills and markers."

With one last considering look at Alex, the valet lurched to his feet and waddled over to one of the hunting prints. Lifting it off the wall, he exposed a small wall safe. Alex felt the back of his neck prickle again.

"He keeps most of it here," the valet said. "He always said he had proof against people if somethin' happened."

"Something did happen," Alex said. "Me."

Bixby got a crafty look in his eyes. "What's the combination worth?"

"Continued mobility. Open the safe."

It was a treasure trove. No money, just as Bixby said. A neat stack of papers, letters, account books, and one beautifully chased gold locket the size of a guinea on a chain. When Alex picked it up, he froze. The gold was inscribed with a Tudor rose. Alex had seen the design before, on items relating to the Lions.

Hoping his hands weren't shaking, he pried the locket open. Another jackpot. A thin strip of paper with that too-familiar grouping of letters. And beneath it... Alex sucked in a breath. The inside of the locket was inscribed with a line from that damn poem Chuffy was trying so hard to pull apart in hopes of finding a cipher key:

Three times thryce I begged of you

Alex almost cursed out loud.

"Where did he get this?" Alex asked, holding it up.

Bixby shrugged. "Think he was helping to clean up a mess somebody made that had to do with the people who hired him. Might've gotten light-fingered. All I know is that he brought it home and stuck it right up there, even though he was three months behind on rent and five on payin' me."

The insurance, Alex assumed. Alex had to get this back to Drake. They had to go through all of the stash from the safe.

Alex squeezed his eyes shut. *His father.* The only way to tell Drake was to reveal the truth about the letters.

Had he run out of time? Would he have to turn evidence in, even if it meant compromising the man he respected and loved most in the world?

He had to get to his father. He needed to talk to him first, no matter what it cost. Closing the watch, he slipped it into his coat and reached into the safe for the rest of the papers. He saw only one letter in Amabelle's handwriting. Just one. *Another teaser*, he thought, bleakly. Another chance to disgrace Sir Joseph or turn traitor himself.

Or play the Lions against themselves. Couldn't he pretend he was submitting? The Rakes had tried it before without luck. Maybe it was time to try again.

"Is that enough?" Bixby asked.

Alex lifted the letter on its watermarked lavender stationery. "Do you know anything about this?"

Bixby grinned. "Musta got another one. Sent out the last one right before I left. Opened it and laughed himself sick. Said as how this would serve some toplofty dandiprat right. Couldn't wait to send it."

Alex knew he should wait until he was alone. He couldn't. Slipping his thumb under the wax, he cracked the seal and opened the packet. Another indicting letter from Amabelle to Geoffrey Smythe-Smithe. Another of his father's letters inside, this with information about the Russian compact. Another plain white note folded in the middle.

We know you won't say no. It's time. We've watched you take
good care of the girls. Now it is our turn. Let us have them and
we will leave Sir Joseph in peace. We will contact you.

Alex thought his chest would explode. Fiona. Sweet God, what had he done? Had he inadvertently led the Lions right to her? He had to get back to her. He had to make sure his father was safe first. He needed to speak with him, or no amount of caution would do any good. And somehow he had to find Weams and shut him up.

"Is this all?" he asked, making sure the safe was empty.

Bixby shifted uneasily. "I don't know. Mr. Weams wasn't smart enough to hide his secrets all over. Would have lost 'em. Has a secret drawer at the top of his wardrobe."

Alex looked up. "Let's go look."

Preceding Alex into the bedroom, Bixby stepped up to the wardrobe and pulled on the doors. They moved a bit and creaked, but failed to open, as if the catch were stuck. He frowned and pulled harder. This time the latch gave way with a snap and the doors slammed open, pushing Bixby back on his bottom, just as the dead and very blue body of his employer came spilling out of the wardrobe onto the floor at his feet.

Bixby screamed. Alex cursed. Well, at least he didn't need to worry about Weams talking.

Chapter 14

In the end, they left Weams where he was, the garrote still around his neck. It was the only thing they could do if they didn't want to become embroiled in questions they couldn't answer. Alex did take the time to check the body over for anything pertinent. Another scrap of paper, an address. The Lion manifesto that would save them all the trouble of investigating other aristocrats and could get him back to Fiona and his father sooner.

He didn't find anything, of course. Not on the body, which Alex suspected had already been searched, not in the secret drawer in the wardrobe, not anywhere else in the rooms. It went against every instinct, but he ushered Lennie and Bixby out the door and relocked it, as if they'd never been there. And then he went home.

Well, he went home after depositing Bixby in a room at an inn down by the docks to be close to leaving ships for when they finished grilling him. Then he guided his curricle back to Grosvenor Square. It was time to talk to his father.

"I cannot wake him, sir," Sweet, his father's valet, said.

"Cannot or will not, Sweet?" Alex asked, his patience paper-thin. "There is an important difference."

He would have been far more upset if he didn't know that Sweet would literally lay down his life for the man who had bought his freedom from a Georgia planter. A fussy little negro with frizzy gray hair and a permanent stoop, he was more mother hen than all of Alex's governesses combined. "He won't admit it, suh," he said in his molasses-slow drawl. "But he's worn himself to a shade. Can't stop him from waitin' on the gub'ment types. You know him. He don' want to disappoint nobody."

Alex rubbed at the headache that was blooming behind his eyes. "Should we ban those gentlemen from the house, Sweet?"

The little man had a wry smile. "You gonna tell 'im, suh?"

Alex suddenly felt exhausted. He couldn't ask his father about the letters. He couldn't go to Drake until he did. He couldn't protect Fiona until he cleared his own mess up. And somehow he had to convince his father to hand off his responsibilities for a while. And that all had to be handled before he even thought of what he felt for Fiona and what that meant.

Then it occurred to him. The man who had threatened Alex about his father's letters was dead. How could Alex know his father was safe? How could he leave him behind with no more than his house staff to protect him?

He was still rubbing his eyes when Soames approached. "Excuse me, sir. There was a note left for you. From a gentleman Sir Joseph contacted."

Bugger it all. The runner. Didn't that just put the icing on the cake? Alex didn't say a word as he collected the slip of paper.

Have answers. At your disposal.

He pulled out his watch, which did nothing but remind him of the locket he had in his other pocket. All of the papers and books he hadn't had a chance to peruse yet.

The threat to Fiona and Mairead.

"I have some messages to send, Soames."

* * *

If she had been there for any other reason, Fiona would have been completely charmed by Chuffy Wilde's house, with the wainscoted hallways that meandered up and down any number of staircases, the mullioned glass windows, and the flagstone floors. Even the garden out back was dear, a hodgepodge of paths and hibernating fountains to enrich what Fiona suspected was a quintessential English garden.

She so wished she could see it in high summer, with its lavender and hollyhocks and daisies, its marigolds and lupin and foxglove, crowded about one another like debs at a season squeeze. Now it was cold and silent and spare, the gardeners efficient in their work. The bees were asleep and the birds flown, except for a few raspy crows, and the little cement benches seeped cold through her clothing.

She was still so tired. The nightmare had effectively killed any hope of sleep. She felt restless and impatient, as if she were holding her breath. As if the world around her were holding its breath, waiting for some upheaval.

Nobody else seemed to notice it. Fiona could see Lady Bea sitting in the lady's salon, with its hand-painted wallpaper that ran riot with violets and pansies and primrose, its overstuffed chintz sofas and cheerful fire, a piece of embroidery in her hands covered in black-and-yellow bumblebees. The old woman was humming to herself, her head rocking a bit, as if she were hearing the music in her head, and the afternoon light gleamed in her silver hair.

Fiona knew that Mairead had sought out Chuffy, ostensibly to discuss the telescope. Fiona had seen them outside no more than an hour earlier, measuring angles and checking skycharts. Fiona looked up to see clouds scudding in from the west. If those did not clear by sunset, it would be a very long evening indeed.

If Alex didn't return tonight, she wasn't certain how she would sleep. But if he did, she wasn't at all certain she wanted to. She unconsciously ran her forefinger across her lower lip, as if she could re-create the delicious texture of Alex's kiss that morning. As if she could call him up to continue it. To expand on it, until her breasts ached and her knees lost their support. Until, just for a few moments, she could rest within a strong pare of arms.

She closed her eyes briefly and relived that moment. That sharp, hard kiss that betrayed so much more than Alex had thought it did.

She had so few dreams left. Her future was written, a place where she would spend her days creating a safe haven from which Mairead could set her stars to dancing. Even her brother's return could not change that. Ian loved them; Fiona knew that. He would do his best to help. But Ian had never had to deal with Mairead. He wouldn't know how to calm her furies and soothe her fears. Soon he would have a family of his own to shepherd, his attention captured by growing children and an ascent to the highest ranks of the aristocracy. His sisters, long since strangers, would drift into the background once more.

And never again would anyone hold her the way Alex had, just for a moment, imparting strength and warmth and understanding, his body wrapped around hers, offering sanctuary. Life. Promise. Alex hadn't meant to; she knew that, too. But with that one act, he had done for her body what he'd long since done for her poor heart: woken it to astonishing and painful life.

She knew she should avoid him. Refuse his touch, his embrace. The nerve-sapping wonder of his kisses. She needed to protect herself just as much as she ever did from wanting too much. From expecting too much.

Couldn't she just once think only of herself, though? Couldn't she take this brief moment and fulfill one dream? He wouldn't love her, not the way she wanted. He couldn't. But would it be so awful to ask him to pretend, for no more than a night, that she was just like him? That she had been raised in a country estate, just as he had, with servants and kind parents and a lock for the front door? That she had a right to feel love, respect, friendship? That she deserved his love?

She sat where she was for a long time, the cold seeping into her bones, her throat clogged with tears she refused to let fall, her chest hot with grief for what would never be. For what she had never allowed herself to want until Alex had knocked on the front door of her school.

Her school, which was gone, too. She didn't have the money to fix it, and she had nowhere else to take it. She and Mairead would have to start again.

If it weren't for Mairead, Fiona would have gotten up from the bench and just started walking. If it weren't for Mairead, she would have had no past and no purpose. If not for Mairead, she would have been alone.

As if she had called her sister to her, Fee suddenly realized that she had been hearing Mairead's voice for the last few minutes, and that it was rising. It was when Fiona heard her sister scream, "Fee! Make him stop!!" that she jumped up and ran into the house.

The staff were all caught in a gaggle by the green baize door, as if wary of wild animals. Fiona fought the sharp edge of frustration. Couldn't Mae rest even for a minute? At least it sounded as if Chuffy was giving as good as he got, which stunned her more than Mae Mae's tantrum.

She slammed into the breakfast room to see the two of them faced off in front of a table full of papers and books, red-faced and screaming at each other.

"You don't have any right!" Mairead shrieked at him, all but wringing the skin from her hands, a sure sign of panic. "You don't! You don't, and I won't let you."

"You're the one with no right!" Chuffy yelled, his hands on his hips, his head pushed pugnaciously forward, his glasses completely missing. "How dare you hold valuable information from us? Don't you know what that means?"

"It means it's mine, it's mine, it's *mine*! I solved it, not you. It was my gift, not yours. You can't *have* it!"

Chuffy actually shoved a hand through his hair. "You have to *listen* to me, damn it. Don't you realize that people could die? People *are* dying, and you stand there acting like a petulant child? It's unconscionable!"

It took that long for Fiona to overcome the paralysis of shock. She had never seen Chuffy upset before, but he was impressive. She swore he was several inches taller, staring right into Mairead's wild eyes. And he wasn't backing down, or soothing her rage or apologizing.

Well, good for him.

"Children," she said, stepping into the room and shutting the door. "The staff are beginning to complain. They're afraid that you'll put the cows off their milk."

Both whipped around at her and began to shout at once. Chuffy looked impatient and frustrated. Mae looked panicked. This was something big.

Stepping into the room, Fiona caught hold of Mairead's hands. "We won't get anywhere by screaming at each other." Mae's hands were wet, which meant that she was terrified. Shaking and cold. The first thing Fiona did was meet her sister eye-to-eye and just hold her still. Just ease her away from the brink. "Let us sit and talk, shall we?"

It was as she was settling Mae into one of the chairs that Fiona realized where Chuffy's glasses had gone. He was bending to pick them up from the floor.

"Now," she said, letting go of Mae. "Chuffy. It seems you want something."

Mae bounced up like a jack-in-the-box. "He can't *have* them. Didn't you hear me?"

Fiona stared her down. "The curate down at church heard you, Mae. Now sit down before I take away your right to choose. Because you know I will."

For a long moment Mae stood faced off with her, face red, eyes restless. Just as abruptly she sat. Chuffy shoved his hair into odd little peaks again. Fiona wasn't as surprised anymore that Mae reached over and patted them down.

"The word puzzles Lady Mairead got from her grandfather," he said. "I think they might be important."

Fiona blinked. "Important? Why? They were games. Besides, those are long gone. We've played them for years."

Chuffy turned those puppy-dog eyes at her, and she felt something catch in her chest. Suddenly he reminded her of Alex.

"I believe Miss Mairead still has them," he said. Mairead was stone-faced. Chuffy ignored her. "And I don't think they are games."

He lifted a page with the familiar letters all gathered into groups of four. "This is from the last puzzle she was working on."

"He *stole* it," Mairead protested, wiggling in her seat.

"Copied it down," he said, the mottled red leaching from his face. "Part of it."

"Yes," Fiona said, her hand on Mae's shoulder. "I saw you do it. But why?"

He lifted another paper and handed it to her. "Because it looks like other...puzzles I've been working on. Ciphers."

Fiona's head snapped up, the paper forgotten in her hand. "My grandfather is deeply involved in the government," she said. "Couldn't these be from them?"

Chuffy shook his head. "I don't believe so. The government uses a different method. This—" He pointed to the paper. "This seems to need a cipher key."

"The key doesn't work," Mairead snapped, reaching for the first paper, the one with the copied puzzle on it.

Fiona looked over. "What key?" she asked. "We don't have a key."

Mairead blinked up at her. "This one did. In the watch."

Fee felt her heart stumble and speed up. "What watch, Mae?"

"You're holding that back, too?" Chuffy demanded.

Fiona spun on him and glared. "One thing at a time, please," she said, her voice admirably calm. "That way we have a better chance of getting everything we want."

"No, you won't," Mae retorted, her head down.

Fiona faced her and waited until Mae's head came up. "The watch, Mae Mae."

For a moment, Mae just glared at her, as if Fiona had called her a liar. Then, huffing, she reached into the pocket of her ubiquitous apron and pulled out a beautiful chased gold pocket watch.

Fiona gasped. "My God, Mae. Where did you get that?"

Mae looked at the gleaming case. "Where I found the

puzzle. Two puzzles, really. I solved the other one. Not this one, though. I don't think this is the key."

Gently Chuffy took the watch from her and held it up. "A Tudor rose," he said, pointing to the engraving.

Fiona nodded. "Part of the family crest. The Haweses were very Tudorish."

She didn't miss Chuffy's reaction, a quick, brief frown. He didn't say anything, though. He slid a nail beneath the watch case and snicked it open to reveal more engraving.

"Well, that tears it," Chuffy muttered.

"Non omnis moriar?" Fiona asked. "What does it mean?"

"'Not all of me shall die.' We think it is one of the keys."

Fiona swung around to her sister. "Where did you get that watch, Mae?"

Mairead blinked a couple of times and looked around, as if it would help her find the answer. "The stables. In one of the stalls. I think it fell."

Chuffy closed his eyes and pinched his nose. Fiona felt the weight of Mae's revelations squeeze all the air from her lungs. "What ciphers are you working on, Chuffy?" She lifted the paper. "Why is this important?"

He sighed and looked down at the group of papers he had laid across the table. "We believe they are from a group of traitors."

Fiona couldn't breathe. The implications of his words simply clogged her throat. "Traitors. Lions? You think my grandfather is a *Lion*?"

"I don't know. But we need to find out."

But she wasn't even thinking about that. The true import of what Chuffy was saying hit, and it dropped her to a chair with a plop. "Sweet God. Are you telling me that Mae and I decoded messages for a group that wants to overthrow the throne?"

She looked up, praying Chuffy would smile and say, no, of course not.

He didn't have to say a word. Fiona was truly afraid she would vomit.

She turned back to Mairead. "Do you really have the puzzles, Mae? Still?"

Mae looked down at her hands, and Fee could see they shook. How could she not know if Mairead had kept those puzzles over the years?

"Mae, please."

"No." Fiona recognized her sister's expression. It was implacable. "No. I don't. I lied. I don't have anything but...but *these*." And she swung her hand across the papers on the table.

"Those are mine," Chuffy said.

Fiona could see why he recognized Mae's puzzle. Each piece of paper had the same rows of letters, all separated into groups of four.

"These are ciphers," she said, and waited for his nod. "And the keys?"

Chuffy sighed and ran his fingers across the leather cover of a small book. "Are you sure you want to get involved?"

"I think we already are," she said. "Besides, it will help pass the time while we must remain in quarantine."

Mae was still rocking on her feet. Fiona didn't want to add that if indeed Mae had kept some of their grandfather's puzzles, it couldn't hurt to distract her until she felt more like handing them over. Fortunately, Chuffy seemed to understand.

"I can't seem to find a pattern," he admitted.

Mairead cocked an eyebrow at him. "There is always a pattern."

"Not these," Chuffy said, pulling out a chair for her.

She sat, her attention already on the papers.

If Chuffy had thought all day, he couldn't have found a better way to distract both of them. He was right. There didn't seem to be a pattern. Not one Fiona recognized, anyway. Scooting her chair closer, Fiona pulled a pad of paper over and went to work.

"I am better at seeing patterns," Mae said with pride. "Fee prefers the frequency theory."

"You say the words in the watch might be a key," Fiona said, trying to pick patterns out of the seemingly random letters. "If they don't work, there must be others."

Chuffy was rubbing at his nose as he leaned over the table. "Won't go any further. I know."

"Of course not."

He took the third seat. "Along with these messages, we've intercepted items that had phrases engraved in them. A flask. An embrolio cabochon carnelian. Both carrying a line of an obscure poem."

"You think the key is in those phrases."

He looked up, his eyeglasses flashing in the candlelight. "Exactly." He handed her the book. "In the poem. Underlined. It's an awful poem. Sorry you have to read it."

Fiona saw the title of the book and couldn't help laughing. "*Virtue's Grave: Worshipping at the Altar of Hymen* by William Marshall Hilliard. Oh, dear."

Chuffy blushed like a first-former. "It gets worse."

She opened the book and agreed.

Isn't the first fruit sweet, my love,
When plucked by own hande?
Does not the berry blushes bring to
Every honeybee in the lande.

"Do I have to go on?" she asked, barely able to contain her laughter. A quick skim showed a poet of far more enthusiasm than wit.

"Not out loud," Chuffy assured her, pushing forward his own notebook. "Problem is, the engraved phrases are just a bit different than the poem. 'Is not the fruit sweet, my first love?' See? And another. Poem says 'Not a bit of me shall dye.' The engraving is 'Not all of me shall die.' Means something. Has to."

Well, as she'd said, it was better than pacing the house waiting for the sound of approaching horses. Pulling out the poem, she set to work with Mae and Chuffy.

"My God," she said after a while, smiling on her scribbles. "The devils."

Chuffy was up off his seat. "What?"

"I have a feeling I don't need to tell you about frequency theory, Chuffy. But, see, Es should make up eight percent of the letters. We should see the repetition."

"I don't."

She grinned. "That's because they've simply left out all the Es. I don't think they took out the Ts, since it's harder to re-create words from them. But nothing in any of these equals the number of Es we should be seeing."

Chuffy looked down at all the ciphers and actually cursed. Then he scratched his forehead with the wrong end of the pencil and left a mark.

Mairead began rocking again.

"What do you see, Mae?" Fiona asked.

"Different patterns," her sister said, jabbing at a couple of papers. "Except here and . . . here."

"So those are from the same key."

Mairead nodded and Chuffy separated those two. But Mae began rocking again. Fiona lifted a hand to Chuffy, hoping he would understand and simply wait. This was how Mairead worked best.

"There is a pattern here," she mused, skimming her hand over the papers. "A definite pattern. We just have to name it."

Chuffy smiled as if he had made the discovery himself. "Should have come to you sooner."

"You didn't know us sooner," Fiona retorted, pencil once again in hand.

"I know I would have liked to."

"No, you wouldn't," she instinctively responded, her attention already on the pattern Mairead was beginning to unweave. "We didn't always frequent the most salubrious of environs."

* * *

"A whorehouse, milord," the runner said.

Alex sat down. "A what?"

The runner looked up from his incident book, his wide Irish face wind-chapped and as sorrowful as a hound. "A whorehouse. I had to ask the marquess, ya understand, before I could share the information, like. He didn't consider it so bad the girls found work in an oculist shop, but a whorehouse is a different thing altogether. The marquess said"— here he consulted the page again—"serve the scoundrel right to tie himself to such as her."

Alex's headache was getting worse. If he had ever thought to question the runner's veracity, that would have settled it. He could hear the marquess saying that very thing.

"You're certain," he said, resisting the urge to rub again at his head. "They worked in a bordello."

The runner grinned past a few missing teeth. "Not so

fancy as that, sor. Betty the Badger offered basics, that's all. In and out, if you will."

Now his stomach revolted. "How old were the girls at the time?"

"Girl, sor. Just the oldest, Lady Fiona. Or Red Fee, as they called her, on account o' there bein' another Fiona already workin' there. Dark Fee. Not sure exactly when she started. She'd been there at least a year when the witness remembers a great, swearing soldier come lookin' for her, and she never come back. Didn't talk to Betty, o' course. Died o' the pox years ago, all right. But her daughter remembers. Girl came twice a week like clockwork, Monday and Thursday."

"And this witness saw Lady Fiona take clients."

The runner scowled. "Was but a babe then, Miss Trixie was. Sat in the kitchen with the cook. Saw the girl come and go by the kitchen door. Left with coins janglin'."

Alex fought a wave of pain. He had known that Fee had lived a hard life; Ian had told him. Fiona had told him. But *this*. It was inconceivable that that bright, brave child should have suffered such soul-killing indignities.

"There's…uh, worse, milord," the runner said quietly.

Alex almost shook his head, full to the brim with revelations. "What?"

"It was well known that the two misses used to meet with a group of full-grown men of the evenin's. Fierce anxious to go, they were. A clerk at Mr. McMurray's remembers that specifically. Mr. McMurray only said that the girls ground good glass…whatever that means, now."

It was no longer a surprise that the marquess had treated his granddaughters with such disdain. No matter how Fiona's life went from here, the marquess wouldn't have cared. Her early years would have condemned her in his eyes.

Alex had to get back to her. He had to keep her safe until they could get to the bottom of this. He had to decide how to help her after. If he could help her at all.

"I'm sorry, son," Alex heard, and looked up to see his father.

He almost cried out with shock. Sir Joseph was almost ashen, and he seemed to be out of breath. No wonder Sweet had been protective.

"Sit here, sir," he said, guiding him to the chair. "Mr. Reilly was just about to leave."

Sitting, his father nodded. "I heard. I am so sorry. Poor child."

Alex pulled the bell and asked Soames to show the runner out. Then he held out his hand. "Thank you, Mr. Reilly. You have been most thorough."

"It's sorry I am as well, y'r lordship. Seems a lovely girl and all. It goes no further, o' course."

When the surprisingly agile little man was gone, Alex turned back to his father. "Sir, what are you doing down here? You should be resting."

Sir Joseph smiled. "It bores me. I am fine. Just tired."

"Loath though I am to disagree, sir, you are not." Alex stood, decided. "The government has had enough of you for now. I'll have Sweet pack for you, and you will join us in the country."

"Alex." Sir Joseph was on his feet as well. Alex knew that frown. "I am weary. Not weak-minded. I have told you that I will not succumb to bath chairs and spas. I have commissions to execute here."

Alex straightened, hands on hips. "Well, I hope one of them is to write a letter to your wife that will explain why you preferred to work yourself to death rather than return to her."

For long, tense moments, the two men squared off, each

absolutely certain of his position. In the end, though, it came down to who had more stamina.

With a sigh of frustration, Sir Joseph eased himself back into his chair. "Do not think this is a precedent, boy. I am merely thinking of your mother's anxiety."

Alex managed to keep a straight face. "You're thinking of the peel she'll ring over your head if she finds out how you've been ignoring doctor's orders. I'll notify Sweet." He checked his watch again and fought a fresh wave of urgency. He wanted to leave now. Jump on his horse and ride it to death. But if he left now, his father would find a way to back out of the trip, and Alex knew without a doubt it would kill him before the answers to that letter did.

"What say we leave after dinner?" He snapped his watch closed and considered his father's color. "May I ask, for my own peace of mind, that I have a friend stop by, Michael O'Roarke? Michael is a friend of Lady Kate Lidge's. Brilliant man. Edinburgh and the Peninsula."

"Well, if I'm shot, I'm sure he'll be the first man I'll call."

"Sir," Alex said very quietly. "Please."

His father met his gaze and must have seen how afraid Alex was because his own features relaxed a bit. "Oh, all right. If it will keep you from driving me to distraction. Call him in."

It turned out not to be that easy. O'Roarke was out of town and not due back for another day. Probably better that way, Alex decided. He had a strong suspicion that if Michael took one look at Sir Joseph, he would confine him to the Grosvenor Square house. And Alex needed to get his father someplace safer. So Alex sent Michael a note. Sweet supervised packing, and Alex encouraged his father to rest on the leather sofa in the library with pillows to raise his head as he instructed Alex on what papers to bring.

Alex was snapping his father's satchel when Soames and Sweet returned from their tasks. "I have one more bit of business to take care of before we leave," he told them, ushering them back toward the doorway. "We'll need the traveling coach ready by the time we eat. Is Lennie still in the kitchen eating through our winter's stores?"

Soames begrudged him a rare smile. "All lads are hungry, sir. He'll be fine there. Don't you worry."

"Well, pack him a roast or something for the road. I do not wish to stop."

Alex turned to speak with his father, only to find him sound asleep. He looked relaxed for the first time since he'd been home.

Alex shooed everyone out and swung the door almost closed. "I know you and Sweet will watch over Sir Joseph 'til I get back, Soames." Accepting his overcoat from the butler, he shrugged into it. "Don't forget. If anyone asks, I have taken my father to Bath for the waters. And I mean *anyone*. The only exception is Dr. O'Roarke."

Soames handed off Alex's beaver and cane. "Your father will not be pleased to disappoint His Majesty, Master Alex."

Alex smiled. "I will present my head for washing when he is feeling better. Right now our priority is to get him better."

And safe. All of them safe.

Safe from him.

Chapter 15

Five hours later, Fiona was glad to have something to do. At least it kept Mae from going mad until the sky cleared for the night. If it did. There were pages of notes cluttering the entire table and empty dishes stacked to the sides as they worked to break the code.

"Maybe if you brought down the codes your grandfather gave you, they would help us figure this out," Chuffy suggested, from where he stood with his jacket off and his hair fingered back into uneven peaks.

Fiona glared at him. Mairead began rocking again. "It's not the same. It's not the same at all."

"It isn't," Fiona assured him. She wanted to tell him that he wasn't going to get anywhere with Mairead if he pushed. She wanted to tell him that those puzzles were long lost, but even that might set Mairead off.

So she counted repeated letters and matched them with *T*s, *A*s, and *O*s, the next most frequently used letters after the now missing *E*. There were patterns emerging, except that each message followed a different pattern. In one, the letter that matched the usual frequency for *A*s was an *I*. In another, it was an *L*. In a third, an *M*. But there was something to the pattern. Something that was teasing at her. If only she could get Mae to concentrate, they might recognize the relationship between the different codes.

But Chuffy was right. None of the patterns matched any of the words in the poem. It was more complicated than that.

She had just scratched out the latest possible key word when she heard the rattle of coaches out front. Fiona stopped cold. Alex had ridden away on a horse. Who could this be?

The sound galvanized the house. Chuffy jumped up and gathered all the paperwork. Several large men with shotguns ran from the back of the house, and in the hallway Fiona saw Chilton toss a gun to a footman.

"Kitchen," Chuffy barked, giving Mairead a little push. "With Mrs. Chilton."

"Lady Bea," Fiona protested, running the other way.

She was halfway to the small salon when the front door burst open and she heard the most welcome words she thought she ever could.

"Easy, all, it's only the prodigal son returning."

Alex.

"You almost got yourself shot, old lad," Chuffy said, sounding brusque.

Fiona took a moment to calm her racing heart and shore up her knees before turning around.

"Couldn't exactly sneak up on horseback," Alex said, pushing the door wide. "I have a bit of a surprise."

Fiona reached the front hallway in time to see Alex help his father in the door. She stifled a gasp. His father was so pale and sweaty, and he seemed to be having trouble breathing. She ran forward, as if she could help.

"Here, lads," Alex called as if he were entering a party.

"Form a seat for Sir Joseph, if you will. He'll insist on climbing the stairs, else, and I'll end up throwing him over my shoulder."

"Impertinent...pup," his father growled.

Alex was smiling and stood easy as the two brutes bent as gently as if they were lifting a child and formed a seat for the panting Sir Joseph to get him upstairs. Fiona could see the terrible strain in Alex's shoulders, though, in the eagle eye he kept on his father, the flicker of the muscle at his jaw. She didn't waste her time with prudence or proprieties. Stepping past Chuffy, she clasped Alex's hand.

"I am glad you brought your father," she said. "I think he will rest better here."

She almost cried out herself at the raw anguish in Alex's eyes. "He's too stubborn for his own good," he said, turning his attention back up the stairs.

Before they could say more, they were shoved aside by a very small negro man carrying a large portmanteau, his own anxious gaze on the disappearing Sir Joseph.

"I'm not certain you met Sweet when you were at our home before, Fiona," Alex said. "May I introduce him now?"

The man turned to show a careworn, elderly, chocolate-colored face with eyes of uncanny green. "Oh, my," he sighed, seeing Fiona and then Mairead following in. "A surfeit of beauty heah, no question, Mr. Alex."

"No question at all, Sweet."

Fiona smiled. "A pleasure to meet you, Mr. Sweet. I am certain you would rather be upstairs than conversing here."

The little man bowed and trotted up the steps. Alex was turning to follow him, when Fiona squeezed his hand. "What can we do to help?"

Alex shoved a hand that trembled just a bit through his

hair. "I have a doctor coming. I would appreciate it if no one shot him before he can get in the door. Father also said he was thirsty."

She nodded. "A cup of tea never hurt anyone. I'll see to it."

"Any chance you were followed?" Chuffy asked.

Alex shook his head, his attention up the steps. "We took as much time as we could. But I needed to get father here. He, uh, might be caught up in our business, and I didn't want to leave him behind. It's a good thought, though, Chuffy." He turned to the butler. "Chilton, will you send a few men out to scout the area, just to make sure?"

The butler bowed and disappeared into the back of the house with the rest of the men. Lennie stood perched in the doorway, her face unnaturally pale, her battered hat clutched in her hands, as if not sure where she belonged in all of this.

"Lennie, why don't you help me," Fiona offered. "Alex, I'm sure you'll want to go upstairs."

"Need me?" Chuffy asked.

Alex looked at him, as if weighing something in his head. "If you don't mind."

Chuffy grinned. "Long as he don't chuck books at me."

Alex grinned back. "He didn't bring any. Come on, then."

Fiona was about to usher Lennie back into the kitchen when Mairead stopped her. "What do I do?" she asked.

Fiona looked up the stairs to where Alex and Chuffy were talking in low voices. She thought of the chaos in the kitchen and Mairead's unease around too many people or too much noise.

"Would you tell Lady Bea that the gentlemen are here?" Fiona asked.

Halfway up the stairs, Alex stopped. "Bea," he mused. "Lady Mairead, would you ask if she would sing? Sir Joseph loves her voice."

Fiona blinked in surprise. "Really?" With his nod, she turned back to her sister. "Why don't you ask if you can accompany her."

Mairead bounced a bit on her feet. "It will be dark soon."

"The stars will be up all night, sweetings. And I doubt it will be long before Sir Joseph seeks his sleep."

For a moment Mairead didn't move, as if testing Fiona's word. Fiona never blinked. She didn't want to think that she was getting rid of her sister so she could get back to Alex. But she couldn't deny the relief she felt when Mairead nodded and trotted off toward the lilac salon.

"How did you get along today, Lennie?" she asked as she led the girl through the green baize door.

Lennie looked over her shoulder, as if she could still see Alex. "Oh…tolerable well, I guess. Milord's father's a pretty important toff, isn't he?"

"I would say so, yes."

Lennie just nodded. "Nice bloke, though."

"Very."

She nodded. "Wouldn't want anythin' to happen to him, would we?"

Fiona looked down at the girl. "I imagine we wouldn't. What are you working out, Lennie?"

Lennie looked up with suspiciously innocent blue eyes. "Nuthin'. Just nuthin'."

Which meant that Fiona wouldn't get any answers from the child any time soon.

So she turned her attention back to securing some tea and one of Mrs. Chilton's tisanes for Sir Joseph and getting them back up to the room.

In the end, the ciphers were forgotten for the evening. Fiona walked into Sir Joseph's room and knew she wouldn't leave until Alex did. The older gentleman was sitting straight up, his mouth open to breathe, his forehead damp and pale. Sweet was already squeezing a rag out in the bedside basin to wipe away the perspiration. Alex had his own jacket off and was sitting by the bed holding his father's hand. Fiona walked over to open the door back up. As she did, like a soft breeze lifting through the window, she heard the opening notes of Mozart's "Mein Holdes Leben," a sweet, soaring piece she knew Mae particularly loved.

And then, from the soft piano base, like smoke from a flame, soared a voice so otherworldly that Fiona froze on the spot, not even sure if she was breathing. Not Mae. She knew Mae's voice.

"Ah," she heard from the bed behind her. "Bea...and... Mozart. She...remembered...."

Fiona turned to Alex. "That is Lady *Bea*?"

He smiled. "Amazing, isn't it? Doesn't make sense when she talks, but can sing like a lark."

No, not a lark. Larks weren't that magnificent. Lady Bea's voice sent chills racing down Fiona's spine and made her want to close her eyes, the better to focus on it. She couldn't remember ever hearing such a haunting, compelling sound. Mairead's playing even softened and slowed with it, as if all she had needed to ease her rather martial playing was Lady Bea's voice.

From that moment, Sir Joseph rested better as Mae and Lady Bea moved seamlessly from Mozart to Handel to Clementi, their music easing the darkness and lifting, at least for a while, the weight of Sir Joseph's illness. Sir Joseph's eyes closed. Sweet smiled, and Alex kept his father's hand, his own head cocked, as magic swirled about the room. Even when Fiona walked downstairs to refurbish tea and provide nostrums, she found the house staff clustered at the doors, tears in their eyes, just listening.

And when Sir Joseph finally fell into a fitful sleep, Fiona walked into the music room to find Mae at the old pianoforte, Bea standing alongside her hand on the instrument, as if to inhale its very vibrations through her fingertips, not a page of music anywhere to be seen. And seated calmly on the rose silk settee as if he would be happy never to move again, Chuffy, his spectacles in his hand and tears in his soft brown eyes. Fiona smiled. There were tears in hers as well.

"You two were better than all the medication in the world," she said, bending to give her sister a tight hug, and then Lady Bea, who blushed and stammered at the praise. "Lady Bea, I have never heard the like. And I am used to listening to my sister. Thank you."

"Sir Joseph?" Chuffy asked, finally getting to his feet.

"Is asleep," Fiona assured them. "I believe you are all excused now." When Mae popped up, Fiona kissed her cheek. "Let me know how our stars are, dearest. I am going back upstairs."

And she did, even if she could offer no more than witness to the rare affection the three men in that room had for each other, especially Sir Joseph and Alex, who sat, hour after hour, in silence, the only sounds in the room the crackle of the fire, the faint wheeze of Sir Joseph's breath and the periodic report from the front hall clock.

Fiona, sharing the room and forcing what nutrition she could on Alex, watched the bond the two men shared and knew it was a thing she would always stand apart from. They spoke in a shorthand that revealed commonality, love, understanding, respect. Often, they communicated with simple silence, and she envied them unspeakably. This was not unnatural perfection; there were human foibles betrayed, little sins committed against the other that shaded smiles and gave weight to fears. But the support was mutual, instinctive, and reciprocal. The closest she had to this kind of relationship was with Mairead, and in truth, Fiona knew that there was no balance there. She was the mother. She had no one in turn to rely on.

For a while tears built behind her eyes and clogged her throat. She thought she might actually weep with the loneliness of her place there in the shadows watching real life. In the end, though, the pain of it was too great for tears or envy or regret. It was too great for anything but searing emptiness and silence.

Several times she thought of leaving, tiptoeing out while Alex murmured to his father, knowing he would probably never miss her. But she would only be lonelier, curled in her bed with nothing but an old pillow in her arms, her heart still sitting in the corner of this room. So she stayed, her head resting against the wall, watching. Counting the ticks of the clock as the shadows shifted and the horizon went gray. Wondering if Mairead had begun to teach Chuffy how to worship the sky. Wishing she knew how to break through the boundaries that separated her from people like Sir Joseph and his son. Waiting, because there was nothing else she was good for at the moment.

And then, as the sun began to blanch the horizon and a few birds woke, Alex climbed wearily to his feet. With a look to Sweet, who sat on the other side of the bed, he came around to offer a hand to Fiona.

"Need to stretch a bit?" she asked with a smile as she accepted it.

His hand was cool and dry, as if he were containing life as closely as he could. Standing on stiff legs, Fiona closed her fingers around his as tightly as she could, knowing that any more expression than that would be repelled. He stood behind his own walls now, where he could protect his father and see himself through whatever waited. Even so, Fiona led him out the bedroom door and into the dark, wood-paneled hallway.

"You should probably get some sleep," he said down to her, his eyes completely shaded. "I think we'll be here for a while."

She fought an instinctive flare of pain at his words. She knew he didn't mean to dispense with her. Still, she felt it.

Instead of letting go of his hand, instead of walking away, she stepped closer and smiled. "If I leave I'll only go to the little observatory," she said. "And I have a suspicion Chuffy would not thank me."

Alex cocked an eyebrow. "You're beginning to accept his attachment?"

Fiona shrugged. "I am willing to wait and see."

He nodded, his eyes closing, his hand still caught in hers. She was glad he couldn't see her because for just that moment, she knew she betrayed herself. He would never have missed the emotion in her eyes: the longing, the hunger, the pain. The real reason she would not rest.

"Fiona."

She caught her breath. "Yes."

His eyes opened, and she quailed at the searing pain there. The bleak tide of despair. "How do I tell my mother?" he whispered.

Fiona froze. She had never seen Alex Knight less than certain. Less than in command. She felt as if she were seeing a glimpse of something Alex guarded more jealously than she did her past.

She lifted his hand and wrapped her other around it. "I don't see that there is anything to tell her yet," she said, struggling for assurance in her voice.

He looked down at her, his expression all too clear.

She jabbed a finger at his chest. "Do not dare give up," she challenged. "Did your father say he was ready to die?"

He didn't answer.

Fiona gave a sharp nod. "If Pip were here," she said, "she would box your ears so hard your head would ring. She would not give up simply because your father was exhausted from a ride. *He* would not give up. How dare you?"

There was more; she could see it. Something that colored his grief, that gave it added weight. Something he wasn't telling her. She battled an instinctive feeling of hurt, as if she had a right to all his confidences. As if she deserved, somehow, to help him carry his pain.

Why? Because she loved him? Because she had hopelessly loved him for four years, following his life like a child reading fairy tales? Because from the moment he had kissed her back in that pasture in the rain, he had belonged to her?

"I will not allow you to give up, Alex Knight," she said, as if it were her privilege. "I won't let you consign that lovely man to his grave. Not until he says so. And I do not believe he is quite ready to do that."

For the longest time he just looked down at her, his entire body perfectly still. She wasn't even certain he was breathing. She had hoped to see that she had eased his distress, at least a little. A smile. A nod. Anything. But Alex squeezed his eyes shut, his hands clenched, his head bowed, and Fiona felt his move like a punch in the chest.

She recognized Alex's state all too well. Rage, grief, fear, guilt. The burden of a man who cared. Had there ever been anyone to ease his fears, his furies? He had a wonderful family, she knew. But she had a feeling that like Sir Joseph, he made it his mission to care for all those around him.

If only she could hold him. If only she could wrap her arms around him, her cheek pressed against the hard wall of his chest, and soothe him. If only she could love him.

Suddenly Alex's head came up. Fiona looked up, painfully hoping that he, too, wanted more. That she was the one he would go to for comfort. It was then she heard the approach of a gig up the drive.

The doctor.

Her heart stumbled and righted itself again, suddenly so heavy she thought it might simply fall away. Of course it was the doctor. Before she could react, Alex had let her go and was running for the stairs, leaving her cold and alone in the empty hallway, once again left behind.

She should have left; she knew that. Help had come, and Alex would no longer need her. But when Dr. O'Roarke followed Alex back up the steps, she was still standing there. And when the men walked into Sir Joseph's room, she followed. She wasn't sure why, except that there was nowhere else to go. So she stood in her corner as the doctor introduced himself to the patient and gave instructions to the other men to light lamps.

She was glad she had stayed when the doctor took one look at Sir Joseph and gave a brisk nod.

"Thought so," he said, opening his leather bag and pulling out a hollow wooden tube. "As soon as I examine Sir Joseph, I'll need someone to run down to the kitchen and brew me some tisanes."

Fiona stepped forward. "I would be happy to."

O'Roarke looked up. "Oh, hello," he greeted her, his homely face lighting.

"Dr. O'Roarke," Alex said, "This is Lady Fiona Ferguson Hawes. A guest."

"A...friend," Sir Joseph corrected, his voice breathy.

Dr. O'Roarke spun around on him. "Enough from you, sir, until we get that fluid from your lungs and strengthen your heart. Now be quiet so I can listen."

Unbuttoning the top of Sir Joseph's nightshirt, the physician pressed one end of the tube against his chest, and the other against his own ear. For a long moment, his eyes closed, he just listened.

"You said that Sir Joseph had had rheumatic fever?" he finally asked.

"And some heart damage," Alex said.

O'Roarke nodded. Moving the tube twice more, he listened, then took Sir Joseph's pulse. "I imagine you feel a fluttering in your chest on occasion?"

Sir Joseph nodded.

O'Roarke nodded back. Then, returning his tube to his bag, he straightened. "Tell me the cretins in London have not been bleeding you."

Sir Joseph offered a dry smile. "They have. I felt some improvement for a bit."

O'Roarke seemed to love his nods. "Then worse. Feckin' eedjits. Have they given you any medicine to take?"

Alex handed over several bottles. When O'Roarke read the labels he cursed again. "No wonder you can't breathe. Well, we'll change that, altogether. Sir Joseph, I'm not sure what the cretins told you, but the rheumatic fever damaged your heart, specifically damaged the valves that keep the blood pumping in the right direction. It tends to back up now, all right, and for you it's backing up into your lungs, which is why you can't breathe. To put it bluntly, sir, you're drowning. But that is something I will not allow to happen. *So!*" Reaching back into his bag, he pulled out a bottle and two bags of herbs. "If this lovely young lady will help now, we will dose you with a tea made with dandelion leaves.

Wonderful diuretic. Be pissing like a racehorse within the hour, breathing better soon after. I also have a tincture of foxglove."

"But that's a poison!" Fiona protested. She knew it all too well.

Dr. O'Roarke smiled at her. "Good girl. In the doses I'm going to give, though, it actually strengthens the heart muscle so the blood gets pumped more efficiently. Nature's fierce amazin', isn't it? We should have you feeling better by noon, then, sir. That sound all right to you?"

Fiona knew how stunned she felt by the doctor's brusque efficiency. She could see Alex's jaw drop a bit.

As for Sir Joseph, he let loose a bark of laughter. "You mean Alex...doesn't have to travel all the...way to...St. Petersburg to tell my wife I've joined my ancestors... in...the family vault?"

O'Roarke laughed in return. "Not if I can help it. More rest, of course. Your son advised me that you're harder to hold still than a sheepdog in sight of a herd. Sure, you'll have to adapt. With the medicine, though, I think we can come about quite nicely."

Accepting the herbs and instructions, Fiona made for the door.

"I'll give you a hand," Alex said, his voice suspiciously gravelly. Stepping quickly forward, he opened the door and saw her through.

Fiona was heading down the hall when she heard the door close, and she turned to see Alex leaning against the wall, his head down. Her heart lurched. She turned back to him.

"It's all right to cry," she said, her hand on his arm.

He laughed, his voice a bit wobbly. "Easy to offer that kind of advice, isn't it?"

She smiled. "Harder to accept it. I know. If you'd like, I

will quickly leave so you have no witness to your unmanly collapse."

She had just taken her hand away when Alex grabbed it. Then he grabbed her and all but crushed her in his arms. She didn't even hesitate. Wrapping her arms around him, she held on tightly, keeping her silence. He needed no words. He needed someone who understood. Someone who cared what happened back in that room.

Her own heart seemed to swell in her chest, its every beat almost painful with joy. With the dizzyingly new sense of belonging, even for that moment. Mairead turned to her because Fiona was all she had. Alex had a choice.

They didn't stand there long, certainly not as long as Fiona would have wished. But she had to get downstairs to brew up the tea, and Alex had to return to his father. She had just turned away again when the door opened and Dr. O'Roarke stepped through. Closing the door behind him, he faced Alex.

"I told half the story in there, now."

Fiona barely kept herself from putting her arm back around Alex. He had frozen in place. "The rest?"

O'Roarke took off his spectacles and rubbed at them with his cravat. "I didn't lie. He will be breathing better by noon at the latest. But, Alex, he is still a very sick man. Between the pace you said he's set and the leech-merchants he's been seeing—"

"The Prince Regent's physician."

O'Roarke gave a bark of laughter. "Proves it. They wouldn't know which end of a scalpel to cut with. The point is, I'll be stayin' about for a few days if you don't mind. Hearts are very dicey things altogether, and his is weak and cranky. I'd hate to do such a good job at savin' him only to have to bury him after all."

"Thank you, Michael. I would appreciate it greatly."

O'Roarke grinned. "Good. Then in gratitude I can expect a nice donation to the orphanage Lady Kate and I manage."

Alex managed a grudging grin. "Pirate."

O'Roarke put a hand to his heart. "Philanthropist."

The two men returned to the room in accord. But Fiona saw something new in Alex's expression. A caution. A tension that made her think of the stillness that presaged a storm. Dr. O'Roarke didn't seem to notice anything. But Fiona walked down the stairs feeling as if the easing of his father's condition had exposed something else that troubled Alex even more. She just wished she knew what it was.

At least, she thought, weighing the bag of dandelion leaves in her hand, she could finally get some sleep.

She was wrong, of course. She had forgotten to factor in Mairead.

* * *

Fiona eventually made it all the way to her bedroom and her nightclothes. The sun was edging its way past its zenith, but the dandelion leaves had begun to work so well that she had been forbidden from the room for fear of her seeing Sir Joseph relieving himself. So she had brewed a cup of tea herself and taken it up to bed.

She wasn't the only one. Alex promised he would also rest. According to Lady Bea, who was in the kitchen experimenting with curry recipes, Chuffy and Mairead had come in from the telescope hours ago. Fiona knew she should check on her sister, just to make sure, but she allowed herself a bit of selfishness. It was her turn to follow her own lead for a change. And her lead said to collapse in bed and not rise until dinner.

She managed two hours before one of the maids shook her awake. "Please, miss," she said, her cap slipping down over one eye as she pushed at Fiona, "you need to come."

Fiona groaned and pulled the blankets over her head. "Go 'way."

"But I can't. Lady Bea said to get you.... Well, at least I think she did. That little Lennie tyke says so, and 'e seems to 'ave figured her out. Says you need to get into the breakfast room before there's carnage. Whatever that is."

"What is my sister doing?" she asked.

It could only be Mairead, after all. No one else had such a diabolical knack for knowing when Fiona's deepest sleep came.

"Waving a gun around."

The blankets exploded around Fiona as she launched out of bed. "A *what*?"

The maid looked frightened. "A gun. One o' the loaded ones the grooms've been carryin'. She's waving it at Master Chuffy and threatening his cods, if you'll pardon me."

Fiona groaned again. How could she have thought Chuffy could be good for her sister? Until Chuffy, Mairead had never brandished a gun at another living soul.

"Fine. I shall come."

She didn't even bother to change. She just slid into her slippers and robe and threw her braid over her shoulder before following the maid down the stairs.

She could hear Mairead long before she saw her. She could hear Chuffy, too, and Lady Bea and the Chiltons, all shouting over each other as if they were backbenchers in Parliament.

"*What*," she demanded, bursting in the breakfast room door, "is going on here? Do you even care that there is a very sick man upstairs who does *not* need this kind of nonsense? Edna Mairead Ferguson Hawes, I am ashamed of you!"

Mairead froze midbrandish, her eyes sparkling with tears, her face red, her hair pulled. "He won't... *listen*," she protested. She stood on one side of the littered table and the rest of the people huddled together at the other.

Fiona slammed her fists on her hips. "So you thought a weapon would clear his ears?"

Mairead looked at the gun as if it had come alive in her hand. "He wouldn't... *listen*."

"I keep trying to tell her," Chuffy said, his own hair in its odd little peaks. "Those games of hers aren't games. She needs to hand them over or she might end up in Newgate for obstruction and treason."

"You can't do that," Mairead argued, the gun swinging back toward Chuffy.

Fiona stepped in between them and took hold of the weapon, inserting her finger beneath the trigger so it couldn't be depressed. "Now," she said, yanking it from her sister's hand. "Do you think we might discuss this like adults?"

Mairead curled her hand, as if Fiona had hurt it. "I can't do it, Fee. I told you."

"Even after Chuffy spent the whole night helping you with the telescope?"

Mairead glowered. "He doesn't know a lens from a lemon."

Chuffy just shrugged. "Told you that in the beginning."

"Did," Lady Bea agreed with a sage nod.

"Besides," Mairead said, pointing, "how can you be ashamed, when you're the one in her nightclothes? Now everyone will see you."

Fiona thought that maybe she had had enough. She was

dragging her hands through her own hair. "Mairead and Chuffy, sit down. Mrs. Chilton, could we have some tea? Lady Bea, would you rather escape while you can?"

But Lady Bea grinned and sat in one of the chairs. "No."

Chuffy gathered up some of the pages that littered the table and stacked them in front of his chair. Then, as if he hadn't just been threatened with a gun, he held out a chair for Mairead as if they were at tea.

Fiona thought she had just about gotten the combatants to go to their corners, when the door slammed open again and Alex stomped through. "What in *hell* is going on down here? You woke my father from a sound sleep. And if you've set back his recovery, I will get out a horse whip, I swear to God."

Fiona looked up at him, and oddly, wanted to laugh. Even his hair was mussed into little points, his shirt shoved untidily into his breeches, his feet bare. They all looked quite deranged. It did her own heart no good that he looked more endearingly handsome than ever as well. How, she thought distractedly, could feet look endearing? But his did.

"We were just about to find out, Alex," she said, impressed at how calm her own voice sounded, considering the mad thoughts careening through her head. "Would you rather stay or return to your father?"

He looked around to see Chuffy and Mairead faced off and Fiona just taking a seat. "You're in your nightclothes."

She did laugh then. There was a gun sitting on the table, and he noticed her night rail. "Yes. I heard about a ruckus and wanted to intervene before they woke Sir Joseph. How is he?"

Alex sat. "Resting. Now, what is going on?"

"I believe," Fiona said, motioning for Chuffy and Mae to sit, "that we are picking up an old argument about some puzzles my grandfather gave us to work."

"Ciphers," Chuffy said, yanking off his glasses.

"Mine," Mae spat, plumping down on a chair. "Mine, mine, *mine*."

"Yes, Mae," Fiona said, patting her sister's hand. She would have been a lot more brusque if she hadn't seen real fear spark in her sister's eyes. Why? "Sweetings, would you rather everyone but you and I leave? I need to know why you won't give up the puzzles. You really have them? I don't see how. We've been unraveling them for years."

Mae just stared at her, her hands twisting together. A bad sign. And no one had time for that.

"Did you have a good night last night at the telescope?" Fiona asked carelessly. Both Chuffy and Alex stared at her. Mae blinked.

"It is a lovely piece of equipment," Mae said. "Four inch. Quite clear."

"And Chuffy was gracious enough to let you use it?"

Mae hunched down a bit, obviously knowing where this conversation was headed. "It's not the same," she said, her voice painfully small. "You don't know."

"Then tell me, sweetings," Fee gently said.

Mairead wouldn't even look at her. "I can't."

"Can—" Chuffy blurted out before Fiona stopped him with a look.

"Do you want to tell me only?" Fiona asked, reaching out to take one of her sister's trembling hands.

Mairead shook her head, her eyes now squeezed shut.

"Would you rather tell Chuffy?"

Another head shake. Fiona was really confused. Mairead did not do things capriciously. There was something here Fiona wasn't understanding. But then, she thought, there were a lot of things she wasn't understanding lately.

"Sweetings," she said, sliding off her chair to come to her

knees next to her sister's chair. "Chuffy and Alex believe these ciphers to be vital. Chuffy believes that our puzzles may help break the code and save lives. Don't you think he deserves our help?"

Mae didn't open her eyes, but she nodded. Fiona saw tears squeeze from beneath her lids. She took her sister's other hand. "*Do* you have some of the puzzles?"

Mae's head dropped even lower. She clung to Fiona's hands like a lifeline. "All."

Fiona was even more confused. She still couldn't figure out how. "Mae. You know that we need to share those puzzles with Chuffy."

Mae didn't move. Not a nod. Not a head shake. Not a flinch. She remained that way for a solid hour as Fiona exhorted her and everyone else waited, the silence growing thick with emotion and taut with confusion. Fiona didn't move from where she was, there on her knees. Mae refused to open her eyes. Chuffy refused to back down. Tea came and went, and no one touched it.

Finally, desperate for a resolution, Fiona gave Mae's hands a good squeeze.

"There is nothing else I can do, Mae. Chuffy, I know you wish to share your telescope with Mae, but until she sees reason, I forbid it."

Mae's eyes flew open. Chuffy made to protest. This time Alex hushed him. Fiona steeled herself against the anguish in her sister's eyes, the stark betrayal. The tears that slowly tracked down pale cheeks. She stayed there on her knees as Mae pulled her hands away and stood. She stayed as Mae walked out of the room.

She felt Alex's hands on her arms. "You had no choice," he said.

Of course she had a choice. So she stood to receive her

sister when she returned, her back rigid, her eyes bright and brittle, the battered little pillow in her arms. Fiona almost chastised her. This wasn't the time to rely on old crutches.

And then, the tears flowing faster, Mae handed the pillow to Chuffy.

Fiona gaped. "What did you do?" she asked, hushed.

But Mae couldn't seem to pull her gaze from the lavender thistles. Giving Mae a quizzical look, Chuffy pulled out a knife. Mae screamed. Fiona yanked the pillow out of Chuffy's hands.

"Don't..." She was shaking. "Please, be careful." She laughed, as if her objection weren't primal. "Our mother stitched this. It's all we have of her." Clutching the pillow close, she turned to Mae. "Did you hide the messages in here, Mae? Why?"

Her sister's eyes were awash in tears now as she lifted them to her. She looked so forlorn, more fragile than Fiona had seen her since their mother's death. "I'm sorry, Fee. I'm so sorry."

Fiona dropped the pillow to the table and took Mae's hands. "Why should you ever be sorry, sweetings?"

Now, Mae was sobbing. "Because I've betrayed you. I shouldn't. I knew that. I *knew* it. But it was all I had of him. All I had..." Mae gulped. "And he was so awful to you. I heard him time after time after time. He hated you. He wanted to hurt you. But, Fee...he was my grandfather. And these were all I still had of him."

So she had stuffed the puzzles into the talisman they had managed to hold on to from their mother. Mae had carried the only family they had around in her arms and blamed herself for it. Fiona felt her heart shatter. She felt the weight of Mairead's guilt crush her. How could she have ever made Mairead think that keeping a memory of her grandfather was disloyal to Fiona? How could she have so burdened her sister?

She thought she couldn't feel worse. And then, worse happened. Because when she let go of Mae's hands to hold her, Mae turned to Chuffy and walked into his arms instead.

Chapter 16

As if doing Catholic penance for hurting Mae, Fiona picked the seam out of the pillow on one side, tiny stitch by tiny stitch, to find the interior crammed tight with slips of paper, some of them all of three years old. Fiona fought a tide of pain at the sight of them. Her own grandfather's betrayal and Mae's hopeless yearning. Could she really still believe that the puzzles were innocent? That his puzzles, which were actually codes and cipher games, weren't actually weapons against the throne? Could she bear it that Mae had hidden them from her so that she could keep a piece of their grandfather?

Mae sat in the lilac salon, curled up on the settee, her eyes half-closed, as if it would keep her from seeing Fiona working in the next room. Waiting for his codes, Chuffy sat on the floor at Mae's feet.

"Only need to copy 'em," he said again, his hand on her knee. "Put 'em back."

Mae couldn't seem to look at him, only nodded.

Her fingers working by instinct, Fiona couldn't take her eyes from her sister. She couldn't swallow past the stone that seemed to have lodged in her throat. She felt suddenly cast adrift, her purpose faltering, her pole star shifted. Almost worse than the revelations about the pillow, could it be that Mae no longer needed her? Could her sister really turn to Chuffy when she had only turned to Fiona in the past? Could it be that Fiona would no longer have her sister to give her life focus and reason?

She didn't think she could bear it. All she had was Mae.

"Happy endings," she heard next to her and looked up to see Lady Bea standing alongside, a cup of tea in her hand. The old woman smiled, set it down before Fiona, and patted her cheek. "All's well that ends well."

Fiona managed a smile. Was it? She wasn't so sure.

With another pat, Lady Bea wandered through to the salon, where she joined Mae. In time Chuffy returned to the table and began to sort through the papers. He pulled out that well-thumbed little book again, as if suddenly the key would make itself known. Fiona would have been happy never to see those ubiquitous little letter groupings again.

And then Alex returned and made it worse yet again.

Fiona had been separating out all of the little papers into the different codes that had been used. At least they didn't have to decode them. The messages were written right beneath the code, where she and Mae had used them to prove their prowess.

Bluebird will not sing for us. It must be removed from the cage.

Mother arrives twelfth June with dozen bags and five staff.

Ignio.

The other sentences had never made sense. The last, though, suddenly sent shivers down Fiona's spine. *Ignio.* Latin for "ignite." What could they have been igniting? What had been the results? If only she and Mae had dated their puzzles, she might remember.

She was so caught up in the papers that she didn't hear the footsteps approach. She didn't have to. Suddenly her limbs were tingling and her belly tightened. Alex was here. She looked up to see him settling into one of the free chairs, his features drawn, his shoulders sagging. She ached for him. She ached to hold him, to soothe him. To have him soothe her. She smiled when she wanted to weep.

"How is your father?" she asked, striving hard to keep her hands to herself. The paper in her fist crackled as she crumpled it.

Alex smiled. "Sleeping. I think Michael saved his life." Wearily he scrubbed his hands over his face. "I don't know what I would have done..."

She couldn't bear it anymore. Reaching across the table, she twined her fingers through his. "As Lady Bea told me earlier, all's well that ends well."

When he looked up at her, she caught that darkness again. The flicker of something that didn't belong, and it frightened her. She knew, though, that this wasn't the time to ask.

"Come to lend us a hand, old man?" Chuffy asked, lifting a handful of papers. "Could use it."

Alex's smile was rueful. For some reason, that alone squeezed Fiona's stomach. "I'm here to make your life more complicated," he said. "Or solve all your problems. I'm not perfectly certain which. I've found another line from the poem."

Chuffy immediately went on alert. Fiona wondered what was wrong. Something felt off. Then Alex reached into his pocket and drew out a large round locket on an intricate gold chain and handed it to Chuffy.

"Open it."

Chuffy adjusted his glasses and flipped the locket open. *"Thrice times thryce I have begged you…"*

Chuffy and Fiona both gasped. "It's the third verse," he said and dove into the book. "But again. Different. Here.

> *So oft have I begged thee*
> *to let me dip my pleasure wick*
> *within your luscious honeypot*
> *to cure my heart and soul.*

He was beet red by the end of the reading. "Sorry."

"Three," Fiona said, reaching for the open locket. "Why three?"

"Or is it nine?" Alex asked. "Three times thrice."

Chuffy scrubbed at his face, dislodging his glasses. "We'll have to go over the poem all over again."

"Mae!" Fiona called, turning for the salon. "We need you here! You need to look at these patterns again."

She would never have heard Chuffy a minute later if Mae hadn't come right over. When Mae joined her, pulling papers together and searching for new patterns, Fiona was briefly too distracted to notice that Chuffy and Alex had gotten up. But Mae worked in absolute silence. Suddenly it was as if the two men, coming to a halt in the hallway, positioned themselves at the other end of a whispering gallery. Mae never heard them; Mae was focused. But Fiona did.

"Bad news, old lad," Chuffy said in hushed tones. "There's no question. Most of those notes Mae kept were government codes. And not the kind marquesses on the

Privy Council would have. Somebody had those girls committing treason."

Fiona froze. Pain sheared through her. *Sweet God.* It was true.

"Don't say anything," Alex answered. "Not now. And if they ask about the Tudor rose, it's a coincidence. Fiona said that it is in her family crest. It's also on the locket."

Chuffy hissed. "Worse and worse. Where did you get the locket? Does it have to do with your father?"

Alex took his friend's arm. "Yes and no. I'll explain later. Our focus now is to break that cipher."

"Thought it was to protect the women."

There was an odd hesitation that caused Fiona's breath to hitch. "Yes," Alex said, sounding strained. "Of course. But breaking that damn code can't hurt."

"And connecting the Tudor rose can."

This time Alex didn't answer at all. Suddenly very afraid, Fiona picked up the locket and closed it. And there, on the front, just like on the cover of the watch Mae had found, was etched a ten-petaled Tudor rose. The Tudor rose that was so perfectly echoed in the Hawes family crest. Fiona swore her heart turned to stone. She couldn't think past her own complicity.

Why should she feel responsible? She hadn't known what the puzzles were all about. She and Mairead had solved them in ignorance. But she did. She felt as if the weight of her grandfather's sins rested squarely on her shoulders because she had done his work for him. Because she had enlisted Mae just so she could keep her busy.

Everything was falling apart, falling away. Her honor was superfluous, her honesty long since sacrificed. And now her future was compromised in a way she might not be able to redeem.

The good news was that once Chuffy returned to the table, nobody noticed Fiona leave. Alex had continued up to his father's room, and Lady Bea was embroidering honeybees on handkerchiefs. Mae looked up at Chuffy with a hesitant smile, and he dropped a kiss on her forehead. And then, as if there had been no crisis, no threats or tears, the two sat down together and bent their heads over the codes.

The kitchen staff noticed Fiona come through to collect her redingote. The guards in the back garden noticed her settling on the little stone bench as the sun sank behind the west wood. But no one thought to ask why. No one thought to wonder why she would go outside bareheaded and alone into the deepening dusk. Which was just as well. Fiona wasn't certain she could tell them.

* * *

Alex wasn't quite certain where he meant to go. He just needed to move. Michael had just turned to him and smiled.

"Faith, and aren't I the most brilliant feckin' doctor on this cretin-infested island?"

Alex looked over to see his father sleeping, real color in his cheeks for the first time since he'd seen him, his breathing easy, his body relaxed.

"He's better?"

Michael gave a considered nod. "Better, yes. Well, no. I'll tell you now, my lad. The last thing he should do is trek back to that frozen wasteland, king or no king. Can you figure a way to get him to stay?"

Of course he could. Break his father's trust and call his mother home. She would take care of matters. But that would take weeks, and Alex wasn't certain how to control his father that long.

"I'll find a way."

Michael nodded. "Now, if you don't mind, I'm going to leave Mr. Sweet here to keep watch, and I am off to sleep. You want to show me where?"

And so here Alex now stood at the head of the staircase with no idea where to go or what to do. He just knew he had to get away from everyone else. He headed down the steps and toward the back of the house, deliberately avoiding the main rooms.

Dinnertime was past, but everyone had been served on trays anyway, the demands of his father and the work over-riding social convention. So the only noise came from the kitchen and the only light from the various fireplaces and a few well-placed candles. Even so, he headed straight through to the library and out the French doors.

The brisk night air brought him up short. He was in no more than shirt, breeches, and boots, and the breeze was playing devil with his overheated skin. He should go in.

He didn't. He began to pace. He would have preferred to ride, pushing his chestnut gelding hard over the harvested ground, the wind pulling at him and the darkness soothing him. Security forbade it, though.

So he walked. And all but stumbled over another resident of the garden.

"Fiona? What are you doing here?"

Fiona startled so badly, she almost fell when she jumped to her feet. Alex grabbed her arm to steady her, but she pulled away. He halted, oddly hurt by her rejection. She stood as stiffly as a nanny, her head erect, her hands folded at her waist, her head turned away, the dim starlight slipping through her untidy hair.

Something was wrong. She was too silent. Too still.

"Are you all right?"

"Yes." And yet, instead of turning, it seemed she continued to look for something in the other direction. There was a waxing moon out tonight, and the sky was thick with smoke. And yet, Fiona's head was thrown back as if she could peer through it to the lights she followed.

"I can't find him," she said, her voice curiously small.

Alex found himself looking up. "Who?"

"Orion. No matter how bad things got, no matter the changes and upheavals, he has always been there. Kind of my rock. My anchor." She pointed toward the southwest sky. "He should be right there."

Alex stepped closer, the unconscious pain in her voice embedding itself in his chest. "He is. You know that."

She lowered her head, but still didn't look at him. "I'm not quite so sure anymore."

He caught an odd shudder, as if she were struggling to hold still. As if...

"Are you crying?" he demanded, taking hold of her and turning her around.

And in that moment he lost his heart.

He had seen women cry. He was surrounded by them, after all. Amabelle had been a genius at tears, instinctively orchestrating them for the best effect. Mistresses had used them for money, and his sister's absolution from petty family crimes. But Fiona was like none of them. It seemed, he thought, seeing the rigid control she attempted to hold over herself, that she resented them. Resented herself for being even this vulnerable, as if it were a betrayal, an unforgivable weakness.

She was not even a pretty weeper. Tears tracked down her cheeks and along her neck. Her hair straggled like a bird's nest. Her eyes were puffy, and he suspected her nose was red. And she was trying so very hard to hold the flood back, as if once breached, the waters trapped behind that dam would destroy her. He wasn't certain she wasn't right.

"Oh, Fee," he murmured and pulled her into his arms. "What have we done to you?"

For a long moment, she didn't react, her body unbending, her hands clenched against his chest. He foundered for something to say, something to do that would ease her distress.

"Didn't you hear Lady Bea?" he asked, resting his cheek against the silk of her hair. "All will be well."

"I'm not...so sure...it...will...." Finally her will seemed to falter a bit, and she eased against him, her face tucked against his shoulder. She shuddered, and shuddered again, her defenses beginning to crumble.

"Tell me," he demanded, his own heart battering at his chest. He couldn't bear this Fiona, lost and vulnerable and shaky.

"I can't see...a way forward," she admitted, her voice unbearably small, her hands still clenched into fists. "I heard you speak to Chuffy, you see."

Alex reached down to cup her chin and lift it until she could not avoid him. "I'm sorry. It was unfair of your grandfather to do that to you both."

Her eyes looked preternaturally bright, swollen with tears she refused to let fall. "You have to realize," she insisted. "Mae couldn't have understood. She would never have helped if I hadn't coaxed her into it." She shrugged, her eyes wandering. "She needed something to do. Something to keep her challenged. I thought..."

"You thought these games would be perfect. And you thought that it was a lovely surprise that your grandfather would actually share something with you."

Her smile was grim. "Not me. He couldn't abide me.

I could never seem to be sufficiently grateful for his largesse. But sometimes... sometimes he would send Mae little gifts. He let her have her telescope, and these... well, these games. And she kept them hidden away, like a dirty little secret, because she didn't want to hurt me, because... because..."

She kept shaking her head, her eyes squeezed shut, her hands clenched. Alex felt her distress in his chest, in his gut and heart.

"I had... one job," she protested. "Only one. Mae. See her safe... happy... I... I failed so badly...."

Surprised by his own vehemence, Alex pushed her away until he held her by her arms. "Are you *mad*? You failed her? *You?* How dare you believe that? You kept her alive. You kept her safe. You let her dream, for God's sake! If you made any mistakes, you made them out of love for her."

She glared up at him, pulling away. "Didn't you see her in there? She was so ashamed. How could I have made her feel ashamed because she wanted a family like everyone else, even if she had to construct it from paper and yarn? How do I make that up to her?" She looked away as if it were too difficult to face him. "How do I atone?"

He frowned. "Atone? For what? Certainly not your sister. And not the messages. You aren't the one who committed treason."

Her smile was a pale thing. "But I was. And I think people died because of it."

Alex was sure of it. But this wasn't the time to discuss it. Fiona didn't need explanations. She needed expiation. Comfort. Support. She needed his arms around her, and he couldn't think of anything he wanted to do more.

It had nothing to do with the comfort he felt in return, of how the sensation of her arms around him felt like a haven, a shelter against his own unbearable future. How the thrum of her heart against his chest stirred him in ways few things ever had.

There were so many things he should be doing. He couldn't think of one he wanted to, except be here with this fascinating, infuriating, endearing woman.

"Whatever else you believe," he said, cupping her face in his hands, "believe this. Your grandfather is responsible for any treason in that house. And Mae is just fine. You did an amazing job raising your little sister."

That actually got a small grin out of her. "Actually," she admitted, "Mae is the elder." Her focus drifted, as if she saw her sister there instead of Alex. "I think Chuffy really does love her," she whispered, and Alex thought he had never heard a more heartbroken sound.

"I think he does," he answered because it was the truth. "Will you survive that?"

Her head came up again, and she peered up at him. "I don't know."

"There can be another future for you than merely to care for Mairead," he insisted.

Her smile carried the sadness of time. "No, there can't."

His own smile wasn't as assured as it might have been a few days ago. "Oh, I think there can. Even after what you survived in Edinburgh."

Ask her, you fool, he heard in his head. In his heart. He couldn't because he was the unworthy one. He didn't deserve her; not until he cleared his name.

She blinked and tried to draw away. He wouldn't allow it. "You know?" she asked. "About Edinburgh? I didn't think anyone knew."

"Your grandfather does. He shared the information with me."

Alex might as well have taken the stuffings out of her. She didn't slump, exactly. She sighed, a long, weary sound that sent a shaft of pain through him. He had heard capitulation before. He had never held it.

"Fiona," he said, "it doesn't make a difference."

She didn't lift her head. "Of course it does. My grandfather will make sure of it."

"Not after I get through with him."

That got her head up, but her smile was unbearably sad. "Blackmail, now? Don't you think I have enough sins to atone for?"

He rested his forehead against hers, his gaze never leaving hers. "I keep telling you. You have no sins to atone for."

She closed her eyes and shuddered. "You know perfectly well that I do."

He couldn't bear the feeling that even though she was still in his arms, she was separating herself from him. Tangling his hands into her hair, he pulled her head back again and met her mouth with his.

He could smell the soft soap in her hair. He could taste vanilla and coffee on her tongue. He could feel her stiffen, only a moment, before melting against him. Before opening to him, inviting him in, meeting him with her own tongue.

He thought his body would explode. He knew his heart somersaulted and his gut clenched. He knew his cock went rock hard. He arched against her, desperate to feel the soft curve of her belly against it. He pulled her closer and tilted his head, needing to plunge deeper, and she met him, tongue to tongue in a frantic dance of need. She arched against him, suddenly as aggressive as he, the hard feel of him obviously not frightening her. She tangled her hands in his hair and held on, as if they weren't close enough.

Alex's brain disintegrated. All he could think was that he

wanted her. He wanted her naked and spread before him, he wanted her around him, hot and wet and tight. He wanted the comfort of her silken skin beneath his fingers.

His hands were moving before he even thought about it, sweeping down her back, measuring the sweet swell of her bottom, the hollow of her waist, the plump temptation of her breast. He nibbled at her lips as if they were sweets and savored the sensual slide of tongue against tongue. He gasped for air and knew nothing except that he needed her like oxygen, like sunlight and rain.

It was the slam of a door that brought him to his senses. Suddenly he remembered that he was standing outside, where anyone could see him, and in the cold. He lifted his head and gazed down at Fiona, who was breathing as hard as he.

"I'm sorry," he said, trapped by the depths of those luminous eyes. He lifted a hand to brush back a strand of dark copper hair. "I didn't mean to do that."

For a long moment she didn't answer. She just stood in his embrace, her arms around his waist, her body trembling. He had to close his eyes for a moment, as if that could help yank his randy body back from the edge of disaster.

"Alex?" he heard, her voice breathy and uncertain.

He didn't move. "Yes."

Her voice was unbearably fragile. "Will you do something for me?"

"Anything."

He heard a gasping laugh and opened his eyes. She lifted back her head and looked up at him. "Don't stop."

Chapter 17

Alex knew his heart simply seized to a halt. "Fiona..."

She met his gaze, unflinching. "Chuffy and Mae are out with the telescope. Bea has retired. And you and I are—"

"Alone." In so many ways.

His body leapt back to life. His hands began to shake. "Are you sure?"

She didn't nod. She didn't have to. There was not merely invitation in her eyes. There was need, a need that called to his. A need he understood. A need for solace, for intimacy, for absolution. For respite from an uncertain sea.

Later he didn't remember going in. He couldn't quite say who made the decision or moved first. All he knew was that he resented having to let go of her hand. That they never spoke of a plan to avoid exposure, but that she went upstairs first, past the footmen, past the butler, as if she had finally given up on the day and simply wanted to sleep. He knew that, left behind, he counted heartbeats until he could follow. He knew he planned out her seduction as he waited, step by step, clothing article by clothing article. And he knew that

when he opened the door to his room to find her standing
limned by the firelight, he forgot all about his plan.

They came together as if they had been completing an
action begun four years earlier, mouths melded, hands moving, clothing falling in piles across the floor. They didn't
speak. Speech was superfluous. What was needed was contact, communion, consummation. What was needed was
proof that they weren't alone anymore, that tears could be
kissed away and despair held off, that the other person knew
the fragility of control, the fallacy of independence. That
fear and loneliness can be dispelled with a touch, a kiss, a
caress, and that the union of two people would last beyond
that moment of discovery.

Alex couldn't get enough of her, the otherworldly satin
of her skin, the silk of her hair, the sleek, strong sweep of
her hips and legs, and the secret landscape of her spine,
small, serial ridges made for nothing but the delight of
a man's fingers. He held her face in his hand only for a
moment, only until he could remember how to remove a
dress, a chemise, a pair of practical cotton stockings. Until he could set her to giggling as he stroked her heels and
nibbled her toes.

The bed was soft as air, the room warm, the only sound
the lazy crackle of a low fire and the wordless murmurs of
discovery and delight. Alex felt as if his heart would explode
with wanting her. His body was hard, so hard he was afraid
of breaking her. Except Fiona was strong. Strong enough
to carry the load of two hearts through the despair of slum
streets. Strong enough to survive the worst of Edinburgh and
still look at the sky.

He cherished her. He worshiped her body like a pagan,
feasting on her as if she were riches withheld. Her long,
swanlike throat, the small hollow at its base that tasted salty

from her tears. Her shoulders and arms and hands and fingers, elegant, capable, clever fingers that were never still. That weren't now as she sought her own discoveries and set off firestorms in him.

Her breasts. Sweet God, her breasts, as plush as pillows, with large nipples the color of spring roses that pebbled into tight buds with attention. He cupped them, stroked them, tweaked them with his finger and thumb, just to see them rise. To feel them swell beneath his hand, to test the pace of her heart beneath as she bucked off the bed in response to his touch. To taste the faint salt of her skin and suckle, drawing her back into a bow, bringing her hands to his head to hold him close, driving him mad with the little murmurs that purred against his mouth.

He had to be in her. He couldn't wait. He couldn't remember ever wanting a woman this badly, needing completion so desperately, hunger and wonder fusing into impulse that urged him to spread her legs, part the rich copper hair that curled at the apex of her thighs, discover the wet heat of her with his fingers and set her to gasping with his touch, torture himself with the heat and wetness and dark scent of arousal on her.

She was ready. He thought she had been before she'd lost her clothes. He wished he could have taken more time, eased her to climax and followed her down, savored the ripple of her body as it came apart beneath his fingers. He couldn't. He slipped a knee between her legs and urged them wider. He bent down to her breast and suckled hard. And when she opened her mouth in a near-silent keen and arched, he met her with his mouth and ravaged her as he positioned himself between her thighs. And then, because he needed her, because he wanted her, because he knew she wanted the same, he plunged home.

And damn near came to a shuddering halt. He might have if she had flinched or pulled away or cried out. But she didn't. She wrapped her legs around his back and her fingers in his hair, and she held on. She met him thrust for thrust, her body so tight around his that he almost exploded on his first thrust.

He couldn't stop, couldn't slow, couldn't on his life be gentle anymore, not with her urging him on, and he plunged deep and deeper and deeper, the bed bumping the wall and her head thrown back, her eyes closed, her hands curling into claws, her body sweat-sheened and taut, her murmurs lifting to cries that he captured with his own mouth rather than be heard and stopped. He couldn't allow it. Not now. Not, he thought, ever.

And then, she clamped around him and she stiffened, whimpering, pulling, pushing, milking his cock of every last dreg of control, and before he could gather the sense to pull out, he exploded into her, pumping his seed into her womb, his own body seizing and galvanized, until he collapsed, damp and exhausted, into her arms, his face against her breast, his heart battering his ribs, his strength gone. Until panting and damp, the two of them simply lay there in the shadows, replete, stricken. Until slowly, inevitably, his sense came back and he lifted on his elbows.

"You were a virgin," he accused.

She blinked up at him. "I know."

She looked so languorous and sated, her lips swollen and her hair tumbled about her on the pillow. His cock stirred and his heart picked up speed.

"But how could you be after working in the brothel?"

For a moment she didn't answer, just stared at him. He thought he saw hurt deep in that lake blue. He thought he saw withdrawal. Wriggling out from beneath him, she climbed off the bed and grabbed her chemise. "You mean, how could I remain a virgin if I'm also a whore?"

He leaped off the bed and grabbed her by the arms. "You are *not* a whore."

She peered up at him, that scrap of linen caught between them, her body alabaster in the dimness. "I know," she finally said, her voice small. "I just wasn't certain you did."

"I could tell from the first kiss, Fee. Whatever you had been forced to do, it wasn't in your nature. But what did you do there?"

Her smile was rueful. For a moment she resisted, her body as tense as her mouth. Then, gently, she pulled away from him. "The accounts. Betty the Badger was terrible at numbers. One of my friends in the vaults told me. So I offered my services. Twice a week." She shrugged. "She paid me well. Would it have made a difference if I *had* done more than the books?"

He couldn't lie to her. "Yes," he said. "Because I would have mourned the innocence lost back in those years. I spent an awful few days thinking that you had been forced into the trade at such a young age."

"I wasn't completely ignorant of it," she said, looking away. "It was rather hard to miss. And people saw me."

"The men on Calton Hill?"

Finally she seemed truly amused. "John Playfair? Good heavens, no. He would have died if he'd known. He taught Mae and me astronomy. They set up their telescopes on Calton Hill."

Alex frowned. "It didn't seem odd to them that two twelve-year-olds wandered around the city late at night?"

She shrugged. "I paid one of the assistants at the shop where we worked to act as our big brother. The gentlemen thought we were always chaperoned."

Alex pulled her back into his arms and gently and thoroughly kissed her. "I'm so sorry," he said, dropping quick kisses across her cheeks and eyelids, trying hard not to betray the depth of his relief. "I should never have jumped to the obvious conclusions. Especially with you."

She lifted up and returned his kiss, her breasts rubbing deliciously against his chest. "So nothing has changed?"

He chuckled and slipped a hand down her back. "Oh, something has changed. It's changed in a big way."

Grinning she wriggled against him. "Yes. I can tell. Shouldn't we take care of that?"

"Eventually," he murmured, nuzzling her neck. "But first, I think you deserve a bit more attention."

He felt her knees weaken. "Any more attention and I will turn into a puddle."

He lifted her in his arms and returned her to bed. "Good. That was just what I was hoping."

"Me, too," she agreed, lifting her arms to welcome him. "Everything else is too complicated right now."

She had no idea, Alex thought. Because after what happened tonight, they would have to marry.

But that was not something he needed to address immediately. Certainly not before addressing Fiona's other needs. Or his.

* * *

Mae woke her, of course. After the second time. No, make that the third. She was back in her bed and the sun well up, when Mae tapped on the door. Her eyes snapping open at the sound, Fiona quickly lifted the covers to check her attire.

Night rail. Good. She had remembered. She almost giggled out loud. After the night she had spent, she was a bit surprised. Faith, she was surprised she had any modesty left at all. If the first time she had made love had been cataclysmic, the second... *and* third... had been languid. Sensual. Unforgettable. Her breasts still ached. Her skin was tingling and glowing and impatient for his touch. And her memory finally, *finally*, had something to offset the rest, something joyful, wondrous, and enthralling. The rasp of his beard against her throat. The soft curl of hair across his chest and that wonderful, enticing, naughty little line of hair that began at his navel and proceeded south. The line that begged exploration, discovery, satisfaction.

Her fingers still remembered his shape. Her mouth held his taste of brandy and coffee long after he'd left. And her body, that body that had been nothing but a tool, carried the imprint of his touch. The deliciously raw soreness that told of repeated invasion.

She had known, all those years ago. She had seen this consummation in that kiss, and she had suffered guilt for it. The guilt was gone, leaving only joy behind. Relief. Resurrection.

"Fee," Mae whispered urgently, knocking again.

Fiona sat up and smiled at every ache and twinge that reminded her of the night before. "Come in, Mae."

Her sister was frowning as she strode in, obviously long since dressed. Without invitation, she climbed up and sat on Fiona's bed, still frowning.

"What's wrong, sweetings?" Fiona asked, taking her hand.

Mairead didn't answer right away, which really caught Fiona's attention. Usually by the time Mairead asked for help, she had an entire script in her head. This morning, Fiona had the patience to wait.

"Something is wrong, Fee."

"What, love?"

"Well, Chuffy and I . . . we . . ."

Fiona's smile spread, even as her heart turned over. "Oh, Mae, I think I know where this is going. I don't suppose you remember the talk we had when you began your menses."

Mae's head came up and she scowled. "I remember everything everyone has ever said."

Of course she did. "I am not quite sure if you understand that particular conversation. I mean about the relations between men and women."

Suddenly Mae was grinning, and she looked like an imp. "You mean about sex? Of course I remember it. Who could forget? I simply thought I would never need it."

Fiona's breath caught. "And you do?"

"Well, yes, soon, I imagine. But that isn't what this is about. Chuffy and I were working, and I had to get up to the convenience, and I saw Alex outside. Just beyond the garden. And something is wrong. That man is wrong."

Suddenly Fiona was paying attention. "Man? What man? Wrong how?"

But Mae could manage no more than a shrug. Mae was terrible at reading people. She took everything at face value. But some vestige of self-preservation alerted her when there was danger. It had gone a long way to keep her alive over the years, especially when Fiona couldn't be there. Even when Fiona *could*.

"Are they still there?"

Mae nodded. "You can hear them from the garden, I think. So you're not seen."

"Stay here, sweetings. Promise?" She only waited for Mae's nod before hopping down and throwing on her clothing. "I'll be right back. I promise."

She hated that her heart was already racing, and that her

palms were damp. She had just had the most wonderful night of her life. Why should she immediately assume that whatever waited for her would destroy it?

There was no one in the garden when she stepped outside. No one within view anywhere. Very carefully, she paced along the tall hedges that marked its boundaries. She was halfway along the back border when she heard them. Alex was whispering. He sounded urgent, as if there was some great secret. "I don't understand. What more could you want?"

"I understand you have the note," another voice answered. "What does it say?"

"To hand the girls over. I've obviously led you to them. You know where they are. That should be enough. They're innocent in all this."

"That's not what I was told. Doesn't matter. Not your place to argue. Your place is to hand them over or the truth about your father's treasonous activities comes to light and he's ruined."

Fiona froze. Her heart stumbled and righted itself. Her stomach, long since the habitat for her most terrible premonitions, squeezed and squeezed. *No, Alex. Please, no.*

She waited for Alex to say that the man couldn't have them. That he would protect them with his life, no matter what.

But he said nothing.

Nothing.

Closing her eyes, she drew a breath. Well, at least she thought she knew what that darkness was that had been dogging Alex. She understood too the dilemma he found himself in, and she hurt so badly for him. How could an honorable man choose between the father he loved and the women he'd sworn to protect? The only thing she could do was to take his choice away.

She wasted only a moment mourning. She didn't think anything could have hurt as much as Ian's loss. Oddly, it did. And then, just as she had always done, she turned to what must be done. Her mind already sorting through things like ready cash and where she had stashed the gall of Aleppo, she turned to go back inside.

Chapter 18

Alex's body thrummed with frustration. His brain reeled with questions, ideas, plans. And he stood perfectly still, facing off with the man who had come to ruin him.

One of Finney's men, a hulking, balding brute named Ben. Alex couldn't believe it. The man had been patrolling the grounds for two days now, and suddenly out of nowhere, he pulled Alex aside and delivered the ultimatum.

"You'll understand, sir, I have nothing but respect for yourself and yours," the man said, as if he didn't have a pepper pot shoved into his belt. "But the gentleman what told me to bring the message has me dad watched. Threatened to burn down his store."

"Do you know who the man is?"

The guard's smile was rueful. "Now, sir, you know I won't tell you. Not when me dad's at risk. You know how much your own dad means to you."

Alex struggled to contain his fury. He had to, or all was lost. "This is ridiculous. What threat could two women be to them?"

The man shrugged. "Don' know, do I? Said they'd stolen somethin' from them they want back."

"What?" Although he had a terrible feeling he knew. "If we know, I can get it back myself."

The man shrugged again. "Said they'd tell the girls themselves."

Alex's gut twisted harder. "What did the man look like who talked to you?"

Ben gave him a gap-toothed smile. "You don't think I'm that dumb, do ya?"

No, sadly, he didn't. "Exactly how do they expect me to... *deliver* the women?"

"There will be a carriage available from tonight. Up to you how you get 'em in."

"And you don't know anything more about this man?"

"Didn't ask. Not my business."

"It will be if you're hanged for treason. How would your dad like that?"

The man shrugged his oversized shoulders. "Least he'll be alive, won't he?"

Alex had actually been hoping for this moment, when he would draw out the blackmailer. But he'd thought to meet one of the Lions. Not another blackmail victim.

It didn't matter. He would figure something out.

"Tomorrow," he said. "Tell them to be ready tomorrow."

And without another word, he walked back into the house. He had to tell Chuffy; there was nothing else for it. He had to make sure his father learned nothing of what was transpiring. Dr. O'Roarke could see to that. After he talked to Chuffy, he would figure what to tell the women. If anything.

For a second as he stepped into the shadowy hallway by the library, he stopped to rub at his eyes. He'd known all along that this was where this would lead. Fiona or his father. The woman he loved or the father who was the whole world to so many people. To him. The man who lay upstairs too weak to even feed himself, who had damn near killed himself to serve his government.

Well, Alex wasn't going to finish the job with this revelation.

But Fiona. Courageous, loving, brilliant Fiona. Beloved Fiona, with her uncompromising honesty, her sly wit and agile mind. Fiona, with whom he was falling in love and whom he only wanted to protect. He felt as if the choice were ripping him apart.

He was headed for the stairs when the door to the breakfast room slammed open and Chuffy burst out like cannon fire.

"Hold there, man," Alex cautioned, catching him before he caromed into him. "What's the rush?"

Chuffy's glasses were sliding off the top of his head and his neckcloth was yanked nearly off. "I have something."

Alex's heart stumbled again. "What?"

Chuffy held out one of the ubiquitous papers, with its coded message. "The paper in that locket you found. Not the Lions' code. Not the government code. Much simpler. Too simple."

"What about it?"

Chuffy gave the paper a wave. "Says everything is in the safe at Hawes House. Everything. Just that. Then, by God, a location. What do you think 'everything' is?"

For the longest moment, Alex just stared at his friend, struggling to catch up. Everything. *Everything.* Alex grabbed the paper and read it. "You're sure? Hawes House?"

The information Weams had that could bring everybody down. *Everything.* Did that mean information on the Lions, or the blackmail material they had been using? Was it his lever to protect those he loved?

"We need to tell Drake," Chuffy said.

Alex grabbed his arm. "Not yet."

First he had to get to that safe. He had to make sure nothing was left that could indict Sir Joseph. He had to get rid of that carriage.

"Why?" Chuffy asked

Alex took a breath. "Because I'd rather as few people as possible knew where we are until we get more answers. I sent a message to Drake that we're safe and secure. Until I know more of the threat from the Lions and the marquess, I'd rather not put the women in any more danger."

Chuffy frowned, rubbing at his nose. "Drake needs to know what we found."

Alex frowned right back. "I'll send him a note that we're on the right track. Maybe that will keep him satisfied for the time being."

Chuffy was staring. "You want to go to Hawes House."

Alex grinned. "Exactly."

"What about the ladies?" Chuffy asked. "We need to tell them."

Alex faltered. "No. No, I don't think they need to know this yet. It would only distress them. Above all, they must be protected."

Chuffy slid his glasses back up his nose. "Because their grandfather has stored important Lion information at his town house?"

No, Alex thought, trying to give nothing away. Because if he didn't find anything in that safe, he'd have to devise another way to keep his father's secrets from being exposed. And right now his only other option was handing over the girls to the men who'd tried to burn down their school.

* * *

Of course Mairead didn't want to go. Fiona had expected it. She hadn't expected Lennie to be so compliant.

"Better f'r everybody," the girl said, feet planted wide in a pugilist's stance.

Fiona ached for that hard little child. "I swore I would never make you go back to the streets."

The little imp grinned. "But if I don't go, how are you two gonna survive? You don' know London. I do."

Fiona felt the burden of that child's future weigh on her. She was running again and dragging along Mairead. She didn't know how they would come about. How could she expect Lennie to face that as well? Except that Lennie was right. Fiona knew where to buy secondhand clothing and bruised fruit in Edinburgh, where to find work, where the marginal neighborhoods met the outright slums. What was safe and what wasn't for a girl. She had never spent enough time in London proper to learn it. Lennie had.

"But I have just begun measuring my stars again," Mae protested, sounding suddenly like a little girl. "I will lose too much time. Chuffy said he'd protect me."

"Alex has a choice," Fiona said, taking her sister by her shoulders. "Us or his father. If you were given that choice, Mae, say Chuffy or our mother, who would you choose?"

Mae looked away, her head down. Fiona thought her own heart would break. Mae had found real human affection with a man. A man she could respect. And now, just like every time they seemed secure, she was being yanked away.

"We couldn't go to the Herschels'?" Mairead asked, still not facing her.

"Sweetings, it would be the first place Alex would look.

Give him a little time to solve his problem." Fiona hugged her rigid sister. "When it's safe, we'll return."

Mae's head came up, her eyes bleak as a late winter sky. "What if it's never safe?"

Fiona dragged in an unsteady breath. "Then we go home to Edinburgh."

That didn't ease Mairead's frown. "But they know you there."

"Not after all this time. Besides, Mr. Playfair is building a real telescope up on Calton Hill. Don't you want to see how it turns out? Don't you want a turn at it?"

For once, even the lure of the sky didn't entice Mae. She just looked forlorn. "Whatever you say."

Fiona pulled her sister into her arms again, just as she had a thousand times before, from the days when they had hidden from their father's wrath in the linen closet to the hard nights in Edinburgh to the spare loneliness of the castle on the moors. This time, though, there was a difference. It wasn't Fiona's arms Mairead wanted to be in, and it tore Fiona apart.

So, she thought, nothing had changed, and yet everything had changed. She should have known that this was how it would be. And she hadn't even begun to contemplate what this would do to *her* heart.

"What first?" Lennie asked.

"Well," Fiona said, stepping back, "first we'll need a plan to get away. We are nowhere near where we need to be. Then we'll need transportation back to London. A place in a neighborhood where we won't be noticed, but won't really be in danger."

Lennie was nodding. "What I know best is Lime'ouse. Down near the docks."

"It would be the second place they would look."

"Seven Dials, then. Where the carters and rag-and-bone men live. I know a boarding'ouse there. Friend of me dad's when he was on the stage."

"Do I have to cut my hair?" Mae asked, her voice small. "Chuffy likes it so."

Fiona considered the bright sun of her sister's mane. "And dye it. We'll do it before we leave. I have the gall of Aleppo. You'll need to tell Chuffy that you aren't feeling well tonight. Lady issues. He will never ask. We'll wait till the moon sets."

Once more Mae asked. "Are you sure, Fee?"

"I am very sure, Mae."

It was the last word that was said on the subject, except when they met to gather their belongings to go. "Only what we need," Fee said, slipping her knife into its holder.

"Miss?" Lennie said, her own few things wrapped in a large kerchief. "Is it stealin' to take a book?"

Both Fiona and Mairead stopped what they were doing. "A book?" Fee asked.

Lennie ducked her head, her neck ruddy. "Found it in the library. About fossils and such. Always wanted to see a fossil. Amazin' creatures, they seem."

Fiona wished with all her heart she had the time to ask Lennie about her interest, of how she'd come to read, how she'd come to discover the world of natural philosophy. She wished she could refer Lennie to her friend Sarah, who lived down where fossils were hunted like partridges.

"I doubt one book will make a difference," she said. "When we gather a bit of money, we can replace it and send this one back."

And that was the sum of discussion about what was to be brought along. Fiona and Mairead had done this so many times that clarification wasn't needed. And Lennie didn't have enough to quibble over.

"I got us some bread and cheese and fruit after cook left," she said. "Last us a coupla days."

Fiona snapped shut her small bandbox. "All right, then. At moonset, we'll be off."

* * *

Marcus Drake's elegant home in Mayfair was usually an oasis of calm. That evening, as the earl stood before his valet deciding whether to secure his neckcloth with the sapphire or emerald pin for his evening stroll through various balls and routs, there came a pounding on the front door.

He looked up, his classic features the image of ennui. "Has no one any manners anymore, Pence?"

"No, milord," the valet answered, returning the unchosen sapphire to its tray. "I do not believe they do."

Drake gave a long-suffering sigh. A commotion had risen downstairs, with the cry of "In the king's name!" echoing up the stairs.

"The poor, mad king," Drake mourned as Pence slid him into his impeccably tailored dove-gray Westin coat. "He is held responsible for more mischief done in his name than Beelzebub." Turning to the mirror, he shot his cuffs, straightened a minute crease in the mathematical he had tied, and exited the bedroom door.

By the time he reached the entry hall, it was to face a small force of scruffy men led by a gentleman with a tipstaff prominently displayed in his hand.

"Wilkins?"

His butler, a twinkle in his green eyes, bowed low. "So

sorry to bother, milord. This gentleman was wanting to know if you knew where Lord Whitmore was."

The evening had just become more interesting. "Knight?" he asked, facing the belligerent little constable. "Good heavens, why? The last even vaguely illegal thing Alex Knight did was help me deposit a female goat in the bagwig's office at Christchurch just in time to birth twin kids. And I assure you, he already paid the penalty for that." Turning to Wilkins, he smiled. "Neither of us could properly sit a horse for a week."

"Ye'll pardon me, I'm sure, milord," the bantamweight invader interrupted. "But this is a matter of treason. Crimes against the king 'isself. Lookin' for Lord Whitmore and 'is father, one Sir Joseph Knight. A warrant 'as been issued."

Alex cocked an eyebrow. "Has it? Treason? My, he has been busy. Constable . . . ?"

"Teastern, milord. Thomas Teastern."

Drake kept a remarkably bored countenance. "Well, Constable Teastern, I don't suppose you know who swore out the warrant, or why you are here instead of the army."

"Not my place to ask, milord. Sheriff signed it and sent me out."

"Admirable. Inconveniently for you, however, Whitmore has not been here. I have no idea where he is at the moment."

"Will you know 'ow I can find 'im?"

"I assume you've been to his home."

"I 'ave."

Drake nodded agreeably. "In that case, I would check some of the spa towns. His father is recovering from a heart seizure. Knight probably took him off somewhere to recuperate." Pulling out his watch, he flicked it open. "Now, if you'll pardon me, I am late for a dinner engagement."

"I 'ave the right to search these premises, milord."

Not by a flicker did Drake betray any distress. "Do you? Why, I suppose you do. Go on, then. Wilkins will be certain to keep track of anything you break along the way, since it will come out of your pay."

"Gladly, milord," Wilkins said with a piratical smile. "Shall we start with the Limoges Room, gentlemen?"

The constable wavered and finally surrendered. "Don't warn 'im off, now," the little man threatened, giving his tip-staff a wave in the earl's face before marshaling his forces back out the door.

Wilkins had barely gotten the door closed when Drake cocked his head. "Most curious. Wilkins..."

"I'll take care of it, sir."

"You know where to go?"

Wilkins held out the earl's overcoat. "I do."

Nodding, Drake slipped into it and accepted his hat. "Well, for God's sake," he said before stepping through the open door. "Don't tell me."

* * *

Fiona wasn't certain whether it was because the three of them had had so much experience fleeing and hiding, or whether it was simply serendipity, but their escape went fairly seamlessly. Mairead pleaded lady problems, and Fiona excused herself to sit with her sister, as if she had ever needed to before. The hardest part was when Alex would look over at her during the dinner they took in the breakfast room, sharing the table with a pile of papers and a small lewd poem. Every time she caught his intense gaze on her, she flushed with pleasure and squirmed with discomfort. Every time he accidentally touched her, brushing a hand across hers, nudging a hip as he moved his chair, backing into her when carrying something, she felt her resolve erode a little more. She needed to leave; she knew it. Not just for her safety, but for Alex's. She could never ask him to choose between his father and her. She could never put either of the two men in danger. But if she took herself and Mairead out of the equation, Alex would have more leeway to solve his problem.

If only she could take him aside. If only he would confide in her, ask her help. Reassure her about his affection. Trust her. But that would only complicate a too-complicated matter and make it harder for her to leave.

And leave she did, tiptoeing out after sneaking some laudanum from Dr. O'Roarke's bag and lacing the guards' ale. As she crept through the deepening night, she was beset by powerful memories.

"It reminds me of the night we ran away the first time," Mae whispered alongside, her hood shadowing her face, her hand in her sister's.

Fiona shivered, the memory suddenly too fresh. "I know."

Her baby brother Teddy had been dead mere days when their mother had woken them from sound sleep, her hand over their mouths, their little bags packed. They had stolen away from the estate exactly the way they were doing now, holding hands and holding their breath lest their father wake from his drunken sleep to notice them gone and come raging after them. She remembered her mother already had bruises on her face. She remembered she had limped the whole way and that they had stopped in the churchyard to say farewell to little Teddy, who had cried too much.

But they had escaped. Their lives had been difficult and poor. But no longer had they needed to live in constant dread of a man's capricious violence and compulsive control. No longer did they suffer the indifference of their family. They protected themselves. Just as they would again.

Only once did she look back, just as they rounded the bend that would take the house out of sight. She could see its black mass blotting the starlight, smoke curling out of a few chimneys. She thought of the people who slept there and how hard it was to leave their kindness. She thought of Alex, sprawled out on his great bed, naked and vulnerable, his hair tousled, his cheeks bristled, his body so sleek and beautiful in the silvered light. She thought of what it had felt like the night before when he had driven into her, as if she had split into two people, before and after. As if from that moment on, she was not an independent soul, but melded to his. As if that melding had ripped apart the fabric of the universe to expose unbearable beauty.

It would not happen again. She was alone once more and would stay that way because Alex still didn't know the whole truth about her, and when he did, he would not be able to stay. But at least once she had known a man's touch. A man's mastery. A man's gentleness and generosity. She knew it was possible, and it had been hers. Once.

From now on, she would rely only on herself.

She just wished that it didn't hurt so badly.

* * *

"Damn her. *Damn* her!"

Alex couldn't seem to move from where he stood at the entrance to an empty bedroom, the door still in his hand, the mumbled excuses of the guards still echoing in his head. Lady Bea had been the one to raise the alarm, running into the breakfast room, breathless and stuttering. Alex had risen immediately, but neither he nor Chuffy had been able to calm her. Then he thought of her voice. That magical, musical voice.

"Sing it," he suggested.

"Oh, how could you let her," Bea sang, her sweet, clear voice throbbing to the tune of "Early One Morning," one of the ubiquitous folk songs about love, loss, and betrayal. "Gone, gone, gone, and left us all behind."

Alex hadn't had to ask any more. He had just run for the guest wing, accompanied by a roused Chuffy.

"Diddled us as sweetly as a second-story man," Chuffy agreed beside him as they looked into the tidied rooms.

Except Chuffy didn't sound like Chuffy suddenly. He sounded like every other man who had been deserted by a woman. He sounded the way Alex felt; bereft, confused, angry.

"What have you done?" Bea sang, her voice wavering. "Why did they go?"

"She must have heard me," Alex admitted, dragging his hand through his hair. "She must know."

Chuffy turned. "Know what?"

Bea sputtered.

Alex took her hand, the pain in his own chest threatening to choke him. "We'll find them. I promise. And when we come back, I will try to explain."

Lady Bea lifted a hand to his face, but her expression didn't ease. "Don't...fail."

Alex's gut twisting, he kissed her hand and turned. "Chilton!" he yelled.

"Know *what*?" Chuffy demanded, his hand firmly on Alex's arm.

Alex looked down at his friend. He wasn't certain he could feel worse. "I'll explain once we get the search started."

"Yes," Chuffy answered, suddenly not vague or bumblish at all. "You will."

Chilton and half the staff ran up the stairs. "Sorry, milord. We...er, slept a bit late. Only woke 'cause there was a messenger at the back door."

Alex glared. "Thick heads?"

Chilton straightened like a shot. "It wasn't the drink, sir. No one got more than a mug of ale."

What had she done? Because she had surely done something. This was a staff that was up to all rigs and rows. "And nobody heard anything untoward."

"Nothing, sir. Not 'til Davers showed up. I'm sorry, milord."

But Alex was already distracted. "Davers?"

"Says he's from Lord Drake. I was just comin' to get you."

Alex felt a headache begin to form behind his eyes. "Bring him to the library then, Chilton. Then find Finney's man Ben for me. And don't take no for an answer. Lady Bea, I would appreciate it if you would sit with my father. He is not to know that there is any kind of problem. All right?"

"Where will you look?" Bea sang as Chilton charged back down the stairs. "Where could they go?"

"Those Herbal people live nearby," Chuffy offered.

"Herschel." Alex shook his head. "She'd know we'd head there first."

"Milord?" Mrs. Chilton interrupted, her chapped hands tucked in her sharp white apron, her narrow face creased. "Don't know if it means anything, but that Lennie's gone as well."

"Regular exodus," Chuffy groused.

Alex's head came up, disparate pieces fitting together. "They've gone to ground."

"Ground?" Chuffy echoed. "What do you mean?"

"The slums, Chuff. They're going to lose themselves in the London slums, and let Lennie guide them. After all, they survived the Edinburgh slums. These can't be worse."

"Different. London."

"A slum's a slum, you pardon my sayin', sir," Mrs. Chilton spoke up. "Long as you look the part and know y'r way around. And that Lennie'd do that f'r 'em."

Look the part. Suddenly Alex remembered Fiona's smiling critique of his attire the night he'd been at the Blue Goose. She'd told him he never would pass, no matter what he wore. He knew without even thinking that she would blend in like a shadow. But he and Chuffy needed help.

"Where is Thrasher?" he demanded. "Find him."

"Right after we talk to Drake's messenger," Chuffy said.

Alex rubbed at his eyes. "This has turned out to be a busy morning, hasn't it?"

He couldn't escape the sense of impending doom. Drake wouldn't contact them unless it was important. And Alex could think of several important things Drake could have found out.

Well, he thought, if it had really been bad, Drake would have come himself.

* * *

He had underestimated Drake's good sense.

"Treason?" Chuffy demanded. "You practicin' treason, old thing?"

Alex fought down the panic that lodged in his chest. "Not that I know of. What else did Wilkins say, Davers?"

Davers, a scrawny jockey of a groom, twisted his cap in his hands. "'e said as 'ow you should warn Sir Joseph, too.

An' if you learn somethin' you was to send y'r messages through me, y'r lordship. He'd get 'em passed along. Lord Drake'll work on 'is end, but says it's better if 'e don' know what y'r up to quite yet."

Alex noticed that Chuffy failed to react this time.

"Good of him," Alex muttered, the heels of his hands pressed against his eyes. "Do they have any idea where this mysterious warrant originated?"

"Naw. Lord Drake spent all night lookin'. Somebody 'igh up, Mr. Wilkins says."

Alex nodded. It would have had to be, someone like, perhaps, a marquess. Hell, they'd just sent the coach and the threat. Why would they change tack so soon?

It was more imperative than ever that he get into that safe at Hawes House.

After he found Fiona. After he made sure she was safe and whole and tucked away somewhere secure. "Thank you, Davers. Mrs. Chilton will feed you. Where will I find you if I need to relay a message?"

"Been given a week off, sor. Stayin' with me mum in Soho."

Alex nodded. "In that case, be handy. And find me five men you can trust. Ask Wilkins. He'll know. I need you to meet us at the Peacock in Islington in the morning."

"The Peacock?" Chuffy echoed. "You think they went there?"

"I think that if they want to get to Edinburgh, they'll have to go past it, since it sits at the first tollgate on the Great North Road. Besides, no one would ever think to look for us there. In the meantime, we'll have Thrasher help us search London."

"Happy to," Thrasher piped up as Chuffy ushered the groom out.

"Go get a muffin," Chuffy told him and closed the door in his face.

Silence fell. Chuffy turned, leaning back against the door. "Don't seem surprised," was all he said.

Alex gave the brandy decanter a longing look and turned instead to the fireplace. "Neither do you," he said.

At first Chuffy looked away. "I am about you."

Alex came to a halt. "And Sir Joseph? You can't imagine he would be involved in something treasonous."

Still Chuffy didn't face him. "There were some odd rumors going around. Year you were on the continent. Lost and found money and all. Some odd friendships."

"And you didn't think to tell me?"

Finally Chuffy met his gaze with implacable blue eyes. "Rather like you're not telling me what's going on now, I'd say. It's not like I haven't wondered."

Chuffy had been with Alex when he had failed to protect Ian Ferguson. Chuffy had never asked why.

"Blackmail?" he asked gently now, hands in pockets.

Alex looked up to see an amazingly benign expression on Chuffy's face. If it had been he, he would have been raging. Alex had betrayed the Rakes, and Chuffy knew it.

"It's complicated," Alex finally admitted, then laughed, a dry, sour sound. "Well, if that isn't the most banal statement I have ever made, I don't know what is."

"Your wife was involved, too?"

Alex's head snapped up and he stared at his friend. "You knew?"

Chuffy shrugged. "After she died. There were some odd coincidences." For a moment he looked down, as if his boot-shod foot were the most interesting thing in the room. "Unfaithful," he said without looking up. "Not a secret."

Alex sighed, once again rubbing at the headache behind

his eyes. "I know. I'm not sure it was her fault, though, Chuff. She was broken...."

"Unfillable," Chuffy said succinctly, finally looking up again. "Happens sometimes. Especially with orphans who changed hands. She did."

Alex met his gaze, wondering why he was surprised at Chuffy's insight. Chuffy saw more than anybody gave him credit for. "Good way of putting it. I thought I could save her." He shook his head with a rueful smile. "How could I have ever been so bloody young, Chuff?"

"Everybody is, sometime or other. Picked a winner this time."

Alex halted, stricken. "Yes," he finally said, suddenly certain. "I did. And I don't plan on losing this one. She deserves better than what she's had, and I mean to give it to her."

Funny. He'd said that before. How could this time be so different? Because the two women were so different. Because he suspected Fiona had disappeared to prevent harm to his father. Because he knew that Fiona had fought tooth and nail to survive, to protect her sister. And because she had not needed him to complete her. He hoped, however, she would let him shelter her.

"What about the blackmail?" Chuffy asked. "Need to get on with it."

Alex nodded. "The affairs weren't the secret," he said, lifting a small crystal vase from the mantel. "The secret was that she had been sending letters to Smythe-Smithe containing all manner of government information. He was her last lover. The one she broke herself over."

The one she killed herself for.

"Man's a bounder." The man was also, at least temporarily, out of their reach on the continent. "You were going to turn her in."

So certain. Alex shrugged, still not certain after all these years. "They have letters from her with information Sir Joseph allegedly shared. Troop numbers and movements. Diplomatic information. It's enough to ruin him."

Chuffy nodded. "You don't believe they're true?"

"I can't. If I did, it would mean there was no honor left anywhere."

Alex noticed how the fire glinted off the segmented glass in his hands. He had the most unbearable urge to heave the thing, just to see it explode against the marble.

Chuffy blinked as if faced with a bright light. "Didn't you ask him?"

"You saw him. How could I put more strain on his heart?"

"Seems you did. Warrant out for his arrest."

Alex set the vase down before he destroyed it, his patience suddenly gone. "Which is why I have to get to Hawes House before anyone else. If there are more letters, I think that is where they are. I need to get that evidence."

"You're sure about that?"

Alex faced Chuffy, but he didn't answer. Because, of course, he didn't know. "I was threatened by Ben last night. The Lions have threatened his old dad. I was told to hand over the girls." He couldn't bear the rest. "Fiona must have heard and thought I'd hand them over to the Lions."

Chuffy's gaze was unwavering. "Was she right?"

And for the first time Alex admitted the whole truth to himself. "I don't know."

* * *

How could stunning redheaded twins who stood as tall as any man simply disappear? And yet it seemed that they had. There was no trace of them anywhere along the route to London. Alex even traveled the Thames, just in case they had taken a water route to throw him off.

Alex and Chuffy finally checked into the Peacock Inn on Islington High Street and plotted to search London. Thrasher went shopping in the stalls of Seven Dials, and Chuffy took their horses around to his parents' mews, exchanging them for less showy hacks. Alex left word where he could along the north route to report the passing of redheaded twins.

And then he received a message from Willowbend. One of the sculleries had discovered two thick red-gold braids in the trash pile and two bath towels smudged with black stain. That beautiful flame-bright hair, sacrificed to necessity and fear. Alex felt sick at the desperation of such an instinctive action.

Standing in the drab, close quarters he had taken in the Phoenix, he shut his eyes. Suddenly he could see it again, that moment four years earlier, when he had had to saw off that glorious banner to free her from the brambles. He could smell the sunlight and feel the lush flaming silk in his fist, lifting in a chill breeze like a battle pennant. It wasn't fair. It wasn't right. And yet she had done it again without hesitation, just to escape him.

Suddenly he wasn't so certain of success.

"You sure you wanna come?" Thrasher asked an hour later as they readied to face the slums.

Buttoning the last button on the stained, crumpled pantaloons Thrasher had provided, Alex grabbed the patched broadcloth coat. "You're going to show us how to blend in, Thrasher. I've been told I don't."

Thrasher tilted his head. "Oh, y'r worshipfulness, you jus' don' belong there."

Alex frowned. "I know that. You know that. How do I keep them from knowing that?"

After a moment's consideration, Thrasher shrugged. "First, don't look like you got someplace important to go. 'n y'r too awake. People in the Dials're tired. Real tired. Walk tired. Think tired. Move tired. Nobody looks anybody else in the eye. That'd be dangerous, like with dogs."

Behind Alex, Chuffy shoved a flat cap on his thick curls. "Act tired. Can do that. Haven't slept in days."

"Not that kinda tired," Thrasher said, wrapping a tattered gray wool scarf around his throat. "Tired like ya got nuthin' and you ain' getting' nuthin', and ya still have ta feed y'r kids. Tired like ya wanna give up."

"I can't imagine Fiona acting like that," Alex mused.

Thrasher huffed in amusement. "If she survived the streets, she did. She didn't jus' act it, neither." Another unconscious indictment on them all. "You got a barkin' iron, y'r worship? And not one o' them fancy pieces you wave around in the park."

Alex pulled out the pistol he had gotten from Finney, a scratched, battered old thing Finney swore shot straight.

Chuffy pulled on a tweed coat that looked as if it had been plucked from the river and pocketed another of the guns, wrinkling his nose. "Well. Ready as I'll get."

"An' you got no idea where they'd go," Thrasher said. "There be a lotta places ta 'ide in them streets. Like I already tole you, all I know is Lennie tole me 'e lived in Lime'ouse and Seven Dials."

Alex checked the priming on the gun. "Our searchers have already scoured every business and boardinghouse between here and the river."

His own fear had mounted with every negative report that had come in. He needed to find her. He needed to beg her forgiveness and then beg her to stay.

"Which leaves the places you 'ope the ladies don' go,"
Thrasher said.

Alex looked up. "What kind of places?"

Thrasher shook his head. "Boozing kens, f'r a start. Flash
'ouses. Then worse."

Worse. Suddenly Alex found himself laughing. It
couldn't be that easy. Could it? He swore his heart was suddenly skipping like a child's. "Not boozing kens," he said,
clapping Chuffy on the back. "Thrasher, take us to some
whorehouses."

Chapter 19

Fiona had thought that there couldn't be a worse place than Betty the Badger's. She had been wrong. After spending the last few days trudging from one end of Seven Dials and Soho to the other, she could honestly say that Betty had been fairly successful. Some of the madams along these streets were successful as well. Tight-fisted, sharp-eyed women who kept closer watch over their girls than a schoolroom nanny and never saw a loose ha'penny leave the building. But those weren't the women who really needed Fiona's help. The unsuccessful ones did. Too flamboyant, too wasteful, too unaware of all the schemes and cons that could siphon their money away, and too uneducated to know how to keep books.

Fiona would have worked anywhere but a brothel if only she could have found a business that would have accepted a female bookkeeper. Butchers, chandlers, cent-per-centers. But long experience had taught her that she wouldn't merely be shown the door, she would be remembered for her bold request. Whorehouses made a practice of forgetting inconvenient problems.

Her approach to the brothels was made easier by the acquaintance of her new landlady. A costumer for theater, Mrs. Tolliver also helped with stage makeup and kept her own paints. So the once-statuesque, redheaded Fiona was now a stooped spinster of middle age with hair scraped into a gray-dusted brown bun, dark glasses, and skin that bore a rather unhealthy yellow tint. Her bosom was compressed beneath muslin wrappings and her posterior increased by the judicious use of theatrical padding. She was, if the people who passed her in the street were anything to judge by, completely forgettable. If she had but known it, she had already avoided the attention of at least three searchers who had been told to keep an eye out for a Scottish queen.

She snuck in and out of fetid alleys and back doors, trying her best to block out the noises and smells and sights, and she spent her time hunched over a variety of desks, tables, and upended crates going over the jumbled, often indecipherable accounts of whores. And then every evening she returned to the room Lennie had found them on the top floor of what would loosely be described as Mrs. Tolliver's boardinghouse.

Exiting Miss Fancy's Parlor into the cold late afternoon, she reached up beneath her brown coal scuttle bonnet and scratched at the wig she wore, irrationally sure that she had brought bedbugs out with her. It would only be for a while longer, she kept telling herself day after day as she trudged from Miss Fancy's to Madame Trixy's to The Cat House to Seven Sins, all vetted by both Lennie and Mrs. Tolliver. Only until Alex and his father were safe, she kept assuring herself. Only until she could earn enough to get Mairead and her back to Edinburgh.

Where she would probably be forced to do the same thing.

How could she already be so tired?

"Ya think you'd like to add one more place, miss?" Lennie asked alongside her.

Startled out of her reverie, Fiona looked around at the fading light and then down at the smudged, smiling face of her cohort. "Do you have something in mind?"

The girl nodded and shoved her disreputable hat back on her short blond curls. "I 'eard as 'ow Nan Blessing 'as set up shop. Knew 'er when I was a littlun. On stage in the pants parts."

"When exactly did you live hereabouts?"

Lennie shrugged and pushed her way through the crowd. "Afore da died. He was an actor, too. Shakespearean. Ma said she fell plumb in love with his Benedick when he came to play at the house where she was governess."

"And your mother died..."

Lennie's shoulders slumped. "Coupla years ago. We'd moved on to Lime'ouse by then. Nan's is two streets over, now," she said as they returned to the center of the dial from which the seven streets radiated. "That red door there."

That red door and the dingy, listing brick building with red curtains at the windows and a light barely lifting the gloom by the door. Fiona felt depressed just looking at it. She knew what she would find inside. Women in faded, dingy drawers, their faces painted like clowns, their eyes older than death. She would have to overcome the urge to hustle them all out the door and away before their lives grew even worse.

She couldn't. She had nothing better to offer them.

It had always been hard to bear these places, where women traded away everything but the will to live. Where the fantasy of love wore a painted face and had an outheld hand. It was so much harder now that she knew how beautiful the act of love could be, how transcendent, so that a person's soul could truly feel connected to another, so the glow in a lover's eyes could light the way ahead. So every touch and kiss could be a blessing. Not a burden.

Lennie knocked on the red door and ushered Fiona in as if she were coming on a morning call. Nan Blessing was in, a corpulent, slow-moving woman with execrable taste, brassy blond hair, and a ready smile and hug for Lennie.

"Sit, sit," she offered, motioning to the threadbare settee next to the overcrowded drinks table. Fiona briefly entertained temptation.

"Happy to know any friend of Lennie's," the woman said. "She told you of our old days, eh? I was quite the high-stepper in those days, wasn't I, eh, Lennie?" Her laugh was booming, her breasts quivering over the edge of her corset with each move. "Couldn't high-step now, could I? Couldn't so much as see my feet."

Fiona sat down as primly as a vicar's wife and clasped her hands in her lap. "I've come to offer my services, Nan."

Nan took one look at the pinched, pale face, the graying hair, and the unfortunate figure and almost choked with laughter. Since that was precisely the reaction Fiona had hoped for, she laughed right back. It was easier that way to bring up her real business, which went quite successfully, until the moment she stood to leave.

"Good thing you came in with Lennie," Nan said, settling her voluminous puce skirts. "I don't trust strangers much. Well, and I'll be honest. With that reward posted, I'd be tempted to turn you in for it, no matter you don't look like the mort they're looking for at all." She shrugged. "Worst they can do is take it back when they see you."

Fiona did her best not to react. She didn't even look at Lennie. "Reward? If it looks like a good deal, I might go in with you. Could always use a few quid."

The older woman laughed until her top button popped. "Oh, lovey, don't. You'll make me pee. Man was here looking for gentry mort. Red hair, he said, tall, womanly, beautiful. No offense…"

"None taken. I am what I am. Who wanted her, constables?"

"Naw. Some poor sod, says she's been barmy since the last babe's born. Been wanderin' all over. Poor bloke looked right fatched. Says the wee ones are pinin' for 'er."

"I ran inta a mort with red hair," Lennie piped up. "Tall, too. What's this cove look like? If'n I find him, I'll split the lot with you, Nan."

"Where'd you see 'er?" Nan asked.

Lennie grinned like a gypsy. "Aw, Nan. Not that I don't trust ya."

Nan laughed again and tousled Lennie's hair. "Tall, brown 'air, brown eyes. Real sad-lookin', you c'n imagine. Just lost 'is job at the brewery, then this."

Fiona's stomach lurched. Who could it be? Alex would never convince this streetwise madame that he belonged here. She would have recognized his worth in a second. Could it be the man who had threatened him? Could it be emissaries of the Lions? She didn't have the luxury of finding out.

She got Lennie out of there as fast as she could. "We might need to go," she told the girl, hustling her along the walkway. "Leave."

"Where?" Lennie asked, skipping to keep up with her long stride.

She shook her head. She couldn't think. Should she trust

her disguise, or should she just run again? Was she quite as invisible as she'd thought? Could it really have been a co-incidence that she was being searched for in whorehouses? Alex knew how she had supported herself in Edinburgh. Had he spread the word?

She wished, desperately, that Alex were here. That he would somehow know where she was and how to get her out of this mess. At least hold her, so she didn't once again feel so alone. She was so caught up in her thoughts that as she turned the street, she bumped into a man coming the other way.

"Excuse me," she apologized, caught for a moment by the color of his hair.

He lifted a hand without turning toward her and kept moving, another in a stream of sorry men in search of work. "It's all right."

"If Nan didn't see through you, nobody will," Lennie said, as if she'd heard Fiona's thoughts. "Believe me, Miss Fee. Y'r mammy wouldn't know ya. Minnie Tolliver does such good work you look like a crone hasn't dropped a babe in a decade."

Fiona was surprised into a laugh. "Once we have you back in petticoats, we'll have to work on your language, Lennie. You mother would be appalled."

Shoving her hat back on her head, Lennie shoved her hands in her trouser pockets. "Aw, I know when to use cant and when not to. Me mam made sure of that."

Fiona knew better than to hug the girl, even though she wanted to. "Well, then let us just say that when we get settled I'll carry on your mother's job."

They had just reached Shaftesbury Road and been forced to stop. The traffic here was heavy, drays and beer wagons and hackneys, horses and pushcarts and the odd stage, barreling through as if they were the only ones in the road. Seeing a break, Fiona had just laid her hand on Lennie's shoulder to urge her forward when she saw the mail coach approach, its bright red wheels and maroon panels splattered with mud. She hesitated, her foot midair, her now-full reticule clutched like the pillow to her chest. She had just turned to tell Lennie to wait when she caught a flash of something behind her, a face she thought she knew. And then, suddenly, she was cartwheeling toward the road, ruthlessly pushed right into the path of the thundering coach.

She saw the lathered horses, and the gaping mouth of the guard, his blunderbuss in his arms like a baby. She heard a shout, and thought a scream, and wondered if it had been she.

Mairead, she thought, and then, *Alex*.

She wasn't sure, even after, how she missed being trampled beneath those steel-shod hooves. One minute she was tipping inexorably toward disaster. The next, she was yanked back so hard she landed on her bottom, right there in the street.

"Oh, miss!" Lennie cried, down on her knees beside her.

The coach went thundering past, the breeze from it blowing Fiona's bonnet back. She struggled to catch her breath, her hand still holding her reticule to her flattened chest, her glasses hanging off one ear. "Who…"

She looked up, finally, to thank whoever had saved her. A man stood there, hand out, his face in deep shadow. She could smell hard work on him, horses and beer, and smiled her gratitude.

"Thank you ever so much," she said, taking his calloused hand in hers and letting him pull her up.

He had thick dark hair and broad shoulders. For a moment her heart skipped around. She felt a moment of joy, relief, gratitude. Then the man turned so that Fiona could see his face, and she realized it was unfamiliar to her. He was pale-eyed and broad-cheeked, with a gentle smile and a missing arm, clad in the faded uniform jacket of the 95th Rifles. Older than she'd thought, with a face marked in creases and old pockmarks. A savior who had risked himself for a stranger. But not Alex.

Did every man suddenly remind her of him? Only a week away, and she was imagining him everywhere.

"You all right now, miss?" not-Alex asked, doffing his cap. "Gave me a scare, no question."

"I gave me a scare as well," she admitted, reaching up with shaking hands to right her bonnet. "I think you saved my life, Mr...."

"Mitchell, ma'am. Tom Mitchell."

"How can I pay you back, Mr. Mitchell?"

His smile broadened ruefully. "You got a job for a man with one arm, I'd surely take it, ma'am. But if you're walking these streets as well, I fair doubt it."

She could barely feed the people she was responsible for. And yet how could she fail to reward such an act? "Tom Mitchell, can you read and write?"

"I can."

She nodded and turned to Lennie. "Don't you think our enterprise could use a strong arm?"

Lennie squinted up at him, as if sizing him up. "D'ya see who pushed her?"

He stared at Fiona. "You were pushed? I just thought you slipped."

Resettling her bonnet, she shook her head. "No. Someone must have thought I wasn't walking fast enough. Did you see, Lennie?"

Lennie shook her head.

"I saw," Fiona heard just behind her, and her heart did another somersault.

She whipped around and gaped. It was the man she had just bumped into coming out of the brothel, the one she thought had been looking for work. She froze, her breath caught in her chest, her heart threatening to break free. It looked as if he was doing the same thing, his mouth actually sagging a bit, an odd glitter in his eye.

She had imagined him all week, but now when she'd seen him, she hadn't recognized him. Somehow, he had learned to mix in. Somehow, he had become hopeless and shabby and worn. She couldn't take her eyes off his beloved face.

But he wasn't looking at her. He had turned to Thomas Mitchell, her one-armed savior. "You know who pushed her, don't you?" he asked.

Fiona looked up at Thomas. But it wasn't the Thomas who had introduced himself. This one was hard-eyed and grim. She caught that in an instant before he gave her another great shove and ran.

Alex caught her handily and set her back on her feet. She tried to run after Thomas Mitchell. How dare he push her? Who was he? Who had sent him?

But Alex held her still right there in the middle of the teeming sidewalk, his face almost as grim. "You're not going anywhere, sweetheart. Chuffy needs the exercise. Are you all right?"

She couldn't seem to manage more than a nod. Her heart was still pounding so.

"You, Lennie?" he asked without looking away from Fiona.

"Right as a trivet. We're gonna get trampled, we stay here, though. Shouldn't we go?"

Alex nodded. "We should. Where?"

Oddly, Fiona couldn't remember. "How did you find me?"

"Pure accident. I was checking all the brothels. You said it yourself. I've been up and down all the streets singing a sad song of my mad wife."

She grimaced. "I heard."

"You did a good job of camouflaging yourself," he said, his eyes soft with hurt. "I wouldn't have recognized you at all if I hadn't heard your voice."

She struggled to take in a breath. His hand was still on her arm, and it burned her. It stirred her, just like always, until she couldn't think or move. "You weren't supposed to," she finally managed.

She couldn't take her gaze from him, drinking in those deep, delicious brown eyes like water in a desert. Desperate, suddenly, to run her fingers along his jaw, over his cheeks, his eyes. Needing to know he was more than her imagination.

"You shouldn't be here," she finally protested, trying to pull away. "You shouldn't be anywhere near us. Get back to your father. He needs you."

He smiled. He actually smiled, and she thought she would weep. "My father is quite well and more closely watched than an heir in the royal nursery. It is you who ran off into the night, Fiona. Couldn't you come to me?"

"No." She wanted to get away. She wanted to curl up into his arms. It wasn't right. It wasn't fair. She had worked so hard to protect him, to keep him from having to make an impossible decision. "No outcome would have been fair."

"I'm sorry, Fiona," he whispered, so that only she could hear it. "I'm so sorry."

Tears brimming in her eyes, she lifted a hand to his scruffy face. "I know."

"I wouldn't have handed you over," he averred, then,

shaking his head, dropped his eyes, his hand holding hers tightly enough to hurt. "I don't think I would have."

She squeezed his fingers. "I'm not sure I would have blamed you if you had. Your father is far more precious to the world than an orphan brat with a knack for numbers."

That brought the thunderclouds. Glaring, he shook her hard. "I *never* want to hear you say that again. Do you understand me?"

Tears again, useless and frightening. She couldn't lose control now. Not now.

"And on top of everything else," he mourned, a broad finger up to stroke the fringe from her forehead, "you had to lop off your hair again. I'm almost most sorry about that."

Her smile was less assured. "It is nothing. Hair grows. At least that is what I have been trying to impress on Mae."

"Mae's with you?" she heard behind her and turned to see Chuffy approaching, completely out of breath.

"Lost him, huh?" Alex asked.

Chuffy shook his head in wonder and wiped his sweating face with his sleeve. "Hardy devils, those riflemen."

Finally, Fiona pulled herself back into the moment. "Why would he do that?" she asked. "Push me and then save me."

"Get in your good graces, I imagine," Alex said.

Chuffy nodded. "Easier to take control if he knows where everybody is. Lowers defenses. Mae?"

Fiona managed a smile. "In our room working on the puzzles."

"The puzzles?" Chuffy leaned close. "She can't be. They're in the safe at Willowbend."

Fiona smiled. "It doesn't matter. She never really needed the slips. Not that way. She just needed to believe that grandfather felt some affection for her."

"But she'd need the poem."

"She had it memorized the first time she read it."

Chuffy's face scrunched up in a scowl. "Too bad. Awful poem. Bad metaphors."

"You wanna jaw all day, it's nothin' to me," Fiona heard at her elbow. "But I'm gettin' hungry."

"Where is she, Fee?" Alex asked. "We need to get the two of you someplace safe."

Fiona looked around, as if calling up Tom Mitchell and the mail again. "How did they find us? I've been so careful."

All she had wanted to do was protect Alex, and she had failed. She wanted to cry.

Alex stroked her cheek. "You ran out into the open. I obviously haven't impressed on you well enough that the minute you came under my care, you were safe, no matter what. I'll have to do better next time."

"Why are we so important?" she demanded. "Mae and I don't know anything."

"But you do." Alex took her hand. "We'll talk when we get you and Mairead to safety."

She looked up, seeking the warmth of his eyes, the strength. Bathing in the nearness of him, as if his very presence provided armor.

"Lennie," Alex said, never taking his gaze from Fiona, "I assume you know where you're staying." The answer was an indignant huff that produced a smile. "Why don't you take Chuffy along so he can make sure Mairead is safe? We'll follow right behind."

Only hard-won instinct pulled Fiona's gaze away from Alex. The light had faded, and they were still standing like a boulder in a fast-moving stream and were receiving more than a few glares as people had to move around them to get home. The cacophony of wagon wheels and hooves and hawkers and broadsheet sellers singing about murder.

Lennie set off running in and out of the passing vehicles like a sparrow among the rooftops, Chuffy following with surprising agility. Fiona didn't breathe until they made it safely to the other side of Shaftesbury and onto Mercer, where the pedestrians outnumbered the vehicles.

Turning back to Alex, she found herself once again completely distracted. "You look particularly handsome as a rogue, you know."

He cocked an eyebrow at her. "I wish I could say the same for you. You look like a Methodist handing out tracts."

That broadened her smile immensely. "That was what the brothel owners said."

Placing her hand on his arm, as if they were strolling the park, Alex made to turn her in the other direction. "I will make the Lions pay for making you think you needed to return to the streets like this, Fee. I swear it."

Fee's smile was a bit wobbly. "It never hurts to reacquaint yourself with old skills," she said, suddenly strong in his company. "For an entire week I was invisible."

She had hoped for a smile. She got a thoughtful frown. "I'd much rather you be allowed to forget. I'd always be afraid you'd slip away and I'd never find you."

Fiona was too afraid to look at him now, not at all certain what she wanted to see. Did he realize what he was saying? Or was he just being polite? She simply didn't know.

She couldn't shake the sense of disorientation. She had been hiding for more than a week, so careful to remain a nonentity, so vigilant. And in a matter of moments, she found herself walking alongside Alex through the noisome alleys of the Dials as if it were the park during the afternoon stroll. The only thing that gave away the danger they faced was the tension in Alex's arm, the constant swivel of his eyes.

The touch of him distracted her; the sound of his voice resonated in her chest and skimmed along her skin. She needed to remain alert; they still had a way to walk. But a frantic kind of giddiness rose in her chest like a tide, and she couldn't seem to breathe past it. Alex was here. Alex had been looking for her. She had run to protect him, and yet she was too thankful for words that he walked by her side.

It was when they walked right past Nan's place that she finally regained her senses. "We seem to be going the wrong way."

"I know. It's safer to take a different route from Chuffy. Where are you staying?"

She looked around, as if she could spot a lurker intent on their passage. "Back the other way across Shaftesbury on Stacey Street, just across from the new charity school."

He nodded and turned down Monmouth as if they were heading toward one of the myriad gin shops, both of them surreptitiously scanning their environment.

The tension fast became unbearable for her. She had so many questions. But she couldn't imagine asking about the people who were blackmailing him or the danger from the Lions as they walked down the narrow and teeming streets.

"We should probably be talking to each other," Alex said, giving her a quick glance. "You look like I'm walking you to the gallows."

She caught sight of a man watching them. Small, thin, furtive. She was about to warn Alex when she caught a telltale motion that actually made her smile. "Beware the pickpocket," she warned.

Alex looked over. "He can't think I have anything."

"You have more than he does."

Alex considered the man for a moment and nodded. "You're right."

"You can never trust the poor," she said. "There is always temptation."

He turned to her, looking unsettled. "Even you?"

He still didn't realize then how far they had sunk. It would have been pointless to tell him, so she just lifted her free hand and opened it. In her palm lay his pocket watch and some change. Then his eyes did get big.

"I was a dab hand at the knuckle by the time I was ten," she said, handing them over.

"Is that the worst thing you needed to tell me?"

Her heart plummeted. Her belly went hot. "No."

"Will you tell me?"

She looked up at him under her bonnet, trying so hard to anticipate him. "You tell me why you're being blackmailed, and I'll tell you why in the end I will leave."

For the longest time he only glared at her, as if challenging her to change her claim. She couldn't, so he began to talk, and talked all the way across to New Compton and back down to Stacey.

And Fiona heard of Alex's doomed Amabelle, the woman Fiona had envied so unspeakably four years ago, the woman she had drawn in her mind as perfect as Alex deserved. The woman who had been so troubled that not Alex, not lovers, not excitement or danger or threat, could satisfy her. Who, in the end, had been destroyed by her own imperfections.

At first Fiona was furious that the woman could have so capriciously wasted a gift as precious as Alex's love. She wanted to hate her. But Alex made her see how pitiful Amabelle had actually been. He admitted that rather than one villain, the marriage had joined two imperfect people in a futile attempt at happiness.

"I was too young to help her," he finally said, his voice low. "I didn't know how."

Fiona felt the old desperation well up in him and held on more tightly. "She was still a very lucky woman."

He looked surprised again, this time in a more profound way. As if struggling to understand Fiona's words. *Oh, Alex*, she thought. *You have blamed yourself too long.* She couldn't make him see his mistake, not here on the street with the world passing by and the threat of curious eyes on them. Later, she hoped. When they were alone. When they had time, time enough for honesty and comfort.

She thought of the magic of that last night at Willowbend and wanted to think it meant more than simple pleasure. She wanted to know whether he felt the same way. She knew she shouldn't expect him to. She shouldn't hope for what would in the end hurt them both.

But perversely, she did.

It seemed he did, too.

She had no sooner ushered him into the dingy front hall of Mrs. Tolliver's house than he dragged her into the parlor and kicked the door shut. Ignoring the horsehair sofa, the sputtering fire, and the tallow candelabras, he pulled her hard into his arms.

"Come here," he rasped, yanking the knot on her bonnet and tossing it on a couch. He was about to kiss her, she thought, suddenly feeling suffused with light. Her heart stumbled and ran. She lifted her head and closed her eyes.

But nothing happened. Frustrated, she opened her eyes to see him looking wistfully at the top of her head. "My poor girl. Look what you did to your lovely hair."

She looked up, as if she could see where it lay flat against her skull, the stain robbing it of gleam or luster. "I did what I had to."

"No," he said, his gaze darkening. "You didn't have to do

it. For God's sake, Fee, after what we shared, how could you think I would desert you?"

He simply took her breath. How could she tell him how she hoped, but wasn't sure? How could she ask if he loved her a fraction as much as she loved him?

"You were given an impossible choice," she insisted. "I couldn't bear to be part of it. I wanted you and your father safe. Mae and I have survived just fine on our own before. We could have until you dealt with those men."

He was shaking his head, as if she made no sense. His eyes were so hot, so sweet, so torn. She brushed aside his hair and stroked his face. She thought she saw tears glisten in his eyes as he twined his fingers through her short locks, pulling her face very close to his. "Don't ever do that to me again, Fee," he commanded on a rasp. "Don't ever frighten me that way again."

She felt tears fill her throat as well. Reaching up, she laid her hand against his stubbled chin. And then, lifting on her toes so they were eye-to-eye, where her intent could not be mistaken, she kissed him. And in that moment, she knew that no matter where she went in her life, no matter what became of her, this was where her home was.

She didn't have to wait long for his response. His arms came around her so tightly he almost lifted her off the floor. His mouth opened, hot and urgent over hers. His tongue plunged into her mouth, met her tongue, mated. His body, so strong, so welcoming, trembled as if he were in a fever. His touch was incendiary, and she relished it, burning up, burning away until nothing was left but the touch of him, the rasp of his breath, the taste of his mouth, dark and hungry and fierce.

"Promise me, Fee," he demanded, pulling his mouth away, until she lifted again, seeking its return. "Promise."

"Anything." She reached up and tossed off his hat, wrapped her fingers in his hair, and yanked him back to her, meeting him in a frenzy of need and joy and wonder. Relief, as if she had been holding her breath since leaving his bed. "What am I promising?"

"You won't ever leave me again. Promise."

Suddenly, it was as if he'd doused her with cold water. From one heartbeat to the next her delight died into ashes and she pulled away. He stared at her, his hands still on her arms. "What?"

"I can't promise that," she protested, her voice thick with tears. "I can't."

He looked furious. "Why not? Don't you love me?"

He might as well have hit her with a club. How could he? "Yes."

She couldn't say another word. Not until he did.

But he didn't.

"What is it?" he asked instead, standing there unmoving as granite, his earth-brown eyes dark as night. "What haven't you told *me*? What can you have done that was more scandalous than working in a brothel or having a wife who betrayed her country?"

Fiona felt the blood drain from her face. *Scandalous.* Oh, sweet heaven, if it were only that. If only she didn't paint him with her crime if she told him. Because she knew that he wouldn't let it rest. He would not let the matter drop until it was finished. And the only way for it to be finished was for her to be hanged.

"I…"

And then the moment was lost. Mae began pounding on the door. "I know you're in there! Lennie told us. Fee, you have to come here! I need help figuring this out!"

Fiona pulled in a sobbing breath, never looking away

from Alex. Daring him to speak, to commit even without her answer. To give her something to take with her.

"Isn't Chuffy here?" she asked, not moving. "Have him help you."

"Fee!"

Fee pulled out of Alex's arms. Alex reached for her, but it was too late.

She shuddered with the impact of loss. "What is it, sweetings?" she asked, pulling the door open.

Mairead was bouncing on her toes, her eyes gleaming, her fingers twisted around each other. Behind her stood Chuffy in a flat tweed cap looking like a beer carter and Lennie, a hunk of bread stuffed in her mouth.

"Mrs. Tolliver has soup and bread," the girl offered, on her own toes to be seen.

"No!" Mae protested, trying to brush the girl away. "I'm close. I can feel it. I need Fee to help me first."

"You need to eat first," Fiona disagreed, taking her sister by the shoulders and turning her for the kitchen. "We'll solve puzzles afterward."

"We'll leave afterward," Alex said, following, "and solve the puzzles when we get where we're going."

They had just reached the staircase when they were interrupted again. Someone was pounding on the front door with something heavy. Everybody turned toward it.

"Open in the name of the king!" a strident voice cried.

"Damn and bugger!" Alex spat. "How did they find us?"

Fiona spun around, agape. "How did they *what*?"

Chapter 20

Alex turned to Lennie. "Is there a back door?"

The pounding began again. "Open in the name of the king, I say!"

Suddenly Mrs. Tolliver was squeezing into the hall, unhurriedly pulling a key from her bodice.

"You just wait!" she yelled before spotting Alex. "Well, hello. You must be Lord Whitmore," she said with a pat on his leg on the way by. "My, you are the pretty one."

Fiona battled a mad urge to giggle. The look on Alex's face was priceless as he stared down at their landlady. Mrs. T was the size of a child, round, rolling, and with the sweetest old face Fiona had ever seen.

The older woman cackled. "I'd have to wager this call isn't for me, so it might be better you all run upstairs and use the roof exit. Lennie, you know the way."

Lennie laughed and took the first steps up. "How we got out of paying that last month's rent. Thanks, Minnie! See you again soon."

And as Mrs. Tolliver made quite a show of yelling back

and forth to her cook and whoever stood outside, claiming she couldn't get the door open, the rest of them scurried up the steps, stopping only long enough to collected Mairead's work. Chuffy stuffed it into his coat pockets while Fiona and Mae grabbed bags.

A scrawny young maid edged into the room, waving at Fiona. "Run! I'll get this stuff. You can come back later."

Fiona thanked her and pushed Mae toward the door Chuffy held open. From downstairs, there came an ominous creaking.

"You stop that!" Mrs. Tolliver shrilled.

"I'll break the door open if you don't answer!" came the voice. "I got information y'r hidin' Lord Whitmore and 'is fancy piece Mizz Ferguson in there, and they's wanted for 'igh treason."

Fiona stumbled to a halt in the middle of the hallway. She swore she felt her heart stop. "*Me?* What did *I* do?"

Alex grabbed her and shoved her toward the stairs. "I'll explain later."

She glared at him. "You certainly will."

Lennie had just led them up the stairs to the attic, when Fiona heard the front door squeal open and boots pound into the entryway. Mrs. T was dramatically weeping, cook shouting, and the constable demanding information. By the time the intruders reached the stairs, the attic door was closed and Lennie was pointing the way across the dusty and cramped room through what seemed to be the prop department for the local theater. Fiona gasped more than once upon coming across a fully dressed mannequin.

Lennie just chuckled. "Warehouse, isn't it? I used to play up here for hours."

Then when all were in, he shut the door and threw a lock. "Ingenious," he told them with a mad grin. "Seems like it's locked from outside. No one'll guess we came through here."

As quietly as they could, they pushed open a suspiciously well-oiled dormer window that led out onto the roof. Chuffy climbed out and reached back in for Mairead.

"Get to the Peacock," Alex told Chuffy as he helped the women through. "Take everyone with you. I'll meet you there in a bit."

Chuffy stopped, frowning. "Ain't the time to go for the safe, old boy."

"It's the only time I have."

Fiona spun around. "Safe? What safe?"

"At your grandfather's," Chuffy said, already halfway across the roof.

Fiona wasn't certain how many more surprises she could take tonight. "My grandfather?"

"Nasty old man," Mae snapped.

Alex grabbed Fiona by the arm again. "Fiona, please..."

For some reason, that settled her. She turned again and waved at Chuffy. "Get Mae and Lennie to safety. We'll meet you. Now go!"

Alex glared. "No, *we* won't. You're going with Chuffy. Trust me. I'll meet you in a few hours."

Her heart was pounding even harder. "You didn't listen, did you? I'm coming."

He shook her arm. "How do you expect me to protect you if you don't listen to me?"

She cocked her head. "I don't."

"Fiona, don't push it. I'm trying to keep you safe."

"I am not Amabelle, Alex. You don't have to keep me safe. I assume you are breaking into my grandfather's house to find something pertinent to my being wanted for treason?"

He couldn't hold her gaze. "It might be."

"Then I have a right to help recover it. Besides, I can hardly be seen in public with a charge of treason hanging over my head."

Treason. Sweet heaven. She had faced many things in her life, but never had she been considered a threat to the state. She wasn't certain whether to laugh or weep.

She knew Alex thought it was the worst mistake of his life, but he took her hand. "Headstrong woman."

Mae tugged at Chuffy's coat. "We need to go. I need a bonnet. My hair hurts."

"Don't have enough hair left to hurt, my girl," Chuffy said, ruffling what was left.

She scowled. "That is what hurts. I don't want you to see."

"Chuffy is in charge, Mae," Fiona threw over her shoulder as she and Alex began to move off. "Do you hear me?"

"Clearly," Mae answered with a casual wave of her hand before they headed off the other way. Fiona prayed that Mae meant it. Nothing would be more disastrous than Mae digging in her heels at the worst possible moment.

Then, in the deepening dusk, Fee saw something that changed the entire equation. Chuffy turned to make sure Mae was with him, and Mae reached out to take his hand. Just that. But Fiona knew this was a crucial shift in balance. She felt it deep in her chest where the weight of her sister had always rested. The minute Chuffy took Mae's hand, he accepted the weight, too.

Fiona had always thought its easing would relieve her. She wasn't so certain now.

Trying to ignore the cold that seemed to seep into the hollows of her chest, she turned around and faced Alex. "Now what?"

He glared at her, as if it were all her fault. "Now," he said, "we run over the tops of these roofs until we find access into a building. And then we run for our lives."

"Oh, I am an old hand at that. Lead on, MacDuff."

He huffed, but set off, still holding her hand.

"Why are we wanted for treason?" she asked, hopping to the next roof after him. "Do they think you helped Amabelle?"

"They think my father helped Amabelle."

She almost pulled him to a complete stop. "Good heavens."

It was getting darker. Fiona had more trouble seeing Alex's dark eyes. She hated not being able to read them.

"There are letters that incriminate him."

She did stop then, right beside a crumbling brick chimney. "In the safe?"

"In the safe."

She nodded. "Forgeries. I've known some dandy forgers in my day."

"I'm sure he'll appreciate your staunch support."

"How am I connected, though?"

Alex began to move again. "There are two theories. One, you're with me and I need a bit more pressure put on me to cooperate."

"And two?"

"The watch Mairead walked off with. We believe it to be very important, and someone might have realized you took it. They want it back, and they have enough power to use whatever means necessary."

Something sharp lodged in her chest. "My grandfather has that power, you mean."

He briefly looked back, and this time she saw sympathy in his eyes. "Not only him. These traitors are all high-placed. We've already stopped a bishop and a duchess."

Fortunately the roofs were all cheek-by-jowl, and Fiona and Alex wove among the chimneys to reach the farthest roof, finally coming upon a crumbling old place at the corner with a broken dormer. Fiona carefully poked her head inside to see nothing but blackness. She could smell no more than dust and damp, a good sign that they would have the house to themselves on the way down.

"Damn and *bugger*," she heard behind her.

Turning she found Alex peeking over the edge of the roof onto Stacey Street. "What?"

He returned, his stride quick. "We won't be going down just now. The constable brought support."

She instinctively moved to see, but Alex brought her up short. "Don't show yourself. There are militia in the street, just waiting for us to come out."

Suddenly the threat became much more real. "What about the back?"

They weren't as obvious in the back, where lawns grew seedy and fences were knocked over. But she felt them there like burrs under her skin.

Giving up, she plopped down where she was. "Now what?"

He crouched before her. "Now we wait."

She nodded, bringing her knees up, folding her arms and resting her chin. "I have been in a similar situation before," she admitted. "It just takes creativity."

"It takes," he disagreed, "waiting."

She grinned up at him, as if this were all a lark. "Oh, good, then I have time for a few more questions."

She could see the defenses immediately rise. "Possibly."

She felt so weary, suddenly. Overwhelmed by the mare's nest she had stumbled into. Frustrated by Alex's attitude. "So let me see if I have this straight," she said, and held up a finger. "My grandfather is looking for us to get the watch back."

"We think so."

She nodded and held up two more fingers. "Minette Ferrar is trying to hurt us to either get back at Ian or smoke him out. And we're undoubtedly in danger from other Lions because we are helping crack their cipher."

He looked away. "Very possibly."

She sighed and rubbed at her eyes. "Is there anyone who *isn't* angry at us?"

"Me."

She looked up and wished that would remain true. "Thank you. It would be helpful to know if there is anyone else I should worry about. Mae doesn't notice that kind of thing."

"Chuffy does."

That hurt all over again. Mae was leaving her; she could feel it, and she didn't know what to do. So she nodded. "Do you know where my grandfather's town house is?"

"Yes, I do."

"Is it any more welcoming than Hawesworth Castle?"

"No."

A bleak grin. "Then I will be more than happy to invade and desecrate it."

"No desecration," he retorted. "We don't want them to know we've come."

She couldn't think of any more questions she wanted answered, so she sat staring at the crumbling roof lip. "I don't suppose we could wait inside somewhere. It's getting bluidy cold out here."

His face eased a bit. "Do you realize your accent is becoming more pronounced?"

She scowled. "I imagine I am reminded of home."

He was silent for a moment. She refused to look up, afraid of what she'd see.

She needn't have worried. He was looking around. Then, suddenly, he jumped to his feet. "Wait here."

She did wait there and watched him almost soundlessly run back the way they had come. She watched him until the darkness swallowed him and the street noise below covered the sound of his steps. She waited, her heart only speeding up a little in instinctive dread that he wouldn't return.

He would, she kept repeating to herself, ashamed at how quickly the veneer of control eroded. It was the dark, she decided, and the cold and the fear of being found. She was so tired and so sad and so tumbled about that the ghosts were able to get close.

She sounded like a whinging brat to herself, but she couldn't help it. She had to keep reassuring herself that he wouldn't leave her this time, even though the night was descending fast, the cold was settling in her hips, and she could hear nothing except street traffic and a Charlie calling the hour. Alex would not leave her, she swore, even as the minutes grew and expanded, the darkness threatened to smother her, and the urge to call out for him grew unbearable.

The chill little wind snaked its way up under her skirts and stole the feeling from her nose, and still she didn't move, mortified because she felt like that child who was told that only by staying in one place would she insure a safe return, only to still be huddled in a forlorn corner hours later.

In the end, she dropped her head into her arms so she could not see, not be tempted for the thousandth time to look the way he'd gone, her heart in her throat, her hope dying by painful inches, the cold seeping into her heart and then her brain as she waited as uselessly as she had before.

By the time she heard the soft footfalls approach, she was tucked into a tight little ball, the kind that could almost convince a person she was invisible. By the time the footsteps stopped in front of her, she was trembling, old instincts too powerful to quell.

"How far away did you think I'd gotten?" he asked, his voice even with her eyes.

She couldn't look up. She didn't want him to see the tears, stupid tears of relief, of gratitude. "Mayfair," she whispered, hating how tremulous her voice sounded.

He didn't say another word, just sat beside her and drew her into his lap. And then, still silent, as if he knew that words would be too much, he wrapped himself around her like a blanket, like a nest, bowing his head over hers, his body flooding hers with warmth and strength, his breath infusing her with life until the tears spilled over her lids and down across his arms and her trembling gradually receded.

Even she hadn't realized how certain she had grown that he wouldn't return.

"It really is quite ridiculous," she said with an untidy sniff as she wiped tears with her wrist. "I wouldn't have ended up in any worse a place than I have been before."

He stiffened, as if she had hurt him. "Yes, you would have," he said, his voice unbearably gentle. "You would have been betrayed one too many times."

She lifted her head and met his gaze, so suddenly close, soft as warm earth, brimming with sweetness.

He lifted a hand and tenderly brushed back her hair. "I had to go to the other end of the block to see if there was a way past the militia. Chuffy seems to have made it out just before the militia covered the whole block. We, however, will have to wait."

She couldn't pull her gaze away, certain that if she did

she would freeze. "Well," she said, taking a deep breath, "I would say our choices are here and Mrs. T's. Here would be colder, but there might have the militia."

Briefly brushing her jaw with his fingertips, he nodded. "We'll try here. Let me go down first, just in case the house is occupied."

Fiona let him help her to her feet. "It isn't. I checked."

He stared at her. "You went in while I was gone?"

"No. I can tell from just a peek. It's a gift." He was still staring, so she gave him a big smile, exactly the way Thrasher or Lennie would have. "It is what made me such a good snakesman. I could crawl into any house, know if there was danger before I let the burglars in. Not everyone has the talent."

She was hurting him with such talk; she saw it and couldn't stop. She needed to prepare him. She needed him to know that when she finally told him the truth, she wouldn't be exaggerating. She needed him to know that if she stayed, she would ruin him faster than a charge of treason.

Not just yet, though. She was too much of a coward. When he lifted those soul-deep eyes to her, she couldn't batter at him anymore. He knew the world; she could tell he did. But he didn't know her world, and maybe that was better.

"Food?" she prompted.

"No matter how good your instincts," Alex said, peeking into the same dormer window Fiona had checked, "I will go first. They're undoubtedly searching the empty houses for us."

Which was when Fiona was struck by inspiration. She looked down at her dull dress and the duller figure concealed beneath. She looked at Alex's rough-hewn exterior and thought how handsome he would be in a uniform.

"They won't be looking for two soldiers," she said.

Which was how they ended up back at Mrs. Tolliver's. The officious little constable could still be heard droning on about something a few stories below, and militia still surrounded the building. But Lennie had been correct. Evidently no one had done more than a quick check of the attics. So Alex locked them from inside and leaned a chair under the handle just to be sure. And they went hunting through the treasure trove within for costumes.

And found a bed. And not the bed one should find in an attic, dusty and tattered and shoved in a corner out of the way. The kind of bed someone retired to for comfort and quiet, piled with thick comforters and flower-colored pillows. Wide and soft and silent when a woman sat on it, just because it was there and she was tired, and she was sad, and she was frightened.

And she wanted comfort.

Standing there in the deep shadows surrounded by an army of someone's imagination, she saw that bed and suddenly forgot about food, about rescue and salvation. She actually shivered, as if she had just touched lightning. Her breath caught and her breasts tightened, and suddenly from nowhere she could see herself entwined with Alex in this bed, sweat-sheened and exhausted, murmuring, stroking, soothing after another furious joining. Ravenous for more. Certain in those moments that nothing mattered but what happened in that room.

She knew better, of course. But no logic could ease her sudden need.

She was turning away, hoping to regain her senses, when she caught sight of Alex's gaze on her. In that instant, her decision was made. The raw need in his eyes flayed her. The bleak hunger that echoed in her belly. It wouldn't be pretty. There would be nothing to write odes about, good or bad.

But for this moment, they needed each other. And for this moment, they had been given just enough space to make it happen.

Never taking his gaze from her, he held out his hand. Never saying a word, she took it. For a very long moment, they stood just that way, hand in hand, the silence stretching into shreds.

"Come along," he said finally, his voice raspy. "Surely we can find some kind of comfort here."

It was as if he'd heard her. He wasn't speaking of mattresses or pillows; she knew it. Her body certainly knew it, his voice setting off a harmonic tremor that should have sounded like wind instruments. "Well," she said, "we do have a bit of time to waste."

And she knew he could hear the wanting in her voice as well. They were locked in a room born of make-believe, caught in the eye of a storm, and for that moment, nothing made as much sense as what they were about to do.

"This wasn't how I wanted to make love to you again," he whispered, cupping her face. "I wanted to give you roses and champagne and featherbeds."

"Next time," she said with a tremulous smile. "For now, this is perfect."

They both smiled at that because of course it wasn't, except that they were coming together again at last, here in the anonymity of a strange room, veiled in the night and bared by their need. They disrobed each other, the chill somehow disappearing as they shed layers, and laughter rising when Alex discovered the camouflage Fiona had worn, wrapped like a mummy until her breasts ached and padded enough that if she fell on her behind she would bounce. He unwrapped her, making it a sensual pas de deux, his face infused with heat as he watched her pale breasts slowly appear.

She turned on her toes, smiling for him, arms out, head back, wishing with all her heart that this were her life, laughter and discovery and wonder. They lay coats down beneath them and pulled the patchwork blanket over them, and for a long time simply explored.

Oddly, this was when they felt the luxury of time. This was when they stroked heating skin and tasted hollows and angles and soft, tender flesh. This was when Fiona delighted herself on the soft curling hair that crossed Alex's chest and then arrowed south. It was when Alex measured her feet and traced every inch of her legs, from ankle to inner thigh, his touch reverent and thorough. This was when they laughed and smiled and teased, here in the poor darkness while the rest of the world waited.

"What is all over your face?" he demanded, wiping at it with his thumb. "You're yellow."

She giggled, which just made her breasts brush against the soft hair on his chest and pull her toes tight. "Mrs. T," she admitted. "Stage makeup. She said it would help me go unnoticed."

"She was right."

Fiona inhaled the scent of his skin. "You smell like a workman."

He pulled back a bit. "Is that bad?"

She smiled up at him. "Not on you. Not now. Honest work never smells bad on a man."

His own smile was wry. "None of my work is honest, Fee."

"Of course it is. If not honest, certainly honorable."

That stilled his hand. "I thought of giving you to murderers."

She stroked his stubbled cheek. "Of course you did. Your father was desperately ill. You wouldn't have left me there, though."

She hoped. But she didn't press. She had more important things to think about, like how delicious his breath felt against her skin.

He looked down on her, his eyes deep and solemn. She smiled, hoping for a response. But he didn't smile back. He frowned, and she could have sworn she saw a gleam in his eyes. "How could I ever be worthy of you?"

She blinked, openmouthed. "Of *me*? You feel you aren't worthy of *me*? Are you mad? Didn't you hear me tell you that I stole to survive? Coal and food and handkerchiefs and on occasion coins. I lied and I cheated and..."

She got no further because he brought his mouth down on hers with a force that took her breath. "You," he whispered between long, furious kisses, "are...perfect."

And when he drove into her, filling her almost beyond bearing, she almost believed it. When he murmured endearments and praise and encouragement, and when he let his hands praise her all on their own, his sweat-slick body arching taut above hers, his gaze locked into hers, his mouth relentlessly seeking, soothing, supping, she thought that very possibly she deserved the desire that wound through her body. Perhaps it wasn't wrong for him to waste this attention on a scrubby Scottish brat. Just maybe she was worthy of a good man's love.

And then, so suddenly it swept every coherent thought before it, her body seemed to explode into fireworks, into lightning and colors, coursing through her, seizing her like madness, every inch of her on fire, freezing, singing, until she wept and, for the first time in her life, was surprised to know that there were tears of joy.

And even that joy wasn't the sharpest, clearest, sweetest. That joy happened when right after her, Alex called her name, his hands tight around her, his mouth on hers, pumping, pumping until he had emptied himself into her and collapsed, languid and boneless, in her arms.

* * *

She should tell him, she thought a while later. He had told her the truth. He had risked sharing terrible secrets, secrets that could see him hanged, even though his wife had been the traitor. He had bared himself, body and soul, and entrusted both in her hands. Couldn't she do the same?

She looked to where her hand lay splayed across his strong, broad chest, and thought of the past few hours. And she thought, no, not now. This isn't the place. This is a place of dreams and possibilities and pretend. There would be a perfect time to tell him. A time when she would have the leisure to explain the whole so the light in his eyes didn't go cold. So he understood, even though most days, she didn't.

There would be a time.

She couldn't seem to find it, though. Not when they rested, curled in each other's arms, sharing heartbeats and silence. Not when Alex turned to her twice more, each more trenchant and delicious than before. Not when she turned to him, because she knew their time was disappearing and she couldn't bear even the space of a sheet between them.

Not when they managed to finally sneak out of the far house in the early hours of the morning and stroll nonchalantly up to Upper Brook Street, a Hussar officer and his faithful batman, nodding to late revelers and waving to the Charlie as they passed his box. Not when they came upon the duke's town house, corpse white against the uniform line of redbrick town houses, where they suspected watchers waited in the deepest shadows.

"Binkley," Alex roared, weaving just enough to betray a

man desperately trying to hold his balance against a surfeit of gin, "are we close to the barracks?"

"Nowhere's near, sir," Fiona answered him with a gentle shove to the shoulder to keep him from toppling. "Nearer Mr. Wickersham's drop."

Alex shook his head, only Fiona seeing the mad twinkle in his eye. "Not stayin' with Wickersham. Farts somethin' fierce. Melted me best brass buttons back in Badajoz." Suddenly he barked and slapped his knee, almost toppling again. "Say that fast, Binkley! Dare ya!"

Which left the watchers smiling and the Charlie chuckling as he set out on rounds, his lamp lifted high. And which left Alex and Fiona unmolested as they strolled down the street where they snuck around to the mews behind.

The time to tell Alex the truth wasn't right when they cased the house, nor when they found the house locked tighter than a nun's knees, or when Fiona brushed Alex aside and used her wicked little stiletto to jimmy open the back window. Not even when they crept through a house so similar to the Yorkshire mansion, with its white marble and priceless artifacts and stiff, pale furniture placed at precise angles, that Fiona's stomach rolled sickeningly and she kept listening for the sound of her grandfather's precise footsteps.

The time to confess would be soon, Fiona thought, her heart climbing into her throat with each step. She felt its approach like a storm closing on the horizon, so dreaded that she couldn't even remember how they had reached the dining room and the Gainsborough portrait of her proud, hawk-nosed grandmother, which Alex drew aside to reveal a wall safe.

"The dining room," Fiona mused with a nod. "Who would think to look here? Hope it's not a Bramah lock. Those are the very devil to get into."

Alex turned around, a set of lock picks in his hands. "Is this another of your skills?"

"No. This is specialist's work. I nicked handkerchiefs and ribbons. Stuff I could carry easily." She shook her head. "I never really thought I'd make use of those talents again."

"Well, this is your last time."

She pointed to the picks. "I see you know your way around a burglary."

"Only for England."

When Fiona saw all that was in the little safe, her fingers began to itch. Enough money for her to build another school for Mairead, velvet jewelry boxes, official papers. And that was in addition to what Alex pulled out and stuffed into various pockets.

"Is this what you wanted?" she asked, making herself look away.

He closed the safe and returned the portrait to its precise position. "More than I could have hoped for. Now let's go."

Good, she thought, her stomach curdling with dread. *Now we will have time for the truth.*

As it usually did, the truth came at the worst moment. They were walking down Oxford Street a little later, Alex with his hand raised to hail a cab like any intoxicated soldier. Suddenly the hair went up on the back of Fiona's neck and she found herself drawing her stiletto.

"Alex, I need to tell you something," she whispered, her head on a swivel.

When she saw Alex's was, too, she knew her instincts were correct.

"What?" he asked.

"I committed bigger crimes in Edinburgh than pickpocketing."

A jarvey was just pulling his hack to a jangling, creaking

halt next to them when the men came out of hiding. Four, five, with cudgels and knives. Alex turned to Fiona. "What were they?" he asked, already pulling his gun.

The leader of the group pulled a gun of his own and pointed it at Alex.

"I murdered two men," Fiona said and threw her knife.

The man dropped like a stone onto the cobbles, a knife in his throat. The last thing Fiona saw before the rest of the men came at them was the look of horror Alex turned on her.

Chapter 21

It wasn't Fiona's admission that rocked Alex to the core. It was the flat, purposeful expression in her eyes when she sent that knife flying at the attacker just as he lifted his gun. Suddenly the assailant was on the ground, twitching his life away, blood pumping from his throat. The gun clattered across the cobbles, and Fiona was pulling another knife from her sleeve.

"Just so you all know," Fiona announced.

Alex didn't wait for a reaction from his attackers. He ran at them.

"Stay here," he yelled at Fiona, and wasn't surprised at all when she ran after him, her long legs unfettered by skirts.

He couldn't think about what she'd just said. What she'd just done. He couldn't react, even though it felt as if a ball of ice had lodged in his gut. He could think of nothing but the fight because if he didn't, his intrepid Fiona would be dead.

From the start, the fight was a melee. Quick and silent and deadly. Alex stopped only long enough to retrieve the attacker's gun and Fiona her stiletto before wading in.

"'ere, gov!" the jarvey yelled, and Alex looked up to see a telltale red band around his top hat as he scrambled off his perch. Could Chuffy have notified Drake and gotten help?

He got his answer when the jarvey pulled out a couple of guns and tossed one to Alex. Alex swung back to the oncoming rush and fired point-blank, dropping a man three steps away. He wished, suddenly, that he had a sword to go with his elaborate uniform. Two other men reached him, one with a cudgel and one with a knife. He pulled his own knife, spinning, lashing out with his feet. The cudgel went down. The knife didn't.

Fiona was dealing with her own assailants. In the brief snatches he could spare, he saw her dancing about, agile and quick, knife in one hand, a recovered cudgel in the other, a deadly smile on her face he thought he would see every time he closed his eyes for the rest of his life.

"Here, jarvey!" he yelled. "To my batman!"

"Don't be mad," Fiona retorted. "We'll all fight together."

And they did, the three of them back to back. The fight was silent except for the grunts of exertion and gasps of pain, a shout or two of warning, and finally, down the street, the shrill whistle of the Charlie, who had spotted them.

"Now, go!" Alex commanded of Fiona. "I don't want to have to worry about you."

She gave him a lopsided grin. "I feel the same about you," she said and sent a knife skimming into a man's thigh. He went down screaming and lost his cudgel. Another man picked it up and ran in.

There were three attackers left. They ignored the Charlie's warning and bore in on Fiona, as if they knew she was the vulnerable link.

"Here!" Alex yelled and tossed her the empty blunderbuss from the coach.

She wielded it like a club.

If Alex weren't so busy trying to get to her to protect her, he would have been mesmerized by her. She was agile. She was deadly. She was magnificent.

She was scaring him to death.

The jarvey was down, blood streaming from his head. The attackers were out of shots. They came on anyway, with cudgels and knives and fists and feet. Alex was grappling with one when he saw another attack Fiona, taking a knife to the shoulder as he wrapped his arms around her and lifted her straight into the air. Fiona battered at him with her fists and feet. She yanked the knife from his biceps and fought to plunge it into his chest. He wrapped his massive hand around hers, where he still held her up in the air and squeezed. She took her other hand and gouged at his eyes, and he screamed, just before he threw her hard to the ground. Her knife went flying. Her mouth opened, her head snapped back, and she gasped like a landed fish trying to get air into frozen lungs.

Alex saw the behemoth lift his cudgel high and ran right at him. Fiona was rolling over, trying to get away. Taking his nearest attacker out with a roundhouse punch, Alex tackled Fiona's assailant at the waist, sending them both flying back against the wheels of the carriage. The horses skittered about, dragging the coach forward. Alex's attacker pushed hard, trying to force Alex's head beneath the moving wheel. Alex was panting from the exertion, his hands wrapped around the bastard's throat and his legs wrapping round the brute's knees until he could manage to get leverage. As quick as a blink, he flipped him, smashing the bastard's head against the street. He saw the man's eyes glaze and fade, and pulled himself up.

One more left. The jarvey was beginning to stir, but

Alex was out of weapons. Then he turned to help Fiona, only to freeze. Standing before her, a gun lifted in his one hand, was Thomas Mitchell, the one-armed soldier who had pushed her into the street. He was aiming straight down at Fiona's chest where she still lay sprawled on the cobbles, and Alex didn't have time to get to him. He thought in that moment that he died, his heart simply crumbling.

"I'm sorry," Thomas Mitchell said, and looked it.

"Let me stand," Fiona begged. "At least give me that."

The soldier just stared at her, as if he couldn't understand. But she got to her feet, standing as tall and beautiful as any Scottish queen. Alex would have gladly died for her. He gauged his distance and edged closer.

"Put the gun down, Mr. Mitchell," Fiona said gently. "Go away from here and never come back, and we need never speak of it."

Alex wanted to scream at her. How dare she forgive this beast? He began to slowly bend, intent on the knife protruding from a still chest at his feet.

Then Alex saw what Fiona had. There was flat, hard despair in Thomas Mitchell's eyes. "What for?" the man asked, letting the gun sag. "I got nothin' to go to. Nothin' left. At least they helped me eat."

Alex couldn't believe it. He was about to do something that could get him hanged faster than his father's letters. "*Can* you read and write?" he asked the man.

Mitchell swung his head toward Alex, the surprise stark. "I said I could."

"Are you attached to your name?"

The man shrugged. "Me da was a right bastard, and me ma died 'fore she saw me. I can do with another."

Alex nodded and surrendered. "Then there is work for

you on an estate I just inherited. You can help me find jobs for other men tossed ashore from the war."

He couldn't help seeing the shining approval in Fiona's eyes and knew he would make this decision again for that look.

Mitchell looked around at the bodies strewn across the street. "What about this?"

"If you know any names, you'll give them to me. Unless you like to talk when you drink, no one will know."

Mitchell drew himself up to a dignified height. "I follow John Wesley, sir. We don't hold with drink."

Fiona laughed, her voice high and breathy. "I think John Wesley probably didn't hold with murder, either, Thomas."

"And *you*," Alex accused, swinging her way. "Did I not tell you to stay out of this?"

She shrugged. "You needed help. I have experience. I think I told you that."

"You told me you stole things."

She shook her head. "I protected Mairead."

His gut crawled. "But it's been eight years."

She looked up then, and he saw a terrible bleakness fill her eyes. "Mairead still needs protecting." Straightening, she wiped her knife on her leg and slipped it back up her sleeve. "Now, could we retrieve our jehu and go home before the watch gets here?"

Alex desperately wanted to kiss her. He wanted to wrap his arms around her so he knew she was safe. She looked like an ensign with her chopped brown hair, broad cheekbones, and bold steps. Her face was sweaty and pale, and blood marred the blue of her costume. She was trembling with delayed reaction, her eyes still dark, her hands restless. He had never seen a more erotic woman in his life.

Which was not a thought he had time for at the moment.

He bent to collect the jarvey instead. That gentleman was sitting up holding his head in his hands and not looking fit to drive. Thomas Mitchell pocketed his own gun and walked up to help.

"Did Chuffy send you?" Alex asked the driver, pulling him to his feet.

The man nodded. "Lord Drake. Said you might need help. Much help I was."

"You know him?" Fiona asked Alex, stepping forward and wincing. "Oh, heavens. I think I shall ache for days."

"See the red band?" Alex asked, lifting the jarvey's hat to hand back to him.

Fiona stared at it a moment, as if she was not comprehending very quickly. "Why, I remember. The coachie who was hired to take Sarah home from school that day wore one of those. Are they . . . ?"

"Yes."

She nodded and turned to the jarvey. "A pleasure to meet you, sir."

"Likewise, miss. Devil of an aim with that knife. Should be in a circus."

She laughed again, a high, breathy sound, and again she winced.

Alex frowned. "Are you all right?"

She looked up. "Oh, yes."

Then she took a step and wobbled. She had her hand at her waist as if pressing against a cramp.

"Miss?" Thomas Mitchell asked, stepping up.

Alex pushed him back. "Fiona . . ."

She lifted her hand and looked at it. It was splotched and dripping. Alex swore his heart stopped.

She looked up at him, surprise written on her suddenly ashen face. "Oh, the devil. I knew I was sore."

And then her knees gave out.

Alex caught her before she reached the ground, lifting her in his arms. "Damn you, Fiona Ferguson. *Damn* you!"

Suddenly everyone was in motion. Alex ran for the coach. Mitchell pulled open the door and the jarvey jumped for his seat. "Where we goin', gov?"

Alex froze at the door, his head spinning, unable to breathe past the rock lodged in his chest. How could she do this to him? How could she risk herself so blithely?

Where should they go? His first instinct was to go home, but there was no doubt it was being watched. He wanted to go to Willowbend, where Michael O'Roarke waited, but he could feel how wet her side was and fought down panic.

"Drake's," he snapped and climbed in, trying so hard to keep from jostling Fiona.

"Hey!" the watchman yelled as the coach lurched forward. "Stop! What's going on here?"

The jarvey never even paused. They hurtled down the street as if being chased by highwaymen.

"I'm sorry," Fiona apologized, her voice even breathier, as if she didn't have enough life force left for volume or, please God, it just hurt to inhale.

"What did you think, exactly?" he demanded, pulling her as close to his chest as he could, trying to warm her. "Did you think that it was going to ease my mind, knowing you had experience committing murder? Did you enjoy it as much this time, or has it become old hat to you?"

He was ashamed at his outburst, but he couldn't seem to stop, fear fueling a rage such as he had never known. Rage at her family, at her struggle, at her isolation when she should have spent her life wrapped in comfort and certain that she was the most precious thing in a person's life.

How dare she risk the chance to know that by trying to save his bloody life? After all, who was he? Just another person who had failed her.

"If you *ever* do anything so monumentally stupid again," he shouted, "I swear I will lock you up in Bedlam and keep your sister away to protect her from your influence. But then, I won't have to worry about locking you up, will I? You just took care of that all by yourself by confessing to murder in front of witnesses who will be more than happy to testify against you. It's a damn good thing Chuffy came along so your sister has somebody to take care of her, because you certainly won't be in any position to."

"Here, y'r lordship," Thomas Mitchell protested from the opposite seat, his face thunderous. "Who do you think you are, yellin' at her?"

"The man who saved her from you," he snapped at Mitchell. "So shut up."

He kept rocking her back and forth, his breath wheezing in his chest, too afraid to look down at Fiona, certain she would be dead and he would be lost, no matter what happened from here on out.

"I didn't...mean it," Fiona whispered. "I mean to...to reassure you that I could...help."

Help? She'd saved his bloody life. Damn her. *Damn* her. He remembered suddenly the moment he had walked into Amabelle's room and found her floating in that obscene red water. He remembered the crushing weight of guilt, the gouging loss, the futility of such waste. He had always remembered it as being unbearable.

He'd been wrong. He had tried to help Amabelle. He had been infatuated with her. But he had never really loved her. He had never respected her. He had never been in awe of her courage and candor and bright, sharp intelligence or her devotion to her sister. He had never wondered how he could live without her.

Finding Amabelle dead had been terrible. Wondering if Fiona would die was unbearable.

Wilkins met him at the door and sent him up to the guest bedroom with Fiona.

"O'Roarke is with my father," was all Alex said.

Wilkins took care of that, too. By the time Alex gently laid Fiona on a bed in one of the guest rooms, he could hear a horse clattering out of the mews.

"Oh, and this is Thomas Mitchell," he told Wilkins. "He is about to tell Drake everything he knows about the Lions' attempts on the Ferguson ladies' lives. He is not to be let loose or introduced to any law enforcement entity. Am I clear?"

"As glass. T'other lady is here, just so you know."

"Mairead is safe?" Fee asked from the bed.

"As houses, ma'am," Wilkins assured her, then coughed politely. "Lord Wilde is with her."

Fiona actually smiled. "I'm glad. Don't let her know I'm here until I'm feeling a bit better. She . . . she has bad memories of some other times we . . . er . . . had trouble."

Alex remembered the night of the fire, Mairead keening in Fiona's arms. Fiona seeming so calm, as if the reaction was all too familiar.

His stomach dropped away and he thought he'd be sick. He had just assumed he'd known the worst of what Fiona had lived through.

No, he admitted honestly, he had refused to admit how bad it could have gotten. He hadn't been able to bear the idea of worse.

"Are you about to finish the confession you began out on the street?" he asked.

She turned wide, bleak eyes at him and then looked away. "I suppose I am."

"You were living alone in an impossible place," he said, "forced to survive on your own. I can't imagine anyone would indict you for self-defense."

Her smile got even sadder. "Even if it was with foxglove?"

Alex could barely breathe. Foxglove? She had poisoned someone? He felt as if he'd taken a leveler. He'd just assumed that Fiona had found herself in a situation like tonight, forced to protect herself and her sister from an attack. But poison took planning. It took a cold heart and colder calculation.

Every time he wanted to open his mouth to say something, he knew it would be wrong. Pat. Trite. Patronizing. So he coughed and shook his head. "How about we save the rest until I'm quite sure you'll be around to finish?"

She looked at him with pain-darkened eyes and then simply closed them.

Alex wasn't certain if she had fainted or simply wished to avoid further discourse. He didn't blame her. He sure as hell didn't know what to say. He didn't know how he would manage to say it past the hot, hard grief that ate at his chest. He wanted to pick her up and run until she could outdistance her past. He wanted to close her so tightly in his arms she could finally feel safe. And yet, he was finally realizing that he could do neither. He couldn't save her. He could only stand with her as she fought to save herself.

Then he pulled off the braided blue jacket and costume shirt to expose the wound on her side and forgot everything else. The issue of saving her suddenly became all too tangible. The cut was narrow, deep, and bleeding freely. A stab rather than a slice. Much more dangerous. Much more easily fatal.

Damn it, Fiona Ferguson. Damn it!

He didn't say a word, just pulled over a chair and bent over his task. Fortunately Wilkins knew him well and had already called for hot water, towels, and basilicum. So Alex kept busy treating Fiona until O'Roarke could make it there to help.

O'Roarke, who was a good fifteen miles away.

So Alex bent to his task, washing the wound and applying the basilicum. He knew he was hurting her. She flinched and clenched her hands, her silence taut and heavy.

"It would be easier if you could faint like any self-respecting woman," he growled, pressing down hard.

Her chuckle was breathy. "Sadly, it usually only works that way in Minerva Press novels and on the stage."

"You've never met my sister Cissy. Does it hurt to breathe?"

"With you...leaning on me like that, yes."

He eased back a moment. "There. Any trouble?"

"My lungs are fine. I think he missed them." She still hadn't opened her eyes. "A good beefsteak should take care of the rest."

Wilkins had been busy gathering lamps and setting them up around the bed before he stoked the fire until the room almost sweltered.

"Anything else?" the butler asked, his hand on the door.

Alex looked at the blood on his hands, how it still trickled past Fiona's ribs. "I wouldn't mind a stiff brandy or two, if you find it."

"I think you know me better than that, milord."

Fee raised a hand. "I'll join you."

Wilkins grinned and bowed. "I was gonna pour yours first, beggin' your pardon, ma'am."

And so saying, he briefly decamped to return with the de-

canter and two filled glasses. Setting them down, he helped
Alex resettle Fiona on her back so she could drink.

"Thank you," she said with a smile to the butler and a sip.
"I think I might survive after all."

Wilkins's grin was delighted. Alex saw that Fiona's hand
trembled and wanted to gather her close, where she couldn't
be afraid or injured ever again. Where he didn't have to be
afraid for her every minute.

"You did send somebody for O'Roarke?" he asked
Wilkins.

Amazingly, Fiona all but reared off the bed, spilling a bit
of brandy over the back of Alex's hand. "You called the doctor away from your father? Alex, how could you?"

She was ashen-pale, and dark rings had begun to show
beneath her eyes, and she wondered how he could have
called for the best physician he knew. He didn't know
whether to laugh or soundly kiss her. "My father is resting."

She huffed, then winced. "He was resting a week ago
when you left. I will be fine. Women suffer blood loss on a
regular basis. We manage."

Never in his life had Alex thought a woman would bring
him to blush, much less Wilkins. But she managed it quite
handily.

"As intrepid as your sex is," he said with a grudging grin,
gently resettling her, "I would rather have the reassurance of
an actual physician. Now, then, Wilkins, that is all."

Alex folded a cloth pad and laid it against the wound,
wrapping gauze all the way around Fiona's slim waist. The
waist he had explored only the night before, tracing it like a
treasure map, following the bend of her hip like the curve of
a river, her belly, her breasts.

It was tainted by blood now. Defiled by violence and
avarice. If Alex let himself be distracted by what had hap-

pened to his beautiful Fiona, though, he would never be able
to work. Wilkins picked up the decanter and refilled Fiona's
glass before departing. Alex sat by the bed waiting for the
linen strips to soak through. He picked up his own drink
and sipped, and he hoped Fiona would drink enough to not
mind what was coming. He was making her uncomfortable
enough. No matter what O'Roarke did, it was going to hurt
her worse.

Besides, he thought, ashamed at his own selfishness.
Couldn't this be the chance he'd been waiting for? Could it
hurt for her to relax enough to actually be completely honest
with him for the first time? There was so much he wanted to
say. So much he needed to know. She was at least marginally
comfortable now. He was more certain she wouldn't die.
Could he finally learn who the real Fiona was?

Did he really want to?

"Fee…"

He wasn't certain whether he was relieved or not that he
was interrupted.

"So, this is the other half of the famous Ferguson twins,"
drawled a voice from the door.

Alex gritted his teeth. "Apologies for abusing your hospitality, old man. Our options were limited."

For her part, Fiona was squinting at the newcomer who
stood just inside the doorway, still clad in evening attire, his
opera cloak thrown over a shoulder.

"I don't know if I like you, sir," she said simply.

One of Drake's eyebrows slowly rose. Alex turned to see
a rather martial light in Fiona's eyes.

Laying his hand against his heart, Drake bowed. "I am des-
olate, Lady Fiona. May I introduce myself? Marcus Drake."

"Oh, yes," she said, only slurring a bit. "I know. I know
all about you."

He didn't smile. "And I know all about you."

Alex gave Drake a quick look, not at all sure he wanted to know what he meant.

As for Fiona, she let her glass rest back on the bed and surrendered to the pillows. "I wish you had told Alex. It might have saved time. Since we're here, are you going to give him the watch, Alex? Or does Chuffy have it?"

"Watch?" Drake asked, suddenly sounding alert. "Is there a watch?"

"There is far more than a watch," Alex said. "You and I will discuss it after I am finished here."

"I strongly suspect we should discuss it now," Drake said.

Alex turned on him. "I'm not certain what Chuffy has told you," Alex said. "But I was able to retrieve a treasure trove of what looks to be Lion material tonight. If you don't want me to toss it in the fire, you'll allow me the time to see to Miss Ferguson."

"From Hawes House," Fiona added quietly, taking another long sip of her drink. "From bloody Hawes House."

This time Drake betrayed surprise. Both eyebrows lifted. "My. Does this trove include whatever they were holding over your head, Knight?"

"It does. I will share it all."

"And does it involve your father?"

Alex faced his superior with unsmiling eyes. "You don't seem surprised."

"Well, the treason warrant was for you both. And...his trip to St. Petersburg wasn't entirely his idea."

Alex found that he was gaping. "You *knew*? And you didn't say anything?"

Drake didn't look particularly penitent. "There were some suspicions. Your father and your wife."

Alex came off his chair, only to be forestalled by Drake's

raised hand. "Don't be absurd, man. I'm speaking of state secrets, not sordid gossip. We'll talk about it when you come downstairs."

"Gladly. But you will stay away from my father."

Fiona opened her eyes and grabbed his hand. "That is not what we decided."

Alex turned to find her gaze suddenly sharp, afraid. For him. Considering how afraid she was of her own final revelation, it almost made him smile. So he raised her hand to his mouth and kissed it. And then he refused to let it go.

"I wouldn't be interfering if I were you, Miss Ferguson," Drake mused gently. "There are at least two dead men in Edinburgh who were known by you."

"So I've been informed by the lady herself." His expression steely, Alex glared at Drake. "In case you weren't certain."

For some reason, that was enough. With a sudden smile, Drake vanished without another word, and Alex turned his attention back to Fiona.

But she wasn't looking at him. She looked after Drake, as if he had left the scent of dread behind. She didn't seem to even notice Alex anymore. Her hand, rarely still, as elegant in flight as a swan, lay limp in his. Her eyes seemed to have lost their light, oddly gray in the early morning. Alex fought a creeping sense of foreboding.

Suddenly he wanted her to stop. To keep every secret to herself, no matter how bad. He would want to ease them, solve them. He would find a way. But he was suddenly sure that some truths Fiona protected were best left in the dark of those vaults beneath a bridge in Edinburgh.

Lifting the decanter, he refreshed them both. She didn't even seem to notice, her eyes unfocused, her fingers rubbing the etched glass in her hand. Alex waited.

"Mae was so beautiful," she finally said as if continuing a conversation, her eyes focused somewhere else. "I tried so hard to mask it, but she was extraordinary. Even when she was a child, people in the street stopped to stare at her." She looked down to where she kept picking at the knitted green comforter across her lap, and her voice grew even quieter. Flatter. "There was a banker. Very powerful. Very well respected. Family man. Member of the kirk. We were on our way home from the optical shop one day when he caught sight of Mae."

Tears welled in her eyes, and Alex squeezed her hand, amazed at the strength in her grip. The expression in her eyes never changed: vague, flat, hopeless. "I was holding her hand because the street was busy. I didn't want her to be hurt. She was only eleven."

Alex was struck by a rage such as he'd never experienced in his life. He wanted to batter at something, tear it apart until it was unrecognizable, shards scattered across the ground. He wanted to lay waste until he was thigh deep in blood, to every predator who had tormented those girls, every good Christian who had turned their backs, every politician who cared more for his own comfort than the children who roamed the streets.

He'd suspected. Tormented himself with the possibility that Fee could have been caught in a web of coercion. But Mae. Mae, who still saw the world refracted through the prism of her sister. Mae, who had needed her hand held after living under a bridge for a year.

"He kept...appearing," Fiona said, her voice scraped raw now. "Following us. Talking to her. Giving her things. Baubles. Sweetmeats. Then one of my friends told me that the banker had hired a bullyboy to separate Mae and me. To...*secure* her. I couldn't wait any longer."

Alex swallowed bile, his unoccupied hand fisted. "What did you do?"

She actually smiled, although it was grim. "Made friends with the scullery at his house. Found out he was partial to a particular chop from the butcher. Nobody else ate it but him. Every night. So I paid the butcher's boy to let me make his delivery."

It was then, oddly enough, in the silence that followed, that the full weight of Fiona's words struck him. Mae had been eleven years old when the banker had spotted her. And if Mae had been eleven, so had her twin. Which meant that when she was only eleven years old, Fiona had been fierce enough, devoted enough, intelligent enough, and remorseless enough to poison a man rather than let him destroy her sister.

It was incomprehensible. Fiona had been created for the skies, for the bright light of the sun, for rapier-sharp debate and sly humor. It was the way he'd always seen her in his mind, as a primal force.

But Fiona was not only that bright spirit waving from the carriage, or the tight, controlled lady who had survived her grandfather. She was the muck of the gutters. The thin, honed steel of survival. She was so much more than he had fallen in love with, and he didn't know how to absorb it all.

For the moment, he didn't have to. He only had to make sure she lived so they could solve the conundrum together.

"I assume the other man you killed was with a knife?" he asked gently.

"I got there just in time." Her voice was flat, thin. "Poor Mae."

"What happened?" he asked, thinking this might be the only time she would tell him. Thinking she needed to. Her eyes were so bleak, haunted with ghosts he would never see.

She shrugged. "It was the vaults. He surprised us.... I hoped nobody noticed."

He had thought once before she would trust him enough to share completely with him. He'd thought he could at least let her weep, hoping she could purge some of the poison from her past. He'd hoped for it. When he saw tears well in her eyes now and begin to track down her cheeks, he was no longer so sure. These tears were different; darker, more bitter. Real poison welling from an ancient wound.

She seemed to be crumbling right before him, the change quick, as if a dam had let go with her admission and she was being consumed. Overrun. She looked frantic, suddenly, frightened. Her breath seemed caught in her chest, causing it to spasm without effect. Her mouth opened, but there was no sound except wheezing, and her hands kept clenching. As if it would keep him from seeing her, she closed her eyes.

Alex knew then that he'd been wrong. He didn't want to see this. No human should ever see this.

No human should ever have to suffer it.

And then he heard it and the hair went up on the back of his neck. It was worse, far worse than with Mae. Mae had keened with distress, with shock and trauma. Fiona keened with despair.

Alex didn't even think about it. He climbed up on the mattress and pulled her into his arms, even though she was stiff and unyielding and frightened him to death. "Hush, sweetheart," he murmured into her ear. "You'll alert Mae if you don't."

The noise stopped. Fee looked worse, her eyes glittering. Slowly, she turned to look up at him. "How *do* I atone?"

He thought his heart would simply shatter into dust. "You foolish girl," he grated, his throat too tight. "Don't you understand yet? You spent your life atoning. You saved Mae countless times. You saved your brother by letting him focus on his job." He dropped a slow, sweet kiss on her rather salty mouth. "And what would have happened to me without you? There would have been no Fee to save me. No Fee to remind me what was important and true."

"Is it enough?" Her voice was so small, so fragile.

"Well," he said with a smile, "if not, you could always marry me. That should even the score quite nicely."

She blinked at him, but it was as if she hadn't understood. Alex wasn't surprised. He hadn't realized until he'd said it that he meant it. Suddenly, though, he knew that it was the only future he wanted. She was the woman he saw working beside him. The spirit that would help guide his feet.

But she didn't answer.

He couldn't bear the distress that thrummed through her body, the decade of struggle and loss and betrayal that was reflected in the depths of her gaze.

"Sweetheart," he murmured, cupping her chin and gently easing her gaze back to his. "You have more than earned a bloody great cry. Why don't you let me watch out for the world a while?"

It was as if she had been waiting for those words. Tears welled, hot and thick, and spilled over. She sobbed, and then sobbed again, her chest heaving. Her body began to shake as if she had the ague, and, rising from deep inside her, from places too old and torn to protect, the keening rose again, unstoppable, unbearable.

Alex held on as tightly as he could, his own throat on fire, his hands shaking as he stroked her hair and uselessly wiped at tears, as he wrapped around her in a futile attempt to protect her from her own memories. It was then, finally, that he learned what Fiona Ferguson had been holding to herself all these years. It erupted from her like infected blood, drawn from the deepest core of her, where the worst memories crouched, the worst fears, the most dreaded truths, and it spilled down her face, down his chest, down onto the comforter and bedsheets as he rocked her. It scoured her lungs and drew her body tight into a ball, as if she could protect herself from the kind of grief that can only be purged with deep, wracking sobs, the pain that had been carried too long in marrow and tendon and bone.

And finally, finally after both Wilkins and Chuffy had popped concerned faces in the door and been silently admonished to leave, after Alex's waistcoat suffered irrevocable damage and his own heart lay wasted and sere in his own chest, Alex felt her sobs begin to ease. He held her all the tighter, murmuring, murmuring, his forehead against the top of her head, her hand in his, his body once again instinctively shielding hers.

Very gently, he bent to set his lips against the damp tendrils at her temple. "Better?"

She didn't smile. Alex understood. He didn't ask if all the poison had been drained. He asked if it was bearable again. "Yes," she said, sounding surprised as she laid her hand against his chest. "I believe it is."

He dropped another kiss on the tip of her freckled nose. "Then why don't I check your dressing one more time, and then you and I will curl up and finally get a bit of rest until O'Roarke shows up?"

She nodded, gently rubbing her hand against his shirt, as if settling. "Alex."

He looked down to see that she lay with her eyes closed, as if she, too, were walking the edge of dreams. "Yes, sweetheart?"

"Ian doesn't know. Please. It would do no good to tell

him. He was doing his best for us. I don't want him to bear this burden, too."

She kept taking his breath. He stroked her hair, not even minding anymore that it was short and uneven. It was her hair, and every part of her was precious. "Only if you'll marry me."

She didn't tense up. She didn't relax, either. Not for a long while.

When she finally relaxed into sleep, her breathing deep and even, her head tucked safely into the crook of his shoulder, Alex felt as if he had attained the kind of victory that stayed embedded in a man's soul. It filled him like light, softening the raw wounds that had been laid bare tonight. It would have been perfect if he didn't remember that Fiona had never answered his proposal.

Chapter 22

Fiona woke to sunlight and silence. She wasn't certain how she felt about either. She was alone in the sparely elegant room into which Alex had carried her the night before, the fire trimming the edge from the chill and the sun pouring in through the high window.

It must almost be midday, she thought, gingerly sitting up and swinging her legs over the side of the bed. Her head hurt. She felt as if she had stuffed it with grimy cotton from the crying and a surfeit of brandy. She should have felt more sore. After all, she was stitched up like a Christmas goose. But really, only her bum ached from when she'd landed on it out in front of Hawes House. All in all, she had gotten off lightly, and she knew it.

Alex had long since gone. Even the dent from his head had erased itself from the pillow next to her, although she could still smell him, vetiver, and horse. She pulled his pillow to her and inhaled, just as if it had been her mother's, as if she could resurrect him from no more than the memory of his touch and a faint, lingering scent.

She wouldn't have slept without him. Just as she'd known they would, the tears had released memories. Jerky, stuttering images of darkness and grime and tallow-tainted candlelight flickering off weeping brick walls. Snow-dusted cobbles on the steep streets. Leering eyes and grop-ing hands. She could still feel the bite of cold against her toes and fingers, the fretful grip of an empty belly. She could smell offal and old drink and cabbage.

Fear. She could smell fear and remembered it on herself. Worse, because she hadn't been able to prevent it, she re-membered it on Mae. Nothing would absolve her for that because Mae had never understood. Not really. She had just looked to Fiona for answers. And Fee had only had reasons.

And yet, this morning as the chilly sun splashed across her covers, the guilt felt blunted. Diluted by the tears that had drenched her. That had drenched Alex. She felt quieter than she could remember in her life.

He had been right. It had been time. It had been well past time. She had spent years holding it off, and Alex had finally forbidden it any longer, forcing the wound open with gentle eyes and the sanctuary of his arms. And no matter what hap-pened from here on out, she would love him for the courage it took for him to face it with her.

He had been so gentle. So kind. So understanding as she had washed him in contrition. She had heard his offhand proposal. Proposals. Both of them. And yet, how could he possibly mean them after what he'd said in the carriage? How he had reacted to her admission? She had seen the look of loathing. She swore she could still feel its impact, a punch to the chest. A strangulation of strangely resilient dreams.

And yet, when he had bent to lay gentle lips against her forehead, she had dreamed again.

Foolish girl indeed. There was nothing more pitiful than

a girl who insisted on a depth of feeling that simply didn't exist. He felt sorry for her. But he couldn't respect her. Not a woman who had admitted what she had. How could he and respect himself?

Enough, she thought, setting the pillow aside. She would know soon enough. She would know everything about her future. Gingerly sliding off the bed onto wobbly legs, she settled cook's night rail about her and looked around. The room was so sleek, a symphony of blues and greens with slim Chippendale furniture and watercolor landscapes. Another place that reflected its owner, she suspected.

And yet there was nothing that might help her. No dress, no shoes, no hint of what she should do next. What she needed to do, besides find Alex. She simply didn't know, and it left her standing by the bed staring at the door like a witless fool.

Every other day of her life, she had jumped from bed with some purpose, be it tedious, exciting, or determined. She could think of a thousand different things she would have been doing even a week before. Even a day before.

Before Mae had turned to Chuffy Wilde and relieved Fiona of the weight she had carried with her for her entire life. Before Fiona realized that even though Mae would always love her, she would no longer need to rely on her. Before Alex had offered his devil's bargain, to take care of her, whether he loved her or not.

Fiona was a bit surprised by how afraid she felt. After all, hadn't she dreamed of this day her whole life, no matter how she loved her sister? Hadn't she wanted to be able to ask more than *What does Mae need?* to start her day?

But what did she ask now?

As if she had been called by Fiona's distress, Mae was suddenly standing in the doorway, her head tilted to one side, as tidy and pretty as if Fiona had helped her with hair and dress as usual, clad in a salmon-colored morning dress, her hair classically arranged around a lovely topknot.

"There you are," Fee greeted her, struck by a new calm in her sister's great blue eyes. An ease that had never sat well on Mae. Fiona thought of the reason and felt another surge of ambivalence. Everything was changing, had changed. She just didn't know her own place in the future anymore.

Mae strode in, scowling. "I want you to sit down, Fee." She dragged forth an overstuffed chair. "Here. Did Dr. O'Roarke fix you?"

Easing onto the chair, Fiona looked sharply up. "What do you mean?"

Mae shook her head, her eyes suddenly old and wise as she perched on the bed. "Fee. You have never fooled me once. If Chuffy had not promised that I would have upset you far more by breaking in, I would have been in here. I assumed your injury wasn't life-threatening, since people simply walked fast, not ran."

Fiona couldn't help but smile at Mae's logic. "I wondered if you knew. Well, I am fine. A few stitches only. Do you know where my attire is?"

Mae giggled. "In the trash bin, I assume. There was quite a lot of outrage about you playing a breeches part."

Fiona scowled, even as her heart sped at the memory of that flight. "It is impossible to run across rooftops in a dress."

"Or fight assailants, I assume." Looking down for a minute, Mae fingered the pretty cream ribbon that fell from beneath her breasts. "I didn't like you being alone last night, Fee. Not when you...when you..." Her head came up, betraying real anguish. "I have never heard you sound like that. But Chuffy said..."

Her heart melting, Fiona reached out to her sister, to find herself engulfed in a careful hug. "Chuffy was right. You would have been submerged in salt water. Alex was quite brave to face it."

Mae hugged Fiona one more time and let her go, her obvious distress easing. "He'll make a good husband, won't he?"

"Chuffy?"

"Don't be silly. Alex."

Fiona's breath caught. "Who?"

Mae huffed in indignation. "He asked you, didn't he? He told Chuffy he would."

Unable to bear the hope in Mae's eyes, Fiona turned toward the window and the cold sunlight. "I'm not certain, actually. But if he did, I fear it may be from misplaced altruism."

"You are nothing like his last wife," Mae protested. "Chuffy told me that, too."

"I am also in need of saving," Fiona said. "At least in Alex's mind. What about you, Mae Mae? Is Chuffy going to make an honest woman of you?"

And for the first time in Fiona's life, she saw a look of pure joy in Mairead's eyes as she considered something other than the heavens. *Breathtakingly incandescent*, Fiona thought distractedly, her own heart contracting painfully at this fresh evidence that she no longer needed to base her life on her sister's.

"It's official, then?" Fiona asked, her voice betraying her ambivalence only a little. "He knows enough math for you?"

Mairead's expression collapsed into frustration. "Do you know, I do believe I am the only one who realizes."

"What, sweetheart?"

"Why, how really brilliant he is." Her smile returned,

sharp, protective. Determined. "I'm not even certain he knows."

"Then it will be your job to make certain that he does." Fiona took her sister's hand and wove fingers. "To paraphrase Mr. Bennett, I could not have parted with you, my Mae, to anyone less worthy."

Mae squeezed hands, bouncing a bit. "I do not know how to feel, Fee. Is it all right to be frightened?"

"If you aren't," they heard from the door, "you're daft."

Mae spun around, her smile once again lambent. "You eavesdrop, sir. How did you know I wasn't discussing personal matters?"

"You were," Fiona retorted easily. "But I suppose a husband has some rights."

Chuffy flushed brick red and ducked his head, sending the glasses sliding south. Mae skipped over to right them. Chuffy slipped an arm around her. "You don't mind? Take care of her, y'know. More devoted than that Halberd fella."

"Abelard," both women answered.

Chuffy rubbed an ear. "Wrote your brother for permission. Proper and all. He said to ask you, Fee."

"Me?" Fee echoed. "Why me?"

Chuffy frowned. "Well, ain't you the oldest?"

She chuckled. "Heavens, no. Mae is, by a full seven minutes. Ask *her*." She grinned. "Oh, wait. You did. That must mean we all approve."

Gaining her feet, she leaned in to drop a kiss on the blushing man's cheek. "I know I don't have to threaten revenge if you don't take care of her."

His eyes twinkled. "Should I say the same to Alex? Waitin' downstairs."

"Make him write poetry," Mae insisted. "Chuffy did for me."

Fiona turned a surprised smile on him.

"Terrible stuff," Chuffy huffed, still red-faced.

Mae stepped up to restore his glasses. "Do you really think the poem is more important than the poet?"

Mae paused, hand still extended, eyes going vague. Fiona wanted to chuckle. For their wedding gift, she suspected she was going to need to get them a sitter to make certain they didn't simply wander off in thought and right over a cliff.

"Mae? Mae!" she called. Mae startled to attention, but Fiona could see that her sister was still distracted.

"All right, children," she said, shooing them out the door. "Find me some clothing, please, Mae, or I will never see anyone."

Which was when Chuffy realized that she was obviously *en déshabillé*. Huffing and muttering in his distress, he dragged Mae back out the door. "Get you…er…attire. Need to come down. Alex can't come up. Ain't proper, not engaged and all. Besides, Drake's looking for you."

And here Fiona had thought she was feeling better. Even so, it took her no more than thirty minutes to present herself at the library door, clad in the first pretty dress she'd had in months, a spring-green muslin with long sleeves and high ruffled neck, her hair pulled off her neck much as Mae's was.

The first person Fiona saw upon entering Drake's library was Lady Bea, standing foursquare before the desk, glaring. Fiona wanted to smile, but she could see the hurt in those gentle blue eyes.

"I am sorry, Bea," she greeted her, hands out. "We didn't want to leave. But we thought we could protect you."

Bea's eyes filled with tears and she squeezed Fiona's hands. "Gudgeon."

"Are we forgiven?"

For that she got a quick, convulsive hug. It was only as

Lady Bea was stepping back that Fiona realized the room was actually rather crowded. Three gentlemen were standing at her arrival: Drake and Alex, seated opposite the Chippendale desk along with another empty chair, and one more gentleman, who sat comfortably ensconced in a deep red leather armchair.

"Sir Joseph!" Fiona greeted the older gentleman in surprise, walking up to take his hand. "What do you here, sir? How do you feel?"

He still looked tired and a bit pale, but far better than last she'd seen him. "Didn't Dr. O'Roarke say that he was better than all the imbeciles in London?" he asked with a broad smile. "His foxglove cure was a miracle. He says that with good sense and moderation, I should regain my strength in no time."

Her smile was heartfelt. "I am glad."

Then it dawned on her that Alex had been holding incriminating letters, and that he'd meant to tell Drake. Her hand still in Sir Joseph's, she turned a worried gaze toward the desk.

"It's quite all right, my dear," Sir Joseph said, reclaiming her attention. "All is known."

Drake was not smiling, though. "Sir Joseph admits to playing deep games with his former daughter by marriage," he said, an envelope in his hand that he tapped against the desk. "No one is pleased, but the matter is now moot. The lady is dead."

Fiona instinctively looked to Alex. He held out a hand to her. Without thinking, she let go of Sir Joseph and reached for Alex like landfall after a storm. He wasn't smiling, either, but his face had never frightened her. Now it soothed, reassuring her in ways words never could.

"He wanted to protect me," Alex told her, claiming both

hands and smiling down on her. "Every bit of information he shared was deliberately misleading. No one knew."

"I'm afraid I used Amabelle in hopes I could reel in her contact," Sir Joseph admitted ruefully. "Sadly, they almost reeled in my Alex instead."

Fiona looked back and forth among the men, letting that information sink in. Suddenly, her knees seemed to soften, and she found herself sitting, gaze locked in on Alex's earth-brown eyes. "Then you are..."

"Gudgeon," Lady Bea repeated from where she was now seated beside Sir Joseph.

"An idiot," Lord Drake growled, and everybody else took seats. "I would like to officially plead with the Knight men to forestall thinking they can protect the crown all on their own in the future. It is far too wearying. I have spent the last twelve hours correcting a misapprehension by a London sheriff that you two were bent on the violent overthrow of the government."

As easy as that. As innocuous. Fiona's heart beat a strong tattoo as it sank in. Alex was safe. His father was safe. Their activities at Hawes House had been worthwhile.

"My grandfather?" she asked, her voice pitiful.

Drake's face became a mask. Alex held on more tightly. "We're not sure," he said. "It is being investigated. If only he hadn't given you those codes himself, we might be able to assume some innocence."

She blinked. "Himself? Alex, what would ever make you believe that my grandfather would hand anything to me himself except our marching papers? And I believe he only did that because Mr. Bryce-Jones was in London."

Suddenly everyone was paying close attention. "Then who did you get them from?" Alex asked.

"From Mr. Bryce-Jones, of course. Along with our mail,

our directions for the week, and our chastisements for petty offenses. The only reason I was there the day you came to tell us about Ian was that you asked for me before you asked for grandfather."

The room stilled in a way that told Fiona she had said something very important. "You don't think Mr. Bryce-Jones..."

"We don't think anything until certain investigators get back from Yorkshire," Drake said.

"Would you like me to help?"

"No!" all three men shouted at once.

She scowled. "You might want to rethink that. As Alex witnessed, I am no wilting flower. And I know everyone involved quite well. Think about it."

Drake pinned her in his oddly sharp blue gaze. "I believe you have quite enough on your plate," he said, his hands on an open file in front of him.

She'd meant to get to her feet. His words put paid to that.

"Oh, is it my turn, then?" she asked, dread curling in her belly. "My acts were in no way innocent, as you reminded me last night. Nor were they in service of the king."

He looked away a bit, focused on the papers he held. She didn't move, caught tightly in Alex's clasp. Comforted more than he could know by his silent support.

"In point of fact," Drake said, flipping the file closed, "both cases have been cleared. A clear case of self-defense with the knife, and the other..." He looked up, and Fiona finally saw real compassion in the man's eyes. "Let's just say that the Edinburgh police were not shocked or saddened at the gentleman's demise."

He slowly got to his feet. "Next time, though, you might find a less notorious poison to use. The symptoms of fox-glove poisoning are evidently obvious to any Edinburgh-trained physician, since they are teaching the use of the substance in treating heart conditions."

"And thank God for that," Sir Joseph said with a smile as he, too, gained his feet. "Is that all, then?"

Drake shut the file on his desk. "It is. You all may go about your merry way. Hopefully, that will leave my poor domicile in peace."

Alex helped Fiona to her feet. "Fee...," he was saying, when the door slammed in and struck the wall. Alex was just pulling Fiona behind him as she bent for her knife, when in stalked Mae, Chuffy close on her heels.

"You cannot arrest my sister," Mae declared like a tragedian onstage.

Drake leaned a hip on his desk, humor flickering at the edge of his expression. "I cannot?" He turned to Chuffy. "Do you have any idea what this is about?"

"None. Was sitting there talking about the wedding, and suddenly she leaps up, yells, 'That's it,' and runs. Can't wait to find out m'self."

"Orange blossoms?" Bea echoed in excited tones.

"Hello, Lady Bea," Chuffy and Mae greeted her in identically unflustered tones.

Drake sighed. Fiona, so recently relieved, almost giggled aloud. "I am quite safe, Mae," she assured her sister. "In fact, we were just about finished here."

"But you cannot be," Mae protested, hands on hips. "I haven't saved you."

Fiona spread her arms. "You are a bit late. Lord Drake already did."

Mae frowned. "Did Alex ask you to marry him?"

It was Fiona's turn to blush. "No, not that it is any of your business. Why don't we all decamp? Aren't we late for luncheon?"

"Gut-foundered," Bea said with a nod.

Mae was glaring at Alex. "Why not? Do you have cold feet? Are you afraid of being stuck with me as well? You won't. Chuffy will."

"But I did ask," Alex protested easily. "I have not been answered."

Everybody turned to Fiona, who wanted to sink into the ground. "That," she told her sister with a meaningful glare, "is not a topic for a crowd."

Mae turned back to Alex. "You'll take care of her? You have an estate? Money in the funds? Family? I have the right to ask."

"She *is* the oldest," Fiona said with an escaped giggle. The day was becoming far too outrageous.

"She is?" Drake retorted, as surprised as everyone.

"That's what I hear," Alex said, not looking away from Mae, who still stood, arms akimbo, in the middle of the Oriental carpet, Chuffy at her elbow. "Well, you've met my father...." He pointed. Mae and Sir Joseph exchanged nods. "And when you get married, you will frequently see my estate."

She scowled. "Frequently? Why? Chuffy has his own place."

He cocked an eyebrow at Chuffy. "Didn't you tell her?"

Chuffy shrugged. "Didn't think of it." He turned to Mae. "Next door."

Fiona's attention was definitely caught. "Next door? Next door to what?"

Alex grinned. "Chuffy. His estate runs with mine. He and I met when I used to summer at my uncle's preparing to be his heir. If it weren't for Chuff, I wouldn't have had any fun at all."

Chuffy nodded brightly. "Parents love him. Think he is perfect."

Alex grinned. "He is."

Chuffy was the one Mae glared at now. "He is not. You are."

Chuffy grinned at her. "Not. Don't care so much anymore. Now, need to let Alex get to business. In the way."

Mae made one last stand. "Make her marry you," she said with a finger raised in Alex's decision. "She needs you. So do I. I can't marry until I know she's happy, and right now she isn't happy. So get to it. Or I won't tell you how I figured out your code."

She almost made it out the door before everyone reacted.

"Wait!" Fiona cried along with the rest of them, including Chuffy, who seemed as surprised as everyone else. "What do you mean?"

But Mairead didn't turn back to Fiona. She turned instead to Chuffy, her eyes preternaturally bright with the triumph of discovery. "You really didn't guess?" she asked. "I figured it out when you spoke of your own poem."

Alex choked. "You . . . wrote a poem?"

Mae glared at him. "It is a beautiful poem. Likening Fee and me to twin stars."

Smiling on Mae as if she had just discovered the new world, Chuffy had Mae's hands in his, and Fee thought, suddenly, how they now were twin stars themselves, shoving Fee out of orbit. She laid her hand against the fresh pain in her chest. Mae had taken the big step away. She had turned to Chuffy first. Fee had thought she would never live to see it. She hadn't realized how sour her hope had grown until it was swept clean by the excitement Mae and Chuffy hoarded between them.

"I knew it," Chuffy crowed, squeezing Mae's hands. "Figured all along you'd be the one to do it. What part of the blasted thing is it?"

Mae grinned, looking supremely satisfied with herself. "No part."

Chuffy actually howled. "It's not the poem? After all this work?"

Mae gently pushed his glasses up. "I didn't say that. I said it wasn't a part of it."

"Well, what does that mean?" Drake asked, his patience worn thin.

But he was ignored. Fiona knew she and Chuffy were frozen in similar poses, eyes off to the side as they both attempted to once again see that little leather-bound book. Fifteen calfskin pages, leather binding, words printed in gilt letters on the cover. *Virtue's Grave; Worshipping at the Altar of Hymen by William Marshall Hilliard.* Not the poem. Not the title; they had tried that, too.

Leather. Gilt. Cover.

She and Chuffy grinned at the same time. "The poet!"

Mae actually laughed. "The ordinal in each stanza shows you how to use the key. Skip the first letter, the first two, none. The key is his name. It works beautifully. Did you know that Pippin's friend is on a list? So is Lady Mercer Elphinstone, the princess's particular friend. And you need to find those guns before they're used."

Drake froze. "Guns? *What* guns?"

Mae blinked at him. "Well, I don't know. They were stolen from the Royal Arsenal. Or they will be. I wasn't quite sure."

Drake all but went on point. "Show me."

But Mae was nothing if not stubborn. "Not until he asks Fee to marry him," she said, leveling a finger on Alex.

"He'll be happy to," Alex retorted, "if you would all just leave him alone with her for a moment."

It was all Mae needed. With a big grin and a wave of her

hand, she led everyone else out of the room like a children's parade. Only Lady Bea stopped on the way by to bestow kisses on both Alex's and Fiona's cheeks.

"Love abides," was all she said.

And then, suddenly, the door was closed, and the room hummed with silence. Fiona found herself standing flat-footed, not at all sure what she should be doing. Knowing that she felt sick with sudden apprehension. She swore her heart would take flight, and Alex hadn't said a word.

He didn't right away. Instead, he stepped up to her, just that. Just looked down on her, as if challenging her to look up. To meet his gaze and challenge him back.

She simply couldn't. Suddenly her world was upside down, and she didn't know what to expect. What to hope for. What to admit.

"Why *haven't* you answered me?" he gently asked, stroking her cheek.

She felt an overwhelming urge to lay her cheek against his palm and just rest. She couldn't. Not yet. Not until she understood.

"Because I don't know why you asked," she admitted and finally raised her head.

His eyes were liquid, deep as night, soft as earth. For the first time since she had first met him, he looked oddly vulnerable, as if something she said could hurt him. As if this moment were the most important in his life, and he didn't know at all how it would turn out.

"Well," he said, gently taking hold of her arms, "let's see. Because you're the smartest woman I've ever known. Because you know how to be thrifty, so you could support me if needed. Because I'll never have to worry that you can't balance the house accounts. I also doubt I would have to worry about my safety with you around. Oh, and because Chuffy

will abuse me no end if I don't bring you to live next door to
your sister."

She knew he meant to ease her tension. He accomplished
the opposite. She didn't need comfort. She needed truth.

"And if you don't marry me I have nowhere else to go,"
she said baldly.

He was silent a long time. She could feel the warmth of
his eyes deep inside where the cold lived. She should step
away from his touch, as it sent new heat curling along her
limbs and into her heart. He was being unfair, she thought
distractedly. She wanted him to hold her. To tell her wonderful things. To promise more. She was terrified he would,
when he didn't mean it.

"Fiona," Alex said, frowning, "do you truly believe that
any of the people you have met since coming to London
would allow you to be alone? Do you think Mae would simply trot off to Berkshire without a wave? If you don't know
it, I certainly do."

The warmth blossomed into something heady. He was
right. He had brought all of these wonderful people into a
life that had been meted out only to Mae, to Pippin and
Lizzie and Sarah.

"Your father would adopt me if I asked, wouldn't he?"
she asked.

Alex dropped a kiss on her nose. "Of course he would. So
would Lady Bea and Michael O'Roarke and Lady Kate. And
you haven't even met Lady Kate yet. I promised you, remember? No matter what it took, you would never be alone
again."

She held her breath. "Even if it took marriage?"

"Oh," he breathed, his smile disappearing. "You think I'm
being noble again. You think that the only reason I want to
marry you is because you might need me to."

Well, isn't it? she wanted to ask. She held her silence, her heart seized with fear.

He didn't answer. Instead, he pulled her into his arms, and he kissed her. His hand caught in her hair to hold her head still, he coaxed her mouth open and plundered it, without permission, without apology, without hesitation, his tongue not searching but invading, his heart thundering against her breasts.

At first she froze, too surprised to react. Her body knew how, though. Suddenly she had her hands in his hair, sating herself on the thick silken curl of it. She lifted on her toes to get closer, to abrade herself on the faint whisper of beard along his jaw. She met his tongue with her own and dueled, the dance fueling fires beyond anything she'd ever known. Just that, a kiss, with bodies pressed tight and hands curved against scalps and chests straining for air.

And then his arms were around her, wrapping her tightly enough to show her exactly how she affected him, his straining cock hard against her belly, and she wanted to drag him down right there and demand he fill her, as if they could fuse, as if they could create fires that rivaled the sun itself.

Instead, he pulled away. He pulled her head down to his shoulder and held her as they regained control. He stroked her hair, as if it were still long and lush, and not a flat brown cap.

"No," he mused, "I didn't think so. I never kiss like that when I'm being noble."

Surprised into a bark of laughter, she hit him in the chest. "I don't think there has ever been a question as to our mutual attraction. But marriage is more than that, Alex."

"As I know far better than you, my dear." He lifted his head and waited for her to look up to see the arousal still flushing his face. "I've been a coward, Fee. I've been afraid.

You see, I think I fell in love with you four years ago when I saw you lean your head out of a speeding carriage. But that wouldn't have been right."

She blinked, thinking maybe her lungs had collapsed. She could barely breathe. "You fell in love."

He nodded, never taking his eyes from her. "I've decided that I was given a second chance, and I'm not going to pass it up. Marry me, Fee, because I cannot live without you. I can't wait to see what you're going to do next. I want to see how you put your stamp on our children, and how you teach them about the stars."

For a long time they just stood in the shadowy room, gazing at each other, communicating with eyes and hands and smiles.

When Fiona looked up at him, it was to see something wonderful. It was as if, she thought later, she could see the whole sky in the depths of her lover's eyes. She could see wonder and adventure and certainty and mystery. And she knew without a doubt that she would spend her entire life exploring it.

"Yes," she said with a slow smile. "I think I will."

He laughed. He actually laughed, as if he were relieved. "Oh, Fee, I promise you won't regret it," he crowed, swinging her around.

"But will *you*?" she asked, only half kidding. "I won't stop my studies. I don't think I can."

He kissed her again, a long, slow kiss of exploration, of communion and commitment. And then, he laid his forehead against hers and smiled. "I'm already way ahead of you." His grin grew impish. "Chuffy and I are building an observatory, did I tell you? Right on the border of our properties. That way if we don't see you or Mae around, we'll know where to find you."

"You could always come with me," she answered, her

heart in her throat, her knees going all soft again. "I would love for you to meet my other gentleman."

He grinned. "Orion? I don't know. I get pretty jealous...."

"What about you?" she asked. "What dreams can I help you realize?"

"A home," he said. "Friends. Family. I think after all this time, I am tired of traveling. I'll be happy to make limited visits, of course. Long enough that my wife might see some of her scientific friends. But I want to make Uncle Pharly's estate ours."

She was no longer certain she was breathing. These were opportunities one only dreamed of when looking up at the sky from a grimy dormer window. "Do you...do you think there might be dispatches to deliver south of the equator?" she asked. "Just think of the sky you could see there."

His smile was so dear she wanted to cry. "To inspire that look in my wife's eyes, I would take her around the world." Another kiss. Another long, swollen silence. "Can I tell the others now?" he asked. "Your sister will not wait much longer."

They told the others. Drake broke out champagne and toasted both couples. Fiona simply didn't know how to believe that it was all happening. And when Mae sidled up to her, she wrapped her arm around her sister's waist.

"Fee," Mae whispered as the men discussed travel and diplomacy. "Can you believe it? We have a family. A real one, I think, even if it is just the four of us."

"No chance of that," Chuffy assured her, looking up. "Alex's family's massive. Cousins everywhere and a plague of sisters. And you haven't even seen my family."

Fiona smiled up at her fiancé. It was true. He had brought her friends, and now he had offered to share his family. She had no idea what to do with one, but she desperately wanted the chance to find out.

"You won't mind the noise and crowds?" she asked her sister.

Mae wrinkled her brow and looked around. "It's quite perfect, I think."

Which seemed to be a challenge. For not ten minutes later, noise erupted once again, this time in the entryway. Drake turned that way with a long-suffering sigh. "And I'd planned on such a quiet morning."

"The Colonel Ian Ferguson, Viscount of Hawes," Wilkins announced. "Viscountess Hawes."

And there stood Ian, tall and broad as a highland mountain, bold as March, poised in the doorway holding on to Sarah's hand as if she were a miracle. And Fiona began to laugh. Suddenly she couldn't seem to stop, as if far more than tears had been tamped down too tightly in her chest and needed release.

It truly was Ian, even if he wasn't in his Black Watch kilt. She and Mae stood stiffly still, not at all certain what to do. Not knowing him enough anymore to know if he would accept their excitement. Then she saw a flash of hurt in his equally blue eyes, and she lost her reserve. She and Mae and Ian and Sarah were a mass of hugging and chatter and laughter, as if Ian and Sarah had merely been late to a party.

"Wait," Chuffy said, pointing at Ian. "How can he be here? Ain't you worried about the Ferrar woman?"

It was Drake who answered. "Interesting, that. I got a note yesterday from one of our...informants. Seems he was instructed to help a woman who smelled a lot like oranges onto a packet to France. She was accompanied by two very large gentlemen, who were decidedly not there to entertain her. It seems Madame has worn out her welcome, even among her friends."

"Don't count on it," Chuffy warned.

Drake smiled. "One of those large gentlemen is ours."

They were safe, Fee thought, one arm around Alex and the other around Ian. They were all safe and together and happy. She had lived in silence for so long, broken only by Mae's insistent chatter, that the chaos of the crowd tumbled over her like a bright waterfall. And she knew that she had been given a gift few had. She had a love, a partner, a friend. And from the ashes of her childhood, she had been rewarded the family she had long since despaired of. She couldn't imagine it getting any better.

Until Alex's mother arrived.

The front door slammed open. More people poured through. Luggage dropped onto the marble floor with echoing thuds, and Wilkins once again appeared in the doorway, by now laughing outright. "Lady Knight and company," to be followed in by a short, round mound of furs that were shed to reveal a short, round, graying middle-aged woman with an exceptionally plain face and Alex's brown eyes. "I went home, but they said for some reason you were all here. Hello, Marcus. Hello, Bea. Is this the girl you're to marry, Alex? I believe I approve."

By the time Fiona was once again alone with Alex, she was exhausted, overwhelmed, and suffering a surfeit of Knight affection. And, as Chuffy had said, she hadn't even met *his* family yet. "Mad as snakes," he'd told her. "Every one of them."

Tucked into Alex's shoulder back in the Knight conservatory, where they could escape all the racket that Mae suddenly thrived on, Fiona found herself chuckling over it all. It was the only thing to do.

"Still want to marry me?" he asked. "You haven't even met my other sisters."

She cast him a suspicious glare. "Trying to back out?"

She could feed for the rest of her days on his smile. "You should know better. I'm just warning you. If you think this is chaotic, you haven't seen the families in full cry."

Her heart swelled and wept with the wonder of it. With the wonder of him. "Too late," she said. "I fell in love with the son. I have to take the family."

Her chest suddenly felt so tight. It took her a moment to realize that what she felt was joy. Unfettered, untamed, unfamiliar joy that fizzed like a rocket and sparked from her fingers.

"Besides," she said, "I have dreamed of this family my whole life."

He kissed her then. "Well, you asked for it."

She kissed him back with all the love in her heart. And when the clatter rose from the entryway outside, she barely registered it, until she heard a well-loved voice yelling like a fishwife.

"Yes, Mama, I married him. Now I am here. Will you take me in or not?"

Fiona and Alex were on their feet. "Pip?" Fiona asked.

"*Married?*" Alex demanded.

But then they looked at each other and laughed.

"You were right," Fiona admitted. "This will take a while to get used to."

He smiled, and her toes curled again. "Oh, you never get used to it, sweetheart. The good news is I know all the places to hide."

They hid so well that they weren't found till morning. By then, Fiona had learned her first lesson not only in families, but in happiness. Miracles, she found, were not woven merely in the heavens. She could be loved, and she could love, and there was no greater magic in the universe. No more spectacular show than the love in Alex's eyes. No greater joy than sharing the love in her own.

It was a lesson she repeated often and learned well.

Fleeing from the law, fugitive Colonel Ian Ferguson finds himself at the mercy of country widow Sarah Clarke. But one kiss with the achingly beautiful woman will ignite a passion that neither can escape . . .

Please turn this page for an excerpt from

Once a Rake.

Chapter 1

Sarah Clarke was not going to let a pig get the best of her. Especially not this pig.

"Willoughby!" she called as she scrambled over the broken fence.

Blast that pig. She had even tied him up this time. But the pen was empty, the wood on one side shattered, and precise little hoofprints marched away through the mud.

Sarah took a brief look at the stone outbuildings that clustered around the old stable. She could hear rustling and creaking, which meant the animals had heard Willoughby escape. But there were no telltale porcine snortings or squeals. If she knew her pig, he was headed due south, straight for disaster.

Sarah rubbed at her eyes. "The cliffs. It had to be the cliffs."

She hated the cliffs. She hated the height and the uncertain edge and the long, sudden drop she had almost made on more than one occasion all the way to the shingle beach below. Just the thought of facing them made her nauseous.

"I have better things to do," she protested to no one.

It was closing in on evening, and she should be feeding her animals. She needed to help Mr. Hicks rescue the sheep who had taken advantage of another fallen fence to wander in among Sir Magnus's prized Devon Longwools. Then she needed to inspect the debris that seemed to be diverting the stream into her wheat field. Instead she would be dancing on the edge of death to collect her pig.

She sighed. She had no choice. Willoughby was Fairbourne's best source of income. And he was in imminent danger of tumbling off the edge of Britain.

Ducking into the barn to retrieve her secret weapon, she picked up her skirts and ran for the path that snaked through the beech spinney. It was the same route Willoughby had taken the day before and the week before that.

Oh, why couldn't he become enamored of an animal in his own farmyard?

"If it weren't for the fact that you are such a good provider," she muttered, pushing her hair out of her eyes with one hand as she ran, "I'd leave you to your fate. Stupid, blind, pigheaded...well, I guess you would be, wouldn't you?"

Both pigheaded *and* blind. One of her husband, Boswell's, few good ideas, Willoughby was a new breed called the Large Black, which produced lovely gammon and even lovelier babies. He also had ears that were so large they flopped over his eyes, making it difficult for him to see. The problem was, Willoughby didn't seem to notice until he was trapped in mire or running right over a crumbling escarpment.

Why couldn't Fairbourne have been situated farther away from the sea? Sarah mourned as she wove her way through the wood. Somewhere like, oh, she didn't know, Oxford.

Quiet, dry, and relatively clean. Away from oceans or high cliffs, with libraries that held more than Debrett's and gothic novels. Yes, especially libraries.

Not that she had ever actually seen Oxford. But she had always thought how wonderful it must be to stroll the stone walks and smooth greens that stretched beneath golden spires, soaking in the history, the culture, the learned discourse of men in flapping black robes. Books and lectures and good dinner conversation. No mud, no mucking out, no pigs of any stripe. But especially no Great Blacks with a predilection for falling in love with inappropriate species.

His latest amour resided in Squire Bovey's pastures, which were reached by way of the coastline. The coastline, which at this point was a cliff several hundred feet above the Channel and apt to crumble for no reason.

Sarah was still running when she burst through the trees into a hard blast of cold Channel wind. She stumbled to a halt, her heart stuttering. Beyond her the land rolled away, barren of all but bracken as far as the jagged, uncertain cliffs. She could see the better part of a mile both ways. She did not see her pig.

Oh, lord, please don't let him have gone over. He's the difference between getting by and going hungry.

She was still standing fifty feet from the cliff, working up the nerve to get close enough for a look down, when she caught the sound of a plaintive squeal. Whipping around, she gaped. She couldn't believe it. There, tucked into the spinney not ten feet away, stood Willoughby, securely tied to a tree. He didn't look happy, but Willoughby never looked pleased when his plans were thwarted.

Sarah looked around, expecting to see the squire's boys, or Tom Scar, who did odd jobs in the neighborhood and could always be seen walking this way at end of day.

But there was no one there. Just the grass and bracken and never-ending wind, which tugged impatiently at her skirts and tossed her hair back in her eyes.

Could it be her mysterious benefactor again? For the last few days she had suspected that she had a guest on the estate. She had been missing eggs and once found evidence of a rabbit dinner. Probably a soldier, discharged after ten bloody years of war and left with no job or home. He wasn't the first. He certainly wouldn't be the last.

At least he had attempted to repay the estate's meager bounty. Sarah had come out each morning to find some small task done for her. The breach in a dry stone wall mended. Chicken feed spread, old tack repaired, a lost scythe not only found but sharpened. And now Willoughby.

Another aggrieved snort recalled her attention. Willoughby was looking at her with mournful eyes. Well, Sarah thought he was. It was difficult to see past those ears. She walked over to let him loose and was butted for her troubles.

Whoever had tied him had known what they were about. It took ten minutes of her being goosed by an anxious pig to get the knot loose. Wrapping the rope around one fist, Sarah reached into her apron pocket for the piece of coarse blanket she had plucked from the barn. Fluttering it in front of the pig's nose, she tugged at the rope. Willoughby gave a happy little squeal and nudged her so hard she almost toppled over. She chuckled. It never failed. She pulled him into motion, and he followed, docile as a pet pug.

It had been Sarah's greatest stroke of genius. Willoughby might not be able to see all that well, but a pig's sense of smell was acute. So Sarah collected items belonging to Willoughby's current amour to nudge him along. Her only objection was the fact that her pig couldn't tell the difference between her and the squire's mare.

"Come along, young man," she coaxed, striding back through the spinney with him in tow. "You truly must cease this wandering. Your wife and babies are waiting for you. Besides, I have four very pretty sows coming next week to make your acquaintance, and you needs must be here. It is iniquitous, I know, but I need that money to tide us over the winter."

If Willoughby finally did manage to tumble off that cliff, she would have no money at all to make it through. She would have no pig to sire new babies, and no stud fees. So the first thing she must do when she returned was fix the pen. Then she still had lost sheep and a diverted stream to attend to before finishing her evening chores.

As she did every autumn, when the farmyard was perennially muddy and her skin chapped, Sarah wished she were somewhere else. It wasn't as bad in spring or summer because then she had growing things, new babies to raise, the comfort of wildflowers and warm skies. Every spring she imagined things could be better. Every autumn she admitted the truth. She was caught here at Fairbourne, and here she would stay. She had nowhere else to go.

She wouldn't think of that, though. It served no purpose, except to eat away at her heart. Tucking the bit of blanket on the fence where Willoughby could smell it, she tied him up with a scratch of the ears and an admonition to behave. Then, rewrapping her muffler against the chill, she went about her work, ending with a visit to the henhouse.

It was when she slipped her hand beneath Edna the hen that she knew for certain who had tied up Willoughby. Edna was her best layer, and yet the box was nearly empty. Sarah checked Martha and Mary and came up with similar results. Someone had taken their eggs. And it hadn't been a fox, or at least one of her birds would have been a pile of bloody feathers.

Well, Sarah thought, collecting what was left, her visitor had earned his meal. She wished she had seen him, though. She could have at least rewarded him with a few scones for rescuing Willoughby from sure disaster.

On second thought, she considered with her first real smile of the day, maybe not scones. They would be Peg's scones, and Peg's scones could be used for artillery practice. No one should be rewarded that way.

Sarah might have thought no more of the matter if the men hadn't ridden up. She was just shoving the chicken coop door closed when she heard horses approaching over the rise from Pinhay Road. She sighed. *Now what?*

Giving up the idea that she would eat any time soon, she gave the coop a final kick and strode off toward the approaching riders. She was just passing the old dairy when she caught movement out of the corner of her eye. A shadow, nothing more, by the back wall. But a big shadow. One that seemed to be sitting on the ground, with long legs and shoulders the size of a Yule log.

It didn't even occur to her that it could be anyone but her benefactor. She was about to call to him when the riders crested the hill, and she recognized their leader.

"Oh, no," she muttered, her heart sinking straight to her half boots. This was not the time to betray the existence of the man who had saved her pig. She closed her mouth and walked straight past.

There were six riders in all, four of them dressed in the motley remnants of their old regiments. Foot soldiers, by the way they rode. Not very good ones, if the company they kept was any indication. Ragged, scruffy, and slouching, they rode with rifles slung over their shoulders and knives in their boots.

Sarah might have dismissed them as unimportant if they

had been led by anyone but her husband's cousin Martin Clarke. She knew better than to think Martin wished her well. Martin wished her to the devil, just as she wished him.

A thin, middling man with sparse sandy hair and bulging eyes, Martin had the harried, petulant air of an ineffectual law clerk. Sarah knew better. Martin was as ineffectual as the tides.

Just as Sarah knew he would, he trotted past the great front door and toward the outbuildings where he knew he could find her at this time of day. She stood where she was, egg pail in hand, striving for calm. Martin was appearing far too frequently lately.

Damn you, Boswell, she thought, long since worn past propriety. *How could you have left me to face this alone?*

"Martin," she greeted Boswell's cousin as he pulled his horse to a skidding halt within feet of her. She felt sorry for the horse, a short-boned bay that bore the scars of Martin's spurs.

"Sarah," Martin snapped in a curiously deep voice.

He did not bow or tip his hat. Martin knew exactly what she was due and wasn't about to let her forget it. Sarah wished she had at least had the chance to tidy her hair before facing off with him. She hated feeling at a disadvantage.

"Lady Clarke," the sixth man said in his booming, jovial voice.

Sarah's smile was genuine for the squire, who sat at Martin's left on an ungainly looking sorrel mare. "Squire," she greeted him, walking up to rub the horse's nose. "You've brought our Maizie to call, have you? How are you, my pretty?"

"Pretty" was not really a word one should use for Maizie. As sturdy as a stone house, she was all of seventeen hands, with a Roman head and a shambling gait. She was also the best hunter in the district and of a size to carry Squire's massive girth.

Maizie's arrival was met by a thud and a long, mournful squeal from the pigpen.

The squire laughed with his whole body. "Still in love, is he?"

Sarah grinned back. "Caught him not an hour ago trying to sneak over for a tryst."

The squire chuckled. "It's good someone loves my girl," he said with an affectionate smack to the horse's neck. Maizie nuzzled Sarah's apron and was rewarded with an old fall apple. Willoughby sounded as if he were dying from anguish.

"Thank you for the ale you sent over, Squire," Sarah said. "It was much enjoyed. Even the dowager had a small tot after coming in from one of her painting afternoons."

"Excellent," he said with a big smile. "Excellent. Everyone is well here, I hope? Saw Lady Clarke and Mizz Fitchwater out along the Undercliff with their paints and hammers. They looked to be in rude health."

Sarah smiled. "They are. I will tell them you asked after them."

"This isn't a social call," Martin interrupted, shifting in his saddle.

Sarah kept her smile, even though just the sight of Martin sent her heart skidding around in dread. "To what do I owe the honor, then, gentlemen?"

"Have you seen any strangers around?" the squire asked, leaning forward. "There's been some theft and vandalism in the area. Stolen chickens and the like."

"Oh, that," Sarah said with a wave of her hand. "Of course. He's taken my eggs."

Martin almost came off his horse. "Who?"

Shading her eyes with her hand, Sarah smiled up at him. "'Who'? Don't you mean 'what'? Unless you name your foxes."

That obviously wasn't the answer he'd been looking for. "Fox? Bah! I'm talking about a man. Probably one of those damned thievin' soldiers wandering the roads preying on good people."

Did he truly not notice how his own men scowled at him? Men who undoubtedly had wandered the roads themselves? Well, Sarah thought, if she had had any intention of acknowledging her surprise visitor, Martin's words disabused her of the notion. She wouldn't trust Napoleon himself to her cousin's care.

"Not unless your soldier has four feet and had a long bushy tail," she said genially. "But I doubt he would fit the uniform."

The squire, still patting his Maizie, let out a great guffaw. "We'll get your fox for you, Lady Clarke," he promised. "Not great hunt country here. But we do. We do."

"Kind of you, Squire. I am certain the girls will be grateful. You know how fatched Mary and Martha can get when their routine is disturbed."

"Martha…" Martin was getting redder by the minute. "Why haven't I heard about this? You boarding people here? What would Boswell say?"

Sarah tilted her head. "I imagine he'd say that he was glad for the eggs every morning for breakfast, Martin."

For a second she thought Martin might have a seizure, right there on his gelding. "You're not going to get away with abusing your privilege much longer, missy," he snapped. "This land is…"

"Boswell's," she said flatly. "Not yours until we know he won't come back."

"Bah!" Martin huffed. "It's been almost four months, girl. If he was coming back, he'd be here."

Sarah stood very still, grief and guilt swamping even the fear. Instinctively her gaze wandered over to what she called Boswell's arbor, a little sitting area by the cliff with a lovely view of the ocean. Boswell had loved sitting there, his gaze fixed on the horizon. He had planted all the roses and fitted the latticework overhead.

His roses, though, were dying. His entire estate was dying, and Sarah was no longer certain she could save it.

"He will be back, Martin," she said, throwing as much conviction as she could into her voice. "You'll see. Men are returning from Belgium all the time. The battle was so terrible it will be months yet before we learn the final toll from Waterloo."

It was the squire who brought their attention back with a sharp *harrumph*.

Sarah blushed. "My apologies, Squire," she said. "You did not come here to be annoyed by our petty grievances. As for your question, I have seen no one here."

"We've also been told to keep an eye out for a big man," the squire said. "Red hair. Scottish. Don't know that it's the same man that's raiding the henhouses, but you should keep an eye out anyway."

Sarah was already shaking her head. After all, she hadn't seen anything but a shadow. "Wasn't it a Scot who tried to shoot Wellington? I saw the posters in Lyme Regis. I thought he was dead."

The squire shrugged. "We've been asked to make sure."

"I'm sure you won't mind if we search the property," Martin challenged.

He was already dismounting. Sarah's heart skidded, and her palms went damp. "Of course not," she said with a faint wave. "Start with the house. I believe the dowager will be just as delighted to see you as the last time you surprised her."

Martin was already on the ground and heading toward the house. With Sarah's words, he stopped cold. Sarah refused to smile, even though the memory of Lady Clarke's last harangue still amused her.

"Just the outbuildings," he amended, motioning to the men to follow him.

Sarah was a heartbeat shy of protesting when she heard it. Willoughby. The thudding turned into a great crash and the heartfelt squeals turned into a near-scream of triumph. She turned just in time to jump free as the pig came galloping across the yard, six hundred pounds of unrestrained passion headed straight for Squire's horse.

Unfortunately, Martin was standing between Willoughby and his true love. And Sarah sincerely doubted that the pig could see the man in his headlong dash to bliss. Sarah called out a warning. Martin stood frozen on the spot, as if staring down the specter of death. Howling with laughter, the squire swung Maizie about.

It was all over in a moment. Squire leapt from Maizie and gave her a good crack on the rump. With a flirtatious toss of the head and a whinny, the mare took off down the lane, Willoughby in hot pursuit. But not before the boar had run right over Martin, leaving him flat in the mud with hoofprints marching straight up his best robin's-egg superfine and white linen. Sarah tried so hard to keep a straight face. The other men weren't so restrained, slapping legs and laughing at the man who'd brought them as they swung their horses around and charged down the lane after the pig.

Sarah knew that she was a Christian because she bent to

help Boswell's unpleasant relation off the ground. "Are you all right, cousin?"

Bent over and clutching his ribs, Martin yanked his arm out of her grasp. "You did that on purpose, you bitch."

The squire frowned. "Language, sir. Ladies."

Martin waved him off as well. "This is no lady, and you know it, Bovey. Why my cousin demeaned himself enough to marry a by-blow..."

Sarah laughed. "Why, for her dowry, Martin. You know that. Heavens, all of Dorset knows that."

The only thing people didn't know was the identity of her real father, who'd set up the trust for her. But then, knowing had been no benefit to her.

"What Dorset knows," Squire said, his face red, "is that you've done Boswell proud. Even kind to his mother, and I have to tell you, ma'am, that be no easy feat."

Sarah spared him another smile. "Why, thank you, Squire. That is kind of you."

The squire grew redder. Martin harrumphed.

"Climb on your horse, Clarke," Squire said. "It's time we left Lady Clarke to her work. We certainly haven't made her day any easier."

Martin huffed, but he took up his horse's reins. He was still brushing off his once-pristine attire when the soldiers, bantering like children on a picnic, returned brandishing Willoughby's lead, the pig following disconsolately behind.

With a smile for the ragged soldier who'd caught him, Sarah held her hand out for the rope. "Thank you, Mr...."

The man, lean and lined from sun and hardship, ducked his head. "Greggins, ma'am. Pleasure. Put up a good fight, 'e did."

She chuckled. "I know all too well, Mr. Greggins." Turning, she smiled up at her neighbor. "Thank you, Squire. I am so sorry you had to send Maizie off."

The squire grinned at her, showing his gap teeth and twinkling blue eyes. "Aw, she'll be at the bottom of the lane, right enough. She knows to get out of yon pig's way."

Tipping his low-crowned hat to Sarah, he turned to help Martin onto his horse. Sarah waved farewell and tugged a despondent Willoughby back to his pen. She was just pulling the knot tight when she caught sight of that shadow again, this time on her side of the coop. Casting a quick glance to where the squire had just mounted behind the pig-catching soldier Greggins, she bent over Willoughby.

"I wouldn't show myself yet if I were you," she murmured, hoping the shadow heard her. "And if it was you who let Willoughby go a moment ago, I thank you."

"A search would have been...problematic," she heard, and a fresh chill chased down her spine. There was a burr to his voice. A Scot, here on the South Dorset coast. Now, how frequently could she say she'd seen that?

"You didn't by any chance recently shoot at someone, did you?" she asked.

As if he would tell the truth, if he were indeed the assassin.

"No' who you think."

She should turn around this minute and call for help. Every instinct of decency said so. But Martin was the local magistrate, and Sarah knew how he treated prisoners. Even innocent ones. Squeezing her eyes shut, Sarah listened to the jangle of the troop turning to leave.

"Give you good day, Lady Clarke," the squire said, and waved the parade off down the drive.

Martin didn't follow right away. "This isn't over, missy," he warned. "No thieving by-blow is going to keep me from what is mine. This land belongs to me now, and you know it. By the time you let go, it will be useless."

Not unless the shingle strand sinks into the ocean, she thought dourly. The only thing Martin wanted from Fairbourne was a hidden cove where boats could land brandy.

Sarah sighed, her mind made up. She simply could not accommodate Martin in this or anything. Straightening, she squarely faced the dyspeptic man where he stiffly sat his horse. "Fairbourne is Boswell's," she said baldly. "Until he returns, I am here to make sure it is handed back into his hands in good heart. Good day, Martin."

Martin opened his mouth to argue and then saw the squire and other men waiting for him. He settled for a final "Bah!" and dug his heels into his horse. They were off in a splatter of mud.

Sarah stood where she was until she could no longer hear them. Then, with a growing feeling of inevitability, she once more climbed past the broken pigpen and approached the shadow at the back of the coop.

And there he was, a very large redheaded man slumped against the stone wall. He was even more ragged than the men who had ridden with Martin, his clothing tattered and filthy, his hair a rat's nest, his beard bristling and even darker red than his hair. His eyes were bright, though, and his cheeks flushed. He held his hand to his side, and he was listing badly.

Sarah crouched down next to him to get a better look and saw that his shirt was stained brown with old blood. His hands, clutched over his left side, were stained with new blood, which meant that those bright eyes were from more than intelligence. Even so, Sarah couldn't remember ever seeing a more compelling, powerful man in her life.

"Hello," she greeted him, her own hands clenched on her

thighs. "I assume I am speaking to the Scotsman for whom everyone is looking."

His grin was crooked and under any other circumstance would have been endearing. "Och, lassie, nothin' gets past ye."

"I thought you were dead."

He frowned. "Wait a few minutes," he managed. "I'll see what I can do."

And then, as gracefully as a sailing vessel slipping under the waves, he sank all the way to his side and lost consciousness.

Fall in Love with Forever Romance

LAST CHANCE FAMILY
by Hope Ramsay

Mike Taggart may be a high roller in Las Vegas, but is he ready to take a gamble on love in Last Chance? Fans of Debbie Macomber, Robyn Carr, and Sherryl Woods will love this sassy and heartwarming story from *USA Today* bestselling author Hope Ramsay.

SUGAR'S TWICE
AS SWEET
by Marina Adair

Fans of Jill Shalvis, Rachel Gibson, and Carly Phillips will enjoy this sexy and sweet romance about a woman who's renovating her beloved grandmother's house—even though she doesn't know a nut from a bolt—and the bad boy who can't resist helping her...even as she steals his heart!

Fall in Love with Forever Romance

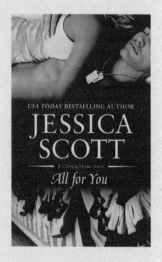

ALL FOR YOU
by Jessica Scott

Fans of JoAnn Ross and Brenda Novak will love this poignant and emotional military romance about a battle-scarred warrior who fears combat is the only escape from the demons that haunt him, and the woman determined to show him that the power of love can overcome anything.

DELIGHTFUL
by Adrianne Lee

Pie shop manager Andrea Lovette always picks the bad boys, and no one is badder than TV producer Ice Erickksen. Andrea knows she needs to find a good family man, so why does this bad boy still seem like such a good idea? Fans of Robyn Carr and Sherryl Woods will eat this one up!

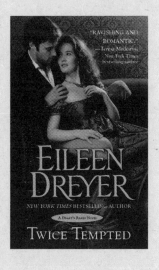
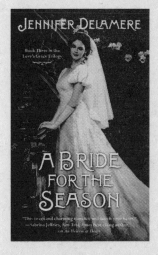

Find out more about Forever Romance!

Visit us at
www.hachettebookgroup.com/publishing_forever.aspx

Find us on Facebook
http://www.facebook.com/ForeverRomance

Follow us on Twitter
http://twitter.com/ForeverRomance

NEW AND UPCOMING TITLES

Each month we feature our new titles
and reader favorites.

CONTESTS AND GIVEAWAYS

We give away galleys, autographed copies,
and all kinds of exclusive items.

AUTHOR INFO

You'll find bios, articles, and links to personal websites
for all your favorite authors—and so much more.

GET SOCIAL

Connect with your favorite authors, editors, and
other Forever fans, and share what's important to you.

THE BUZZ

Sign up for our monthly romance newsletter,
and be the first to read all about it.